Thief

Sarah-Jane Lenoux

Thief Copyright © 2010 by Sarah-Jane Lehoux

All rights reserved under the International and Pan-American Copyright Conventions. No part of this book may be reproduced or transmitted in any form or by any means, electronic or mechanical including photocopying, recording, or by any information storage and retrieval system, without permission in writing from the publisher.

The scanning, uploading and distribution of this book via the Internet or via any other means without the permission of the publisher is illegal, and punishable by law. Please purchase only authorized electronic editions, and do not participate in or encourage the electronic piracy of copyrighted materials. Your support of the author's rights is appreciated.

Warning: The unauthorized reproduction or distribution of this copyrighted work is illegal. Criminal copyright infringement, including infringement without monetary gain, is investigated by the FBI and is punishable by up to 5 years in federal prison and a fine of $250,000.

This is a work of fiction. Names, characters, places and incidents either are the product of the author's imagination or are used fictitiously, and any resemblance to any actual persons, living or dead, events, or locales is entirely coincidental.

A Mundania Press Production
Mundania Press LLC
6470A Glenway Avenue, #109
Cincinnati, Ohio 45211-5222

To order additional copies of this book, contact:
books@mundania.com
www.mundania.com

Cover Art © 2010 by SkyeWolf
SkyeWolf Images (http://www.skyewolfimages.com)
Edited by Skyla Dawn Cameron

Trade Paperback ISBN: 978-1-60659-227-4
EBook ISBN: 978-1-60659-226-7

First Edition • May 2010

Production by Mundania Press LLC
Printed in the United States of America

10   9   8   7   6   5   4   3   2   1

For Sean

Acknowledgments

First and foremost, I would like to thank Skyla Dawn Cameron for believing in *Thief* and fighting for its publication. I couldn't have asked for a better editor, mentor, and friend. I would also like to thank Daniel J. Reitz Sr., Niki Browning, and the rest of the staff at Mundania Press.

Special thanks to L. Gallant Potts, S. Jackson, C. Miller, J. Moss, W. Shaw, A. Wylie-Ellis, A. Yealland, B. Yurkoski, and all of the lovely folks at the Writing Bridge.

Thank you to M. Lamb, J. McCleary, T. Rennick, M. Scalzo, and the staff at BVH.

Thank you to A. Aguiar, P. Arbour, K. Bouillon, K. Carre, E. Crossman, L. Davis, M. Garvie, J. Hunt-Beyer, D. Lagrandeur, B. Madill, A. Mozdzanowski, S. O'Brien, S. Pedra, N. Pelland, M. White, A. White-Wagner, A. Williams, and everyone else who has offered their support and encouragement during and after the creation of *Thief*.

PART 1
STRAY

Chapter 1

She might as well have been invisible. The people of Eloria paid no mind to the redness of her nose or to the wet marks that streaked across her dirty face. She was just another nameless vagrant after all, of which the city had more than its fair share.

It was midday. People flooded the constricted, cobbled streets, busily going about their lives. The perpetual grind and toil demanded that sales be pitched, prices be haggled, and money be made. Each day like the one before—an uphill battle to earn as much as the gods would allow so that, hopefully, their own children would not have the same desperation in their eyes that the skinny girl had in hers.

Had it been any other day, Sevy would have laughed at the curses that flew after her whenever she bumped into one of the merchants. Any other day and she would have been more reckless, more bold, snatching coins right from outstretched hands and then making a game of the ensuing chase. Today, sadly, was not such a day.

The morning had begun well enough. Hopping nimbly over heaps of trash, she had rummaged for breakfast before returning home, a derelict building that once served as stables, decades ago, back when the Axlun royal family still lived in Eloria and the city was in its finest hour. Now abandoned by most of the kingdom's aristocracy, Eloria had descended into a long, drawn out rot. Bad for the economy perhaps, but just right for those like Sevy. The city was littered with ramshackle houses and factories, memories of past prosperity cast off like the shells of sea creatures, readily appropriated and transformed into covert bastions of beggars and brigands.

The stables sheltered any number of street children, orphaned by choice or by circumstance, living together in fluid, drifting groups. It was their sanctuary against the dangers of the city, and though it couldn't hold heat in the winter or lose it in the summer, it was dear to them.

She climbed up to the hayloft and tucked into her meal of a half eaten apple and a crust of week-old bread, quite content. Things were looking up when Trena arrived and dangled a bottle of ruby red wine before Sevy's eager eyes.

"Aww, fantastic! Where'd you get it from?"

Trena popped the cork out with her teeth then took three swigs, each bigger than the last, before answering. "A friend."

"Nice friend."

"Mm-hmm."

If Sevy's attention had not been focused on the savory liquid, she may have noticed the nervous squirming or the edge in Trena's voice. Instead, she simply sighed appreciatively and held up the wine in a mock salute to their health.

All too soon the bottle was emptied, leaving only a pleasant heat in their cheeks and a sickly sweet taste in their mouths. Warmed and sleepy from the drink, Sevy reclined against the wall and picked at random splinters of moldy hay while Trena turned the bottle over and over again in her hands. With the distraction of the wine gone, Sevy finally discerned that something wasn't quite right with her normally bubbly friend. Several times, Trena opened her mouth to speak, but then shook her head and remained silent.

Sitting there, in the musty ruin of an era long past, they were quite the pair of opposites. Trena was a full head shorter than Sevy, but what she lacked in height, she made up for in curves. Sevy often stared enviously at those curves, comparing them to her own spindly frame. Heredity and malnutrition combined to work against Sevy, making her appear much younger than her sixteen years. Her brown hair, loosely tied back with a strip of cloth, didn't have the luster of Trena's blonde curls. The closest that Sevy's pallid cheeks ever came to a fetching shade of red was when she was embarrassed, but Trena's seemed to be everlastingly rouged. Trena's clothes were always neater too. Sevy was forever discovering new rents and tears in hers. And her shoes...

Now that was odd, Sevy thought to herself. She hadn't, until that moment, noticed that Trena was wearing new shoes—slippers made from softened leather. And a matched set as well. First a bottle of wine and now new shoes. An eyebrow rose as she regarded her friend with suspicion.

"What's up?" she asked lightly, drawing her legs up to her chest.

"Nothing," came the sighed response. "It's just...about my friend. He's really nice."

Sevy nodded her agreement even though her stomach was beginning to churn. And it wasn't from the wine.

"Well, um, he said he can get us all sorts of things. More wine, food, clothes. Whatever we want."

In one hurried rush, Trena spoke animatedly about a man named

Gihaf, one who promised them all of Eloria in exchange for certain favors.

"It's nothing we haven't done before," Trena said with a shrug of her shoulders, trying to appear casual. "Just now, he'll give us stuff for it."

"You can't be serious."

"It's not so bad, honest. He promises that we'll be safe and that the men he'd fix us up with wouldn't be horrid or anything."

In her heart, Sevy had always known Trena might succumb to something like this. She was weak willed, more liable to take the easy way out, and definitely more likely to be charmed by anyone with a silver tongue.

The gods had been smiling upon Trena the day they arranged for her to meet Sevy four years earlier. Born from tougher stock, forged by the biting winds and glacial waters of the Melacian Sea, it had been Sevy who discovered such a relatively safe and comfortable place to live. It had been Sevy who learned through trial and error how to pick pockets and steal food. Trena may have been gullible, but she wasn't stupid. She had latched onto Sevy, recognizing her strength and nerve.

As for Sevy, she was just happy to have a friend. Like the majority of Eloria's children, she had already experienced far too much loss for such a short life. Trena was her surrogate family, and Sevy was not about to let anyone, particularly some pervert pimp, take her away.

Indignation blazed within her stout little soul as Trena continued her impassioned speech, punctuated with sobs and frequent hitchings of her chest. She extolled Gihaf's virtues—by the way she spoke, he may as well have been King Grewid himself—while rationalizing her choice with protests against the cold and the hunger.

"I'm sick of this. I mean, look at us, Sevy. Look how we're living. It shouldn't be this way! And Gihaf says—"

"Gihaf is lying!" Sevy at last exploded. "You're so stupid! You wanna be his whore? Fine. Go! Get out and go spread your legs for him and the whole world!"

Trena was shocked into silence for a moment. Then she wailed Sevy's name and threw herself at her feet. "Please, don't be angry! Please!"

She just laid there, a blubbering heap on the floor, crying so pitifully that Sevy's eyes misted over in spite of her anger. Maybe it was all Sevy's fault. She did have an overbearing personality, to put it mildly. Bossy was a description Sevy wasn't likely to ascribe to herself, but it was much closer to the truth. Trena had always simply followed in Sevy's wake, never testing the waters for herself, never learning what manner of sharks swam in Eloria's depths.

It's my fault, Sevy thought. She shouldn't have protected Trena so fiercely in the past. By doing so, she had set Trena up for a life of dependence on others. *I'm so stupid.* But there would be plenty of time later on for Sevy to beat herself up over the decisions she had made. Right now, she had to stop her friend from making a huge mistake.

Her tone softened as she helped Trena up. "You don't have to do this. I'll just start stealing more. I'll take care of you, you'll see. Look, I'll go right now and get some money to pay Gihaf for the wine. You won't owe him anything, all right? You'll see."

Without waiting for a reply, she ran outside and down the alley. She didn't want to hear more excuses, more justifications. Words like that, harmless as they outwardly appeared, had a way of burning what they fell upon, like cinders on the wind. Sevy would prove to Trena that they could get by without resorting to prostitution. She'd prove it to her, and then she'd make Trena grovel for awhile for ever doubting Sevy's ability.

Finally reaching the marketplace, Sevy pushed a strand of greasy hair from her face as she came to a stop. Green eyes with blackened half moons bruised underneath sized up the crowd that was milling about the market. She took breath after slow breath to calm herself and gain focus. She couldn't afford any mistakes, not today.

She needed to gather as much as she could, as fast as she could. She needed an easy mark. Not the dwarf over there sloppily drinking from a rain bucket. She would bet that his purse was in danger of bursting, but dwarves guarded their money like wolves guarded their dens. No point in risking injury. The two men discussing rhetoric over rum cakes and coffee were suitably distracted, but they were most likely students, and the pockets of students rarely contained anything more than lint and dreams of grandeur. What about the elf dancing on the corner? She could skim from his earnings while he had his limbs tangled up in a bizarre impression of a bird, but as she walked past him, she saw that his hat held only two half pieces of copper. He'd either have to learn some new steps or start stripping before the crowd tossed him anything worth stealing.

No, no, no! This wasn't going well at all! What the hell was wrong with these people? Why did they have to make things so difficult? What had started as a simple task was turning into something infuriatingly problematic.

But then she saw him. A tall, dark-haired young man dressed in a smart blue jacket. His attention was fixed on a busty merchant, though his eyes drifted more to her chest than to the wares laid out on her table. The pair flirted and laughed freely. Whatever they were bantering back and forth was certainly more engrossing than the scrawny girl sneaking up behind them.

Sevy could see a money bag hanging on his belt, and it was plenty full too. Perfect! She smoothed back her hair and wiped away the fine layer of sweat that had broken out across her brow. *Breathe!* she commanded herself. *Quit acting like such a beginner! This guy is a complete patsy. Not worth the worry, so just relax!*

She brushed against him, pretending to peruse the trinkets for sale. Oh my, what a pretty set of wooden earrings, and goodness me! Those bone bangles are absolutely to die for. She felt his eyes pass over her as he politely attempted to shift out of her way, but they quickly returned to the buxom beauty behind the table.

That's it, buddy. You just take your time with her tits, and I'll be gone before you can wipe the drool off your lips.

Trembling fingers slipped around the bag, carefully working it off his belt. Almost had it. Just one more tug. Success! Sevy could scarcely suppress her snicker of victory while she moved to sidle back into the ranks of the invisible underclass.

Before she could, a hand gripped her shoulder, halting her escape.

"I'll take that back, sweetheart."

"Take what back?"

He laughed as he turned her to face him. She glared at him in defiance, looking straight into his face for the first time.

Beautiful. The word almost escaped her lips in an awed whisper as she found herself mesmerized by the twinkle of his oceanic blue eyes, but, luckily, her tongue was so tied by the sight of his bewitching smile that she couldn't speak. The way the sun lapped at each strand of his flowing black hair was so engrossing that she forgot to struggle against his hold until his voice, mellifluous and tinged with mirth, broke her out of the spell.

"Nice try, really it was. But your technique is terrible."

"Wh—what?" she stammered, remembering her predicament. "You're crazy! Let me go or I'll call the guards."

"Oh really? All right, call them then. We'll wait here together and let them sort it out." Without waiting for her reply, he pulled her closer and reached into her pocket.

"Let me go, you lecher!"

Smirking, he scooped out the bag of coins and made a show of tucking it inside of his jacket. Sevy felt her face grow red, but was it from the chagrin of being caught or from the intensity of those eyes shining down at her?

She had to look away, and it was only then that she noticed the people gathering around them like ravenous dogs primed for the scent of blood, no doubt hoping for a spot of entertainment to help break up the day. There's nothing quite like a public thrashing to lift the stupor of drudgery.

"What's going on, Jarro? Gonna teach her a lesson?" someone shouted.

"Give her to me. I'll teach her real good," another man jeered, thrusting his pelvis.

She had been caught in the act. By city law, it was his right to dole out her punishment, but in his face she saw none of the hatred and righteous indignation she had come to expect. There was only merriment, as though the two of them were sharing in a joke that the others were not privy to.

"Shut up!" he yelled to the yammering horde before flashing her another brilliant smile. "Listen, sweetheart, how's about I let you go this time? Just promise me you'll work on that technique."

∽∾

Though he had shown her mercy where others would not, the dark-haired man had quashed any confidence she had in her abilities that day. It was hours before she could return to the stables, dolefully appraising the meager offering she eventually managed to steal for Trena. A bit of food, a bit of coin, a few odds and ends that could be sold. In all, maybe enough to keep their bellies full for about three days.

She prayed that it would be enough to persuade Trena against her foray into prostitution. Sevy would be lying if she said she hadn't considered it at some point. It did seem like easy money, but that notion didn't hold much water if given more than a half second of thought. They had both seen too many of their young friends ruined that way to be able to pretend that it was a bright idea.

No one concerned themselves with the hundreds of women and children who sold their bodies for food and money, certainly not the city guards who were more liable to demand free services than they were to offer any sort of protection. Whores were routinely beaten until their faces became unrecognizable. Many were found dead in back rooms and alleys. Still others disappeared completely. And if violence didn't get you, disease certainly would. The infected were left to die alone, unable to care for themselves anymore. When happened upon, their bodies were tossed into the furnaces of the charnel house alongside rapists and murderers, and their ashes scattered to the four winds so that they could never enter Promyraan, a final punishment for their lives of debauchery. Sevy felt sick to her stomach picturing Trena ending up like that.

That won't happen, she thought, gritting her teeth.

She climbed up to the hay loft, plastered on what she hoped was a convincing smile, and held up her stolen goods. "I'm back! And look what I..."

The smile fled from her face. Trena had company: a rather large man with a heavy, sloping brow and oily hair slicked into a ponytail. Sevy staggered back a step as he rose to his feet, instinctively noting the size of his hairy-knuckled hands.

"Sevy, this is my friend, Gihaf."

"Well, hi there. Tre's told me all about you," he said cordially.

She couldn't help staring at them. Those hands that were large enough to dwarf her own. She pictured them running over Trena's curves, over her own tiny bumps, and she shook from head to toe.

Gihaf turned towards Trena and laughed. "What's her problem?"

Hands large enough to wrap right around her neck if he so wanted. Or to squash her skull like a grape.

It wasn't a conscious decision. Sevy reached down to her boot and pulled out a dagger. "Get out."

"Sevy!" Trena gasped.

Gihaf's eyes widened and his nostrils flared, and her gaze shifted once more to those hands, expecting them to strike out at any moment. He surprised her when he appeared to collect himself, his voice remaining agreeable and calm. "Little girls shouldn't play with knives. Tre and I are just talking nice here. Nothing to worry about."

Nothing to worry about, except for the fact that such a beast of a man was in her home, smiling at her as though they were intimate friends, speaking to her with the same honeyed tongue that had so deceived her friend.

Unable to find words to express her loathing, Sevy spat onto his chest.

"Oh gods! Gihaf, she didn't mean it, I swear. I'm so sorry." Trena rushed to wipe the gob off of his shirt.

Gihaf pushed her away and stomped forward, making the floorboards creak and sway, backing Sevy into the wall. This near to him, she could see the beads of sweat and oil that rested in the pores on his nose. His scent was sour, a mingling of body odor and beer. How had he managed to sucker Trena in? He was repulsive.

Sevy held tight to her dagger. "I'm not afraid of you. Get out and leave me and my friend alone." She hoped that he wouldn't hear the quiver in her voice.

He snorted. "Big words for such a little girl. You need a lesson in manners."

"No, Gihaf, please! She's just trying to protect me. Leave her be!"

"Shaddup. Now listen, Sevy, I'm a nice guy. I take good care of my friends. You do want to be my friend, don't you?" Up came those hands, calloused and cracked and rubbing across her cheek. She shuddered and turned away, but he forced her to face him by grabbing hold of her chin. "It's all up to you, Sevy. Tre here, she's a good girl. Does what good little girls are supposed to do. And I reward her for that, don't I, Tre? I can give you whatever you want, Sevy. Just be a good little girl."

He leaned down and shoved his tongue into her mouth, probing her as if he were her lover. She gagged.

This isn't happening...

A part of her begged to retreat deep inside her mind, to hide inside herself until he finished and left her alone. Maybe if she stayed still long enough, he'd forget she was there. Maybe if she prayed hard enough, she'd sink into the walls, safe from his touch within the rotting wood. But these were wild, nonsensical thoughts, and now was not the time to give in to flights of fancy.

There was another part of her mind that screamed for her to fight, and in spite of her fear, she knew what she had to do. She rallied her courage and stabbed the dagger into his arm. He yelped and jerked away, staring at the wound in shock.

"You bitch!"

Sevy tried to run, but he was too quick. He had her pinned before she could think to stab him again. He seized her hand and slammed it against the wall until she was forced to drop her weapon.

"Stupid little cunt!"

She closed her eyes against the spray of his saliva. His fist cracked across her jaw, once, twice, and the skin on her lip popped open, filling her mouth with salty warm fluid.

"Help me," she managed to squeak out.

"Tre won't help you. I told you, she's a good girl. Now I'm gonna show you what happens to bitches like you!"

Sevy screamed as he thrust his hand down the front of her shirt, groping so savagely it was as if he wanted to tear off her skin as well as her clothes. She jerked her knee up as hard as she could and the result was instantaneous. He doubled over, groaning. This was her one chance and she knew it. She kicked him again and again, and didn't let up when he fell onto the floor.

"So I'm a bitch, huh?!"

Blood spurted from his nose and mouth, and he wept like a nursling. Sevy laughed, loving the sight of him crippled like this. Each crunch she felt in his ribcage helped to mollify her disgust and fear. She couldn't stop even if she wanted to.

Then suddenly, she was seized from behind. Startled, she whipped around to face her new assailant and saw that it was Trena.

"Sevy, don't! Leave him alone. Please!"

"Trena, I—"

"Just go. Go!"

"But you're coming too. Come on!" Sevy grabbed her hand, but Trena shook her off.

"You don't understand. He's all I've got. I need him!"

"That's crazy! He'll use you, he'll hurt you! Come with me," Sevy pleaded. "I'll protect you!"

Gihaf stumbled upright, splashing rubied clots of blood onto the floor as he slurred, "You're gonna pay, bitch!"

"Get out of here!"

"I'm not leaving without you."

"Shut up and go! Please, if he hurts you..."

"No! Trena!"

"Oh, you stubborn bitch, just go! Leave! Now!"

Sevy stared, unable to move until survival instinct took hold and made her scramble down the ladder.

Blindly, she raced through the city. She ran until her lungs burned, street after street, not caring when she overturned a vegetable cart, deaf to the cries of people she crashed into. She knew he wasn't following, but it didn't matter. She was spurred on by pain like a horse lashed by a wicked master.

Finally, exhausted, she slumped against a brick wall and slid down until she was sitting, arms wrapped about her knees. She gasped for breath, forcing the air to pass by the fiery knot that had taken up residence in her throat, and tried to blink away the tears that blurred her vision.

How could she? Her best friend. Her only friend. Her only family. How could she?

Chapter 2

A bottle exploded against a slab of stone, shattering not only the glass but the daze Sevy had sunk into. She must have fallen asleep because it was now dark. The lanterns had been lit and were burning cheerily, one of the few remaining public services that Eloria had left. The light not only illuminated the main streets, but acted as surrogate stars since smoke from the multitude of chimneys smudged out the sky.

Sniffing and wiping her eyes with the palms of her hands, Sevy stood, at first not recognizing where she was. She was fairly certain that she was in the north-eastern quarter, but none of the seedy brick and wooden buildings looked familiar. Wrapping her arms around her chest protectively, she hurried up the street, trying not to draw attention to herself. She focused on the ground to avoid eye contact with those she passed.

Raucous music drifted on the wind, drunks stumbled about while preaching and singing to anyone who would listen, whores called out to men walking by. Sevy realized that this was probably just the sort of place a man like Gihaf called home.

Then she saw a building that made her eyes double in size. She couldn't read the words, but the picture on the plaster sign was easy enough to figure out. The Bloody Heart. And even though she had rarely been to this section of the city, she now knew precisely where she was.

The reputation of this particular tavern and the surrounding neighborhood was well known amongst her fellow pickpockets. It was home to an organized gang, one of the most powerful and influential in the city and therefore one of the most dangerous. The street kids knew to avoid them. Gangs were always looking for new recruits and they didn't take no for an answer.

She sniffled, feeling terribly sorry for herself. She had lost her best friend and her home, and now she was stuck in gang territory in the dead of the night.

A good dose of self-deprecation snapped her back into action. She needed a plan. *Think, Sevy, think.* Obviously it was best not to tarry here, but where to go next? Not back to the stables. Safety came in numbers, but she knew that none of her friends would rally round her if she got into another fight with Gihaf. Loyalty was a rare thing when you actually needed it. Trena had demonstrated that perfectly, hadn't she?

She decided to head for the river. Lots of kids lived underneath the bridges that crossed the Elor River. Sevy could fit in pretty well. No one would question why she was there or who she was. She could eke out a living scavenging along the shoreline. Who knows, maybe the sound of the gulls or the smell of the sea that followed the river would provide her with comfort as they reminded her of home.

That decision settled, she turned her attention to her bearings. The river was west and to get there, she'd have to go down some questionable alleys. Even the lantern lighters could not be persuaded to venture into these alleys, and left them to the black of night. They were crowded with enough debris that any number of dangers could be concealed along the path. Sevy glimpsed figures moving through the shadows. Maybe just harmless drunks, but why take the chance? She reached down to her boot before realizing that her dagger had been left back at the stables, along with the rest of her small possessions.

Oh, brilliant. Just fucking brilliant!

Just another detail that added to her miseries. She wanted to curl back up and cry some more, but she would not allow herself to be undone so easily. That's just what that asshole and Trena expected, didn't they? Well, she'd show them.

With a sharp intake of breath, Sevy entered the alley. The walls closed in on her like a vice, but she assured herself that this was just her fear and that alleyways could not really shrink at will. Barely in four yards, she heard a low growl and a wet, chewing noise to her left. She peered towards the source out of the corner of her eye, spying a sewer troll hunched over a dead body. The shock of hair that ran down from the crown of its head to the small of its back sprung up like a cat's. It scuttled atop the body, protecting its meal with a snarling flash of fangs. Gore dribbled down its chin as it glared up at her and took another bite from the arm. She averted her eyes and picked up her pace. Sewer trolls may have been the smallest and most animal-like of their kind, but they were wiry and vicious, certainly not something to be trifled with when defenseless.

Another bottle smashed and she jumped.

Gods, get a hold of yourself, woman, she admonished herself.

Lot of good it did though, as she jumped again when someone lying at her feet laughed, "Scared, baby? C'mere. Come gimme a hug."

Steady breaths, in and out, not going to give in, not going to run. And then something laden with slime and fur wrapped around her ankle. That was it. She bolted forward.

She almost shrieked a prayer of thanks when washed out light came from up ahead. The alley was opening onto a wider, better lit street and she was mere seconds to safety when she crashed into something and was knocked backwards onto the ground.

"Oh, I'm sorry, miss! I didn't see you."

There was a man standing above her. Ignoring the outstretched hand, Sevy scrambled to her feet and tried to push past him.

"Whoa, whoa! It's all right, I won't hurt you," the man said, taking hold of her shoulders.

"Don't touch me!"

"I'm not going to hurt you, miss. Hey, don't I know you? Yeah, you're the girl with the bad technique."

She had heard that genial chuckle before. Sevy blinked, taking a moment longer before she recognized him as the dark-haired man she tried to rob earlier that day.

"Let me by," she whispered. He stared down and, mortified, she realized that he was looking at her torn shirt. She pulled the pieces together in a vain attempt to cover herself.

He frowned. "Are you all right? Did someone hurt you?"

"No, just get out of my way!"

He touched her shoulder again. "Wait a second, sweetheart."

"No!" She beat his chest with her fists. "Let me go! I'll kill you, let me go!"

"Stop that! I'm just trying to help you." He took off his jacket and held it out to her. "Here, take this."

She squinted in suspicion. What sort of twisted trick was this? Then he smiled at her the same way he had in the marketplace, and she felt washed with sunny, friendly warmth. Against her will, she felt herself melting under his gaze. Thank the gods it was too dark to get drawn into his magnetic eyes again.

Maybe that's what he wanted. Maybe he was just another creep, another pervert, a spider who used good looks to lure flies into his web. But she really did need something to cover herself with. She didn't have much, but she didn't like the idea of flashing it for everyone to see. After a few more seconds of deliberation, she snatched the jacket out of the man's hands and ran from him.

"You're welcome!"

The rising sun reflected off of the water, sending soft ripples of light into Sevy's eyes. She groaned and covered her face with her arms. Upon making it to the river, she had picked out a spot to sleep, nestled under the beams of the Gerio Bridge. She wasn't alone. There were others huddled around tiny bonfires in groups of three or four, but no one had tried to talk to her. That was how life was. You stayed out of trouble by minding your own business. Strangers were avoided. Sevy knew this, knew it would take time to make new friends, but she still felt miserably lonely.

She walked to the river's edge, kicking at random pebbles and making a face at the chunks of grey scum that washed ashore. Factories up river made no qualms about dumping their refuse into the Elor, the tannery being the biggest culprit. She didn't even want to wager a guess as to the origins of the flotsam and jetsam. Some things were best not known.

Her tired reflection greeted her in the brackish water. The circles under her eyes had darkened by several shades, matching the nasty bruise Gihaf's fist had left upon her cheek. Her tongue gingerly ran over the split in her lip, and once again, Sevy tasted copper from the blood caked around her mouth. She scooped up a handful of water and washed her face as best she could, forcing herself to ignore the rotten egg and cabbage smell that invaded her senses.

That futile bit of toiletry accomplished, she inspected her shirt. It could be mended with a quick sewing job, but with the effort needed to get a needle and thread, she might as well just nick another shirt. In the meantime, she had the dark-haired man's jacket for cover and warmth.

It was too big for her, but it was a gift she was grateful for because although it was late spring, the nights were still cold. It was a nice jacket too. She figured she could probably sell it for a few coin. In the morning light, she was better able to examine it. It was made of thick blue wool, had no tears or patches, and all of its horn buttons were still in place, a rarity in clothes on the streets. Whoever that man was, he must have been pretty well off to have such a jacket, let alone give it away so freely.

There was a bulge on the left side. Sevy patted it, realizing for the first time that there was something hidden inside one of the inner pockets. To her astonishment, she pulled out the very same bag of coins she had tried to steal the day before.

Instinctively, she curled her body, shielding the bag so that none of the people around could see. She fingered through it, doing her best not to jingle the coins.

There must be thirty silver in here!

Never in her life had she seen so much money at one time. It was a fortune for a girl like her. She instantly pictured how she would spend it, so happy she could have cried.

Maybe a warm room with a bed for a few nights. Food and wine. A new shirt, maybe even a cloak! A dagger, I should get that first. Wait until Trena...

Her celebration came to a halt. Funny how one's memory can be suppressed by something as simple as circles of metal. She wouldn't be sharing her good fortune with Trena. She'd probably never see Trena again. An undertow of emotions threatened to pull her down, but she fought against it. After all, why should she care?

Trena had made her choice more than clear. If she wanted to be a whore for that bastard, fine! Serves her right for setting Sevy up like that.

See if I care, Sevy repeated, convincing herself that it was the truth.

She picked herself up, ran her fingers through the tangle of her hair, and straightened her clothes. The markets would be opening soon and Sevy was going shopping.

꽃

"Whaddya mean? I've got money." She held out a handful of coins.

The merchant remained seated on the chair that groaned under the weight of his fleshy form, and crossed his arms on top of his ample belly. "Your money's no good here. I know you, you stinking thief. Probably just use the knife to rob me blind in a couple days. Get lost!"

Sevy kicked the table, which didn't do much besides make her foot and her pride sting. "Just give me the goddamned dagger!"

"Keep that up and I'll get the guards on you! Now get! You're scaring the real business."

"Ass!" she retorted before stalking off.

She shuffled aimlessly around the square, berating herself for trying to get the knife honestly when she should have just filched it. She would have been long gone before the fat oaf had noticed, and now thanks to that little exchange, the surrounding vendors had their hackles up so she wouldn't have much luck stealing from any of them either.

To add insult to injury, a pair of girls her age, arms loaded with bolts of damask, were sneaking glances at her. Sevy knew their type. They were the spoiled princesses of the upper middle class, putting on the same airs as royalty even though their families still lived meal to meal and still picked nits from their hair at night just like the rest of the ignoble. Sevy hated them instantly, from the tops of their expertly crafted coiffures to the shiny brass buckles on their shoes. The tallest of the pair leaned to whisper something into the other's ear and they both giggled. Sevy saw red.

"What are you laughing at?"

The girls became fixated on the woven detail on the damask, but Sevy was not about to let them off so easily.

She stomped up to them. "Eh? Something funny? Care to share it with me?"

"Hey, you! Get away from them! Miserable good-for-nothing! Away with you!" the fat merchant called over.

The girls smirked. Sevy did likewise back at them, then punched the tall girl in the face and took off in a sprint, raising her hand above her head and extending her middle finger back towards the two girls specifically and the entire marketplace in general.

She stopped running a few blocks away, quite pleased with herself even though she wouldn't be able to go back to that neighborhood for awhile. Those snobs looked like the sort to blubber to the guards, and that bloated behemoth of a merchant would no doubt rat her out at the first chance.

But it was worth it, she thought with a cheeky grin.

Invigorated, Sevy decided to indulge herself with a couple of drinks. If the gods should decree that you be homeless and friendless then at the very least you should be able to get hammered enough to forget your troubles. It was only fair.

There was a pub a few streets over that she liked to go to whenever she could afford a pint. It was simply called Sally's. No one could remember who Sally was, but the name had remained the same for years despite the high turnover of owners. It was a dirty dive, mostly frequented by street cleaners and other grunts—a class of men who just wanted to get shit-faced and didn't care about the ambience and décor of the fancier establishments or the dancing girls and roaring music of the scummier ones. Sevy strolled up to the bar, slammed a coin down, and placed her order. Heady, malty, brown ale. She licked her lips in anticipation.

"Hi, sweetheart."

She started at the unexpected intrusion into her space, and then stared at the puddle of ale that had spilled onto the bar. What a waste! And just because some prick decided to test his luck with her? Not gonna happen, buddy. Not in a million years. She was all set to tear into the luckless fool, but was confronted with that now familiar smile.

"Feeling any better?"

A tingling sensation broke out across the back of her neck. Cast in a dreamy beam of sunlight that crept through the pub's mucky windows was the dark-haired man, just as cheerful and carefree as he had been the day before. But Sevy was not about to let those blue eyes befuddle her again. "So, what? You stalking me now or something?"

He laughed and took the seat next to hers. "I saw you in the market. Just wanted to know how you were doing today."

"Why? I'm not for sale if that's what you want."

"Please. I don't have to buy my women. And anyways, you're a bit young for my taste." He signaled the bartender over. "Whiskey, straight up."

Sevy drank her ale, but the thrill of the frothy treat was gone. The man made small talk with the bartender: the weather was improving, wasn't it nice now that winter was over, and have you heard what's going on at the Vasurach border? Terrible shame that. Nothing remotely interesting and nothing important enough that it should warrant him trailing her. So what did he want? His jacket? His bag of coins? Pretty eyes notwithstanding, there was no way he was getting those, or anything else, back. Sevy decided to slip out while he was distracted, and inched off the stool.

"Leaving so soon? You didn't even finish your drink," he said without looking at her.

"What is it with you? Got nothing better to do than harass me?"

"Sit down, stupid. I don't want to chase you out of here." He chuckled, before quietly adding, "Someone mess with you?"

"No."

And then for reasons she couldn't explain, she sat back down. She felt his gaze settle on her, scrutinizing her, unnerving her. She began to play with her glass, sliding it hand to hand.

"So you just like punching yourself then? Seriously, if someone's messing with you, tell me. I'll handle it."

"Why do you care?"

"Because I do. Sick of seeing kids like you. It isn't right."

"Yeah, well, lots of things aren't right. What else is new?"

He smiled again and her traitor of a stomach wobbled. Determined not to be swayed by those deep blues, she glanced at his classically chiseled cheekbones and then at his broad shoulders, but found those just as captivating. She was filled with the urge to run her fingers through his wavy hair to see if it was as soft as it looked. Without realizing it, she smiled back at him.

He finished his whiskey. "Well, I guess I'll be off now and leave you to drink in peace. The name's Jarro, in case you're wondering, and I meant what I said."

"My name is Sevy," she mumbled.

"Well, Sevy, see you around. By the way, the jacket looks good on you."

He winked at her and walked out of the pub, whistling. Sevy, cheeks aflame, watched until he was gone from sight before turning back to her ale with a small sigh.

Chapter 3

The weeks dragged on. Time seemed reluctant to pass, clinging covetously to each second, stretching out each day for all that it was worth. When the sun finally dripped down into the horizon, the bleakness of night yawned out before Sevy like a vast impenetrable fog.

If she wanted to count her blessings, she'd admit that boredom was a far cry better than unrest and upheaval. She hadn't seen any sign of Gihaf, she had new clothes and a dagger thanks to Jarro's money, and she was adjusting to life by the Elor. Sevy supposed she should be grateful. She should be, but she wasn't.

The cold hard truth was laid plain. No sign of Gihaf also meant no sign of Trena, the thirty pieces of silver were long since spent, and the Elor just plain stunk.

In spite of her attempts to fit in, the river kids were still ignoring her. Sevy chalked it up to jealousy on their part. She was older, wiser, and obviously more adept to this lifestyle than they were. She pretended not to care about their indifference to her greatness, although the solitude was becoming unbearable. She had taken to stealing food to give to them, hoping to win them over with kindness.

"Hey, kid, look," she whispered to a child with crusted sores covering her arms. "I brought you something to eat." Sevy held out a wedge of cheese with a friendly smile.

The girl reached for the food, but then pulled her hand back, eyes darting to her friends playing by the edge of the river.

"You can share it with them if you like."

The girl snatched the cheese and ran it over to the other children where it was divided and devoured. Sevy sulked as they went back to throwing stones into the water without so much as a nod to her.

Her stomach rumbled its disapproval. That cheese was all she had stolen that morning. Why had she given it away to a bunch of ungrateful brats? Now she'd have to go and grab something else unless she wanted to go hungry.

She mulled over which market to try. By watching the others climb the joists of the Gerio Bridge, she had learned how to cross the river without having to pay the toll. If you were strong and nimble enough, it was the simplest way to get to the western quarters where Sevy had, in her daily wanderings, discovered new markets carrying much finer and more expensive goods than those east of the Elor. That meant tighter security of course, guards on patrol at every corner and the best of things locked behind glass and bars, but the payoff was worth the extra effort.

And as her hunting ground expanded, so did her luck. She rotated her time between a handful of markets both sides of the river, never visiting the same one more than once or twice a week. It was working out wonderfully. They weren't wise to her the way they used to be. Anonymity was her benefactor.

Today though, she didn't scale the bridge. Without making a conscious decision, she headed towards the old neighborhood, junky and cheap, but familiar. She scanned through the faces of the shoppers, recognizing more than a few. She waved hello to some young acquaintances, but there were no curly blonde heads to be seen. She didn't know if that should make her relieved or worried.

Before stepping into the square she paused to adjust, straighten up, dust off, and compose herself. She still wore the jacket Jarro had given her even though common sense told her that it should be sold. She just couldn't bring herself to part with it. It was the first time in years that she owned something so nicely made and it made her feel quite proud. She walked confidently, her head held high.

Ambling up to the tables, she was pleasantly surprised that the merchants didn't raise the alarm as soon as they saw her. Either they had forgotten her face or she looked more like a respectable citizen now that she had proper clothes. She chatted casually with a few of them, picking up different objects and pretending to examine them with one hand, while the other snuck things into the jacket's deep pockets.

When they were full, it was time to head to another area to sell the swag. Counting in her head, she figured that she'd be able to get maybe three or four pieces of silver. She hummed to herself and smiled at everyone she passed. All in all, it was shaping up to be a great day.

Then Sevy heard a voice that made her heart skip. Just up the road, a group of men were going into Sally's pub. The one holding the door open, the one laughing the loudest and clapping each of the men on the back as they passed, was Jarro.

Over the last weeks, he had crossed her mind frequently, but she scolded herself each time. Sure, he had been kind to her and, true, he was very attractive, but that shouldn't be reason enough to daydream about him like some daft schoolgirl. So what if she had analyzed every word he said and gesture he made? What did it matter if she had the image of his smile stamped into her memory? It didn't mean a thing. Right?

She patted her pockets. Though she had no money, she did have a newly stolen bracelet made of colored beads linked together with a copper chain. Just costume jewelry, but quite pretty. Maybe the barkeeper would take it in exchange for a pint. And maybe she'd sit at the bar.

Oh grow up, stupid. What good would that do?

She moved a few paces down the street before feeling compelled to stop. She was thirsty. Awfully so now that she thought about it. She peeked through the pub's door. Jarro, still laughing, was holding up a shot glass. His exuberance was infectious and the other men joined in the toast. Before Sevy knew it, she was inside.

Her sweaty little palm gripped the bracelet so hard that it left an imprint on her skin. On tenterhooks, she slid onto a stool near to him. He hadn't appeared to notice her yet. Should she say hello? Well, it really couldn't hurt. Just a casual, "Hey, how's it going?" Nothing special. No big deal. She opened her mouth. Nothing came out except a squeak of air.

"You deaf or something? What d'ya want?" The bartender stared down at her.

"Sorry. I didn't hear you."

"Gonna buy something or what?"

"I have this," she said, offering the bracelet. "Can I trade it for a drink?"

"What do I look like, eh? I don't need no stolen crap. Either you got coin or get out."

She was painfully aware that the area around the bar had fallen silent and that the men, including Jarro, were watching with amused interest. The absolute last thing she wanted to do was lose face in front of him so she squared her shoulders and met the bartender's glare with her own frost filled scowl.

"It isn't stolen! Now get me a drink!"

The men laughed and Sevy grew hot. She failed to see the humor in this and felt like a complete idiot, which made her more angry than embarrassed.

"Well, you heard her," Jarro called. "Get her a drink."

She looked at him in shock while tiny prickles of pleasure stole through her and a grateful but goofy smile stretched across her face.

"Hi!" she said, a bit too loudly.

"Hello, sweetheart. How are you? I haven't seen you around in awhile." He moved to sit next to her. "I was worried."

"Worried? About me?"

The bartender returned with a mug of ale and glanced at Jarro when Sevy held out the bracelet to him. Jarro tossed some money onto the bar.

"Keep it, Sevy. I don't think it would look very good on old Hal here."

"Thanks."

She took a sip and hoped that her cheeks weren't betraying how excited she was that he remembered her name.

They drank in silence; it was torture for Sevy though Jarro seemed at ease. She snuck furtive sideways glances at him when she thought he wasn't looking, agonizing over what she could say that wouldn't sound completely moronic.

Thankfully, he spoke first. "So where've you been?"

"Around."

He laughed. "Not the talkative type, I see."

She pinched her thigh as punishment for such stupidity then cleared her throat. "Thanks for the jacket."

He nodded, taking another drink. Was he getting bored?

"I, um, did you need it back?"

"A gift is a gift. You keep it." There was another pause, briefer this time, during which he yelled over to Hal for another whiskey before turning back to her. "So you're not from the city, are you?"

A hint of misgiving returned. None of the street kids ever discussed where they were from or what their lives had been like before coming to Eloria. Too much information was a dangerous thing in the wrong hands. "What's it to you?"

"Nothing. Just making conversation."

"Oh. Sorry." Another pinch, harder this time.

He waved her apology away. "That's all right. I understand. How about I guess where you're from?" He looked at her thoughtfully. "I'd say somewhere along the coast? Am I right?"

She nodded. "How'd you know?"

"Your accent is a dead giveaway."

Sevy blushed hotly.

He seemed to catch the flush in her cheeks. "Don't worry. It's not that noticeable. I've just been to the coast enough to recognize it."

"Where are you from?"

"You don't want to take a guess?"

She shook her head. "I haven't been anywhere."

"I'm from a town called Devenbourn. West of the city, in the farmlands."

"You don't look like a farmer."

He laughed and she gave a sheepish grin, wondering why what

she had said was so funny. One of the men he was sitting with earlier approached and whispered in his ear. She caught the word "fight" and the name "Duyan", but that was about it. Jarro finished the rest of his whiskey in one gulp and stood up.

"Well, sweetheart, I'm sure glad to know you're all right. See you around."

"Bye!"

As soon as Jarro was out of sight, Hal appeared and refilled her glass. "Don't want any trouble. A friend of his is a friend of mine."

She held up the mug in a salute to him, brushing off the cryptic comment and reveling in the moment. A friend of his. A friend. That's right. He was her friend now, wasn't he? That's what it meant when someone gives you a jacket and buys you a drink and asks where you're from, right?

So to hell with those snobby, scabby kids by the river. They weren't going to get one more morsel of stolen food from Sevy. In fact, she should go to them now and demand recompense for the food they already took. She didn't need them now.

Not when she had a friend like Jarro.

Chapter 4

Every day for the next week, she returned to Sally's, eager to see Jarro again, but was disappointed each time he failed to appear. On a more positive note, whenever he saw her, Hal the bartender wordlessly handed her a mug of ale. She didn't question this new found luck, though she did wonder how long she could get away with getting free drinks.

After one such visit to Sally's, she wandered over to check out the old neighborhood, with eyes keen to see a certain someone's handsome visage and ears straining to hear that merry laugh. Instead, she found herself confronted with a head full of blonde tresses.

If it hadn't been for the hair, Sevy wouldn't have recognized Trena at all. In the interim since their disastrous parting, Trena had discarded second-hand trousers and frayed linen shirts for a corseted blouse and a slitted red skirt, becoming a convincing cliché of a fallen woman.

She was alone, walking with arms crossed, ducking in and out of the crowd, eyes fixed on the ground. Not open for business at the moment, Sevy surmised with a frown. She was making her way back to the stables, which Sevy found strange since she was certain that Gihaf would have taken Trena to live somewhere of his choosing, sequestered from anyone who had known her. Isn't that what men like him always did? Keep a python's grip on their women so there would be no chance of escape?

Sevy wondered if Gihaf had lost interest in Trena. A fragile speck of hope floated through her heart. Maybe she could talk to her, convince her to come and live by the river. Perhaps Trena wanted to apologize, but was too afraid of rejection.

Didn't matter though, did it? Who cared if Trena was bursting to say that she was sorry? That didn't change the fact that she had betrayed Sevy. Sevy should take the sight of Trena with bowed head and slumped shoulders as a victory. She had been right and Trena had been wrong. Sevy should be happy. She should be indulging in some well earned self-righteousness.

But she wasn't.

She lingered to make sure the coast was clear then followed Trena down the alley that led to the stables.

It was eerily quiet. Where were all the other children? The grifters trying to trick her into a game of cards, the buskers practicing their latest songs, even the littlest ones who hadn't yet carved out a niche for themselves and relied on the mercy of their friends: all of them gone. *This isn't normal*, Sevy thought as she looked around. At any time of the day you could always expect to see at least a dozen or so. Her fellow street rats had apparently jumped ship. Well, maybe they had moved on to better things. Not likely, but anything was possible.

One final scout to make sure she wasn't being followed then she slipped through the open door and climbed to the loft. Trena didn't look up when she came in, but visibly flinched.

"Hi."

"Sevy! What are you doing here?"

"I saw you. In the market. I just wanted to see how you were."

"You shouldn't be here. If Gihaf finds you, he'll kill you."

So Gihaf was still in the picture. Sevy laughed so that Trena wouldn't see her disappointment. "I'm not afraid of him. I was doing a pretty good job kicking his ass. Until you stopped me."

"If you're here to lecture me, save your breath and leave."

Dust danced in the thin threads of sun that slipped through the cracks in the walls. It was enough light for Sevy to see angry, ugly impressions of handprints up and down Trena's arms, a colored account of beatings past and present. Noticing her line of vision, Trena wrapped a blanket round her shoulders.

Sevy felt a surge of protectiveness, a manner of maternal fury building in the pit of her stomach. Trena's betrayal didn't matter now, but her safety sure as hell did.

"Come with me, Trena. I have a safe place to take you. And I've been getting better at stealing. I have a whole new system worked out."

"It's too late for that," Trena whispered with more than a hint of regret. "Gihaf would find me. It's easier this way."

Sevy reached out to her, but was promptly spurned.

"You need to leave. Now."

An emotional protest died on Sevy's lips. As much as she wanted to, she couldn't force Trena to leave. The line had been drawn and Trena had decided that Gihaf was on the winning side.

"All right, if that's what you want," Sevy said as she climbed back down the ladder. "See you around."

In her mind, Trena came running after her, apologizing for being such a fool. They'd figure out how to get rid of Gihaf and then things would go back to the way they were before. No, even better than before. Together, they'd beat the odds and forge a decent life for themselves. It would be nothing but good times from here on out. But Trena didn't come running. She didn't even say goodbye. Sevy brushed a tear from her cheek.

"Aww, are you crying 'cause you were so mean to me?"

"Gihaf!"

"That's right, bitch." The brute was right in front of her, blocking her way out of the alley. "Nice to see you again. We've got some unfinished business to take care of."

She whipped out her dagger and brandished it menacingly. "Get away from me, pig, or I'll mess you up worse than last time!"

"Oh, I'm gonna enjoy this."

Gihaf charged, but she jumped out of the way. He roared in frustration and came at her again, this time seizing her arm and backhanding her across the face. Sevy kicked him in the shin and though it hurt him, he didn't release his hold.

"Not getting away that easy, bitch!"

She jabbed with her dagger, aiming for his heart, but missed. He swatted the blade from her hand then grabbed her by the neck, lifting her thrashing and clawing into the air.

"What's wrong? No more sassy comebacks?"

Stars flew up in front of her eyes. She went limp, her body deciding for her that it was inevitable that she should die this way, at the hands of the one who had destroyed her life. The burning and the pain were replaced by a sense of tranquility. Then suddenly she was on the ground, clutching her throat, coughing. She looked up in bewilderment and there was Jarro, standing between her and Gihaf, drawing a sword.

"You all right, sweetheart?"

Gihaf was lying across the alley. He staggered to his feet and Sevy saw a welt rising on his temple. "You ain't got no business here, Jarro. She's mine!"

"Like hell! Touch her again and you're dead. I'm sick of you preying on these poor kids."

"Oh, fuck you and your bleeding heart!" Gihaf yelled as he took two throwing knives from his belt. He hurled one at Jarro's face that was effortlessly blocked with a simple spin of his sword. Gihaf sneered, but there was something else, apprehension or maybe even outright fear, surfacing in his expression.

Trena appeared. "What's going on?"

Gihaf then confirmed that he was only brave when bullying teen-aged girls by pulling Trena against his chest and pressing his remaining knife against her throat.

"Trena!"

"Let her go."

"Quit meddling in my business, Jarro. This one's mine, aren't you, Tre?" Trena didn't answer so he shook her violently. "Aren't you?!"

"Yes! Yes!" she sobbed.

"Now you're gonna let us by and you're not gonna try and stop me, got that? And you, bitch, I'll be seeing you around real soon."

Trena lurched, tripping over Gihaf's feet as he pushed her ahead. Jarro remained steadfast. "You're not leaving here with her. Let her go and I'll let you live."

Gihaf's eyes went wild with rage. "Big Man, Jarro! Big Man! Well, I'll tell you something. Your rat ain't here to back you up so you ain't so tough now."

He threw Trena at Jarro, using her as a distraction so that he could dart in and swipe at Jarro's hand. There was a flash of blood. The sword fell. Now that Jarro was disarmed, Gihaf rushed at him, tackling him to the ground. They rolled on the ground, punching and kicking at each other. With his size and his knife, Gihaf had the advantage. He flipped Jarro onto his back and tried to gouge him in the throat. Jarro wrestled for control of the blade.

"Trena! We've gotta help him!"

A wasted appeal. Trena sat huddled against the wheel of an overturned cart, clutching white-knuckled at the spokes. Her vacant stare was focused on the brawl, but she made no move to run to either party's aid. Sevy, on the other hand, frantically tried to break the men up. She kicked and scratched at Gihaf's back. She wrapped her arms about his thick neck, striving to pull him off. It was then that Jarro cried out. Gihaf had sliced a yawning gash into his cheek. Blood spattered onto the ground under his head.

Sevy gaped in shock. How dare he? First he had taken Trena from her and now Jarro? *No. Never!* She trembled from the amount of anger that coursed through her veins, and her body moved on its own. She grabbed the discarded sword and thrust the tip against Gihaf's shoulder. It took all of her will not to hack into him. He stiffened, but did not drop the knife.

"Leave Jarro alone!"

"Sevy, no!" Trena screamed, springing to life.

"You don't have the guts, bitch."

"Don't call me bitch!"

Raising the sword for momentum, she used all her strength to drive it through his back. Blood exploded upwards when Sevy pulled the sword out again, and startled, she backed away. Gihaf made a strange panting noise, to speak or perhaps just to try to breathe, before collapsing.

There was an ungodly screech, which Sevy could not identify until she looked at Trena and saw that her mouth was open in a seemingly never-ending scream. Jarro struggled up from underneath Gihaf's weight, pushing the body aside, his own blood pouring out from between his fingers as he clutched his face, mingling with Gihaf's. So much blood. It pooled on the ground as though the earth itself were hemorrhaging.

Sevy stared at Jarro then back at Trena who was bawling over Gihaf's body. "What did you do? What did you do?"

Dazed, she raised her hands and watched them quiver. *What did I do?*

"Sevy!" Jarro shook her from her trance. "Take your friend and get out of here. I'll take care of the body."

"Body?" she murmured.

"Snap out of it! Quick, get going before the guards find you here!"

"But you're hurt." She reached for his face.

"Don't worry about that. Just go!" He yanked Trena to her feet. Pushing her towards Sevy, he yelled again, "Go!"

The urgency in his voice forced her into action. She dragged Trena along as she dashed down the alley and out into the streets. Jarro had told her to go so she was going. To where, she didn't know. She needed to think. She needed a plan.

It was going to be all right. No one but them and Jarro knew what had happened, and Jarro had promised to cover for her. No one would miss a monster like Gihaf so everything would be all right. Trena was safe now. They both were. That was the important thing.

If she could only get the sight of all that blood out of her head. She was still seeing it, no matter where she looked, as though she had a colored screen held over her eyes.

Trena stumbled and cried for Sevy to stop because she couldn't breathe, but that didn't matter. They had to keep running until Sevy could think of what to do next. But Trena wasn't content to wait for that. She wrenched free of Sevy's grasp.

"You bitch! Why did you do that?"

Sevy's mouth fell open in surprise. "He was going to kill us!"

"No, he wouldn't have done that! He wouldn't hurt me, he loved me!"

"Trena, he was going to slit your throat to get away."

"He wouldn't have done that if you and your stupid friend hadn't shown up. You've ruined everything! You bitch!" She slapped Sevy soundly.

"What the hell are you going on about? You're free now! He can't hurt you anymore!"

"You just don't understand. I didn't want to be free. Now what am I gonna do?"

"Come with me. Jarro will help us out, I'm sure of it."

"Jarro? That man back there was Jarro? Oh my gods, Sevy, you're so stupid! He's worse than Gihaf ever was."

"No, that's not true. He's nice. He's my friend."

"He's a gang lord, idiot! Gihaf warned me about him and his men, bunch of murderers."

"Gihaf lied! Jarro isn't like that."

"Yes, he is. And now look at you, you're a murderer too! Get away from me!"

Trena spat on her and fled before Sevy could say another word. She stood frozen as the spittle moved in a sluggish path down her neck.

Murderer?

⁓⁓

Back at the river, she replayed everything over and over again in her head. Death wasn't new to Sevy; she'd seen more than enough of it in her life. One of her earliest memories was the time the body of a sailor had washed up onto the beach and she squatted beside it, poking at the stinking bloated mass with a piece of driftwood, watching the tiny blue crabs scuttle in and out of the gaping mouth, until her shrieking sisters came and yanked her away. The carnage that had forced her to come to Eloria, the nameless corpses encountered throughout the city on a regular basis, she'd seen it all. But this was the first time she'd ever taken a life. She examined her hands as though they were completely foreign to her, puzzling over if they had really done it, if it was really her fault that a person was dead.

"You had to do it. It was him or Jarro," she reassured herself. But the words were hollow, meaningless.

Should never have gone back there.

The most bizarre part of it all was the guilty thrill she felt, and how much stronger she now perceived herself to be. She was more powerful than she imagined. She knew it was wrong so she tried to suppress it, but it was there, a susurration of wicked pleasure inside of her, making her ashamed.

There was also the matter of Trena's revelation concerning Jarro that caused her confusion. Sevy could dismiss the accusations as spite or even something Gihaf had invented to scare Trena into submission. But she couldn't stop thinking about the coins and the jacket. What regular man could afford to give those away without hesitation, especially in this part of town? The words of the bartender kept floating back to her: "Don't want any trouble..."

If it was true, then what did Jarro really want with her? Why would a gang lord show kindness to an orphan except to butter her up for some underhanded reason? Trena had been fooled by new shoes and a bottle of wine, and Sevy had thought her naïve, yet was she not just as gullible? A new jacket, some friendly chitchat, and she had committed murder for a virtual stranger.

No, it was not the same thing. She was almost positive of that because while her instincts had blared a warning the very first second she met Gihaf, she just didn't get that same impression from Jarro. He had risked his life to save her even though most people would see her as nothing but a worthless little wretch.

Groaning, she stood up. There was no hope that she'd be able to sleep tonight. She decided to walk until she tired herself out. In the dying light, she made her way across Eloria, right then left, through streets and alleys, always heading north, following a path she wasn't fully aware of until she'd reached her destination. The Bloody Heart.

If what Trena said was true, then Jarro was probably around here. She'd seen him in this area—another damning sign—so maybe someone knew him and knew where he was. Somewhere along the way, she had come to the conclusion that it didn't matter if he was heading up a gang or not. He could be on the royal guard's most wanted list for all she cared. She only wanted to find him and make sure he was all right. Steeling herself, she marched into the tavern.

It was poorly lit by a handful of greasy kerosene lamps whose scent mingled with that of alcohol and sweat to produce a rank aroma, so oily that it coated the inside of her nose and throat with a noxious funk. The patrons of the tavern were crammed wall to wall, laughing and drinking and brawling. She got a couple of stares and cat calls as she slinked to the bar, and for the first time in her life she was happy that she didn't yet have the assets that would have been sure to draw more unwanted attention.

An elf fell before her feet, neck slit open, exposing the juicy vestiges of his visceral column. His mouth worked open and close, reminding her of the fish her father used to throw flopping onto the deck of his boat. The eyes had that same glassy stare as the life leaked out of him in a dark puddle on the floor. Sevy's legs felt like they'd give out on her, but she persevered. She stepped over the body, skidding in the blood.

At last, she made it to the counter and peered up at the barkeeper, a portly, balding man whose apron was covered in red and brown stains.

She straightened her shoulders, sucked in a lungful of the fusty air, and loudly proclaimed, "I'm looking for Jarro."

The barkeeper's eyes widened then narrowed in what had to be the worst bluff she'd ever seen. "Never heard of him."

"Don't give me that bull. I need to talk to him. Where can I find him?" She threw a half piece of copper onto the bar.

Laughter. She glanced into the glittering red eyes of a dark elf who sat three stools over. "She's got quite a pair!"

"What'd you want with Jarro, eh?" the bartender asked. "He don't take whores, far as I know."

She bristled at his presumption. "None of your business. Now either you know where I can find him or you don't. Don't waste my time."

"Listen, you little snipe—"

"Oh, shut it!" the dark elf said. "He's up the street, girl. Big house with the red door."

"Thanks."

She quaked with relief once she was back outside. Following the dark elf's directions, it did not take her long to find a two-story, timber framed building with a door painted cherry red. All of the windows on the lower floor were covered with shutters, but she could hear people moving around inside. She mustered her nerve again and knocked.

A wrinkled brown head popped out. Sevy did her best not to gawk at the ancient little man who stood before her, with swollen veins under parchment-like skin and, most distracting, one milky white eye that moved around independently of the other. "Yeh? What do ya want?"

"I'm here to see Jarro."

He squinted his good eye at her then closed the door in her face. Snatches of conversation floated through the wood. "Jarro...some girly... dunno...let her in or what...dunno."

She was just about to knock again when the door reopened. This time it was Jarro who answered. She gasped when she saw the raw stitches that lined the side of his face. His cheek, swelled to double its size, pushed his right eye into a slit.

"Sevy? What are you doing here?"

He couldn't open his mouth wide enough to speak properly and as a result his voice was distorted, sounding weak and weary. The wound had drained not only his blood, but his vigor as well. To Sevy, he no longer appeared the dashing quintessence of perfection. He was a real person, fallible as the next. Yet even with this unexpected epiphany and the distressing sight of his battered face, she still found him beautiful. Now more than ever.

"I needed to talk to you."

"You came here? At night? You're even crazier than I thought. Well, come in, you little fool."

He held the door open for her and, meekly, she entered the house. The old man had settled into a chair and was already dozing, but there were more people, close to a dozen in the room, a motley collection of young and old, man and woman, human and non-human. When they saw her they visibly relaxed, sheathing their swords and taking their seats. Were they expecting someone else?

"Who's this, Jarro?" an elven woman asked.

Elves, of course, had the reputation of being blessed with more beauty than any other race. Sevy had often gazed at them from afar, admiring their grace. But the one who stood before her now was truly exceptional. Flawless skin, delicate features including a charmingly placed dimple, a long mane of lavish scarlet; she was stunning. Sevy was uncomfortably aware of how scrawny and childlike she was compared to this woman's comely physique. The new clothes and boots she had been so proud of seemed like mere rags next to the elf's exquisite indigo gown. Sevy shifted uneasily. The elf took notice of this and responded by tossing her hair over her shoulder.

"Just a friend," Jarro replied as he took Sevy by the arm and led her into another room. He motioned for her to sit. "You shouldn't have come here. It's too dangerous."

"I'm sorry. I just wanted to see if you were all right. And to thank you."

He sighed. "I'm fine. Are you all right? And your friend?"

"She's not my friend." She bowed her head. Why had she come here? She felt like such a fool.

Jarro patted her hand, a gesture that made her more self-conscious than comforted. "How did you find me?"

"I asked at the Bloody Heart."

"You went into the Bloody Heart? Alone?" A touch of his regular joviality entered his tone. "You're really something else."

"It wasn't so bad," she said, with a small shrug of her shoulders.

He tried to laugh, but was cut short by the spastic twitching of his injured cheek. Flinching, he raised his hand and pressed it against the stitches, waiting for the pain to pass.

"I'm so sorry. Does it hurt much?" She leaned towards him, wanting to touch him. Instead, not knowing what else to do, she clumsily pulled her hand back onto her lap.

"Nah, not much."

She raised an eyebrow. "You're lying."

"Maybe." A faint smile skimmed across his lips. "But don't worry about it. The ladies love a good battle scar."

"I, um, what did you do with the...with Gihaf?"

"You don't need to know. Now then, it's late. I'm exhausted and I'm sure you are too. Let's get you a room."

"What? Why?"

"Just because you're stupid enough to wander the streets at night doesn't mean I'm about to let you do it again. You'll stay here until morning, all right?"

She got up and followed him out into the common room where the pretty elf was waiting, watching them, eyes alight with some unknown hostility.

"Irea," Jarro said to her. "This is Sevy and she's staying the night. Can you find her a room?"

The elf responded with an aggrieved sigh then started up the staircase. Sevy hesitated, looking to Jarro for reassurance.

"Goodnight, sweetheart."

※

Later that night, Sevy lay burrowing her head into a downy pillow. How many years had it been since she slept in an unsoiled bed? The sheets smelt sweet, like hot house flowers. There was even a pitcher of clean water on the bureau that she used to scrub her face and neck. She felt comfortable despite the horrors of the day, which were now so remote it was as though they had happened to someone else. She could have been dead, could have been just another body for the street cleaners to scrape up. Instead, she was warm and safe. Thanks to Jarro.

She smiled dreamily at the thought of him. He was unlike any other man she'd met. He was sweet and smart. And handsome. For once, it seemed like someone genuinely cared for her. He didn't have to be nice to her. He certainly didn't have to let her spend the night here, especially after she had almost gotten him killed. And yet, here she was. Trena had been wrong about him. He may well have been a criminal, but he was definitely no Gihaf.

Thinking about Trena, who probably wasn't spending the night in such luxury, made her heart constrict. She had always relied on Sevy and then on Gihaf to take care of her. Now she had no one.

It's her own damn fault, Sevy thought with stubborn resolve. *Besides, she'll find someone else. She'll be fine.*

The success of her own future was not so definite. It was clear to Sevy that certain decisions must now be made. She couldn't keep going like she had been. Not if she wanted to live. It would only be a matter of time before her luck ran out.

She knew what she had to do. Now all she needed was the courage to do it.

※

In the morning, with all due caution, Sevy peered out of the room. The house was quiet save for the sounds of gentle snoring that drifted from the rooms across the hall. She tiptoed down the staircase, wondering what to do next. Should she leave? She looked at the front door and chewed on her bottom lip, debating. The clarity she experienced during the night had faded and doubt had stolen back into her soul.

Not for long though. The stairs creaked above her and down came Jarro, blinking sleepily and running a hand through his tousled hair. The sight of him, the smell of him, it made her ache, almost like she was hungry, but it was a different sort of hunger than the kind she was used to.

"Morning. Sleep well?"

"Yeah, thanks."

She tripped down the hallway after him into a kitchen. Her stomach grumbled and her face turned red again, something that happened far too often when she was in his presence. If he noticed, he didn't let on. He gestured for her to sit as he stoked the fire and hung a kettle of water to boil, asking if she preferred coffee or tea. She didn't know as she rarely had either. While she waited for him to join her at the table, she idly traced patterns in the wood grain and snuck glances at him every few seconds.

Finally, he poured two mugs of coffee and then sat down across from her. She mumbled her thanks. Knots constricted her throat. Her hands felt clammy. She still couldn't bring herself to voice the question that she had been waiting all night to ask.

He didn't come to her rescue again by making small talk. He just drank his coffee and watched her with obvious amusement while he waited for her to begin. She blushed yet again and looked away, which made him chuckle.

"I guess, I guess I wanted to ask you something," she said.

"Sure. Anything."

"Trena said you, um, run a gang or something."

He smiled. "Or something."

"Can I join?"

A dark cloud passed over his face. He got up and paced the room. After what seemed like ages, he turned back to her. "I don't think so. This isn't the kind of life for a girl like you."

She jumped up. "But I can help you! I can fight some and I can steal! Please?"

"You're so young."

"I'm almost seventeen! And what difference does that make anyway? I'll do anything you want."

"Go home."

Her lip trembled. "I don't have one anymore. I have nowhere else to go."

"Sevy, please, I don't want to see you get hurt. You're a nice kid. You deserve better than this."

"Yeah, well, since when do people get what they deserve?"

He cracked another smile at that and looked at her intently. What he was thinking, she didn't dare to imagine.

"I'll tell you what. I guess I could use a new thief." She started to squeal with delight, but he cut her off. "Wait a second! You have to pass a little test first."

He pulled out a piece of copper and carved a letter S onto one side with a knife. "If you can steal this coin from me without me noticing, I'll let you in."

"That's easy!"

He winked at her and put the coin into a small pocket on his shirt, right next to his heart. She frowned. "All right, that's not so easy."

"You have until the end of the week."

"What? That's impossible!"

He shrugged. "We'll see, won't we?"

"Well, you have to sleep sometime, I suppose."

"True. But in case you didn't notice, I've got a house full of guards here."

She looked at the floor. "That's it then. It is impossible. If you didn't want me to join, you could have just said so." Her lip quivered again and her eyes welled with tears.

"Aw, come on, sweetheart. Don't cry about it."

"It's not fair," she wailed. "I'm all by myself! My family is dead, my best friend hates me, and you hate me too!"

"I don't hate you. Please don't cry."

Sevy threw her hands over her face and her body wracked with sobs. Jarro patted her shoulder. She kept crying so he wrapped his arms around her, pressing her head against his chest. "There now, sweetie. It's all right."

The tears ceased abruptly. "You're damn straight it's all right." She held up the coin, twirling it before his eyes. "Am I in?"

"Why, you little..."

"Well? Am I?"

Chapter 5

Sevy stood at Jarro's side, shuffling her feet and mumbling words of greeting to the people around her. He pointed to each of them, reciting their names. "And this is Marsus and Isafina. That's Thryn, Firule, Graka, and over there is Ponarelle..." and so on and so forth until the names and faces blurred into one.

She was overwhelmed and knew there was scarce chance of remembering any of them later on. No worries though, as no one seemed particularly interested in her. They grunted their acknowledgement and went about their business, all except for the little one-eyed man. His name was Turlan, and he was Jarro's doorman. Considering that he made sure to tell Sevy this detail several times over, it was evidently a position that swelled him with pride. How such an enfeebled old man could serve as a successful sentry was beyond her, but regardless of that, he was friendly and was the only one who took her hands in his and planted a dry kiss on each of her cheeks, welcoming her to the house.

Lastly, Jarro led her over to the elf with red hair. "And you met Irea last night, of course."

Sevy held out her hand. Irea responded by glaring at her and then at Jarro before stalking away.

"Irea!" Jarro called.

"Oh, don't mind her," a voice said. Sevy turned. Standing behind her was the same dark elf who had given her directions the night before. He made a face at the departing elf, rolling his eyes and curling his lip. "She's always in a bad mood."

"Revik, where've you been?"

"Around. A better question would be what the hell happened to your face?"

Jarro touched his wound, which was less puffy, but more purpled, and sighed. "Long story. I'll fill you in later. Right now, there's someone I want you to meet. Revik, this is Sevy."

He grinned at her in recognition. "Ah, the mysterious girl who stormed the Bloody Heart. Pleased to make your acquaintance." He tipped his head. "You made quite an impression on old man Vipin. Muttered about the lippy little gutter snipe all night long."

"Sevy's just joined with us."

"Has she? That calls for a drink."

"Aye, a drink," Turlan said. "It's about bloody time!"

Jarro laughed. "You already have a bottle in your hand. But you're right. Drinks all around."

The others voiced their approval and brought up a keg from the cellar. A young fellow with strawberry blonde hair and a speckled face—Sevy thought his name was Firule—sprinted upstairs, returned with a rebec, and scratched out a jaunty tune, his enthusiasm compensating for his lack of talent.

Jarro passed Sevy some ale, and then held his own glass up. "To your health, sweetheart."

"To your health!" the room repeated, downing their drinks. Second rounds were poured out before Sevy had a chance to finish her first.

She was self-conscious and nervous, happy and excited all at once. Her eyes barely moved fast enough to keep up with the activity whirling round her, so many weirdly wonderful people talking and laughing and sending foam flying as they danced with their drinks raised in the air.

Jarro crossed the room to sit down and she padded after him. "What should I do first? Steal something? Beat up somebody?"

"Sure, right after you help us with a prison break," Revik drawled.

Her eyes widened. "Re...really?"

The men looked at each other and dissolved into laughter. She was bemused by their sudden outburst until it dawned that they were teasing. She bit her lip.

"You're brave, Sevy, I'll give you that, but—"

"But you don't have much brains," Revik thoughtfully added.

Jarro silenced him with an elbow to his side before continuing. "But you've got a lot to learn. Take some time to get to know the neighborhood, the routine."

"It's all right to go out around here?"

"Of course. You're family now. Anyone that gives you a hard time has to deal with the rest of us."

Family...

She nearly split with emotion, and leaned over to hug Jarro quite fiercely before she could stop herself. He squeezed her back and when they parted, her skin was drenched in crimson. She stuck her nose in her mug to hide the telltale blush, but both men saw and laughed again. Jarro ruffled her hair, putting her at ease, but it was a while longer before she could raise her eyes to his.

The drinking lasted all afternoon and continued late into the evening. It had been quite the party, though after the first hour Sevy realized that they weren't really celebrating her enlistment. They just liked the excuse to drink and carouse. All except for Irea, who had only made a couple of appearances, coming downstairs to give Jarro the evil eye before walking away in a huff.

Sevy hadn't drunk much. She wanted to keep a clear head as she remained glued to Jarro's side and listened to him talk about various things. She hung on each word he said even when his speech became more slurred and his sotted stream of thought became difficult to follow.

Whether it was from his inebriation or his injury, or maybe a combination of both, Jarro faded soon after the moon rose. He bade the room goodnight, gave Sevy another flush-inducing embrace, and headed upstairs. Though the party was on its second wind thanks to the addition of even more people enticed by the music and the constant flow of liquor, Sevy decided to follow Jarro's lead and slipped up to her room. Everyone seemed nice enough, but she thought it prudent to avoid them while they were smashed. After all, she didn't know any of them other than Jarro, and some had looked rather intimidating. Especially Revik.

Eloria was multiracial, growing more so every year, but the different peoples didn't often mingle in matters aside from commerce. While Sevy had seen dark elves from time to time, moving furtively through the markets, more elusive than the rodents they were so often compared to, she had never met any. They kept to themselves and never seemed to stay in one place for very long, which was wise considering their reputation. Elves were tolerated for their cunning, dwarves for their money. Dark elves had no such redeeming qualities and were regarded as little better than trolls.

Sevy had certainly heard enough stories about them. They were not called dark because of the color of their skin, which was actually a pale shade of blue. Rather, it was because of their nature. It was a well known fact that dark elves were fond of human blood, but they were so cagey about their sanguinary samplings that King Grewid could not justly order an edict about them. The kids in the old stables had spoken of many a friend of a friend who had fallen prey to a dark elf's thirst, lured into the shadows like lambs to the slaughter, never to be heard from again. It happened all the time. She was sure of that even if she had never witnessed it herself.

She doubted that Jarro would be foolish enough to let Revik in his house if he were truly dangerous, and granted, he didn't seem menacing. He had a clear voice and a jolly laugh, not the sinister hiss that was expected. When he smiled, she didn't see any fangs salivating with blood lust. He was actually quite attractive in an exotic sort of way. But regardless of this, she found him, with his piercing red eyes, robin egg skin, and yards of white hair, rather disquieting, even as he traded dirty limericks with Turlan.

Laughter and bits of song floated up the stairs into her room as she made ready for bed. Most of the tunes were new to her, recounting the exploits of heroes like Eustropa, slayer of the Great Horned Corlop of Usmadius, or the lives of not so epic folk whose greatest deeds were surviving to be toothless old crones. Every second song spoke of love. First loves, lost loves, bad loves, so many different songs that it seemed to Sevy that minstrels must be just a pathetic bunch of heartbroken rejects.

Finally, Firule played a song Sevy knew: the tale of a middy doomed by the goddess Ulla to sail for eternity, never to return to land or the waiting arms of his bride again. As she hummed along, she was drawn back in time. She was a baby, exhausted from a day of play, lovingly rocked and soothed to sleep by a mother's lullaby and the haunting wail of the sea as it smashed upon the cliffs.

Sevy yawned and stretched out in bed, comforted by the memory which in her half sleep was so real she could almost see her mother's smile and smell the smoke from her father's pipe. Stomping feet and loud voices trod over the vision and snapped her awake. Firule's audience did not want such melancholy fair. They demanded something more lively. Sevy threw her pillow at her door in protest when he began butchering yet another trite love song.

Since sleep had been so rudely stolen, the next best way to kill some time was to snoop around the second floor while everyone else was occupied. A cat would have admired her stealth as she crept along the hallway. The floorboards, as seasoned and worn as Turlan himself, did not betray her footfalls. She listened at each door and stole inside when she was certain they were empty.

Each room was pretty much the same as hers, with a bed and a bureau. Some also had a chair or a wardrobe. The most intriguing belongings were the assorted trinkets and knick-knacks displayed on shelves or tucked away into drawers, giving modest glimpses into the personality of their owners. One room had a wall devoted to children's ink drawings, and judging by the skin color of the figures within the pictures, she guessed it was Revik's. Did dark elf children suckle on bottles of stolen blood? Were they given incapacitated victims to serve as ghoulish wet nurses? That was a very creepy image she wished she had never conjured. Next room!

Fortunately, the subsequent rooms were devoid of such thought provoking paraphernalia. They were interesting for a more tangible reason. On tabletops, in boxes, hidden under clothes, she found enough wealth to feed and clothe her for a year. Her fingers twitched with each new discovery of jewelry and coin, but she resisted the urge to pocket them. Like Jarro had said, these people were now her family, and she couldn't rightly steal from family.

Her luck held. No one had discovered her nosy explorations yet and there was only one room remaining. The door was partially open and a sliver of light spilled into the hallway like a beacon. Tiptoeing up to it, she heard Jarro's voice.

"Don't be like that."

"Don't be like what?" a woman said.

Sevy frowned. *Who's that?* She inched closer, and by peering through the crack she spotted a shirtless Jarro reclining on his bed. The sight made heat stream to places other than her face. He was gazing at someone across the room. Irea. The elf had her back to Jarro, and Sevy could see the pinched expression she wore as she brushed out her hair.

"You're upset with me." He sighed. "What did I do now?"

"You know what you did. Why do you insist on bringing home strays?"

Strays?

"Is that what's bothering you? She's just a kid."

"She's hardly a kid, Jarro! She's not that much younger than you," she said, hands on her hips.

"What difference does it make? She needed a place to stay."

"So do a hundred others, but you just had to bring home a pretty young thing that worships the ground you walk on!"

Sevy pumped her fists and fought the urge to stomp in there and slap that high and mighty elf right across the face.

Jarro just laughed. "Honey, honestly, you're making too much out of this. She's a nice kid, but that's all she is. You, on the other hand..." He clasped her waist and pulled her down on top of him.

"Don't you dare try to worm your way out of this!" Irea protested, though there was a smattering of delight in her tone.

Jarro murmured something that Sevy couldn't hear. She made haste back to her room and closed the door behind her to shut out the image of Irea giggling and kissing him in reply.

"So I'm a stray, am I?" Sevy muttered as she paced to her window and back to the door. "Just a nice kid? Worship the ground he...please!"

She flopped onto her bed. Strangely, it didn't seem as comfortable as it had earlier. She pounded at the pillow and kicked at the sheets. A few evil thoughts crossed her mind; ways she could interrupt Jarro and

Irea, tricks to distract them. Anything to pry their lips apart.

She should have known that he'd have a woman. It shouldn't have been that much of a surprise. And really, what did it matter to her anyway? She could have laughed at how ridiculous it all was. Irea thinking Sevy was out to steal her man, Jarro viewing her as nothing more than a "nice kid", and Sevy allowing herself to think, for even an instant, that a man like him would ever give her a second look. She would have laughed, except for the fact that she felt rather sick.

No, this is a good thing, she assured herself. Now she knew where she stood. Even so, it irked her to no end that of all the women to choose from he had to go and pick that bitch of an elf. Typical man!

Chapter 6

The days came and went, borne away on the wind like a dandelion's clock. Before Sevy knew it, a month had passed.

A safe place to sleep and three hot meals a day were doing her a wonder of good. She felt healthier and stronger than ever before. Her skin was losing its sallow hue. The circles under her eyes were fading. She even fancied that her figure was filling out. The child she had been was receding into the woman she was to become. Appraising herself in her mirror, she wondered if anyone else noticed the change.

Upon the insufferable Irea's insistence, Sevy's hair had been chopped short. To help with the lice, or so the elf claimed. It now fell an inch below her ears. Sevy hated it at first, thinking that it made her look more like a boy than ever before. But then Jarro remarked that he thought the style was becoming, which led Sevy to decide that she liked it as well.

Getting to know the routine, as Jarro had worded it, took longer to get used to than new hairdos. She was accustomed to doing things on her own schedule, basically whenever the mood struck her. Now she was made to work within a semblance of structure. Jarro met with her every morning after breakfast and gave her the day's orders. Sometimes she was told to follow one of the others and watch as they conducted their business. Their business, as far as Sevy could tell, didn't amount to much. It usually entailed visiting shops around the city and spending twenty minutes or so gossiping with the owners. Then just before they left, a small bag of coins would be ferreted into their hands. Protection money, most likely. The exchange was all very discreet and civilized. And boring.

Other days, Jarro would ask her to steal something for him. Sevy was offended by his requests at first, as they were small and simple like a bauble or a loaf of bread. Things even a child could steal. It took her awhile to realize that he was testing her, assessing her skill, slowly pushing her to see just how much she could get away with before being caught. She resolved to make the most of it. If he asked for a ring, she would scour through dozens of markets before selecting the most valuable and beautiful one she could find. It was great fun to her, and she was always so proud when she handed Jarro her tiny trophies.

Except when he turned around and gave them to Irea.

Living in the house not only tested the limits of her abilities, but her fear as well. It was difficult to go anywhere without bumping into Revik, and there were only so many times she could politely refuse his offer of drinks at the Heart. One day, he caught her off guard and, as a joke, scooped her up over his shoulder. Terrified, she had screamed, only to be stunned into silence by the reticent sadness that appeared on his face before he could conceal it. She had hurt his feelings. Dark elves had feelings?

It was after that incident that Sevy decided to give him a chance. The next day she asked if she could tag along with him. It was an experiment in bravery and she was charmed by the results. Revik turned out to be a lot of fun. He taught her neat tricks, like how to drink a shot of gin upside down and how to cheat at dice. Sometimes he'd take her out to any number of pubs, and the pair would get so rowdy that they'd be repeatedly thrown out, and spend the rest of the night caterwauling silly songs on street corners for spare change.

Through Revik, Sevy learned that everything heard on the streets should be taken with a grain of salt. He was no monster. Besides his raging streak of sarcasm, he was never anything but amicable towards her, and it was impossible to believe he was capable of gory violence while he was performing his falsetto imitation of Irea. "Jar-rooo, buy me that dress. Jar-rooo, I need more perfume. Jar-rooo, I'm a big bitchy cow."

Sevy looked forward to the time she spent with Revik, but, hands down, the favorite part of her day had to be mid afternoon. A drowsy hush would fall over the house as most of the members were either out around town or having a nap in preparation for the night's activities. Jarro would take Sevy into his study, a snug nook off of the kitchen with a large picture window opening onto the courtyard, and sit with her at his desk. The sun warmed her back and she nibbled on cookies while he read to her from one of his multitude of books. Growing up, he told her, he had a proper education in a real schoolhouse with a real teacher and everything. He loved to read and spent most of his free time mulling over the history of Axlun or elvish folk tales or made up stories about fairies and dragons and knights.

When he learned that Sevy didn't know how to read or write, he made it his mission to teach her. She wasn't particularly interested and found trying to master the alphabet frustrating beyond words, but she loved to sit at his side and get lost in the tenor of his voice. It didn't matter what he read. It all sounded lovely.

Drinking buddies and educational endeavors aside, she was beginning to grow restless. Life in a gang wasn't proving to be as action packed as she had supposed. Jarro wouldn't let her come with him when he thought there would be trouble and he wouldn't include her in any of the meetings he held, even though they sounded very exciting through the closed door, with lots of shouting and banging on tables. Her requests for inclusion were often met with, "Oh, but it's too nice a day to be cooped up in here. Why don't you go outside and play, sweetheart?" She was beginning to feel that Irea had been right; that she was nothing but a "stray" the men brought sweets home to. Just some stupid kid.

She desperately wanted to prove herself, to show Jarro that he made the right choice in letting her join, that she could pull her weight just like the rest of them. That morning, she resolved to talk to him and try to convince him that she was ready for more responsibilities. She rehearsed a speech detailing her many talents, then headed towards his room.

At his door, she raised her hand, but before she could strike the wood, Revik stormed past her.

"Hey!" she protested.

"Sorry, squirt." He threw the door open and walked into the room. "We've got trouble."

"What is it?" she heard Jarro ask.

Revik hesitated. "Not for your ears," he said to Sevy as he closed the door in her face.

Her teeth gnashed together so forcibly that it made her jaw ache. How dare he? The patronizing attitude they all had towards her was beyond infuriating. She had half a mind to barge in there and tell him off, dark elf or not. Instead, she was able to subdue her temper by pacing outside the door until it opened again. Revik came out first and went downstairs, oblivious to her glower. She peeked inside at Jarro.

"What's going on?"

"Duyan's men are making noise again. Nothing for you to worry about."

Duyan was a rival gang leader. Eavesdropping into their meetings, Sevy had learned all about him. He was trying to push his way into Jarro's territory, and from what she had gleaned, the two gangs had been clashing quite a bit lately. There was something she didn't understand about it all. Something about the latest attacks being acts of retaliation. Retaliation for what, she hadn't figured out yet.

"Can I come with you?"

"Not a chance. Too dangerous."

She trailed down the hallway after him. "Oh, come on! I can fight!"

"I'm sure you can. But can you use a sword?"

"Probably."

"Probably?" he repeated, crooking an eyebrow.

"Well, I've never tried before, but it looks pretty simple."

"Sorry, sweetheart. Tell you what, I'll ask Revik to train you sometime, all right? But until then you stay put, got it?"

"Yeah, got it," she said with a solemn sigh.

She watched in despondence as he and several men left the house and headed up the street. So much for proving herself. That should be her, marching at Jarro's side, chest puffed out with importance. Run of the mill citizens should be deferring to her, not treating her like some petticoated poke-along.

Turlan chuckled. "Chin up, girly! Things ain't as bad as all that."

"It's not fair. I can handle a little fight. Men! Think they're so tough. I bet I could kick all their asses!"

"I believe ya," he said, raising his arms up. "Just don't hurt me."

Sevy did not appreciate his joke, and to make that clear she knocked over a glass vase that sat on the table and let out a growl. Unmoved by her showboating, he hobbled away, still laughing.

Sevy turned to stomp back up to her room and almost slammed into Irea in the process. By the smirk on Irea's face, she must have witnessed the whole display.

Sevy straightened her back and crossed her arms. "What do you want?"

"Oh, nothing," Irea said. "I was just curious. You're supposed to be our newest thief, are you not? Then why don't you make yourself useful and go get me something pretty."

"I don't take orders from you. Go do it yourself."

"Me? Steal something?"

"You're not a thief. You're not a fighter. Just what exactly do you do around here?"

Irea inclined her head so that it was inches from Sevy's ear, and whispered, "It's not a question of what. It's a question of who."

Had Sevy been born with more wit, she would have retorted with something clever and biting. As it was, all she could think of to do was roll her eyes and let Irea's obnoxiously tittering laughter accompany her up the stairs.

※

"A wooden sword?" she asked.

"Safer this way. You don't get a real one until I'm sure you can handle it," Revik replied.

"What do you take me for? I can handle the real thing." She threw the sword onto the ground and kicked some dirt over it for good measure.

"Pick it up, princess, and let's get started. If it makes you feel any better I'm using a wooden one too."

Sevy pouted. After days of hounding Jarro, reminding him of his promise, he finally asked Revik to train her. And now this? A wooden sword? As soon as it looked as though they were going to start taking her seriously, they went and gave her a toy? A dozen curses deluged her mind and she was about to tell Revik exactly what she thought about him and his stupid sword.

Soft laughter interrupted her tirade before it could begin. Jarro and Irea were seated across the courtyard under the shade of the lone tree, sharing a bottle of wine. He purred into her ear and from Irea's giggles she obviously liked what she heard.

Sevy narrowed her eyes and scooped the sword up, pointing it at Revik. "Let's go."

Revik bowed. "Attack."

With a yell, Sevy charged, swinging vertically, aiming for his head. Revik blocked her attack. She slashed at him again, but he parried her strike and then thrust his sword forward. The tip touched her stomach.

"Now you're dead," he said, smirking. "Attack."

This time, she tried to come at him from the side. Once again he parried the blow then swung down. The edge of his sword glanced against her left thigh.

"And now you have no legs."

"This is stupid!"

"No, you're stupid."

She scoffed then took a swipe at him when she thought he wasn't looking. He clamped onto her wrist with one hand and, with the other, bashed his sword right smack on the top of her head. "Nobody likes a sneak, my dear."

"Revik," Jarro called. "Play nice!"

"Yes, Mother. Fine. We'll start with the basics. This, Sevy, is a sword. You use it to kill things."

"Can we just get on with this?" Sevy sighed.

"In a hurry, are you? Have someplace you'd rather be? I can certainly think of a few places I'd rather be, and let me assure you they involve a lot less moaning, and a lot more wine and topless women. Well, maybe a little moaning. But stop trying to distract me with all your talk of moaning, naked women. You're the one who wanted to learn how to fight after all."

"You're the strangest man I've ever met."

"First things first. Your posture is horrible. Stand like so. Back straight. But not rigid. No, no, no!"

It took awhile before Sevy positioned herself the way Revik was, and even longer before she held the sword the way he wanted her to. Then he started on footwork.

"Step step forward. Step step back. Like this. See?"

"Are we fighting or dancing? Can't we just skip to the part where I stab you?"

He laughed. "Here, let's try this. Hold your sword like so." He repositioned her with both hands on the hilt of her sword so that she held it parallel to her body. "Now if I thrust forward like this, simply push my blade away. Perfect. Let's try that again."

Slowly, Revik went through various blocking methods, and Sevy thought she was catching on quickly. It was much easier than learning how to read, that was for sure. And despite his teasing, Revik was an excellent teacher, and he didn't mind having to repeat himself whenever she started to struggle. Her biggest problem, he told her, was her impatience, which would lead to fatal mistakes in a real battle.

"Don't just look for the easy win." He gave her a whack to her side that left her breathless. "You're leaving yourself wide open. Come on now. Don't just stand there like an idiot."

"Well, that hurt!"

"Good. It's supposed to."

Which was worse: Jarro's chuckle or Irea's mocking laughter? It was hard to tell.

With a sigh, she thrust at him half-heartedly. He parried, but she was able to block his counter attack. A bit amazed with herself, she thrust again with more force.

"Nice! Now faster."

She nodded and came at him again, her movements becoming more fluid with each pass. Revik taunted her, calling her a sissy and a milksop until she was goaded enough to call him names back. That helped to liven things up and Sevy relaxed into the rhythm of the fight.

"Looking good, sweetheart!" Jarro said, and she grinned over at him, but was humbled when Revik took advantage of her distraction.

The white sun of summer crowned the sky and focused its rays on the combatants below. The sweat and the heat only heightened Sevy's exhilaration as though she were siphoning energy from the sun itself. She stripped to her undershirt, no longer shamed by her body. It wasn't skinny or childlike. It was lean and wiry. Powerful. The bruises spreading from Revik's hits were marks of valor.

She was ecstatic that Jarro was watching her, cheering her on and shouting out warnings, instead of paying that snooty elf more undeserved compliments. When Revik called a time out to get a ladle of water from the well, Sevy ran to Jarro for more direct encouragement. "How am I doing?"

"Fantastic!" He handed her his glass of wine. "You're a natural."

"Not bad, girl, but don't get too cocky. Revik's going easy on you." Irea leaned her head to rest on Jarro's chest. She lifted her hand and twirled her fingers through his hair. Sevy was suddenly reminded of the sewer troll possessively guarding its food.

And just like that, she was once again an awkward child, her confidence secreted away like the sun behind the clouds. She turned from them, grumbling.

"Hurry up," Revik said. "Let's go again."

"Yeah, yeah."

He laughed. "Well, try not to sound too eager. I'm going to attack. Defend yourself."

He swung horizontally to cut her across the waist; she countered with difficulty. They went back and forth for awhile, but the fun was gone. Revik grew impatient with her lackluster swings and doubled his insults, which did help rally her spirits somewhat. She started pressing forward, backing Revik up. For a moment, Sevy actually thought she was winning. But, as Irea had said, he was just going easy on her, and as soon as he grew bored with her advances, he parried her strike and deftly leapt over her head, landing behind her. Before she could face him, he kicked her in the back and sent her sprawling onto the ground.

Irea's boisterous laugh crackled off the courtyard walls like the sound of ice breaking in the spring thaw.

"No fair!" Sevy groaned, spitting the dirt out of her mouth.

"Nothing in the rules against it."

"Not so rough, Revik," Jarro called at the same time Irea shouted, "Good one!" Sevy cursed her under her breath.

"I heard that," Revik said, not attempting to hide his merriment. He leaned in and whispered, "And I agree."

Sevy couldn't help but slip a smile. At least her nerves weren't the only ones that Irea gnawed upon. She'd seen Irea and Revik butt heads on more than one occasion, usually instigated by one of Irea's snide, borderline racist comments, always said out of Jarro's earshot, of course. Sevy dusted her clothes off and picked up her sword.

"That's the spirit, Sevy. Show 'em what a stubborn little beastie you are!"

"Is that supposed to be a compliment?"

He came at her. She deflected his blow and then swung her sword low. He countered and thrust forward. She was expecting this and instead of trying to parry, she jumped to the side then grabbed his arm, pulling him off balance. As he stumbled, she swung and he just barely avoided her blow.

"Well done."

She smiled and looked to Jarro for acknowledgment. Her face fell when she saw that he and Irea were kissing passionately. There was nothing in Jarro's world but soft red hair and full red lips. Irea winked at Sevy before deepening the kiss, practically climbing on top of him right there.

"Hey! Pay attention!" Revik yelled.

She may not have been a dark elf, but at that second Sevy's eyes flashed with fire just as brightly as any of theirs did. Anger boiled over inside of her and she rushed at Revik with a roar.

Their blades clashed together. They were face to face, Sevy straining to force Revik's sword away, Revik laughing at the abrupt change in her demeanor. "Well, aren't you just a little hellion?"

"Go bugger yourself!" she snarled, though the remark wasn't really directed at him.

Revik shifted his weight forward onto his left leg, and with his right, kicked Sevy in the shin, causing her to falter. She crashed to the ground and managed to roll away just before his sword came down upon her. Eyes narrowed, she rushed up at him, butting her head into his side. He fell back a few steps then pushed her off.

"I guess you're the type who has to learn the hard way, huh? You really think you can get one up on me on your first day?"

"Shut up and fight!"

"Sure. Whatever you say."

Three seconds. That's how long it took for Revik to knock the sword from her hands and strike her not one, but five times, each hit more brutal than the last. Finally, he struck across her legs, rendering them momentarily useless. She lay broken on the ground, panting into her arms, waiting for the stinging to subside.

Revik sat down beside her and patted her back. "Good job today."

"Liar."

"No, really. A valiant effort for a beginner. But tomorrow, what say we go somewhere the witch can't watch? The stink of her dirty crotch was distracting. Hey, Jarro," he said, raising his voice. "Didn't our little girl do great today?"

Jarro was suddenly beside her, helping her to her feet as she wheezed with laughter and pain.

"I'm impressed. I honestly thought Revik would have crippled you by now."

"I think this deserves a celebration, don't you? Booze at the Heart. Wait, no. Let's go across the river and get you one of those fancy drinks all the sophisticated ladies rave about. Jarro's buying."

"Hey!"

"Don't play the miser now, my friend, this was..."

Sevy ignored their teasing exchange as she glanced over to the tree where Irea still sat, lips pursed in a sour pucker. Sevy blew her a kiss before threading one arm through Jarro's and the other through Revik's. While the three of them strolled off together, Irea was left alone, forgotten and muttering.

Chapter 7

The days were barely able to hold the amount of activity Sevy wanted to experience. Much of her time was taken up with lessons from both Jarro and Revik, but she had begun to venture out into the city more, exploring it in regards to her new position in society. Since becoming a member of Jarro's gang, she discovered she could walk through the roughest areas with impunity. This new found freedom was relished, knowing in full confidence that no one could dare to touch her without summoning the wrath of her new family. The merchants, wising up to the fact that wherever she went a senior member of Jarro's gang was not far behind, treated her with respect, going so far as to offer her free samples of their product. Sevy was seduced by the power she now held over them, and more than once Jarro had to rein her in again, reminding her that not everyone appreciated being bossed around by mouthy teenage girls.

But when a wave of scorching heat swept over the city, making even the most basic exertion of energy unthinkable, Sevy's fun came to an end. The usual happy-go-lucky atmosphere of the house turned foul, and everyone seemed to have lost patience for Sevy persistently shadowing them, asking that they teach her whatever it was they were doing.

Even Jarro, who was normally cheerful and good natured, now had a short temper, though he tried to keep it suppressed. While Revik's witty banter took on a sharper and more cutting edge, and Irea did little more than lounge around, fanning herself and complaining, Jarro became withdrawn. He spent a lot of time off by himself, rubbing the bridge of his nose absentmindedly and muttering various self-deprecating remarks. When Sevy asked him why he felt it necessary to call himself a bastard and a spineless rotter, he quietly replied, "I'll thank you to mind your own damned business, sweetheart." He was quick to add a smile, but she could tell that was just an afterthought, an apology of sorts.

All Sevy could do was pray that time would bring a change in the weather.

One particularly humid day, she decided it was best to keep out from underfoot. It was too hot to remain up in her room, and as Irea was monopolizing the courtyard, Sevy headed over to the Bloody Heart.

She ordered a drink from Dril Ray Vipin, just plain Vipin as he was called by his customers, who in the past months had learned to keep his big fat mouth closed and save the snipe comments for other audiences. But while he may have had to serve her, he didn't have to like it. He slid the mug to her with a grunt, about the closest thing to a social nicety as he was willing to give her.

Sevy took a sip and stuck out her tongue. Vipin was known for being the biggest skinflint this south of Wilrendel. He didn't want to spring for an icebox let alone ice so the ale tasted like warm piss. Still, it was booze and it would do for now.

She surveyed the room. Due to the heat, the Heart was left wanting for the patronage of anyone other than a handful of diehard drunkards. None of them would be much company. She thought about going back to the house, but then noticed Turlan at one of the tables, alone, whispering to himself. She walked over to him. "Mind if I join you?"

"Buy me another and you can."

She grinned. Turlan was a nice old guy. She liked him because he always told the most interesting stories when he was drunk, which was often. She readily passed him her ale.

"How's yer training with what's-his-name? Seen you practicing the other day. Not bad, not bad. Yer getting better."

"Thanks. I think it's going pretty well. Jarro said if I keep it up he'll let me come along on jobs more often."

"Good, good." He downed the mug and looked pleadingly with his good eye at Sevy. She chuckled and got up to fetch him yet another drink.

Just then, the door swung open and two men stumbled in. From the way they were hanging onto one another to stay upright, they appeared to be a few sheets to the wind already. She had never seen either of them before. One was gangly and had elaborate tribal tattoos covering his face and neck; the other would have been good looking if he were about forty pounds lighter. They bumped into Sevy on their way to the bar and made her spill ale onto her shirt. She glared at them, but they didn't pause in their incoherent singing to apologize to her.

"What's wrong?" Turlan asked.

"Nothing. Just those two idiots."

He took a sip and smacked his lips in satisfaction. "If they're bothering ya, just make 'em stop. For a little thing, yer pretty spunky. Course in my younger years, I'd step up and get rid of 'em for ya, but I ain't that tough these days. 'Cept for my skin."

She giggled, enough encouragement for Turlan to tell her a story about what he was like when he was her age. Back then, he told her, some of the royal family still lived in Eagleborn Castle in the heart of the western quarters. Once, he had slipped into the treasury room, guarded by fifty of the king's best men mind you, and taken a single strand of pearls. A gift for his girl, don't you know. Sevy listened to him prattle on about his glory days, laughing inwardly that the number of guards had tripled from the last time he had told this story, but was distracted. The two men at the bar were getting louder and were yelling insults at the other people in the tavern.

"Ah, those were the days," Turlan finally finished after ten minutes or so. "Those were the days."

He looked down at his liver spotted hands, rubbing his arthritic knuckles together as though he could smooth away the bane of time. As young as she was, Sevy really couldn't understand his melancholy and didn't know how to respond other than to reach over and pat his arm. He smiled at her, but was drifting in time, perhaps remembering all the girls who had stolen his heart way back when.

"Well, isn't that a pretty picture!" the portly stranger said, appearing by their table. "That your granddaughter or your girl?"

The tattooed man soon followed. Both men now seemed surprisingly sober. "Can you still get it up, old man?"

Sevy scowled. "Bugger off!"

They laughed. The fat one grabbed Turlan's ale right out of his hands and drank the rest of it. Turlan swore and stood up, pulling out his dagger. Sevy did likewise.

"You ain't welcome here, so get out!"

"Better get used to us, old man. We like it here. Think we'll come around more often."

"Like hell!" Sevy yelled. "You heard him, get out! Or else!"

"Or else what?" The fat man flipped the table, causing Turlan to lose his balance and turtle over. Both men took out their knives and looked at Sevy, eyes twinkling with sadistic expectation.

She glanced around the tavern. The other people present were too wasted to be of any help. Most didn't even seem to know what was going on. Only Vipin was watching, his face expressionless as he wiped a dirty glass with an equally dirty cloth. A bubble of panic built up inside Sevy's stomach, but now was not the time to let fear get a hold of her.

"Or else you'll have to answer to Jarro!"

"Jarro? Why should we worry about him, eh? When all he's got for backup is little girls and old men."

"Is there a problem?"

There were no words to describe Sevy's relief when Revik brushed her aside and stared the pair of strangers down. Tattoo man's swagger was sufficiently subdued, but the other continued to crow. "And the party's complete! Good to see you, rat. Jarro let you off your leash much?"

There was a flash of metal too quick for Sevy to follow. The man's eyes widened and his mouth fell slack. Sevy followed his gaze down to the hilt of Revik's sword buried within rolls of flab. A quick jerk of the sword up and out produced a geyser of blood that the man plunged into.

"I've a message for Duyan," Revik said to the tattooed man as he pushed him towards the door. "Tell him that Jarro's rat is hungry and that anyone who sets foot in our territory is fair game. You go and tell him that."

Sevy saw the terror in the man's face. He was gone the instant Revik let go of him, racing down the street as fast as his shaking legs would allow. Revik gave Sevy half a smile as he wiped his blade clean and returned it to the sheath on his back. She watched, waiting in macabre fascination for him to swoop down upon his fallen prey and feast upon the still warm blood. But he did not. He completely ignored the body as he bent to help Turlan up.

"Sorry, Revik. I guess I ain't got any fight left in me."

"Don't worry about it. Sevy," Revik said over his shoulder, "you coming?"

Word traveled fast and a flurry of activity was already underway once they arrived back at the house. Graka was ordered to take some men back to the Bloody Heart and clean up the mess. Others were sent to scout out the area for more enemies. Turlan was ushered up to bed, despite his protests that he was well enough to take his post at the door. Not knowing what else to do, Sevy followed Revik into Jarro's study.

"I'm sorry," she said once Revik finished relating the tale. "Me and Turlan didn't mean to start anything."

Faint creases of worry had etched themselves onto Jarro's forehead. He massaged his temple with two fingers and closed his eyes. "No one blames you. They were looking for a fight. Are you all right? Did they hurt you?"

"No, I'm fine."

Revik stepped forward again. "Duyan is getting more aggressive. We need to take a stand against him. You know this. I've told you this all along."

"I know, I know," Jarro said, sighing.

Sevy looked from one man to the other. There was some sort of unspoken communication going on between them, and suddenly Sevy perceived something she had never considered before. She had to wonder—had they been of the same race, had all things been equal, would Jarro still be leader of this gang?

"We need to stand against him," Revik repeated.

"And get ourselves killed?" Irea asked. Sevy hadn't noticed her. She was sitting on a chair beside the window. "Why start something with Duyan over a bar room tiff?"

"That wasn't a tiff!" Revik shouted, startling Sevy with his volume and anger. "That was a deliberate attempt to throw his weight around, right in our neighborhood! Right down the bloody street!"

"I'm just saying that we shouldn't jump to conclusions. Maybe they honestly went there for a drink. We've all seen how insolent Sevy is."

Sevy let out a small cry of disgust. "What's that supposed to mean?"

"That you're more trouble than you're worth. Just like I've said from the beginning."

"That's enough. Revik saw the whole thing. Sevy didn't start it."

Irea's answering laugh was laced with resentment. "Oh yes, she's just so innocent, isn't she? Let's not forget that Duyan's men have only been acting up since Gihaf disappeared. And we all know who's responsible for that!"

Gihaf...

Hearing that name threw Sevy into shock. It was like seeing the specter of a half-remembered nightmare come shambling out into the daylight. She hadn't realized that anyone knew about Gihaf besides Jarro, and he had never spoken about it since that day.

"But what does that have to do with Duyan?" Sevy asked.

"Gihaf worked for Duyan, you little twit."

"Shut it, Irea!" Revik said. "They've been trying for months to take over, long before Sevy came. So just shut it. Jarro, Duyan isn't going to back down until we make him. I say we take some men and show him we're serious."

"And start a war over nothing? You're a fool! We should make peace with him. He's stronger than we are. Jarro, darling, listen to me."

The creases in Jarro's brow grew deeper, but it didn't take long for him to reach a decision. "No, Revik's right. We don't make deals with scum like Duyan. We fight."

"Fine! Listen to the squeaking of a rat instead of to me. Weakling! You're going to get us all killed!"

Sevy waited for Jarro's reaction to Irea's outburst, but surprisingly enough there was none. His eyes did not trail her as she stomped from the room, nor did he make a move to follow her. Calmly, he spread a map out over his desk and ran his finger back and forth across the width of it before stopping and tapping on one spot. "Find some volunteers.

We'll go to Lornian. A handful of his crew have been making themselves at home there and it's about time we got rid of them."

Revik nodded and strode out into the hallway where he raised a call to arms. The house reverberated with the answering roar. There were shouts and cheers, doors slammed and feet stomped up and down the stairs, so much so that a fine spray of dust wafted down off the rafters.

Sevy stifled a sneeze as she edged towards Jarro, who had moved to gaze out the window. The only one who did not lend his voice to the bedlam, Jarro seemed wearier than he had just seconds before.

"Jarro? I'd like to help."

"No."

"Please? You've seen me train with Revik all summer. I can help, honestly!"

They caught one another's eyes in their reflections in the window. She hoped to convey her strength and her fealty, attempting to emulate the grim seriousness that Revik had shown at the tavern. She had the unsettling feeling that she appeared constipated rather than intimidating. Jarro stared at her for a long while. What was he thinking?

"Fine," he said at length. "But you stay close to me. Go find Revik. Tell him you're coming."

They assembled in the common room an hour later. In addition to Sevy, Jarro, and Revik, ten other men were going to Lornian. The remaining members were instructed to patrol the borders of their territory, and a few were charged with guarding the house. Turlan, ignoring a direct order from Jarro, got out of bed and hobbled back and forth, completely out of breath and accomplishing nothing of relevance.

Only Sevy seemed impervious to the tension as waves of excitement rolled to life within her. Finally, a real battle. This was going to be fun. Jarro handed her a short sword in a black leather sheath and she strapped it to her waist, feeling quite grown-up.

"I don't see why you're doing this," Irea whined from the staircase. "Duyan's a powerful man. You'd do well to join with him. You'd do well to choose your friends more carefully. How long do you think you'll last on the strength of one filthy red-eye?"

Now that got Jarro's attention, and for the first time, Sevy heard him raise his voice to Irea in anger. "Say what you like about me, but don't you ever—"

Revik cut Jarro off by placing a hand on his shoulder. He shook his head.

Jarro shot Irea one last pointed look. "We'll talk about this later."

With that, he led the group from the house. Sevy hung back for a moment, glancing at Irea whose stare of hatred could bore holes into iron. For the first time, Irea actually frightened Sevy. Beneath that pretty face lurked something ugly, something akin to what Sevy had seen in Gihaf's eyes. Unnerved, she turned away from the unblinking glare and ran to catch up with Jarro and Revik.

Chapter 8

The Lornian District was a half mile strip of tenement buildings west of the river. Every second or third building contained either a brothel or a dance hall and, as one would expect, was home to many prostitutes. But Lornian was unique among its kind. It was run by a council of women, steely eyed madams who took great pains to ensure the safety of their workers. Only the very best girls lived on Lornian and only the very best clientele were admitted, an arrangement that caused envy and resentment among their competitors. For a nominal fee, Jarro provided protection against these rivals, and unlike other organizations that offered similar services, he did not allow his men to abuse their position.

Before joining with the gang, Sevy had never even heard of Lornian. It was a guarded secret among the city's well-to-do. She guessed that was to keep out the riffraff. The aristocracy probably wouldn't like sharing their whores with the unwashed masses, and they doubtlessly wouldn't want their high society wives to learn about their dalliances on the sly either.

Three months ago, Sevy would have claimed to know all the ins and outs of Eloria. Now she constantly discovered that she didn't even know half of what really went on. Though it was just one city, it had many different worlds.

She scanned the street, watching the women who strolled arm in arm and chatted demurely with one another like proper ladies. They had no bruises or scars on their bodies; their eyes were bright and their voices were upbeat. Sevy found herself whispering a small supplication, a prayer that Trena would be lucky enough to find a place such as this. A token gesture perhaps, but it was enough to ease the ache that burned in Sevy's chest at the thought of her former friend.

It must have been this same lonely ache that made Sevy suddenly reach out and grasp Jarro's hand. Such a childish action. She was horrified. As soon as she registered what she had done, she released him, but he smiled at her, took her hand again, and continued walking as if this was normal behavior for them.

"Remember what I said, all right? Stay close to me," he whispered to her.

"And keep your mouth shut," Revik said, coming up beside them.

In a clatter of silver bangles, a woman with slate grey hair arranged in ringlets and braids emerged from one of the houses to greet them. "Jarro, love!"

Sevy recognized her as Ponarelle. She occasionally slept in the room across from Sevy's and was Jarro's liaison to the Lornian madams, being a retired prostitute herself. She was pretty, though long past her prime, and had a lilting laugh and a sweet singing voice. Sevy had only met her a handful of times, but liked her well enough, despite her irritating habit of pinching Sevy on the cheek.

Jarro took Ponarelle by the arm and led her out of earshot. Sevy squinted at them, hoping that she could read their lips if she tried hard enough. Ponarelle gestured to a row of apartments at the edge of Lornian then sped back indoors, calling for all the girls to do likewise.

The street emptied as Jarro and Revik started for the building. The others followed at their heels. They were silent now, guided by hand signals and intuition. Jarro pointed and half the men circled round the back. He motioned for Sevy to stay behind him as they went inside. The others went upstairs while Sevy, Revik, and Jarro searched through the lower rooms. They appeared to be vacant, but there were signs that people had been there recently—discarded clothing, scraps of food. She wrinkled her nose at the smell. Somebody didn't like using the latrine.

A quick hunt through the apartments didn't turn anything up, so they rejoined the other men at the foot of the stairs and went back outside. Sevy sighed, crestfallen. She had been eager for more excitement than that.

As if in answer to her wish, two dozen men suddenly burst out of nowhere, emerging from behind rubbish bins and dropping down from roof tops. Their small group was surrounded and Sevy's heart became as a caged bird, flying madly against her ribs.

The tattooed man who had threatened Sevy and Turlan at the Bloody Heart stepped forward. "Well, hey there, Jarro. Here for a piece? Betcha the girls round here charge a lot less than the redhead you keep at home, eh?"

"You're not welcome here," Jarro said, refusing to be baited. "Go back to Duyan and tell him so."

"You're outnumbered. Why don't you leave while you have the chance?"

"Why don't you go to hell?" Sevy piped up.

"Shut it!" Revik hissed.

"You again?" the man said to Sevy. "Resorted to recruiting little girls, Jarro? Is business that bad?"

Without waiting for a reply, he tipped his sword and the rest of the thugs charged.

The men ran forward to meet them while Sevy's bravado vanished. She knew she should fight, but couldn't force herself to step into the fray. The savagery of it all. The clashing of metal and the sprays of blood. It was just like that long ago time. Her mother shaking her awake. The pounding at the door. Her sister screaming, "Run!"

Sevy backed away, breathing heavily, sword shaking in her sweaty hands.

The tattooed man fell next to her, pressing his palm to a gash that split his brow. It was a superficial wound, but looked ghastly and would need several stitches to close. The side of his face was so painted with blood that the ink had all but disappeared. Sevy shrunk against the wall, hoping he wouldn't notice her. Fortunately, he only had eyes for the person who caused the wound, the same person who had trod over his pride at the Bloody Heart.

"Fucking rat!" he sneered at Revik, whose attention was now on another opponent. His cowardice at the tavern had demonstrated that he was no match for Revik, but he wasn't above stabbing someone in the back. When Sevy realized his intent, she cried out and poked the man in the side, cutting him, but doing no real damage. The distraction worked too well. He forgot about Revik and focused on her, screaming out a guttural challenge that chilled her to the marrow. She panicked. She ran. The man gave chase, following her down the adjacent alley until she slammed into a wall. It was a dead end.

Flight had been foiled. She had no choice except to fight. Sevy held up her sword, praying to the gods that it would stop wavering so much. "Get back!"

He swung and she managed to block. She tried to cut him across the legs, but he stepped out of the way and swung again. The tip of his sword sliced her across her chest before she could parry. She sucked her breath in through her teeth as flashes of pain bit into her, hotter and sharper than the sting of sea nettles.

As the blood spread over her breast, Sevy was drawn into a whirlpool of rage that pulled her down to the blackest depths of her soul. Like a leviathan slumbering on the ocean floor, the dark portion of her soul, the part that had taken pleasure in Gihaf's death, was aroused and shot up to the surface.

Revik may have taught her how to wield a sword, but it was anger now that guided it. She stabbed wildly at the man, again and again so that he had only precious seconds to react, barely able to block one strike before another swept down upon him. He stepped back. She pressed her attack, muscles rippling in satisfaction when her blade finally made good and sunk into his arm, cutting through the skin and tendons like an oar through water, coming to a jarring stop when it struck against a bed of bone. His sword fell helplessly to the ground. With a wicked laugh, Sevy kicked it away before swinging again. She studied the stupefied look that came to his face once he realized his belly had been slashed open.

Remember this moment. There's no need to run anymore. From now on, they will run from you.

However, the surge to her ego was short lived. His failing arms couldn't hold back his innards much longer and Sevy gagged at the sight of the gore that slopped onto the ground. She had to rest against the wall until the nausea passed.

Then, in the distance, she heard Jarro calling out to her. "Sevy! Where are you?"

"Here!" she answered, as she hopped over the body and jogged back up the alley.

The battle was over and the street was littered with bodies. Sevy was relieved to note that the fallen were comprised exclusively of Duyan's men, but victory had not come without a price. Firule, the lanky would-be musician, was badly hurt and the others had fashioned a makeshift stretcher to carry him home. As they passed, he stared unseeing into Sevy's eyes, mouthing words that not even he could understand. She shuddered.

"Are you all right?" Jarro asked.

She nodded, so ashamed that she had turned tail at the first hint of trouble that she was unable to speak or even look at him.

The walk back to the house had the air of a funeral procession with Firule providing his own mumbled dirge. Sevy trailed behind, only quickening her pace when Revik turned and barked at her to hurry up.

Once again, word traveled on the wind. Turlan had the door thrown wide before they even passed the Heart. Irea stood leaning against a lantern post, a look of "I told you so" engraved on her face. She didn't even pretend to be sympathetic when Revik asked her to bring some supplies up to Firule's room. She complied with the request, but not without first tossing her head and clucking her tongue. The rest of the house scattered, some to return to patrol, others off in search of a drink to wash away the aftertaste of bloodshed. Jarro heaved a sigh and flopped down onto the nearest chair.

Sevy tiptoed up to him. "Is Firule gonna be all right?"

"Revik's a good healer," Jarro said blankly, not answering her question. "You'd better go to your room. Take care of that cut."

"I'm sorry I ran. I got scared." She glanced at him then quickly averted her eyes. "Are you angry?"

"We'll talk later. Go."

She hurried upstairs, blocking her ears against the sounds of suffering coming from Firule's room.

⁂

The birds bid adieu to the daylight in a cacophony of warbles and twitters, and night descended over Eloria like a hawk on unwitting quarry. Only then did the evening pixies living in the courtyard tree pop out of their nest one by one, stretching and shaking off sleep. They eyed Sevy warily; the sight of the roguish brunette made them anticipate a barrage of pebbles or twigs that could begin at any moment. She kept a reserve of odds and ends on her windowsill for that very purpose, and the tiny creatures had no way of knowing that harassing them was the furthest thing from Sevy's mind this night.

They were still trapped in buzzing agitation when Jarro came into her room. "How's that cut?"

She turned from the window. "I'm so sorry. Please, it'll never happen again! I'm sorry."

"Sevy—"

"I know you're angry with me, I can tell. I let you down. I'm sorry."

"Shut up."

Sinking onto the bed, she placed her head in her hands, not wanting to see the disappointment and disgust she was sure was in his eyes. She flinched when she felt his hand on her back.

"Sevy," he said softly. "I'm not angry with you."

"You're not?"

"I didn't even know you ran away until you told me. I was kinda busy at the time." He gave her a wry smile. "And even if I had seen you, why would you think I'd be angry?"

"Because I'm a coward! All I ever do is run. But I promise from now on I won't. I promise!"

"You're not a coward. So you got scared, so what? Fear isn't something to be ashamed of. It's there to help you. If anything, you should listen to your fear more often and quit being such a loud mouthed brat."

He ruffled her hair until she stopped sulking long enough to say, "But I want to be there for you. Like you've been for me. What if...what if it had been you instead of Firule? I never would have forgiven myself."

"It should have been me. Firule was a good man."

"Was? But I thought Revik—"

"Revik can't make miracles, sweetheart. He's doing his best, but..."

"But?"

The sadness in his eyes was answer enough.

"And there's nothing we can do?"

"Revik and Irea are still tending to him. I tried to help, but Revik told me to check on you. To be honest, I think he wanted me out of the way. We'll just have to wait. And who knows, maybe he'll pull through."

"But what if he doesn't? It's all my fault."

"No, it's not. Firule would have gotten hurt regardless. We were outnumbered. Should've brought more men with us, but we didn't know there'd be so many of them there. Ponarelle said that there were only five of them earlier. She doesn't know when the others showed up. Almost like they expected us or something."

"Still," she insisted, "I shouldn't have run. I'm a coward."

"Pigheaded too. Seriously though, Sevy, I think you're a pretty amazing girl. You've got more guts than I did when I was your age."

"Yeah?"

"I was training in the King's army back then. Didn't want to be. It was my dad's idea. I hated it. I just wanted to stay home and be a farmer like him."

"The army?" Somehow, picturing Jarro as a soldier was even harder to do than picturing him as a farmer. "What happened?"

"Five years ago, I had enough of fighting and I deserted. Of course, I couldn't go back home. Dad would have disowned me. So I came here, started over." He leaned on his elbows and sighed. "Funny how sometimes no matter how fast you run, you wind up in the exact place you were trying to escape."

"What are you trying to escape from?"

"A little bit of everything."

"Oh." She frowned, unsure of what he meant by that.

"Sorry. I'm probably not making much sense. Maybe you'll understand when you're older."

"What're you saying? That I'm not mature enough?"

"I didn't mean it like that."

"Or maybe I'm not smart enough to understand?"

"No, no. That's not what I—"

"Well? Which is it?"

"Yemet save me from temperamental women," he groaned, flopping back onto the bed. Then he yawned into his hand. "The moon's not even up yet, and I'm completely knackered. Pathetic, huh? Guess I'm not really the man you thought I was when we first met, am I?"

"No, not really. You...you're even better. But," she said hastily, burning with embarrassment, "if you're not happy here, then why don't you leave?"

"It's more complicated than that. I have obligations that I can't just walk away from. And I do have fun here. You and Revik and Turlan and the others, you're like my family. But on days like this, I wish I could just leave the city, get a piece of land somewhere, start a real family..."

Sevy wrinkled her nose. "With Irea, right?"

"Are you kidding me? Irea, a poor farmer's wife? That'd be the day."

"I'd pay to see her mucking out a horse stall," she added, pleased when he joined in her laughter.

"And what about you, Miss Sevy? You're somewhat of a mystery even after all these months. Revik and I have a running bet about you, you know."

"What?"

He grinned. "Yeah. He thinks you have some sort of dirty little secret in your past, and that's why you don't talk about it."

"Tell Revik he's an idiot."

"Consider it done. But you never did say why you came to the city, and I've got to admit, I'm curious. I know you're from the coast, but you never said where."

"Willing's Cove."

"Never heard of it."

"It's not there anymore. Pirates."

"I'm sorry." He squeezed her shoulder, obviously appreciating the full implication of her few choked words.

"These things happen. Besides," she faked a smile and tried to sound positive, "I'm glad I came to Eloria. I'd make a terrible fisherman's wife, don't you think?"

He chuckled and they sat in silence for awhile, lost in thought, but thankful for the other's company. A shift had occurred in their friendship. Sevy felt it even if she couldn't explain it. And when, at the same moment, they reached out to embrace one another, Sevy didn't feel embarrassed or self-conscious. There was no need to anymore.

Someone cleared their throat and Sevy raised her head from Jarro's shoulder to see Irea standing in the doorway, arms crossed, scowl on her lips. "Firule is dead."

Chapter 9

Sevy sat at her window, alone once more. The pixies, puzzled but pleased at her lack of interest in them, had long since left their tree in search of food and wouldn't be back until dawn, so there was nothing for Sevy to watch except for a few moths mystified by the torchlight.

She could tell from the movement downstairs that the house was full of people, although there was no laughing or dancing this night. They were planning strategies and keeping watch. And holding a wake over Firule's body.

Sevy didn't want to join them. She had enough of death for one day and didn't want to sit up with it all night long. She didn't like that particular tradition. It came from the west, brought back to Axlun by traders and travelers. The seafaring folk from whom she descended, an admittedly superstitious lot, believed that being close to a corpse for an extended period of time was liable to attract bad spirits. There were some parts of her upbringing she couldn't shake off, despite her irreverent nature.

A soft knock on the door broke her out of her reverie. She called, "Come in," and frowned when she saw red hair falling gracefully against a silken green dress. "What do you want?"

Irea held out a cup of steaming liquid. "From Revik."

"What is it?"

"Tea. A special brew. He was worried about your scratch." Irea smacked her lips as if she had just swallowed something very distasteful. "Can't have our precious Sevy falling ill, can we?"

Sevy reached for the cup. "Thanks. You can go now," she added when Irea made no move to leave.

"I'm supposed to make sure you drink it all. It's more effective that way."

Sevy glowered as Irea perched herself on the corner of the bed and folded her hands on top of her lap. "If he's so worried, why didn't he bring it?"

"Well, he's just a little preoccupied right now. Or have you forgotten about poor Firule already? Ah, such a waste. He was so young."

"Oh. Of course. I, ah, did you know him well?" Sevy asked, shamed into a semblance of cordiality. She took a sip of the tea. It was sweeter than she expected. Like honey, but more subtle. She drank some more.

"No, not particularly. But I am acquainted with his wife."

"I didn't know he was married."

"Mm-hmm. And a baby on the way. It's just too terrible. I wonder what's going to happen to them now. Oh well, I'm sure Jarro will take care of them. He's got a soft spot for charity cases. I suppose you'd know that better than most, wouldn't you? We're just going to have to get used to giving all of our money away to widows. What happened today is only the beginning, you realize. Duyan will retaliate. And he is not as soft as Jarro. You look pale. I understand. This is a lot for you to take in, isn't it? Drink your tea. It will help you feel better."

Sevy was light-headed. She closed her eyes and rested against the window pane while taking another drink. "Jarro's smart. He'll figure something out. We can beat Duyan."

"Time will tell. It really is such a shame. If you hadn't killed Gihaf, none of this would have happened."

"But Revik said..."

"Oh, he just said that so you wouldn't feel too badly. I, however, believe that you need to accept responsibility."

Sevy tried to stand up, but felt rather dizzy. "Revik said..."

"Oh dear, what's wrong? Not feeling well? Can't stand to hear the truth?"

There was a clattering noise and Sevy was surprised to see that the tea cup had fallen from her hands. She looked at Irea, confused.

The elf smiled. "I see how it is. Jarro takes you into his home, feeds you, clothes you, and this is how you repay him. You brought on this war with Duyan. Don't you care about Jarro? About any of us?"

Sevy wanted to protest, but her tongue was so thick and heavy, too cumbersome to form any words.

"You're just using him, aren't you? Trying to crawl your way up in the world however you can. You don't care about him at all."

"No," she managed to say. "I lo..."

"You what? Love him? Oh dear, I feared as much, but a part of me thought you were smarter than that."

Sevy tried again to stand, but her legs had disappeared. No, she confirmed they were still there by lolling her head downward. She just couldn't feel them anymore.

"You poor girl. Don't you know anything? True, it's not so strange to suppose that one day he would come to you and whisper sweet nothings in your ear. But that, dear child, is not love. You're a plaything, Sevy. A temporary distraction. What do you have to offer except a cheap thrill? Men don't take interest in you because they actually care. Remember that."

A scream ripped through Sevy's head. She couldn't move and it terrified her. She stared at Irea, pleading for help with her eyes, the only part of her still under her dominion.

"You'll just have to trust me on this. I've been alive long enough to know what men are like. They're really very simple creatures, led by lust not love. It's not fair at all, I know. But why fight it when you can use it against them? It's astonishing what a pretty face can get them to do. Now then, it looks like we're about ready. Stand up, please."

An unfathomable flood of horror coursed through Sevy as she rose to her feet. She didn't know how she had managed to move. She still couldn't feel anything.

Irea clapped her hands in delight. "This is too delicious! I've hated you since the first second I saw you, but it looks like you're going to be of some use to me. Come along, follow me."

Sevy struggled to stay where she was, but found herself following Irea down the stairs and into the common room where the others were. She screamed again. Not a hint of a sound would leave her throat. Her mouth didn't move at all.

"Sevy and I are going out for awhile. Just us girls."

"That's not a good idea tonight, honey," Jarro replied. "It's not safe."

Jarro! Jarro, help me! Jarro, please!

"Silly boy. We're just going to buy poor dear Firule some flowers, and maybe some incense. He deserves that much, wouldn't you agree?"

"Then I'll go with you."

"No, you're needed here. Don't worry. We'll be careful and we'll be back soon."

Oh gods, Jarro, please! Can't you tell something's wrong? Help me!

Jarro was about to say something, but Irea placed her finger against his mouth. "Honestly. What sort of example are you setting for your men, hmm? That we should be afraid to walk about in our own neighborhood? And considering that you trusted Sevy enough to join you in your little fiasco this afternoon, you should trust her enough to escort me down the street! Isn't that right, Sevy?"

"Yes," Sevy heard her voice say.

For a moment, she thought Jarro would continue to object. Instead, he walked away.

Jarro!

"Let's go, Sevy. Quickly now."

She fought the entire way. Nothing was working. She couldn't control her movements any more than she could control Irea's.

Irea gestured to a waiting carriage. "Get in."

She did as she was told. Irea climbed up beside her, yelling at the driver to get going. Sevy heard the snap of the lash and the carriage jerked into life. It clattered over the cobblestones as it traveled through the darkened streets, past the Bloody Heart, away from anyone who could help her.

"I suppose you're wondering where I'm taking you," Irea said, relaxing into the seat. "You'll see. But I really should thank you. Your arrival gave me the push I needed to do something I should have done a long time ago."

Given their relationship, Sevy could only dream with dread what that something was. Irea grew quiet, looking as happy as though they were on a pleasant jaunt through the countryside. The carriage took so many twists and turns that soon Sevy lost track of where they were. In the moonlight veiled by smoke, all the houses looked the same. She couldn't pick out any discernable landmarks. It was as if she was in an entirely foreign city, one designed by fear and populated with unknown horrors ready to pounce on her from each corner they rounded.

All too soon the carriage stopped. They were in front of a large brick building. The weathered paint above the entrance said "Ganklan's Meats and Victuals", but the air did not have the unctuous smells normally associated with a butcher's. Even more curious were the two guards armed with spears, standing on either side of the door.

The guards nodded to Irea as she led Sevy inside. The building was filled floor to ceiling with crates and barrels. A warehouse apparently. Sevy saw bottles of wine, animal pelts, weapons, strange powders; all manner of things bundled away. There were a few men scattered throughout the room, picking through the merchandise. They docked their hats or bowed their heads when Irea passed them. She certainly knew her way around the place, expertly navigating through the maze of boxes. Sevy was led to the back of the room, through a doorway and up a staircase. Then they headed down a gloomy hallway towards the front of the building again. At last, Irea stopped before one of the doors and knocked.

"Come," a voice within called.

Irea opened the door, revealing a tall man with a shaven head. He wore only a pair of trousers, and inked over his brawny chest were the same tribal designs that the man Sevy killed at Lornian had. They were likely kinsmen, which told Sevy exactly who he was.

"Well, well. To what do I owe this pleasant surprise?" he said, rising up from his bed. Irea walked forward to meet him and they kissed. It was obvious from the way their lips lingered that they were more than just casual acquaintances.

"I brought you a present, Duyan. What do you think?"

He looked Sevy up and down. "Nice enough, I suppose. Would you like a drink?"

"Love one."

Irea sat on a chaise, arranging her dress so that it wouldn't wrinkle, while Duyan poured two glasses of white wine. He was a gracious host, offering a dish of chocolate truffles, plying her with a plethora of compliments. Except for the fact that there was a girl standing frozen to the spot, staring at them in utter terror, it was all quite proper and civilized. They clinked their glasses together in a toast to Irea's beauty and charm.

"I'm so terribly sorry about your men."

He shrugged. "More where they came from. Let's get to it, shall we? First a heads up about Lornian and now you bring me this girl. I know you well enough to know you never give gifts without wanting something in return."

"You offend me! Can't I do something nice? And here I went and brought you Jarro's newest pet. One would think you'd be more grateful."

"Really?" Duyan inspected Sevy with renewed interest. "The one who killed Gihaf? Now why would you bring her to me? Just what are you up to?"

"Again, you are so suspicious. Don't you understand? Here, let me paint a pretty little picture for you. The lot of them, drunk senseless over that miserable musician's reeking body. Jarro, off a ways by himself because he's guilt stricken and brooding like a foppish poet. I'll pull him outside and, through my tears, I'll tell him that, oh goodness me! How horrible! Nasty old Duyan has kidnapped Sevy!" Irea paused her theatrics, waiting for Duyan to laugh before she continued. "Oh, Jarro, who knows what that evil man is doing to her right this very second! It's just too awful! No, no. There's no time to wait for the others. Go on, my brave darling, and I'll alert that horrid rat of yours. Go. We'll be right behind you." She drank another sip of wine through smiling lips. "He'll be alone. He'll be outnumbered. He'll be at your mercy."

Duyan held up his glass. "Clever elf!"

"I'm always thinking of you and your needs."

"Somehow I doubt that. So tell me. What are you getting out of this?"

"What I deserve. A spot at the side of the most powerful man in

Eloria. Jarro is weak. Pathetic really. What else can one expect from a stupid farmer boy? But you," she said, reaching over to walk her fingers up his chest. "With Jarro out of the way, you can rule this city."

The upsurge of anger inside of Sevy nearly blinded her. She used every bit of willpower she had and was rewarded with a twitch in the tips of her fingers. The numbness was beginning to subside.

Duyan pressed his lips against Irea's hand. "Whatever you want, you'll have."

Irea arched into him. The rage continued to swell as Sevy's whole being ached to strangle the traitorous life out of Irea. She managed to utter a small gasp. Duyan and Irea broke their kiss at the noise.

"Looks like the drug I gave her is wearing off."

"What do you want me to do with her?"

"Whatever you like. I'm sure you can think of something. Just be careful. She'll be able to move again soon and she is quite the scrapper. Let your men know to expect Jarro by morning. Goodbye, Sevy," she said with a vicious smile before departing.

Sevy could feel her arms again, but her legs still wouldn't cooperate. She visualized her blood pumping through her arteries, down into her thighs, taking with it the command to move. It seemed to work. Her legs tingled, the muscles shook. Her knees were next. They wobbled back into life enough for her to shift her weight from one leg to the next.

Duyan watched her struggles over the rim of his wine glass with the rapt attention normally reserved for unusual insects: fascinating enough to poke and prod until curiosity was sated, but still subject to the same fate as all bug-kind.

After awhile, he came to stand next to her. She shuddered when he trailed his hand down her back. "Sevy, is it? You're kind of pretty. Jarro ever tell you that? I don't know what Irea gave you, but I think I'll let you limber up some more. It's more sporting that way, don't you think?"

"Go to hell!" she finally blurted out.

He laughed and drew her to the bed. She was able to resist, but not enough to stop him from sitting her down. Keeping his gaze on her face, waiting for her reaction, he rubbed her shirt down from her shoulders. Her breath came in rasps and the downy hair on the back of her neck rose; exactly the kind of response he appeared to be hoping for. His lips grazed her skin. His hands snaked around her waist. She couldn't stop herself from crying out.

"Now, now, save your tears. There's plenty of time for that later." Then he was on top of her, pinning her hands at her sides. He ran his tongue over her face. "Mmm, you taste good."

"Get off of me!"

"That's it. Fight me. I like it!"

She was pressed deeper into the bed, scarcely able to breathe with his weight crushing down upon her. He tried to kiss her. She kept her lips pressed together, denying him entrance. One hand slipped down her side to pull up her shirt so that he could touch her skin. She screamed and he used the opportunity to intensify his kiss.

The only coherent thought she was able to have was that this was the mouth that would order Jarro's death come daybreak. The leviathan awoke once more and in a flux of fury she bit down on his tongue as hard as she could.

As he screamed, she was able to roll herself off the bed and dart for the door, but she was still too sluggish. He leapt after her with a yell, dragged her back, and threw her down.

"I'm gonna rip you apart and let Jarro find you in pieces before I gut him too!" he bellowed, spitting blood. He took off his belt. Sevy curled into a ball and cried out each time the leather struck and took a lick of her flesh away with it.

She was falling. Falling down a hundred feet or more, down into an umbra that had no end. When she opened her eyes again she was on her stomach. Duyan was straddling her, fumbling with his trousers. She reached back and grabbed his exposed groin, sinking her nails into the sensitive flesh. The pain that came from his throat was a primordial howl certain to rouse empathy in the hearts of men the world over. Sevy wiggled free from underneath him. Her fingers brushed against the discarded belt, and in a flash of pitiless inspiration, she cinched it around his neck.

His eyes bugged out and he made an eerie clicking noise. He scratched at her, but it was in vain. His face turned a violent shade of purple as the rest of him slumped down. Sevy just managed to scoot out of the way before he landed face first into the bed. Still she pulled at the belt, using her legs as leverage. Her arms trembled from the effort, but she wouldn't stop, afraid that he was faking.

In the end, it was her body that made the decision to release the belt. She had exhausted the last of her energy. She panted, lungs burning as if she were the one choked. Then she was swept away by pain.

Her wounds followed her into the darkness, finding her and steering her back to consciousness. When she awoke, it was early morning. Her body was one raw throbbing nerve and her mouth tasted bitter. She hissed when she touched the array of lash marks covering her arms, some already showing signs of infection.

Duyan was still on the bed. That meant no one knew yet. No one knew that he was dead or that Irea was sending Jarro after her. Sevy had to get to him and warn him about Irea's sedition. But how? Duyan's men probably wouldn't just let her leave through the front door and she couldn't remember seeing any other exit.

There was a window high on the right wall. Standing on tiptoe, she pushed the panes open and looked out. It wasn't that far to the ground, ten, fifteen feet maybe. She figured she could probably scale down the side of the building.

As she was trying to negotiate her way out the window, something thundered in the hallway. She heard sounds of a scuffle, men yelling.

"Sevy? Sevy, where are you?"

The door was thrown open. Jarro stood before her, his sword and hands smeared with blood. She was so surprised to see him that she did little more than stare, dully supposing that she must have passed out again.

"Oh, thank the gods!" he cried, rushing to her. "Are you all right?"

There was little time to assuage either of their fears. Footsteps pounded up the stairs. Jarro ran to slam the door shut. He slid a wooden bolt into its lock just as someone banged into the other side of the door. Though it rattled, the door held.

"Are you all right? Where is that bastard? I'll kill him!"

She pointed to Duyan's body. "I...Irea set you up! She...she..."

"What are you talking about?"

She shook her head, trying to clear her jumbled thoughts. "She made a deal with Duyan. It was all a trap!"

"What?" The banging grew louder and the door started to creak on its hinges. "We've gotta get out of here. Can you fight?"

She wasn't sure that she could, just standing upright made her head swim, but she nodded yes. Jarro searched round the room, found a sword, and pushed it into her hands. "Let's go."

"Wait!" she cried, frustrated that her mind was working so slowly. "The window. We can go out the window."

"All right, come on." He picked her up and lifted her to the sill before crawling up beside her. On his count of three, they jumped down together, landing painfully on the ground below. Her ankles bent at an unnatural angle, but Jarro didn't let her rest. She was yanked to her feet and dragged after him as he ran.

"He's outside!"

Duyan's men ran out of the building. Jarro made quick work of the first one to reach them. While he faced two others, Sevy took a swing at a third, managing to hack his hand off. Yet another man rushed her. She darted to the side and stabbed him through the back before kicking his body away.

There were more advancing. Jarro grabbed her hand again and they fled down the street, pushing past slack-jawed bystanders, and ducked into an alley. Their pursuers, more familiar with the area, closed in.

Their progress was slowed when they burst out of the alley onto a marketplace that was just starting to fill with vendors preparing their tables. They crashed into a display of cages, sending the poor birds inside into a screaming frenzy. The next merchant who got in their way mimicked the birds when Jarro's sword ripped through a row of hanging rugs to clear their path. A horse and cart was being led down the middle of the street. Jarro shoved the driver aside, cut the horse free of its harness, and then threw Sevy on top of it. Grabbing the reins from the stunned man's hand, Jarro leapt up behind Sevy and kicked the horse's side. It took off in a gallop.

Sevy looked back over Jarro's shoulder and saw that the mob of Duyan's men was still following. Arrows whizzed by her head, thankfully missing their mark. The horse was too fast for them and they fell further and further behind.

Though it frothed from its effort, Jarro didn't allow the horse to slow its pace until they were far outside Duyan's territory and safely back within their own. At the house, he helped Sevy dismount then crushed her against him. "Are you sure you're all right?"

She nodded, too out of breath to answer.

"Irea said that Duyan had jumped the two of you, taken you away."

"It was a trap! She said, she said you were weak. She drugged me and they made a deal and—"

His mouth formed a taut line. "That's enough."

"Please, you have to believe me!" she begged him, grasping at his shirt. Without another word, he led her inside.

"What in the world?" Turlan gasped when he saw Sevy, the tears in her clothing, the oozing lesions underneath.

"Take her upstairs. Get her cleaned up."

Revik came out of an adjoining room. "What's going on?"

The staircase creaked, betraying Irea as she tried to sneak down to see what the fuss was. She turned to run, but Jarro leapt after her, grabbing her arm and jerking her down the stairs. She fell at his feet.

"You!" he said, pointing at her. "What the hell did you try to do? You stupid bitch!"

"Jarro, I...I..."

"I should cut your lying tongue out!"

"Jarro, what's going on?" Revik repeated.

"Why don't you tell them, huh? Tell them how you lied to us! Tell them how you, you, no! Don't you dare touch me!" he yelled as she threw her arms about his waist. "Gods, Irea! After everything I've done for you. How could you?"

"Jarro, I...let me explain. It was Sevy! It was her and Duyan! Not me! I'd never betray you, Jarro! Never! I love you!"

"Get her out of my sight."

Not hesitating for an instant, Revik dragged Irea outside. Her screams faded into the distance as she was forced down the street.

⁂

The window was open, but the day's heat remained locked in the room. Sevy kicked at the pile of blankets Turlan had heaped over her. He said it was to help sweat the fever out of her. She wasn't very confident in his medicinal knowledge, but Revik had not returned yet so Turlan was all she had.

She hadn't seen Jarro since he had washed and dressed her wounds. Turlan had been put in charge of her care after that. The old man had stayed the entire day next to her bedside, the longest span of time she'd seen him go without a drink in his hand. In whispers, she told him everything that happened. He wasn't so forthcoming, and though he had many hushed conferences with people at her doorway, he wouldn't tell her what was going on downstairs. From the sounds of it, the entire gang had amassed in the common room and it drove her insane wondering what they were discussing, what tactics they were devising. Twice, she tried to sneak out. Turlan shepherded her back into bed, scolding her stubbornness. At nightfall, he finally left her room, bidding her to sleep.

That was unlikely. Her body ached, and no position she tried eased the intolerable pain. Her arms would not stop spasming, as though her wounds wanted to remind her through constant throbs that they were still there. Her mental state wasn't much better. She could feel Duyan's tongue on her skin and no amount of water would wash it away. Disturbing fantasies of what might have happened hounded her. And even though the house was filled with people, she couldn't help worrying about his men attacking. She was concerned for Jarro and, in spite of herself, she actually felt some pity for Irea and wondered what Revik was doing with her.

Eventually, her body's exhaustion curbed the machinations of her mind. Just as her eyes closed, a knock on the door startled them open again.

"Sevy?" Jarro called.

"Yeah?"

"Are you awake?"

"No."

He came into the room and sat on the bed next to her. He didn't say anything. He just sat there. His eyes were focused on the ground as if watching a serious and somber mummer performing an invisible drama amidst the knots of the floorboards.

She couldn't bear the silence. "I'm sorry."

"No, sweetheart, I'm sorry. I should have known what Irea was up to. 'Just us girls'. I should have known."

"I'd understand if you want me to leave."

With uncharacteristic timidity, he reached out to caress her cheek. "I don't want you to go anywhere. This is your home." His hand dropped back into his lap and he frowned. The moonbeam coming through the window highlighted the misery on his face.

"Um, about Irea. What's going to happen to her?"

"I don't know. I don't really want to know. Revik said he took her to the outskirts of the city. She deserves worse, that bitch. But I can't...I couldn't... Guess she was right, huh? I am weak."

"No, you're not. You're the strongest person I've ever met."

A glimmer of a smile skimmed across his lips. He looked away.

"What happens now?"

"I don't think we'll have to worry about Duyan's men. They'll be busy for the next couple of weeks, fighting for power. Maybe we'll get lucky and they'll kill each other off completely. But Revik and I were talking, and we thought that maybe it'd be best if you and I left town for awhile."

For a moment, the throbbing in her arms was redirected to her heart. It raced at triple its normal speed as she tried to decipher the exact meaning behind his words.

"Just until things settle down," he added, probably mistaking her silence for skepticism rather than euphoric shock. "People will forget about Duyan soon enough, but you never know who might want revenge in the meantime. Revik will take care of things here while we're gone. He's done it before. Hell, he's better at it than I am."

"Really? You really want to?"

"Of course. I was getting sick of the city anyway. I could use a change of scenery. We'll travel around, find work where we can. It will be good experience for you. You told me once that you've never been anywhere before. Now's your chance. And, well, I think it'll be fun. We'll start with Wilrendel. I'll take you to see the new palace. What do you say?"

She nodded and he smiled at her, not his regular beaming smile, but enough to alleviate a few of her fears.

"Good. Now get some rest. We'll leave as soon as you're strong enough."

Sevy sighed as he left the room. She really was worried about him. He was acting upbeat, but she knew it was purely for her benefit. He must have been terribly hurt by Irea's betrayal. Regardless of her own opinion of the elf, she had seen the way Jarro would look at Irea in the quiet moments Sevy had been so envious of. He was a flirt, but he had sincerely cared for Irea.

It didn't make any sense to her that Irea could throw away that kind of devotion so easily. Everything Sevy ever wanted—money, friends, a safe home, and most importantly, Jarro—had been laid at her feet and still it hadn't been enough. What manner of life had Irea experienced that she could be so blind?

Sevy whispered a promise to herself that no matter what happened, she would never become as jaded as Irea. She would do her best to see the good in everyone and everything. Just like Jarro did.

Giddy anticipation tingled inside of her despite her worries. Soon she'd be traveling across the land, perhaps even past the borders of Axlun. The maps Jarro had shown her, the towns and the forests and the mountains that had seemed little more than pen marks on parchment would become real. She'd get to see and do things that most people in Eloria would never experience.

Best of all, Jarro would be with her the entire time, just the two of them, with no one else to vie for his attention. It was wonderful. She closed her eyes and her imaginings blurred into dreams as she fell sound asleep.

PART 2
SWEETHEART

Chapter 1

The whiskey blazed a trail down his throat. He slammed the glass on the table, and stretched his mouth as if doing so would help to cool the smoldering aftertaste. Whiskey was Jarro's drink of choice, had been since he first snuck a bottle from his father's liquor cabinet back when he was thirteen and desperately trying to impress a coquettish classmate. But even after all these years it still made him grimace with each swallow.

He drummed the table with his fingertips as he debated pouring another shot. The bottle was already a third empty. A couple more drinks and he would slip into what Sevy called his 'pleasantly pickled' stage, where, through fits of laughter, he would try to explain how wonderful everything suddenly became. He wanted to at least be able to form a coherent sentence when she showed up, but he had already been waiting for the better part of the day and there was still no sign of her.

Dammit, where is she?

Three months. That's how long it had been since he had last seen Sevy. It was the most time they had ever spent apart in the eight years he'd known her. She had gone up north on business, delivering some goods to an old acquaintance of theirs, while he stayed behind in Eloria. He regretted that decision the second he lost sight of her moving amongst the torrent of travelers that streamed in and out of the northern gate, and after only a fortnight he found himself missing her company terribly. Things in the city just weren't the same without her. The days crawled by, humdrum and predictable, broken only by the exasperation of the civil unrest and the street brawls that were becoming far too common in recent years.

When Turlan had handed him a letter earlier that week, Jarro was so excited to see Sevy's distinctive chicken scratch on the envelope that he nearly ripped it in half breaking the seal. Her message was short and to the point, asking him to join her in the tiny hamlet of Mindervale, northeast of the city. No explanation for the request was given, but none was needed. He rushed to meet her without a second thought.

Revik, of course, teased him mercilessly, making cracks about how henpecked he had become. That was Revik for you. He must spend a considerable amount of time coming up with his tongue in cheek insults because it seemed as if the supply was infinite. Jarro just laughed and shrugged it off. He missed his friend, what was so bad about that? Plus, he had the sneaking suspicion that most of Revik's quips were a cover for slighted feelings. He was probably put off that he hadn't been invited along, but someone had to stay behind to keep things running smoothly. And, at any rate, he hadn't the patience to debate whether or not he should ask Revik to come with him. Not when he had an excuse to steal away for awhile.

The trip to Mindervale would provide him with a much welcomed distraction. Not only would he get to see Sevy again, but for a few days he'd be free of the backstabbing, the chicanery, and the clashing of egos that went hand in hand with heading up a gang.

There had been a time when he believed that being a criminal was glamorous and exciting. Deserting the army had marked him a wanted man; he had few options available and had to earn a living somehow. Thievery came more naturally than he would have thought, and with his charm and charisma, it hadn't taken long to forge the alliances that would make him a major player in the city. Then came money, power, loose women and good times—all the things his father had ever cautioned him against. It was addictive, a rebellious slap in the face of every authority figure he had ever known.

More than a few hours had been spent musing on the precise instant the thrill vanished. Maybe it was the time an enemy delivered a message via the riven corpse of one of his young friends. Perhaps the screams of a whore begging for mercy as she was gang-raped took the fun out of rubbing elbows with ruffians. Or maybe, as he thought most likely, there wasn't one defining moment, but a gradual shift in perception brought on by his own growing maturity. A strong sense of duty awoke in him, one that all the money and power in the kingdom couldn't suppress, and because of it Jarro had taken it upon himself to protect the less fortunate from those who would take advantage of them. He had striven to set an example of kindness and compassion. After all, circumstances made him work as a criminal. That didn't mean he had to behave like one.

Sadly, good intentions are reputed to lead only to one particular place and, in the end, cynicism won over optimism. How could it not? For every merchant he helped keep in business, ten more were trampled beneath the feet of bootleggers and bullies. For each child he smuggled food to, a dozen others starved to death. It was a bitter day indeed when he realized that his humanitarian endeavors were about as useful a tool of social change as throwing coins into a fountain.

Eloria was a cutthroat, pitiless place. Cruelty and bloodshed were all the majority of its citizens had ever known. To say that they were resistant to change would have been an understatement. Even amongst his own men, Jarro was an oddity. Most owed him their lives, some he counted as close friends, but they were satisfied with the status quo and more often than not his altruistic nature was met with skepticism and contempt.

He wasn't deaf to their grumblings when he gave away large portions of their earnings to the needy or when he reprimanded them for what they considered justifiable acts of violence. He knew he had become somewhat of a joke, the law-abiding law-breaker of Eloria who'd rather sneak money into someone's purse than out. Jarro had no doubt that his men would have mutinied against him years ago if it hadn't been for Revik and Sevy.

The finest right hand man one could hope for, Revik, thanks in part to his heritage, had a presence that could chill the blood of even the most stalwart man. His prowess with the long sword was renowned, and it was a brave man indeed who dared face the dark elf in combat. In addition to this, Revik had a shrewd mind. Jarro couldn't count the number of times that Revik's council had saved the day, so astute was he at picking up on details others easily overlooked. But above all else, his loyalty was unwavering. There was nothing Revik wouldn't do for a friend and that was something Jarro appreciated more than any knack for weapons or words.

Sevy, likewise, had proved to be an invaluable ally. Gone was the headstrong but unsure orphan who had once conned him with counterfeit tears. Well, she was still headstrong, but she had matured into a self-assured woman, an accomplished thief, and a skilled fighter. He knew most people found her distant and cold, and she could be unpredictable; one moment sitting quietly, the next exploding into a rage if something said or done didn't meet her approval. She had an intense stare that, when set upon you, felt as though it was dissecting your soul while at the same time revealing none of the tumultuous emotions that lurked within her.

A hapless stranger unaccustomed to her ways would find her off-putting to say the least. Not Jarro. Sevy's bluster, he knew, was her shield. When they were alone, she revealed an entirely different personality. She was sweet and loving and actually kind of silly. She could be exhausting and exasperating at times, but she was a devoted friend and his most trusted confidante.

And right now, she was about five hours overdue and it was driving him to distraction. He had visions of her waylaid by highwaymen, lying bloodied and bruised in a ditch somewhere. Not very likely, as Sevy could handle her own quite nicely, but it was a possibility. He couldn't just sit there doing nothing any longer. He decided to go outside and see if he could spot her coming up the road.

With one last drink, he started to rise from the table when a cool, smooth hand slipped over his mouth. His startled attempt to turn was foiled by another hand that pressed on his shoulder, forcing him to sit back down.

"Leaving so soon?" a silky voice breathed into his ear.

His body relaxed. "Dammit, Sevy, you nearly gave me a heart attack!"

"Started the party without me, I see."

He wanted to scold her. Instead, he pulled her into an embrace that must have lingered too long for her comfort. She wiggled away, gave him a peck on the cheek, and took a swig of his whiskey.

"Where have you been? I've been waiting for hours."

"I've been here since this morning," she answered coyly. "I was just preoccupied."

"Well, he better damn well have been worth it, making me worry like that."

"Not really."

He laughed aloud. She could be so heartless when it came to her men. If she wasn't interested she'd rip them apart just for daring to approach her. And even when one managed to catch her attention they never seemed to be able to hold it for very long. Jarro called her fickle, though other men would doubtlessly use a different name. It wasn't her fault though. She knew what she wanted and didn't waste time batting her eyelashes like other women did. He found it refreshing, but he did pity the men that fell for her. She was not one to mince words and it was painful to watch her work over some poor love-sick fool. Painful, but also highly entertaining.

"How are things in the city?" she asked, taking another drink. She scrunched up her nose and stuck out her tongue. "How can you drink this swill?"

"If you don't like it, don't drink it all on me. Things are fine. Boring, but fine. Turlan says hello. I won't repeat what Revik said. How was it up north?"

"Profitable."

"Mm-hmm. Well, sweetheart, you didn't ask me to come all this way just to hear you boast about your riches, did you?"

She leaned in to him, voice dropping to a conspiratorial whisper.

"I have another job lined up, but I could use your help with it."

"Sevy!" Jarro looked up to see a young man, shirt untucked and hair disheveled, dashing down a flight of stairs. "Sevy, where'd you go?"

She sunk low in her chair, but with less than ten other patrons in the bar, it didn't take him long to spot her. He bounded towards her like a puppy, stopping short when he noticed Jarro seated beside her.

"I'm busy," she hissed. "Go away."

"You left without waking me up. Who's he?"

"None of your business."

Sevy gave the man her famously frosty stare. It was enough to take him aback, but with the taste of her so fresh on his lips, he didn't look quite ready to concede defeat.

"Come on, luv. Come back upstairs." He tugged her sleeve.

"Now you've had it." Jarro chuckled, poured himself another shot, and settled back to watch the show.

With meticulous slowness, Sevy took his hand from her arm and squeezed. Jarro winced, imagining that he could hear the bones crunching together as she continued to apply pressure. The man tried to pull free, and as that failed, twisted his body to the side. When he let out a mewling yelp, Jarro snorted on his whiskey. Was it wrong that he found this so comical?

"It was fun, but now it's over. So stop bothering me, got it?"

He nodded and Sevy administered one final squeeze before releasing him. He was a sucker for punishment apparently, as he remained by the table, shaking and rubbing his hand like a bewildered child.

"Well, what are you still standing here for? Get lost!"

He took one last longing look at her before slinking away. The disgust on Sevy's face was priceless. Jarro watched her, a large smile curling up the corners of his lips. They both laughed when they caught each other's eye.

"You shouldn't be so mean to the poor things."

"Mean? I'm not mean. I'm just honest. At least I don't give them false hope like you do with your women."

"Me? Never!" he said, feigning insult. They laughed again. "All right, enough fun. Tell me about this job."

Chapter 2

The air was heavy with leaf-sweetened water. It was refreshing, but sat a tad uncomfortably in his lungs. As the forest shook off the languor of the night's rainfall, it quivered with life, from the ambitious line of ants who had mistaken his boot for a tree stump, to the quail he had unintentionally driven to near hysterics by his presence so close to her nest.

"Would you hurry up?" he called over to a thicket.

"I'm trying," came the grumbled reply. "I can't get it to look right."

"Then come out and let me see."

Much longer and he would have pushed into the plants and pulled her out, decent or not, but a half-minute later Sevy emerged amidst a bevy of curses, clad in a blue dress with a matching handkerchief over her hair. There was a large protuberance around her stomach, so contorted that it appeared as though she were smuggling a sack of potatoes. "How does it look? Real?"

"If your baby is a two-headed freak, then yeah, it looks fantastic."

She paused her struggles with the bulge long enough to shoot him an evil look. "I told you I couldn't get it right. You could try helping, you know."

"Don't get crabby. This was your idea, remember?"

She tossed her head and punched her gut in frustration, looking more like she was attempting feticide than donning a disguise. In the end, it took their combined fussing and prodding, and a great deal more swearing, before the bundle of cloth tied round her waist took the proper shape.

"There," Jarro announced at length. "I think that's better."

"How do I look?"

"Very matronly."

"I hope they buy it." The crinkle of her nose as she inspected herself suggested that she wasn't impressed. "I guess so long as they don't try to touch it, it'll pass."

Jarro had to turn his head to hide his smile. It was just like her to make things more complicated than they needed to be. The objective: to steal a religious artifact from The Pious Progeny of Eewerel, a shrine devoted to the god of birth. It was a simple enough heist until one factored in Sevy's flair for the dramatic, hence the ridiculous pretence. She wanted to investigate the shrine's defenses beforehand and decided that they would arouse the least amount of suspicion if they visited as expectant parents. Too much time spent alone with her over active imagination, Jarro concluded, but he loved the excited glimmer that would come to her eyes as she laid out her plans so he always went along with them if only to make her happy.

He fondly remembered the first time she had been in charge of a job. Their client, a well regarded member of Eloria's elite with an unfortunate weakness for dog racing and dwarvish hookers, had been willing to pay greatly for the retrieval of certain damning documents as they made their way by caravan to his business partner's house in Allerough. Sevy had begged and pestered for the chance to call the shots during the theft. He was reluctant at first so she turned to sulking. He gave in when she got violent and spent the better part of the day either punching his arm or pinching the back of his neck. In her wisdom, Sevy determined that their best bet to get the documents was to travel with the caravan masquerading as Judian and Wilsa Osafagrun, a newly-wed couple on honeymoon. She made up an elaborate but completely useless back story that she insisted he memorize. And she had even used an accent, so affected and unnatural that he cracked up every time she spoke. They had nearly been exposed when Jarro accidentally referred to her by her real name, but in the end they got the papers, their reward, and even a few free congratulatory meals in the interim.

At least this time there were no pseudonyms or lines to rehearse. Just one pitiful excuse for a pregnant belly. Sevy was lucky Revik wasn't here to rip into her, though Jarro would make sure to fill him in on all the details once they got back to the city.

"Are you ready?" he asked, taking her hand.

A quick hike through the forest led them to the village. If it could be called a village. There were barely ten buildings, very simple, very tiny, and most were made entirely out of straw and twigs. More like mounds of kindling, they certainly were not the sturdiest houses he had ever seen. In fact, a number of roofs had buckled from the weight of the night's rain, and what villagers could be seen were standing forlornly around the sodden ruins discussing in low voices how to go about repairs. It was absolutely depressing. He couldn't imagine this place having anything worth stealing.

A gaggle of dirty children found Sevy and Jarro more interesting than their parents did and trailed behind for a while, no doubt hoping for money or scraps of food. Jarro heard the disdain in Sevy's sigh when he threw a few coins to them, but how could he not? They were only children after all.

The path sloped upwards to the top of a hill, upon which stood The Pious Progeny. In stark contrast to the rest of the village, its bloated pomposity was more of a shrine to excess than it was to Eewerel. Large and carefully crafted from beautiful planks of yellow pine, the shrine made it all too obvious where the money round here was spent. The decorative shrubs forming a lane to the front entrance and the blossoming trees surrounding it were not native to this part of Axlun, and their daily upkeep must have cost a week's wages. Jarro had his doubts that Eewerel would want his parishioners to live in such squalor for the sake of one shrine, but who was he to say? He had left religion behind in childhood.

It was show time. At the doorway, they shared a smile of encouragement before Jarro rapped the hefty ornate iron knocker twice. He heard the grating of metal as a lock was undone and an elderly, bearded man in a long green robe appeared. "Welcome, my children. What can I do for you?"

Jarro stepped forward as Sevy bowed her head and placed a hand protectively across her belly. "My wife is expecting soon. She wishes to kneel before Eewerel."

"Of course," the monk responded, his voice dripping with manufactured compassion. "Eewerel will hear your prayers, daughter. Your child shall grow strong and healthy in His love."

"Thank you," Sevy whispered, bowing her head even lower, a veritable picture of diffidence and innocence. Jarro had to give her credit. She always was a good little actress. She could fool just about anyone, himself included, when she wanted to. She even managed to replicate the waddling walk of pregnancy as the monk ushered them down an aisle.

They passed other worshippers who were attempting to pray while also trying to control their squirming, impatient children as they followed the monk to the altar, upon which resided a bulky, marble effigy of a man with the head of a rabbit. Its hands were outstretched to give an air of empathy, but Jarro thought, stifling an immature snigger, that they just served to draw attention to the god's exaggerated manhood. Sort of a 'Hey, welcome to my shrine and, oh yeah, have you noticed my penis?' pose. Maybe Eewerel was an exhibitionist, like those pathetic men in Eloria who got their kicks from flashing strangers. He wondered if Sevy was thinking along equally sacrilegious lines, but no, she was so completely immersed in her role that she appeared unmindful of the holy protuberance. Using Jarro's arm for support, she made a convincing production kneeling down before the statue.

The monk beamed at them. "I'm sure you will find comfort here. Eewerel does look kindly on those who pay proper homage."

He cleared his throat and held out his hand. Jarro scoffed, not about to give a single piece of copper to this con until Sevy reached back and pinched his leg. Reluctantly, he placed a few coins into the monk's outstretched palm. With a cagey smile, the monk pocketed the coins and walked away.

"Damn highway robbery!" Jarro complained under his breath.

"We'll get it back, don't worry. Once we grab that." She nodded to the statue before her.

He couldn't resist. "I guess size really does matter then, huh?"

"Jealous?"

"Ha!" The sound of his outburst resonated through the otherwise hushed shrine and Sevy pinched his leg again. "Ow. Quit it. Anyway, how the hell are we going to get this thing out of here?"

"Not the whole thing. Just the crystal."

He examined Eewerel and saw that set in the god's forehead was a very large, round crystal. "How's it fastened in there?"

"Don't know. Just mortar, I think. Probably should be able to pry it out with a knife. And look up there. The birds."

As if he were directing his prayers to the heavens, he tipped back his head and saw song birds darting high above them. The very top of the walls were lined with stained glass windows detailing Eewerel's various miracles in jewel-toned brilliance—breathing life into a stillborn, returning vitality to a line of dejected looking men, placing a fetus into a barren woman's womb. One of the windows had been smashed and the birds were flying in and out up to the rafters, accompanied by blossoms that wafted in on the breeze and floated lazily about the shrine.

The monk strode past again, making his rounds, no doubt hoping to collect enough to repair the damage to the window plus a little something extra for himself. Jarro flicked another coin to send him on his way. They waited until he was out of earshot.

"Pretty easy, don't you think?" he whispered. "We can climb up one of the trees and get in from there."

"I don't see any guards, do you?"

"No. It's a minor shrine. Far from the main roads. I don't think they'll have many, but they must have some. That village is so poor, I'd imagine break-ins are pretty much a given."

She nodded in agreement. "We'll wait until after dark. I'll go in while you keep watch. Shouldn't take more than a few minutes."

They were still marveling at the lack of security when they returned late that night. Not counting the crystal, he had seen golden chalices, candlesticks inlaid with jewels, tapestries threaded with veins of silver. Even the windows themselves would be worth something. Either the townsfolk were among the most devout in the kingdom or they knew something that Sevy and Jarro did not.

Sevy pointed for him to circle one side while she took the other. There was no light from within the shrine, no voices or footsteps. He couldn't believe their luck. They met again at the front, shaking their heads to indicate that they hadn't seen anything, and then they snuck over to the broken window where he lifted her up to the lowest limb of the nearest tree. Like a nimble squirrel, she climbed to the level of the window. He balked when she jumped from the branch, but she made it, catching the sill with both hands. She pulled herself up, climbed over the sill, and gave him a saucy wink before she dropped inside.

There was nothing for him to do but stand beneath the window, waiting, watching for any sign of trouble. A gentle wind picked up and blew blossoms into his face, their smell sickeningly sweet. Five minutes passed. He grew impatient.

Suddenly, the wind gusted, rattling the stained glass windows. The trees groaned in protest as they were pushed by the gale, a groan that was mimicked by something within the shrine.

"Jarro!" he heard Sevy call. She sounded calm, but there was an odd tone in her voice that made his stomach lurch.

He climbed the tree faster than he thought possible, though with none of the grace Sevy had displayed, and jumped over to the window. Straddling the sill, he peered inside, batting away the blossoms that poured in with the wind. Sevy had scaled the statue of Eewerel and was holding onto its head with one hand while the other held her dagger, her excavation interrupted.

Jarro followed her gaze to a tiny whirlwind dancing between the pews. Blossoms and pages from prayer books were caught in it, and he watched in stunned silence as the whirlwind appeared to pulsate and grow.

"What do you think it is?" she asked.

"No idea. So hurry it up."

"Just a second." She wrenched her eyes away, turned back to the statue, and continued to dig the crystal out.

"Sevy, I think we should go."

"Almost got it!"

A second later the crystal popped into her hand, echoed by a loud cracking noise. The whirlwind swelled, absorbing nearly half the room, and then without warning it drilled into the floor. The shrine trembled and Sevy had to cling to the statue to keep from falling off. The ceramic floor tiles snapped upwards, revealing that the ground underneath had cleaved in two.

The shrine shook so hard that Jarro was thrown from his perch on the window ledge. He fell inside, landing face first onto the floor. He moaned and cradled his nose, feeling warm blood ooze out over his fingers.

Sevy startled him by suddenly appearing at his side. "Are you all right?"

"Yeah. Let's just get out of here."

The split in the floor had doubled in size and continued to grow. He couldn't say how deep it had gone and didn't care to find out. Using his body as a shield, he pressed Sevy to the wall and they inched towards the exit.

Another tremor, this time accompanied by a long, low rumble, knocked them off their feet. The force of it kept them pinned to the ground, unable to move, until just as suddenly as it started, the quaking stopped.

He heard something coming from deep within the earth. He heard the sound of claws digging against rock and dirt. It grew louder. Raising his head, Jarro peered under the rows of pews. Something was crawling out of the fissure.

Sevy swore. She had seen it too, and whatever it was, it was gigantic. It stood on four squat legs as thick as tree trunks, splayed out like a lizard's. The body was fat and distended and covered in scaly armor of glinting gold. A spike-lined tail lashed about angrily, bashing into the pews, tossing them aside as easily as if they were twigs. Jarro looked up, following the line of the neck to a broad head, a pointed snout, four sets of horns, and a pair of cold, black eyes.

When it spotted them as they lay huddled together on the floor, the beast snarled, drawing back its lips to reveal a mouth jammed with dripping fangs. Sevy was the first to jump up and pull out her sword. Jarro did the same not a second later.

"What the hell is that?" she cried.

He didn't answer. The shrine did have a guard after all.

Jarro put his free hand on Sevy's back and pushed her towards the door. The beast roared and moved to block their escape. It spun around, whipping its tail at them. They darted out of the way and the spikes crashed into the wall, splintering the wood. With a yell, Sevy leapt towards the beast and cut it across one of its back legs. It turned on her in a rage of snapping jaws.

Despite its massive girth, the creature moved surprisingly fast. Sevy jumped back and forth, thrusting her blade at the thing whenever she could, but had yet to land another blow. While its attention was on her, Jarro rushed forward and impaled the beast deep in its side. It bellowed and swung its tail. One of the spikes caught him in the arm. He was lifted bodily and thrown against the wall.

"Jarro!" he heard Sevy scream.

He felt faint as the pain set in, but there was no time to rest. He clambered to his feet, barely managing to avoid another blow.

The beast howled again. Sevy straddled it, stabbing its back repeatedly, but regardless of how many times she pierced it, it would not falter. It spun around in a frenzy, rearing up into the air, and finally flung her against the marble Eewerel where she lay stunned. It moved to bite her.

Jarro's sword was still lodged in the beast's side. He had no other weapons, but couldn't just stand there and let Sevy be mauled. He threw himself between her and the beast, and grabbed hold of its lower set of horns. It snapped its jaws furiously and shook its head from side to side, and he was again lifted off his feet.

Thankfully, Sevy came to and scrambled out of harm's way. Then a new problem faced him. There was no way he could move fast enough to avoid those teeth once he let go of the horns. It was a standoff, and with the blood and sweat coating his hands he was sure to lose his grip. And soon. Terrified, his eyes locked with the beast's. Was it just his imagination or did the thing appear to smile at him when it too realized his error?

Above the din made by the beast, he heard a grating noise, rock crunching against rock. Then Sevy's voice came out of nowhere. "Jarro, move!"

He took the chance and let go off the horns, diving to the side just as Eewerel came smashing down.

Viscous lumps of blood squirted across the room as the creature's head exploded under the weight of the statue. It was all over so quickly, it took Jarro a moment to grasp what had happened. There was no question. The creature was dead. Jarro spat out a chunk of something nauseating, brain matter perhaps, as it ran down the side of his face into his mouth. Panting and clutching his injured arm, he collapsed onto one of the remaining pews.

"Hah!" Sevy yelled in triumph. She scrabbled atop the fallen statue, jumping up and down on it to squish it further into the gory mess. "I think it's dead," she said as she kicked through the muck to retrieve their swords. "What was it anyway?"

"Don't...know."

She looked up, noticing his wound. "Are you all right?"

"Yeah, I—"

The wind suddenly screamed through the shrine again and another infant whirlwind appeared. Without another word, they both bolted towards the entrance, threw open the door, and raced out into the night.

⁂

They ran for what seemed like hours, making sure to cross streams and double back every so often so that if anything was trying to track them it wouldn't be able to follow their trail. When Jarro's strength eventually gave out, they picked a sheltered spot to rest.

He was pale and exhausted, aching from the puncture in his arm. Luckily, the spike hadn't hit any major vessels so the bleeding had stopped on its own. Sevy washed and wrapped the wound as gently as any nursemaid. She even made him some ledum tea to help with infection and pain, though she did make a few snide remarks to the effect that, aside from some bruising, she hadn't received any injuries at all.

"That was too easy!" she proclaimed as she stoked up the fire.

He rolled his eyes. "Sure. Whatever you say."

"I wish we could see that monk's face when he sees his shrine in the morning. Betcha he'll cry."

"You just stole from a shrine, we were almost killed, and now you're making fun of a monk? Granted, a crooked monk, but still! Sevy, the gods will strike you down yet."

Her derisive giggle told him that divine retribution was not a concern of hers. She pulled the crystal out of her bag, twirling it so that it caught the light from the fire and sent rainbows into his eyes. "Eewerel may want to, but I think Annu-nial will protect me. From what I was told, Eewerel stole this first so I'm really just setting things right again. For a price."

"Next time you commit sacrilege, leave me out of it."

"Wimp! You needed to get out of Eloria anyway. City life makes you soft." She smirked as she poked his stomach. He swatted at her and she ducked away, ever the agile figurant even after a melee with a monster.

As she puttered around their makeshift camp, he leaned back against a tree and rested his eyes. A smile flitted across his face when she spread a blanket over him, but her doting did not come for free.

"You take first watch," she said, lying down next to him.

"Says who?"

"Says me." She stuck out her tongue.

"Oh, very mature."

She grinned and shifted closer, resting her head on his lap.

"Comfortable?"

"Mm-hmm."

There were evening pixies buzzing over head, attracted by the warmth of the fire. Jarro watched them dart from spot to spot, diaphanous wings beating so quickly they appeared motionless. Their flight paths were erratic, unpredictable, as if they were being tugged around like a child's toy on a piece of string. Combined with their soft hum, the effect was hypnotic and threatened to lull him to sleep. He had to shake himself awake. Absentmindedly, he coiled strands of Sevy's hair around his fingers. He heard her sigh in contentment, an echo of his own sentiments.

Despite being gored by some kind of monstrous guard dog, he did have to admit that it had been sort of exhilarating. He smiled at Sevy. Her brazenness was rubbing off on him. Things were always interesting when she was around. Being with her was so much more exciting than sitting around Eloria, collecting money from scared merchants, and fighting with dimwitted enemies.

"Sevy?"

"Mmm?"

"I was just thinking. Once we deliver the crystal, where do you want to go next? Maybe we could head west, take a ship to the islands or something. That might be fun, don't you think?"

One eyebrow rose, just enough to draw the lid up to peek at him. "You don't want to go back to the city?"

"Not really. It's so boring there."

The droning of pixie wings filled the silence, but the threat of sleep had disappeared. The mere mention of Eloria made his shoulders seize up. That shouldn't be. Eloria was his home. He shouldn't dread the thought of going home.

But he did. He had for years. And over the years, he had taken every opportunity he could to go traveling with Sevy. Oh, there was always some official reason. At first, it was the trip to Wilrendel to avoid reprisal from Duyan's men. Then there was the art theft in Kiming Falls, the smuggling operation to the Tarlugen Coast, the document retrieval from Allerough. Every one of them had been menial jobs better suited to underlings, but that hadn't mattered. He had happily abandoned his post at the slightest prompting, always deliberately overlooking the fact that his gang suffered with each of his absences.

He hated his docile nature, but he couldn't deny it. And he knew that he wasn't being fair to his men any more than he was to himself. Maybe it was time to make a decision, to stop trying to live between two worlds, pretending to be someone he clearly was not.

"Sevy?"

"Yeah?"

"What would you say if I left Eloria? Permanently?"

Her eyes popped open. "Leave? But where would you go? What about the gang?"

"Well, I was thinking I could hand over control to Revik. You know he's the one holding things together anyway. And then I'd be free to just go wherever. Do whatever. I'm so sick of it there."

The expression that came to her face was thoughtful, but there was something else buried there. Disappointment? Dismay? "If that's what you want. But what about...I...I'd miss you."

The firelight reflected on tears pooling in the corners of her eyes. She looked away and bit her lip, reminiscent of the bashful girl she had been when she was younger. He found it very endearing.

"You'd come with me though, right?" He rubbed her cheek with his thumb.

"Really?"

"Of course! It'd be no fun without you, sweetheart. We could do stuff like this all the time. But without the almost dying part. Whatever we want. Just the two of us."

"I'd like that," she said softly.

"Plus," he mused, "that way we wouldn't have to split our profits, wouldn't have the bother of all the petty turf wars..."

"Wouldn't have to put up with those god awful new recruits Revik lets join," she finished for him.

He laughed. "Oh, wait until you meet the latest. Some jackass named Bolozi. I don't know where Revik finds these guys. I tell you, dark elves have terrible judgment in people."

"Must be why he likes you so much." She winced as he gave her hair a tug. "Ow!"

"Well, it's something to think about."

They grew quiet again. Sevy smiled as she stared into the fire, and Jarro suddenly felt self-conscious. There was still more he wanted to say, more he wanted to confess. His feelings of inferiority, of fear and shame. It would be liberating to finally say aloud all the things he had kept hidden, but he was worried that she would think him pathetic. It was better to change the subject.

"So, where exactly are we taking the crystal?"

"I told you, to the priestesses of Annu-nial. They've got a temple about a day's walk from here."

"Priestesses, eh? Interesting."

"Don't get too excited. They've taken a vow of celibacy."

"For now."

She rolled her eyes and he laughed.

"Enough talk, more sleep," she mumbled.

He leaned his head back against the tree and watched the stars, tiny eyelets that let white slivers slip from the heavens hidden behind the velvet mantle of the sky. It was a lovely night. The kind one could imagine themselves remembering decades into the future when they were old and grey and the beauty of simplicity was all there was left to enjoy. After a few minutes passed, Jarro heard Sevy's breathing deepen as she fell asleep. He smiled. He couldn't articulate it, but even though they were in the middle of a strange forest possibly being hunted by another monster, he knew he was safe, and despite the dull ache in his arm, he was content and comfortable. This was the way home is supposed to feel, he surmised as he nodded off, and it felt wonderful.

Chapter 3

"That's it?" Jarro asked, eying the temple skeptically. It was low to the ground, built with stones, and sealed with mud. No windows could be seen and there was only one plain wooden door half-swallowed by moss and creeping vines. Nestled in amongst the trees it was easy to mistake for a natural feature. In fact, he had walked right by without noticing it until Sevy stopped him. "Doesn't look like much."

"They're a bunch of hermits or something. Kind of strange. Let me do the talking, all right?"

He wasn't going to object. It was her transaction, and besides, he was wary of the kind of people they were, vaguely wondering how Sevy had even come across them. One would have to be eccentric to worship the goddess of death in the first place. Adding that to the rock pile they called a temple, they were guaranteed to be a collection of crazy old crones. As he was still nursing his injured arm, he didn't have the strength or patience to decipher zealous gibberish. He'd just hang back while Sevy handled things, and then they'd be off.

Sevy banged her palm on the door. It opened half an inch, rusted hinges resisting with a hair-raising screech. "Yes?" a voice as high pitched as the hinges asked. "Oh, it's you! Did you retrieve the Eye of Annu?"

"Yep, so let me talk to Aliss."

The door was thrown wide. Jarro's jaw fell slack when he caught sight of the priestess standing before them. She was voluptuous and blonde and the ceremonial vestments she wore were delightfully form-fitting. "Oh, hurrah! Annu has answered our prayers!" she said, bouncing up and down in glee. Jarro couldn't stop his eyes from trailing downwards. Nor could he conceal the pleased expression that came to his face, cut painfully short by the swift elbow Sevy delivered to his side.

"Aliss?" she repeated.

"Yes, yes, one moment. Please come in."

The woman motioned them into the murky inner sanctum. Jarro had to duck to get through the doorway before he found himself in a circular room that was bare except for a natural spring bubbling in the center. A few candelabra haphazardly scattered about kept the room from dissolving into complete blackness. *Mood lighting,* he thought with a grin, as the candles and the water married to throw undulations of light which further accentuated the blonde's figure. Jarro watched the sway of her hips hungrily as she left the room to fetch her superior.

"You didn't tell me they were so friendly," he whispered into Sevy's ear. Another elbow, this time to his bandaged arm. He was still clutching it when the blonde returned with a darker haired woman whom he assumed was Aliss, and once again he was thrown by the beauty he beheld. She was spectacular. Tall and lean. Olive skin and smoky eyes. Even though she was a priestess, she deported herself with an air of exotic experience that Jarro found tantalizing.

"Well met, my daughter," Aliss said to Sevy. "Leonetta has told me that you have the Eye." She paused, seeing Jarro for the first time. "Hello. I don't believe we've met."

He flashed a big smile. "Hello yourself. My name—"

"Is not important," Sevy interrupted. "I have the crystal. Now where's my payment?"

"Yes, the payment. As you can see, we are a small fellowship. We cannot afford to pay you much."

"I don't think that'll be a problem," Jarro said.

Sevy audibly clenched her jaw. "Yeah, it will. We agreed on forty gold. Pay up. If not, I'm sure I can find someone else who'd be interested in buying this stupid rock."

"No! No! You cannot! The Goddess will be so upset!" Leonetta, the blonde, pleaded as she threw herself into Jarro's arms. "Please, we must have the Eye!"

His pulse raced just a little faster. "I'm sure we can come to some sort of arrangement," he said rather breathlessly.

"No, we won't. Forty gold. Now!"

"Come now. Your husband is being so much more reasonable," Aliss said, smiling at him.

"Oh, I'm not her husband. I'm, uh, nobody's husband."

Would it be inappropriate if he winked at her? He thought not, but apparently Sevy did. Digging her nails into his arm, she hauled him outside. The look she gave him could have blanched a ghost, and she slammed the door in his face, leaving him alone outside. Using the tone normally reserved for her mortal enemies, Sevy began an impassioned tirade. He couldn't make out what she was saying, but it made him cringe all the same, anxious for the fate of the priestesses if they dared interrupt. Thankfully, they had more sense than that. A few minutes of silence passed, then the door exploded open and Sevy stomped down the path leading away from the temple, tucking a very full money bag into her pack as she went.

"Wait," he called. "We're leaving? So soon?" There was no reply. He followed her into the forest and when he finally reached her, he seized her hand. "Wait a second!"

"Why?" she said, whipping around. She had a murderous glint in her eyes. "So you can flirt with them some more?"

"I wasn't flirting!"

"Oh really? 'Please, we must have the eye!' 'I'm sure we can come to some sort of arrangement.' I mean, seriously, what the hell was that?"

"What was what? I was being nice!"

"Nice? Nice? I didn't risk my life getting that stupid piece of crap just to be nice, Jarro. That was my deal and you had no right trying to undermine me like that."

"They're just priestesses. It's not like they have a lot of money."

"And since when did you become so damn devout? Hmm? About the time the blood left your head for parts south?" She cast another glare at him and continued walking, muttering various curses.

"Sevy!" He knew that she could hear him, but she would not answer. Groaning in frustration, he ran after her again and blocked her path. "Sevy, would you just stop and talk to me?"

"I have nothing more to say. Why don't you go back to the temple? I'm sure they'd be more than happy to talk to you."

"You're being ridiculous."

"Excuse me? I'm being ridiculous? I'm not the one who lets big breasts interfere with business."

"So I flirted with them, so what? Don't act like you've never done it before."

"This isn't about me! It's about you trying to throw my money away, money I worked hard for, on the slim possibility that you might get laid."

"Your money? I've got a goddamned hole in my arm! Half of that money is mine, remember?"

"You want it? Fine! Take it and get out of my sight!" She threw a fistful of coins at him. They bounced off his chest and fell onto the forest floor. He was baffled. He'd been on the receiving end of her anger more than once, but never like this.

He paused in his chase long enough to collect the gold. "Sevy, wait!" She stopped, to his surprise and relief, and he held the coins out to her, little metal peace offerings which he desperately hoped she would accept. "Here, take them back. I'm sorry. Don't be upset with me, all right?" She didn't make a move to claim them, instead stood with arms crossed, eying him sullenly. He reached into her pack, took out her money bag, and replaced the coins. "I'm an ass, I know."

"You're damn straight you're an ass," she said, snatching the bag back. She started walking again. "Well? Are you coming?"

He guessed that meant she had forgiven him. Or at the very least she was thinking about forgiving him. Sevy had always been temperamental and he knew it would be a while before things went back to normal. She could hold a grudge longer than most. Sighing, he followed after her. It was going to be a long day.

Chapter 4

Jarro was a ladies' man, always had been. He had a way with women, a knack, which drew them to him even before he was old enough to realize that he could use his god-given gifts to his advantage. He could remember being a child, still small enough to snuggle up on his mother's lap, surrounded by women oohing and awing over his big blue eyes or the curl of his dark hair. He loved the attention then and he loved it now.

He had often maintained that women were the best teachers. Through the pleasure and the pain they meted out, a man could learn many things, and if he were an apt pupil he could certainly improve his chances of the former. Jarro, making no attempt at modesty, considered himself a quick study.

And right now his years of education were telling him to lie low.

Sevy was still annoyed with him. That was obvious from her posture, the look in her eyes, the sound of her numerous sighs. What wasn't obvious was why she was so upset. He could see it from her point of view, but he had hardly committed a grievous sin. Things should have blown over by now. So why hadn't they?

She did not lay her head on his lap that night. Instead, she placed her bedroll on the opposite side of the fire. She did not say goodnight. The next morning, he was greeted by a frown in place of her usual sleepy smile.

By midday, she began to issue monosyllabic responses to the conversation he tried to strike up. They were more like grunts than words, but would suffice to encourage his reconciliatory efforts. He found some buttercups growing by the side of the road and picked a bunch for her, timidly holding them out like a child would for his favorite schoolmistress. They were tossed aside without hesitation. It didn't seem to matter what Jarro did. She was in a snit and nothing would coax her out of it.

Night fell as they arrived back in Mindervale, and they stopped at the same tavern where they had met at the start of this misadventure. He wistfully remembered the reunion they had shared back then, and prayed that they could recapture some of that happiness.

"Buy you dinner, sweetheart?" he asked.

"Don't care."

That was almost a sentence. He decided to take it as a good sign. He bought her the best meal Mindervale had to offer: a tough piece of steak and a couple of withered potatoes. Luckily, the ale was good and strong. He made sure to keep the supply coming, knowing that she could never resist a drink.

It worked. The wintry veneer that had frozen Sevy's face since his impropriety finally began to thaw. The corners of her mouth twitched, promising an eventual smile. She let her gaze roam the room and Jarro wondered if she was searching out the young man she had spent time with here. *Stupid little sop*, he thought, surprising himself with his bitterness.

A band was playing that night. They were locals, nothing special really. Just the usual trio of pipes, fiddle, and drums that one could find in any given tavern in eastern Axlun, but they could carry a tune and that was enough to get some of the other customers up and dancing. They started into a jig, heavy on the pipes which he knew were Sevy's favorite. He noticed her tapping her glass in time to the music.

Taking one last mouthful of whiskey for courage, Jarro stood and held out his hand. "Come and dance with me."

She cocked an eyebrow. "I don't think so."

"Oh, come on!"

"Why don't you go ask one of them?" she said with a perfunctory gesture to a group of women standing by the bar. Pretty, nubile, just his type. They started giggling when he glanced at them. Ah, clever girl. It was a test and he knew it. Well, he would settle for nothing less than passing with honors.

"Because I don't want to dance with them. I want to dance with you." Without waiting for a reply, he pulled her up. "Please?"

He could tell she was mulling it over, but it seemed to take an eternity. Eventually, she gave her consent with the faintest nod of her head, and she allowed him to walk her to the dance floor. He paused long enough to catch the beat of the song then led her merrily around the room. The music was rollicking, the high spirits contagious. Even though they hurt his still-smarting arm, he made sure to include plenty of spins and dips in his repertoire of dance steps as he knew she loved them. It took almost the whole of the song, but he was finally rewarded with a laugh, the sweetest sound he had heard in two days. By the time the music came to an end, he had his Sevy back.

She did a mock curtsey and turned to reclaim their table. Not wanting to let her go just yet, he kept hold of her hand. "One more."

The band played a soothing, slow tune. The other dancers paired off and the mood of the room glided into dreamy sentimentality. "Please?"

A hint of red spread across her face. He grinned. He had always found her quick blush to be one of her more charming quirks and it heartened him to see. He wrapped his arm around her waist, pulling her close. She hesitated then placed a hand on his shoulder. He moved her in a languid sway, letting the music wash over them and wreathe them together in a private space all their own.

Neither said a word. For an instant, their eyes locked together. Hers held a strange sparkle. They were greener than usual, or maybe it was just the lighting. In either event, they looked different. Good different. He wanted to tell her so, but she blinked and looked away. Undaunted, he pressed her tighter against him and felt her sigh.

His gaze trailed down her face and settled on her lips. Very full and pink, he wondered how it was that he had never really noticed them before. A peculiar sensation then struck him: the desire to know what it would be like to kiss those burnished, mesmerizing lips. He was unexpectedly aware of everything about her—the curve of the small of her back against his palm, the way her left hand tangled in his hair, the soft fullness of her breasts pressed against his chest.

"You're beautiful," he whispered.

She looked at him. Her lips parted. The urge to kiss her was irresistible. Suddenly, her back became rigid and she jerked free of his embrace. "You're drunk." She gave a dismissive pat to the top of his head.

The song ended and she walked away from him without explanation. He stood watching her, filled with misery and confusion, uncomfortably convinced that all eyes in the tavern were settled upon him and had served witness to that irrational exchange.

What the hell was that?

Later, after several more shots of whiskey and a smattering of tongue-tied goodnight wishes, he tossed in his bed. He wished he could say that his inability to sleep was thanks to his arm, but that wasn't anywhere near the truth. What happened back there? He had never looked at Sevy that way before. Sure, he had always thought her attractive. She had a sort of impish appeal, but not by any stretch of the imagination was she the sort of woman he normally went for. He was aware of the starry-eyed crush she had on him when they first met, but she had outgrown that years ago and he could honestly say that he had never seen her as anything more than a friend. He turned on his side and exhaled, as if doing so would purge the odd notions floating around his head.

She was probably right. He had been drunk. But he'd been drunk around her scores of times and had never experienced anything even remotely like that.

He raised his head to look at her lying in the bed across the room. He could hear the soft, steady rhythm of her breathing as she slept. The moon peeked through the shuttered window and in the muted light he saw her chest rise and fall with each breath. Her hand was twisted in the sheets and although her face was slightly turned away from him he could see her eye dancing under the lid. He smiled, curious as to the content of her dreams.

The more he watched her, the more heat built in his body and another strange fancy took possession of his mind. He had a longing to slip into bed beside her and wake her with a kiss. He imagined her eyes opening, gazing up at him, beautiful smile appearing, so inviting, so luscious. "Oh, Jarro, I've dreamed about this for so long," she'd moan, hands running through his hair as he bent to kiss her again.

He forced a laugh to jolt himself out of the fantasy.

Yeah, right! She'd probably scream and beat the hell out of me. What am I thinking?

He rolled onto his other side to stare at the wall rather than her distracting form, and cursed himself. Sevy deserved better than the kind of thoughts he was having. She was his friend, not some ditzy barmaid. How could he think about her like that? There were some lines that were not meant to be crossed.

It must just be from traveling together, he concluded. That and the fight they had. Plus, he was overly emotional about the time they had spent apart. And don't forget the whiskey. That had to be it. Of course. After all, what else could it be?

Chapter 5

The journey back to Eloria was agonizingly quiet. Things between Sevy and Jarro were still strained, but this time it wasn't Sevy's doing.

She tried to engage Jarro in friendly banter, regaled him with tales of her adventures up north, teased him, tortured him with purposely off-key singing, even tackled him a few times, but he remained aloof, managing only the barest of hangdog smiles before sinking back into stoicism. Mortified by his behavior at the tavern, he couldn't even look at her without wanting the earth to swallow him up. It wasn't right the way he had thought of her, the way he was still thinking of her.

What was wrong with him? There were times he would sneak glances at her and be struck near senseless by the simplest of things, like the way the sunlight hit the wisps of hair framing her face. Every night when she changed the dressing on his arm, he had to bite his tongue to divert attention away from the sensation of her fingertips moving across his bare skin. It was maddening being so close to her. The only way he could maintain control was by keeping as much physical and emotional distance as he could without hurting her feelings.

By the third day on the road, she fell silent as well, perhaps sensing that things were different. At first, he was relieved. The less animated she was, the less fuel he had for his inflamed imagination. The relief did not last long however, as he soon took to obsessing over what she was thinking, feeling. Did she have any clue that the reason he wouldn't look her in the eyes was because he now found them so blindingly beautiful that it made his legs grow weak? She couldn't know. He wouldn't let her. She was too dear to him to risk losing over some absurd hormonal reaction. He would not throw away eight years of friendship because of this…whatever it was.

Eloria would provide sanctuary from these thoughts. With the others around to act as a buffer, he'd get over this unwelcome infatuation and then things could go back to normal. Maybe one day, years from now, he would tell her about it and they'd have a good long laugh over what a fool he had been.

"Home sweet home," she suddenly murmured.

Before them lay Tingarny, a shanty town that sprawled for miles before the eastern gate, home to the poorest of the poor who could not even afford to live within Eloria's slums. In the distance behind Tingarny, the city wall loomed like the carcass of a fallen giant swathed in a yellowish haze of decay. Jarro felt sick to his stomach.

"Yeah. Home sweet home."

He fought the impulse to grab her hand and force her to run with him in the opposite direction. It was tempting, but it wouldn't be the right thing to do. Especially not with the way he was feeling. Whether he liked it or not, this was the life he had made for himself. Change may come in time, but for now he had a duty to uphold.

He hadn't even made it through the front door before the weight of that duty was thrust back onto his shoulders. A handful of his men had been caught breaking into the coffer of Eloria's leading shipwright. Many palms had to be greased to have the incident overlooked, and two men were hanged before Jarro was able to secure the release of the others.

Following that unpleasantry, there was little time to plan his retirement or to ponder his peculiar conduct concerning Sevy. The gang was in turmoil and Jarro found himself having to contend with a wave of insubordination instigated by their newest recruit, Bolozi.

"It seemed like a good idea," Revik maintained as they discussed why Bolozi had been allowed to join in the first place. Revik had considered it a gesture of peace and goodwill made towards someone who had the potential to cause a lot of trouble. Bolozi had come from the southern provinces hoping to make his fortune, and though he had only been in Eloria a short time, he had already built a name for himself and was able to procure allies wherever he went, though Jarro was at a loss to figure out why.

He certainly hadn't made a good impression on Sevy. Her jaw set with recognizable loathing after just one look at him. Jarro was ineffably relieved that at least she was able to see Bolozi for what he was: a roughneck, pure and simple. He was arrogant, cruel, just plain belligerent. And, regrettably, less than a month after joining with the gang, he began voicing aloud all the things the others didn't dare to say. Why did Jarro feel the need to play benefactor to every orphan and pauper around town? Was it naivety or sheer stupidity that led him to keep a dark elf as his advisor? And just where had he run off to while his men were sitting in prison? Bolozi avowed that Jarro was weak, at the beck and call of a shrew, and would lead them all to ruination if nothing was done.

Too much time and energy was then spent undoing the damage the coffer incident had managed to inflict. Lines were drawn, stances were taken. A lot of valued men went their separate ways. Bolozi remained, for what nefarious reasons Jarro could only imagine, and for now there was no way to be rid of him without inciting rebellion. Patience was a virtue, his mother had taught him. For now he'd just have to wait and watch and plan his next move. This was exactly what he was doing when Turlan hobbled into his study one afternoon.

He refused the seat Jarro offered him, preferring to lean on his cane instead. "Too much work getting back up," he said, though Jarro could see the pain behind his flippant attitude. He'd been in a poor state for years, long before Jarro had first found him in a gutter, drunk on wood alcohol, but his health had deteriorated dramatically over the past summer. The healers Jarro consulted were surprised the old man had lasted this long. Most likely, he wouldn't make it to see another spring. One more problem to add to the long list of troublesome and unsettling developments that Jarro could not bring himself to deal with.

"Just wanted to let ya know all the men reported. Money's been collected for this month." Turlan placed a sack of coins on Jarro's desk, wheezing at the effort. "'Cept Bolozi. He ain't back yet."

Jarro frowned. "Where'd he go?"

"Northern gate. The smithy there owed plenty so he took a couple guys. Should've been back by now."

"Let me know the second he gets back."

Turlan nodded and shuffled out of the room. Jarro sat, thinking. Obviously, the continued disobedience would not do. Bolozi would have to be taken in hand eventually regardless of the outcome, but the thought of it gave Jarro a headache. Better to let Revik handle it. After all, he was the one who had let Bolozi in.

Jarro found Revik outside in the courtyard sparring with Sevy. As usual, they weren't holding back any blows. Sevy punched him in the face before he could duck. She tried to strike again, but Revik took hold of her arm and twisted her round into a headlock.

"Say mercy," he said with a laugh.

"Fuck you."

"Hey, Revik! Can I have a word?"

Revik's grip on Sevy's neck relaxed as he glanced up at Jarro. She took the opportunity to elbow him in the stomach and flip him over. He landed on the ground with a smarting thud.

"Do you two have to play so rough?" Jarro asked. "Look at you. Your nose is bleeding."

Sevy touched the back of her hand against her nose and shrugged. "He started it."

"Listen, we need to talk about Bolozi."

"What did he do now?" Revik sighed as he wiped sweat off his brow.

"He's not back from collecting dues yet."

"Think he's pocketing the money?"

"I don't care about the damned money. I just don't want him hurting that poor smithy. He pays us to protect him from that sort of nonsense."

"Don't worry. I'll deal with it. And you," he said, challenging Sevy, "I'll be back for a rematch later."

"Anytime, loser."

Jarro contemplated following Revik into the house, but before he could, Sevy began talking, cheerfully ignorant to the discomfort Jarro felt at the prospect of being alone with her. "If you don't like Bolozi, why don't you just get rid of him?" she asked, taking a few swings at the practice dummy.

"Not that simple. He's got a lot of friends. I'd rather not start some stupid feud over this."

"Get rid of them too."

"Just like that, eh?"

"Sure, why not?"

"Because it would end up being me against more than half the gang."

"Come on, it'd be fun to clean house. And you wouldn't be alone. People love you, Jarro. They always have. You're the best boss around."

He smiled. "Thanks, but I think you're overestimating my popularity these days."

She leaned back against the dummy and stretched her arms out over her head, unaware of how enticing her movements were. He shook his head so that he could focus on what she was saying. "You know what your problem is? You're too nice."

"Oh, am I?"

"Yep. Too nice and too forgiving."

"What would you suggest then?"

She grinned. "Let me teach Bolozi some manners for you. Please? I've been wanting an excuse to hurt that guy since I met him."

"You really don't like him, do you?"

She made a face.

"Neither do I. In fact, I don't like most of them anymore."

"So why don't we just take off then? Like you said before, let Revik or whoever deal with them."

Her suggestion took him aback. They hadn't mentioned that plan since their return. He hadn't dared to bring it up. Not with the way things were going.

"You'd come with me?"

She nodded, tightened the leather straps around her hands, and punched the dummy before looking at him again. "Well? It's your call, Jarro."

A thousand thoughts rushed through his head. He pushed the more lascivious ones aside as they only served to complicate matters. If they planned it properly, they could leave within the month. That would be more than enough time to get all the supplies they needed, tie up any loose ends. He'd let Revik know tonight. Revik would be happy. Unlike Jarro, he seemed to enjoy living in Eloria. More than that, he liked having control. Bossing around humans was a guilty pleasure of his, Revik had confessed on more than one occasion.

There was just one more important detail that nagged at him. Sevy followed his line of vision to the house where Turlan could be heard coughing and hacking.

"Maybe we should wait until spring," he said.

She nodded, understanding. "Sounds like a plan. Are you going to let Revik know?"

"Yeah," he sighed. "I'll tell him soon."

"All right. Now! I want to fight some more and since you sent Revik away it looks like you're gonna have to do."

He groaned. "Just go easy on me. I'm only human you know."

"Quit whining. Let's go!"

He tilted his head down and raised his fists, knees slightly bent. They circled each other warily.

"Come on, wuss. Quit stalling and fight!"

"You're all talk, Sevy."

She smirked and jabbed him a couple times in the ribs. He gave her a straight right to the shoulder and they both stepped back. She stepped in again and tried to uppercut his chest, but he deked to the side, avoiding the blow. He delivered a left hook that made her stagger. The pained glare she gave him filled him with remorse.

"I'm so sorry, sweetheart! Did I hurt you?"

He should have known better. With an evil laugh, she jabbed him in the head, gave him a straight left to his chin, then a right hook to his temple. His vision wobbled and he fell backwards onto the ground.

She put her left leg on his chest, staring down at him in victory. "I'm all talk, am I?"

He let her gloat while he caught his breath, then grabbed her foot and twisted it hard. She yelped as she lost her balance. Before she could get up, he rolled on top of her, pinning her arms above her head.

"Bastard," she whispered, her way of saying she was impressed. "Of course, you realize the second you let me go you're gonna get it twice as hard."

This was dangerous territory and he knew it. He would chastise himself for it later, but for right now he allowed himself the pleasure of her sinewy body pressed under his. "Well, maybe I just won't let you go. I don't have anything else to do today, do you?" he said, cocking his head to the side.

She laughed and pretended to try to bite his face. He kind of wished that she would.

"Jarro? Hey, Jarro?" Turlan was standing in the doorway of the courtyard. Silly old codger never did have any sense of timing. "Bolozi is back. You wanna talk to him or what?"

Jarro looked at Sevy. "Truce?"

"Maybe."

Grudgingly, he released his hold on her wrists and stood up, missing her warmth immediately. She kicked him in the behind as he walked away, unwitting punishment for the naughty thrill he had gotten from their game. It was so wrong of him, he knew, but he just couldn't help it. That green-eyed spitfire would be the death of him.

Inside, he motioned for Bolozi to follow him into his study away from the others. "Where's Revik? He left to find you not ten minutes ago."

Bolozi made some kind of unintelligible noise which Jarro took to mean that he hadn't seen Revik, then sat down on a chair and plopped his foot up onto the desk. His demeanor was reminiscent of an unapologetic schoolboy about to receive a tongue lashing from an uptight teacher for bad behavior on the playground. Jarro would have none of it. He kicked Bolozi's foot down. That was enough to get his full attention. "The money?" The bag was produced. "And the smithy?"

"No worse for wear."

"I don't go in for dealings like that around here, understood? If I hear about you laying one finger on my clients—"

"You'll what? Cry to your girlfriend about it?"

The stony smile displayed on Jarro's face promptly dispatched the haughty one from Bolozi's. In one swift motion, Jarro jumped forward, lifted Bolozi out of the chair by his throat, and held him against the wall. "I don't appreciate your tone. You want to be a member of my gang, you play by my rules, got it?"

Bolozi, feverishly trying to remain on tiptoe, nodded his head. Jarro held him a minute longer before letting him drop back to his feet. "Good. Now get out of my sight."

Jarro slammed the door behind the idiot as he scurried out of the room. Now alone, he discarded the macho façade, and paced around his desk to release the suffocating anger and impotence he felt. He didn't know how much longer he could put up with this. But he had to. At least until...

He stopped himself from finishing that thought. Turlan was his oldest friend, one of the first Jarro had made when he came to the city twelve years ago. He couldn't leave, not while Turlan was so close to the end. It was unlikely that anyone, not even Revik, would have the patience needed to care for him as time went on.

Perhaps the reason he felt so strongly about Turlan was because of the remorse he carried. Due to the shame he had brought them with his desertion, Jarro would not be able to be with his family, his father, to tend to them in their final days as was the duty of a good son. He had let his family down miserably. There was no way he would do the same to his friends. He just had to resign himself to the fact that they'd have to stay for a few more months at least. There was no other option.

In the meantime, he would transition authority to Revik. It wouldn't be that hard. No one respected him anymore anyway, thanks to Bolozi. And though it made his ego smart to admit it, Revik was the real power behind this organization. He always had been. Jarro was a figure-head, a human mouthpiece to appease Eloria's bigoted heart, but now it was time to step back and let Revik speak for himself. There were those who didn't like dark elves and would resist, but Jarro was confident they could be won over, or at the very least subdued. Revik was certainly capable of taking care of his own interests and didn't have any of Jarro's qualms regarding violence. He'd do just fine.

He nodded to himself. That was it then. He had a clear plan. With that matter settled, he let his thoughts drift, daydreaming about how nice it would be once he was free of Eloria. A fresh start. A new life. He could do anything he wanted and he wouldn't make the same mistakes he had made before.

Sighing, he rested his head against the window pane and watched Sevy, who was still out in the courtyard. Unlike when he had fled from the army, this time he wouldn't be alone. No matter where he went, or what he did, Jarro would be able to take comfort in Sevy's friendship.

It would be a challenge to wean her off of life outside the law. It was all she had ever known. He chuckled as she mocked the practice dummy and made exaggerated fighting stances. It would take time, but it wasn't impossible. With Sevy by his side, nothing was.

Chapter 6

Did they notice the change in him? He doubted it. For people always lamenting their fate to muck through life as the dregs of society, they never made much effort to improve their situation. And they never looked kindly on those who did. They probably couldn't even begin to fathom why he would want to leave this type of existence. Here it was, another pointless night of fighting and drinking followed by the familiar malaise of a hangover then back to business robbing honest people of their hard earned coins. They sickened him. He sickened himself for ever being a part of it.

"Jarro! Here, have a glass," someone cheered as they shoved a mug of ale into his hand.

Alcohol wouldn't improve his mood. He had been in a funk for weeks now and a little drink wasn't going to change that. Time was ticking by far too slowly. He just wished that...No, he couldn't wish that. Turlan was worth the aggravation. Jarro went to him now, to his chair by the front door where he was snoozing.

"Hey, Turlan. How are you feeling tonight?"

"I'd be feeling a might bit better if you'd pass me that ale."

"Do you think that's wise?"

Turlan chortled. "At my age, nothing's wise."

Jarro conceded and handed him the mug. Absorbed in his drink, Turlan didn't provide much in the way of conversation so Jarro had to settle for watching the others dance and play. A crowd had gathered around Bolozi, egging him on as he attempted to down an entire keg. He passed out half way through and flopped onto the middle of the table with a phlegm-filled snort. Jarro sneered and contemplated having a bit of sport with a razor and Bolozi's fat head. Sevy's influence, no doubt.

The thought of her coaxed a smile from him. She could probably think of dozens of wicked tricks they could play on Bolozi. Jarro looked around for her before spotting her with Revik. They were dancing. Well, in a manner of speaking. Revik was spinning her and she stumbled to stay upright, winded by laughter. Jarro frowned at the twinge of possessiveness that crept up his spine. He shook it off and turned back to Turlan.

"How about a game of cards?"

"Sure! I'd never pass up a chance to get yer money."

Jarro moved over to the table and shoved Bolozi to the floor. He hit the ground with a thump and kept on snoring. Jarro could barely resist the urge to give him a good, swift kick. Turlan sat down and pulled out a deck of cards. A few men joined in, and a lively game was soon underway. For awhile, it was almost like old times.

An hour later, Jarro was down eighteen silver pieces, having lost the last three hands in a row. "Guess it's not my lucky night, eh Turlan?"

There was no answer. Turlan, though he was still clinging to his cards, had fallen asleep. Gently, Jarro picked him up and carried him to his room. It wasn't the least bit difficult. Turlan weighed next to nothing. Jarro cringed at the crunching he felt in Turlan's joints as he tucked him into bed. There was so little left of him now. "Goodnight, old friend," he whispered.

On his way back to the game, he happened to glance over to a corner where Revik and Sevy sat, chatting with one another. The muscles in Jarro's neck tensed. He rubbed them to relax again and resumed the game.

Minutes passed. He couldn't resist looking over his shoulder to sneak a peek at them. Sevy was playing with Revik's hair, making tiny braids in the long white strands while she whispered into his ear. Revik looked up and caught Jarro's eye before saying something that made Sevy laugh.

"Hey, Jarro? You in or what?"

"Huh? Yeah, yeah, I'm in."

He tried to focus on the game, but was completely distracted. What were they talking about? He turned to look at them again. Sevy leaned into Revik, her hand on his chest in a very intimate manner. Then Revik draped an arm around her and she rested her head against him. His lips brushed against her temple, which made her laugh again.

Jarro tossed his cards aside. Ignoring everyone he passed, he stormed out into the courtyard, pushing over some wooden crates as he went. His blood pounded. His chest puffed out with each breath.

He drew his sword. The practice dummy, innocently swaying back and forth in the breeze, became his unsuspecting opponent. He slashed it, splitting it open so that its straw entrails spilled over the ground, but Jarro found that wasn't good enough so he set about hacking it to shreds. Once it was completely obliterated, he took a few swipes at the pole it had been attached to. It was immature, but it did make him feel better. The rage was gone. Now he was left with a subtle, seething resentment that sat like a rock in his gut. Kicking through the remains of his inanimate foe, he puzzled over his anger.

He looked suspiciously at the open door as though it was the source of his bad temper and debated whether or not to go back in. The music and voices inside were creating quite the racket. Smoke drifted lazily out into the sky. Everyone else was having a good time, why shouldn't he? It was his gang, his home. Why should he feel unwelcome there? It wasn't right. He should march in there, take back the money he lost, throw Bolozi out on his drunken ass, and pry Sevy free from Revik's clutches. And if anyone didn't like it, well, they could suffer the same fate that the dummy had.

This wasn't at all like him, he reflected as he circled the courtyard. It was just the result of everything that had been happening lately. He had to be content with the knowledge that things would improve with time. It was silly to get so worked up. Sevy would make fun of him if she had witnessed this juvenile temper tantrum.

Sevy...

The mental picture of her in Revik's arms made his blood boil once more. Logically, he knew that it shouldn't upset him. Why should he care what she did? It was her life and if she wanted to waste her time with the likes of Revik then so be it. No, that wasn't fair of him. Revik was a good man, one of his closest friends.

He wondered what they were doing. Was Revik sweet talking her? Maybe by now they had gone upstairs for some privacy. Maybe he was using that elvish charm of his. Sevy always did have a weakness for bad boys. Jarro paced the length of the courtyard so furiously it made him light-headed. Is Revik kissing her now? Sevy wouldn't fall for that, would she? Of course not, she's a smart girl. She knows what men are like. Then again, she and Revik had been friends for a long time and they had a lot in common.

Jarro pulled at his hair, hoping the pain would purify him. It didn't matter what they were doing. It was none of his business. If he just repeated that enough maybe he'd believe it.

He decided that he didn't want to go back in. He kicked at the ground while he contemplated what to do instead. The attack on the dummy had dulled the edge of his sword. The blade needed resharpening. He stomped over to the whetstone that was in the corner, doused it with water, and worked the pedal with his foot until the wheel reached proper speed. Then he pressed his blade against it.

A soft light grabbed his attention. Though the arms of the courtyard tree partially blocked the window, he could tell that a candle had been lit up in Sevy's room. What did that mean? Was she alone? Was

Revik with her? His concentration distracted, Jarro's finger slipped and rubbed against the whetstone. He pulled his hand away, but not before the skin had been scraped raw. "Dammit!"

He was startled by a low laugh. "You shouldn't play with your sword while you're drunk," Revik said from the doorway.

"I'm not drunk," he muttered, though he suddenly felt a curious jolt of relief.

"The great playboy Jarro leaving a party before he's wasted? Why, that's unheard of!"

"Not in much of a party mood, I guess."

"And why is that?"

"I have to have a reason? Why are you out here anyway? I thought you were..."

"Thought I was what?" Revik moved closer, amusement dancing in his carmine eyes. "Otherwise engaged?"

"Your business, not mine." Jarro ran his finger along the edge of his blade. It was nice and sharp now. He returned it to its sheath and looked around for something else to occupy his time, but there was nothing except for the bothersome dark elf who would not stop grinning.

"You humans. For having such a short life span, you sure do waste a lot of time. You never just say what's on your mind, do you?"

"Well, why don't you tell me what's on my mind then, hmm? I didn't realize you were clairvoyant."

"It's pretty obvious. You're upset that Sevy was paying attention to someone other than you. But instead of acknowledging that, you'd rather sulk out here. And apparently," he eyed the dummy, "break things."

Jarro tried to laugh, but it came out sounding like an unnatural cough. "You think I care what she does? Why should I?"

"Because you're in love with her."

"What? You're insane!"

"You mean you're not? Really? Well, that's wonderful news because I was thinking of trying my luck with her. I just wanted to make sure it was all right with you first. It is all right with you, isn't it?"

Jarro was helpless to do anything other than stutter random noises.

"Oh, so it's not?" Revik asked once he had stopped chuckling. "Hmm. I can't imagine why."

"It wouldn't work," Jarro insisted. "It would be a bad idea. A very, very bad idea."

"Think so? And why's that?"

"Well, you and Sevy, um, the thing is she..."

"I see. So you don't want her, but I can't have her either. Is that what you're trying to say?"

"That's not it at all. It's just, I don't know. It's complicated."

"Why don't I believe you?"

"I don't know. Maybe because you're an ass?"

"Ouch! Well, aren't we testy tonight? You know what would make you feel better?" Jarro didn't bother to ask what, as he knew Revik was enjoying himself far too much to stop there. "A bottle of wine, some candlelight, and a certain brunette."

"Don't be a pig."

"You know you want to. Don't pretend you don't. Look at you. You're practically panting for it."

"You know something? I used to think you were clever, but you are clearly just a babbling half-wit with too much time on his hands. Yes, I love Sevy. She's my friend. But that's all she is. So can you please just shut up?"

"Good gods, man! Quit lying to yourself. Do you have any idea how many bets I've lost over the years waiting for you two to finally get together? What's taking you so long? She's a great girl."

"I know that."

"Don't meet girls like her too often."

"I know!"

"And she's got a nice little body too. Kind of small up top, but I sure wouldn't mind having a go with her."

"Hey! You watch your damned mouth!"

Revik laughed so hard he doubled over. Disgusted, Jarro moved to charge past him, but Revik caught his arm. "Hold on, I'm not finished. If you're worried about me, don't be. I wouldn't do that to you even if I was interested in her. But how much longer do you expect Sevy to wait around for you? Sooner or later, she's going to find a man who won't take her for granted."

"What do you mean?"

Revik brought his shoulders up to almost his ears with his exaggerated shrug. Still chuckling, he headed for the door.

"Wait a minute!" Jarro called after him. "Do you really think that?"

"Hard to say. I'm just a babbling half-wit, remember?"

Jarro stood gazing up at Sevy's window. "Revik doesn't know what he's talking about. I don't take her for granted, she knows that," he mumbled under his breath. "She knows I'd do anything for her."

"Because you're in love with her," Revik's words floated back to him.

He felt like breaking things again. He was anxious and edgy and wasn't sure what was causing it. He wanted to go inside, yell at Revik, set him straight.

Damn smug elf!

What did he know anyway? If Revik couldn't understand that platonic relationships between men and women happened all the time, then it was his loss. After minutes more pacing and brooding, Jarro decided to talk with Sevy. They'd have a laugh about it and that way he'd know that Revik was simply spouting rubbish as usual. He walked inside and up the stairs, ignoring the obnoxious wink Revik gave him. There was no answer when he knocked on the door to Sevy's room.

"Sevy?" He heard her giggle, so he cracked the door open and peeked in. "Sevy?" he repeated.

She was in her nightgown, crouching barefoot with her hands clasped in front of her.

"What are you doing?"

"Look what I got!" She held her hands up. A faint green light slipped through the cracks of her fingers, accompanied by a buzzing sound. "See?" she said, moving a thumb to reveal an angry pixie bouncing off her palms. "I caught it trying to steal my stuff."

"It's too small to steal your stuff," he said, baffled.

"I'm going to keep it. What should I name it?"

"It's a pixie, sweetheart. They don't need names. Now you'd better let it go before it—"

"Ow!"

"—bites you."

"Stupid little...I'm gonna smush it!"

"No, you don't." He pried her fingers apart and let the poor sprite loose. It fluttered about as if in a daze before zipping through the open window, off to re-join its swarm and tell them about the evil giant it had battled. Sevy giggled again and swayed backwards. Jarro caught her elbow to steady her. "How much did you have to drink?"

"A lot!" Before he could say anything else, she threw her arms around him and nuzzled her face into his hair. "Aww, Jarro, you're not angry, are you? You left the party. Where'd you go?"

The warmth of her breath against his neck made him flush, and it really didn't help that there was only a thin slip of fabric between his hands and her skin. "I, uh, the noise was getting to me."

"You wanna go back down? Let's go fight with somebody."

He laughed. "No, you should go to sleep. It's late."

She mumbled something incoherent as he helped her to bed. He pulled the blanket up for her and she gave him a bleary-eyed smile before falling asleep. For a moment, he watched her, fondly smoothing some hair from her face before he caught himself.

He was stunned as the truth revealed itself. Suddenly everything became very clear. The jealousy he had watching her with Revik, the lust that had given him so much guilt, the emptiness he had felt when she was away. The reason he always pictured her with him when he imagined what life would be like after Eloria. It all made perfect sense now.

He loved her. He had always loved her. Leaning down, he kissed her lips, happily thinking that they were just as sweet and soft as he had dreamed them to be, before blowing out the candle and leaving her room.

Now I've just got to find a way to show her.

Chapter 7

Adrenaline swept through Sevy's veins as she navigated the cobwebbed corridor, eyes squinting in the gloom. Footsteps sounded on the floorboards behind her. They were close. She had a good lead over them, but for how long?

Another corner, another identical passage that could bring freedom, folly, or still more turns in the seemingly unending maze of halls. She should have brought twine or a piece of chalk as Revik had suggested to spare herself this stressful setback. Sevy had inherent abilities that lent themselves favorably to her career of choice; sadly, a sense of direction was not one of them.

The jewels stowed in her satchel were not worth this aggravation. Her share should be doubled. That was only fair considering she was the one stuck in this damnable vault while Revik and Bolozi waited at ground level, too craven to shimmy down a length of rope. Too heavy, they had insisted. It would be easier for them to hoist her back up than vice versa. Yeah, sure. She believed that was their sole motivation just like she believed Bolozi was a pixie. It was a good thing she didn't let fear rule her head or they would have had to go home empty handed.

Of course, they still might if she couldn't manage to find her way out of here. The voices of the guards were getting too close for comfort, and though she'd rather die than admit it, sharp little teeth of claustrophobic fright were biting into her skin. Everything looked the same, covered in the same blanket of darkness and dust. How long had it been since anyone had been down here? How long would it be before anyone would come looking for her? She imagined someone opening the vault years from now and finding her skeleton lying in a corner, bony fingers still scratching at the walls.

Enough, she ordered herself. Panicking would not help matters. Besides, this place wasn't that neglected. Someone still cared enough to employ the guards who had followed her down once they had been alerted to her presence. There was more than one way in apparently, and that meant more than one way out. Comforted by that knowledge, she was able to negotiate the passageways with a little more reason and a little less hysteria.

Finally, she saw a spotlight washing the floor in a muted but much welcomed glow. She ran towards it, congratulating herself on a job well done. The light was coming from a trapdoor some twenty feet above her head. It was the same one she had used to descend, but the rope was no longer there.

"Bolozi," she said in a stage whisper. She glanced over her shoulder, hoping that she wasn't revealing her location to more listeners than intended. There was no response so she had to raise her voice. "Bolozi! Where are you?"

This time she was answered by excited shouts. "I hear her! Over this way."

She readied for the fight. There was no other choice. The wall was too smooth to scale. There was nothing that she could climb upon. She was trapped.

The first of the guards gave a yell when he spotted her swathed in the light from above. He charged, but she cut him down in time to clash swords with the next guard. She kicked him backwards then impaled him when he thrust forward again. He fell against her and in the confined space almost pinned her to the wall. She flung him off just as three more men rounded the corner.

"Stay back!" she growled.

They jeered, but approached cautiously, noting the pair of bodies by her feet.

"Bolozi!" she yelled up to the trapdoor. "Revik!"

One of the guards, whose severely pointed nose resembled more hawk than human, laughed. "Looks like you're on your own. Might as well give up."

"Like hell."

They waited for her next move. She wasn't going to make it simple for them. Only beginners and idiots gave up a good defense in favor of a feeble offence. If they wanted her, they would have to come and get her. The stalemate drew on. Sweat trickled down the length of her spine, but it wasn't a sign of surrender. She still had one trick left.

"What's the matter? You're not afraid of a girl, are you?" she taunted, kissing the air for extra effect. "Come on, boys. Show me what you're made of. Or am I the only one around here with balls?"

It worked. She knew it would. Men were so lamentably predictable. The bird-man advanced only to be stopped mid-stride by the arrow that pierced his skull with a wet *thunk*. He reeled back, blindly bumping into his comrades. Sevy took the opportunity to run the remaining guards through while they were distracted. Proficiently placed stabs calmed the residual twitches then she craned her head towards the trapdoor. Bolozi's round face peered down at her.

"Where were you?" she yelled.

"Sorry," he said matter-of-factly as he threw her the rope.

Once she was back on ground level, she let loose her anger and cuffed him upside the head.

"What was that for? Daft bitch." He pushed her away.

"You were supposed to wait here."

"I heard a noise. Thought I should check it out."

"I could have been killed!"

"I said sorry."

Snarling, she grabbed him by the shirt. "Listen, you son of a—"

"Get your hands off me, you cunt!"

"What did you just call me?"

"Sevy!" Revik said, coming up from behind. "Did you get the jewels?"

She nodded curtly, about to launch into his interrogation next. Even if Bolozi was that stupid, Revik knew better than to throw a friend to the wolves like that. She got out the words "And just where the hell" before he cut her off.

"Then let's go. Now."

She complied, but not before slamming Bolozi into the wall to let him know that this conversation was far from over. She received a look of scathing disapproval from Revik, which only incensed her further. They didn't speak again until they reached home.

"Next time I do a job with you, don't bring the dead weight," she said to Revik as she banged the front door open.

"Hey," Bolozi protested, "I saved you, didn't I? You'd have been arsed if I hadn't shot that guy."

"I wouldn't have been arsed if you had stayed where you were supposed to."

"I heard a noise!"

Turlan glanced up from his chair where he had been napping. "Uh-oh! What happened?"

"Nothing." She took a seat at the table and pulled out her sword to clean the blade, a more productive use of her time than arguing with jackasses like Bolozi.

"Yeah, nothing," Bolozi said. "Just women overreacting like they always do."

She glared at him. "Say that again?"

"Never mind."

"That's what I thought."

Jarro came down the stairs. "You're back" he said, single-handedly bringing her out of her temper with his sunny smile. "How did it go?"

Sevy produced the satchel and slid it across the table to him. Revik handed over a second one, which at least accounted for his whereabouts while she was trapped in that cursed hole. Jarro opened each bag and laid out the jewelry for a quick first appraisal. *Good pieces,* Sevy thought. The stones were flawless, nicely proportioned, and had been locked in that vault long enough to have the old-fashioned look that every nouveau riche, make-believe aristocrat clambered for. Being on the cutting edge of style is all well and good, but you can't fit in with the elite unless your bootlegged baubles look old enough to be heirlooms. The only respectable money was old money. Everyone knew that. Yes, Sevy figured they would make a tidy profit. It had been a good heist regardless of Bolozi's ineptitude.

Speaking of that oaf, despite being the only one to return without a prize, Bolozi greedily surveyed the jewels, licking his lips at the sight of them. Sevy huffed as he reached forward and grabbed a diamond choker. "This one's mine!"

Revik snatched it from his grubby grip and put it back on the table. "You'll get your cut eventually."

"But I want that necklace," he whined. "Wanna give it to my girl."

Sevy laughed. "Poor girl!"

"What's that supposed to mean?"

"It means that—"

"Sevy," Revik said. "I've had enough squabbling for one night. Bolozi, we sell the jewelry, end of story."

Bolozi watched in sullen displeasure as Jarro, who Sevy noticed hadn't made a move to put Bolozi in his place, gathered up the pieces. "That ain't right. Why does he get to keep them? He didn't help."

Again, Jarro did not respond with anything more than a slight roll of his eyes. Sevy frowned. Although part of his charm was his kindness and patience, she really did wish that Jarro would take a firmer hand with the men. It would save him a lot of headaches. She watched him leave the room, taking the jewels with him to place under lock and key.

"He's the boss," Turlan said.

"Not much of a boss."

Sevy stopped polishing her sword mid-wipe. "Watch your tongue."

"Hey, just calling it like I see it. Seems to me like he don't do much. Not much at all." She held his eyes until he squirmed. "Don't get pissy with me. I'm just being honest."

She would have leapt at him, but Revik had placed an iron grip on her shoulder. "There's no debate, Bolozi. Things round here are done a certain way, and if you don't like that then you are welcome to leave."

With a sigh that told that he wasn't through complaining yet, Bolozi waddled out of the room in search of a more sympathetic audience. Only then did Revik release his hold on Sevy.

"Should've let me at him," she muttered.

"He ain't worth it," Turlan said.

"Maybe not, but it'd be a lot of fun."

They both laughed. Revik did not join in. He crossed his arms and glowered at Sevy.

"What?" she asked.

"I don't need you stirring up trouble."

"Huh? I didn't! He started it, running his mouth off about Jarro like that."

"It doesn't matter. Just ignore him."

"Ignore him? And should I also ignore the fact that he almost got me killed? I told you he shouldn't have come with us tonight."

"Gods, are you really this dense? I asked him along for a reason. You'll be leaving soon and I don't need you making things harder for me."

"Eh? You leaving, Sevy?"

"Jarro told you?" she asked, disregarding Turlan for the moment.

"He told me," Revik said, also ignoring the old man. "Just back off, understood?"

"What would you like me to do instead? Bend over?"

"Quit being so melodramatic."

"I'm serious, Revik. Oh, I know. Why don't we give him the necklace he wanted? What the hell, let's just give him everything we stole tonight."

"Would you please just shut it?"

"And why stop there? I've got some money upstairs. Should I give him that too? Think then we can all be best buddies?"

Revik's eyes sparked. He looked like he wanted to throttle her. Instead, with what was obviously a great deal of self control, he clenched his fists and stalked to the fireplace. For once, Sevy decided not to press her luck and kept her mouth closed. Revik began speaking a few minutes later, each word exuding restraint. "You and Jarro may not care what happens to the gang, or to me, but I do. And while I admit that letting Bolozi in was a mistake, the fact is that he's here now and he's not going anywhere. Not without a fight anyway."

"Exactly! So let's fight."

"Yeah, wonderful idea. Let's just alienate everyone by making them choose between their good chum, Bolozi, and a blood-thirsty monster.

Brilliant."

"What?"

"In case you've forgotten, my skin is a different color than yours."

"What's that got to do with it?"

"It has everything to do with it! You think people are going to like having a rat in charge? I need all the friends I can get. Just...never mind." He sighed, as though abruptly plagued with melancholy. "I'm done talking about this. Goodnight, Sevy."

The fire had left him, doused by grief that Sevy could not identify with. It was unlike him to appear so down trodden. Revik, her acerbic ally, always up for a game, always quick with a laugh—it surprised her to hear him speak with such sincerity. It almost made her want to apologize.

Almost, but not quite. The easier thing to do was to mock him. "I don't need you stirring up trouble. I don't need you making things harder. Boo hoo hoo."

"Sevy?" Turlan asked. "Mind telling me what's going on?"

She had forgotten Turlan was there. He was such a grizzled fixture of the house that he blended into the background as readily as a portrait hung on the wall. Many things were said and done in his presence without the intent to include him simply because it was impossible to know when he was paying attention and when he was lost to sleep or memory. Only Jarro seemed to be able to tell the difference. He was also the only one who could draw Turlan back to reality whenever he dawdled too long in a spell of time. Their relationship was sweet and poignant, although it did inspire Sevy's jealousy every now and again.

And of late, it caused resentment too. Sevy had been so excited that night Jarro first mentioned leaving Eloria. Her happiest memories were those of their travels together. The good times they had, the escapades, the heartfelt confessions shared in the wee hours of the night soon would make up each and every day. Think of the life they would have out on the open road, free of the yoke of responsibility. The kingdom would be laid at their feet.

It was frustrating that their plans had to be postponed for the sake of one person. She knew she was being a spoiled brat when she thought of Turlan as nothing more than a hindrance, but it could not be helped. He was old and infirm. He would die whether or not they stayed in the city. Why waste their lives waiting on him?

But what was the point of thinking things like this? She would never admit them to Jarro, and she would never purposely hurt Turlan's feelings. So for now, because it was what Jarro wanted, she kept up the lie. "Me and Jarro are gonna go traveling. Just for awhile. Revik's in charge while we're gone."

"That all? You two leave all the time. Why the big fuss?"

"You know how men are," she said lightly. "Anyway, we're not leaving yet. Not until next year. So don't worry about it. And don't tell anyone else, all right?"

"My lips is sealed," he said with a toothless grin before resuming his pre-bedtime snooze. His bald brown head, which reminded her of a dried out barnacle waiting for tides that would never return, sunk onto his chest. Once a globetrotting rogue, a self proclaimed conqueror of great cities and even greater women, Turlan was now slowly being consumed by Annu-nial. Were the prolonged deaths of the elderly a blessing or a curse when compared to the ways that the young were likely to die? Sevy wasn't sure.

The combination of affection and irritation that she felt towards him thoroughly confused her conscience. Rather than waste time playing philosopher, she once again opted for the easy way out. Why think on death when life had more pleasing things to offer? Seeking out some of that pleasure now, she wandered down the hall and into Jarro's study.

He was sitting at his desk, reading. Sevy flopped onto the nearest chair with a dramatic sigh.

Jarro smiled. "Something wrong?"

"Bolozi's an asshole."

"I agree."

"And Revik's being stupid."

"Is he? Hmm. That's a shame." His mouth quirked as though he were biting the inside of his cheek.

"Are you laughing at me?"

"Yes. Yes, I am." He laughed aloud in response to her pout, then got up and crossed the room, crouching so that they were eye to eye. "Sweetheart, don't worry about Bolozi."

"I can't help it. I hate him. Get rid of him."

"You know I can't do that. It's Revik's decision. I told you before that Bolozi is popular with the others."

She tossed her head. "Hah!"

"He could take a lot of men with him if he goes. Or he could turn them on Revik. Things could get rough once we leave."

"That's Revik's problem. Not ours."

"You don't really mean that, do you?"

"No. But how am I supposed to put up with that fool if I can't punch him once in awhile? And Revik...bossing me around like I'm a new recruit. It's insulting."

"Please just let it be. For me?"

She never could say no to those beautiful eyes. "Fine. But you owe me."

"That's my girl," he said, taking her hand and pulling her up. "Come on. Let's go out."

Something in his voice pushed all thoughts of Bolozi from her mind, and the smile he gave her kindled a fire beneath her sternum. Breathless, she followed him out onto the street, waiting while he wished Turlan goodnight. They passed by the Bloody Heart, which she found curious.

"We're not going in for a drink?" she asked.

"Nah."

"Then where are we going?"

"Just for a walk. Does it matter?"

"I guess not."

They strolled in amicable silence. The air was crisp. Aside from the homeless huddled in doorways and the occasional drunk lost in a spirited stupor, the streets were empty. She loved Eloria at night. It was as though the city was theirs.

Soon they reached the Gerio Bridge. Jarro tossed the toll keeper some coins and they crossed, pausing to look down into the dark water. The moonlight hid the river's filth, transforming it into something of beauty. She could almost pretend that they were standing next to a sparkling river in the Northern Jungles instead of the sickly Elor. Movement along the banks far below caught her eye. In the fragile little forms of the orphans living there, she saw herself, a lifetime ago, sloshing through the mud like a castaway from a shipwreck. How long would she have survived had it not been for the man at her side?

"Nice night," Jarro murmured.

"Mm-hmm."

"I guess we won't get many more nights like this before winter."

"Probably not."

"I want to remember Eloria like this," he said with conviction. "When we're gone, I mean. I want to remember the good things. Not the Bolozis or the Ir...the Duyans. I'll never regret my time here. Because if I had never come here, I never would have met you. Everything was worth it because of you."

Her mouth dropped then spread into a timorous smile. They watched the river a while longer before continuing on into the western quarters. Jarro led the way and every time she thought they were going to start back for home, he would take her down another street, farther and farther into the patrician neighborhoods of the city. If she didn't know him better, she'd say that he was stalling.

Eagleborn Castle still held court over this area despite being unoccupied for years. Its towers and turrets were visible above all the rooftops. Like a kindly father keeping watch over his sleeping children, the castle provided the remaining nobility protection from the masses thanks to the contingent of guards stationed there. Almost all of the workers employed by the city labored here, keeping the streets clean and lit, the hedges neatly trimmed, and the gutters free of rubbish. Fancy shops and restaurants catered to the whims of the upper class while the rest of Eloria went to bed on empty stomachs.

Sevy stopped to peer into a couple of windows, looking wistfully at the treasures sheltered behind the glass and metal. She had no need of finery, but it was still fun to imagine being the type of lady who could wear silk and satin without looking like a highly priced whore or a child playing dress-up. Jarro stood next to her, a bit closer than he normally did, which made her slightly nervous.

"That's pretty," he said. "I bet you'd look gorgeous in it." She looked at him out of the corner of her eye and he began to stammer. "I mean, you always look gor...the dress would look good. On you. Because it, you know, matches your hair. Or something. I, um, do you need anything for winter? Boots, I mean. Or a new cloak?"

"No." She wondered where this sudden interest in clothing was coming from.

"Because I'd get you some if you needed them."

"That's all right, thanks."

"I'd get you whatever you want. Or need. You know?"

"I know."

Something was wrong. He never tripped over his words like that. Once, he had been caught in bed with the wife of a jail warden and, thanks to his quick thinking, had managed to so thoroughly confuse and confound the cuckolded man that they went out for drinks together later that night. Jarro did not stutter. He did not ramble. And any other night, it would be Sevy avoiding his eyes, not the other way around. It wasn't like him at all.

She frowned. "Am I in trouble?"

"What? No. Why?"

"Because you're acting strange."

"I am? No, I'm not. I'm just, you know, thinking. Got a lot of stuff on my mind."

"All right," she said, unconvinced.

"All right."

There was a long pause. She pursed her mouth and looked down at her feet. Things were only this uncomfortable when they were fighting. Maybe she had said something wrong back at the house. Maybe he was upset with her. Or maybe he had changed his mind and didn't want her to leave Eloria with him after all.

She stopped him by putting a hand on his arm. "Jarro, you sure nothing's wrong?"

He looked down at her hand and slowly raised his eyes to meet hers. His gaze was so intense that she had to glance away.

"Everything's fine," he said finally, a strange smile on his lips.

He slipped his arm around her waist as they began walking again. At first she was startled, but then saw a pair of guards across the square from them. Jarro must have seen them too. Pretending to be a couple was their oldest trick, done to draw attention away from themselves. A guard would not be suspicious of lovers taking a late night stroll, but two people hanging around posh storefronts for no apparent reason would certainly be stopped for questioning.

Sevy sighed and leaned her head against his shoulder. It may have been an old ruse, but it was her favorite. She shut her eyes, letting him lead her away from the guards, confident that he would not let her trip. She snuggled closer, breathing him in. He smelled nice, reminiscent of a forest warmed by the summer sun. Very earthy and familiar and comforting.

Minutes drifted by before she became curious. Did they really look so out of place that they needed to be followed for so long? She glanced about the street. They were alone.

"Where'd they go?"

"Where'd who go?"

"The guards."

"The...?" he asked, brow knitting together. "Oh. Oh yeah. The guards. They, ah, just turned the corner."

His arm pulled away so quickly she might as well have been on fire. He shuffled his feet then raked a hand through his hair before looking back at her and laughing awkwardly.

"So, um, hey, have you seen this?" he said, pointing to the terrace of an upscale tavern. It was home to a large fountain. Unlike similar fountains around the city, this one was actually running. It had intricate carvings all over its base and at its center were three ornate fish spouting thin jets of water from their mouths. Sevy moved closer to get a better look.

"Do you like it?" he asked.

"Yeah, it's pretty." She trailed her hands through the streams and splashed him. "How much do you think something like this costs?"

"Don't know, but I bet I could make one like it."

"Liar."

"I'm serious! I used to build all sorts of stuff on the farm. This is just masonry work, fancied up a bit. You'll see. One day, I'll make you a fountain just like this."

"Sure, it'll go great with my mansion."

"I'll build you one of those too. Anything you want, you'll have. I promise you," he replied softly.

She saw that he was watching her with that same intense look as before. A hot blush spread up from her neck, and she cursed herself. She was behaving like such a silly child, but he was just so odd tonight. She wasn't sure what to make of it. She shifted her weight uneasily, looking back at the fountain.

"Sevy?"

"Yes?" She focused on the water, continuing to run her fingers through it despite the icy cold.

"Do you ever...I mean, sometimes do you think about...about..."

"About what?" she whispered, a great pressure suddenly building in her chest.

There was a long pause before he spoke again. "Never mind."

"What were you going to say?"

"It's nothing. Forget it."

She heard him mutter "dammit," and he wandered away from her. She stared at the water, feeling as though she had done something wrong. She was so wrapped up in uncertainty that she didn't hear him approach again, and she jumped when he brushed her hair off of her shoulder.

"Sorry!" he said. "I didn't mean to scare you."

"That's all right."

He took a deep breath, then reached out and grabbed her hands. Sevy looked at him in bewilderment. He didn't try to lead her anywhere. He just stood there, holding her hands, smiling that unknown smile.

"Your fingers are cold."

"From the water." She nodded to the fountain.

"Can't have that."

He rubbed her hands between his then raised them to his mouth and blew on them, all the while gazing into her eyes. She swallowed thickly as he lowered her hands and placed them on his chest. His fingers slid up the backs of her arms, gently tugging her towards him.

Her pulse hammered in her ears as Jarro's lips parted. He leaned his head down and continued to pull her forward. They were just inches from each other now. Her breath became ragged. The heat in her breast threatened to engulf her.

The stomping of heavy feet forced them apart. More guards. They tipped their caps as they passed by. If they only knew what they had interrupted. But then Sevy wasn't sure of that herself. Had Jarro really just tried to kiss her?

No, she was mistaken. She had to be. It couldn't be that.

They glanced at one another. He cleared his throat. A second later, he reached for her again. Sevy panicked. She pulled away before he could touch her, and became engrossed in adjusting the sleeves of her shirt. What was he trying to do? And what the hell was she doing?

Sevy, you idiot!

When she finally screwed up enough nerve to look at him, he darted his eyes away. Whatever had been happening had passed.

Say something to him, her mind screamed.

"Well, ah, I guess we should be heading back, don't you think?"

Oh, that's just fucking brilliant, Sevy.

"Yeah, you probably want to get some sleep, right? After the job and all," he said to the ground. Then he peeked up at her and gave half a smile. She smiled back, probably showing more gum than necessary.

Jarro babbled about fountains and mansions and his superior carpentry skills as they walked home. He was overly cheerful, more hyper than his usual self, but at least he was talking. Sevy was relieved that the uncomfortable tension had been broken, but couldn't help but be subdued by the sinking feeling that a very precious window of opportunity had been forever shut.

Chapter 8

Sevy spent the next afternoon training in the courtyard, hoping to burn off the nervous energy that had kept her awake all night. It didn't seem to be helping. She chalked it up to the mysterious disappearance of the practice dummy a couple of nights earlier. Fighting the air just didn't have the same effect.

She hadn't seen Jarro since the hurried and uneasy breakfast they shared that morning, and for that she was grateful. During the night, she replayed every detail of their walk almost to the point of obsession. Something was different. Something that scared her at the same time it thrilled her. But she would not allow herself to get her hopes up.

Despite persistent fantasizing, she had come to accept that he would never see her as more than a friend. That was just the way things were. Sevy didn't have much to offer when compared to the beauties Jarro had bedded in the past. She was not particularly attractive or pleasant, and he was a better man than she could ever deserve. Yet now he was acting so strangely. Almost as if he...

She beat that notion from her head. He was probably just worried about handing the reins over to Revik. That couldn't be an easy thing for him to do. Pride was such an important thing to men, she knew. Not to mention the heart sickness he had over poor old Turlan. As much as she was raring to leave, it was possible that Jarro viewed their departure with mixed emotions.

He had a life here after all. He had a home and friends. Traveling was tolerable when you knew it was temporary, but how long could she actually expect Jarro to roam the wilds with her? He liked having his own space to retreat to when he got sick of other people. He liked settling next to a cheery fire with a good book to read. Parties and adventure and exploration had their merits, but they placed second to his desire to live a simple, quiet life. He'd often talked of putting down roots somewhere and building a house to share with a wife and children.

The thought hit her suddenly—what would happen once Jarro fell in love? Over the years, Sevy had been forced to swallow the sting of jealousy whenever a new woman caught his fancy. Luckily, they never seemed to last very long. A few days, a couple of weeks at most, and then Jarro would find some reason to break things off. But eventually, especially as he grew older, he would start looking for something more enduring.

And then what would happen to her? To them? What place would she have in his life? Obviously a new bride wouldn't want Sevy hanging around, and although it killed her to think of living without him, she didn't know if her heart could bear watching him with another woman like that.

She sighed and looked at the window to Jarro's study. She could see him sitting at his desk, absorbed in a letter. If only she wasn't such a coward she'd march in there right now and tell him exactly how she felt.

But there was no way that was going to happen. What if he didn't feel the same way? What would become of their friendship? She didn't know how it could possibly survive the embarrassment. And the worst part was how nice Jarro would be about the whole thing. He'd give her the old "You're a great gal. I hope we can still be friends," speech she heard him recite to other women so many times before, and then he would never see her as anything but a pitiful, lovesick fool.

She slammed her fists into the courtyard tree, completely disgusted with herself. Why would a man like Jarro ever think of loving someone like her? Why should he? She was pathetic.

But the way he had looked at her, the things he had said—maybe there was a chance.

That was it. She had to know one way or the other, or else go completely insane. She balled her hands into fists to keep them from shaking and rushed into the house.

At the door to his study, she paused, bracing herself, and then knocked. Her heart pounded furiously as she waited for his reply.

"Come in."

"Hi, it's just me."

He didn't look up. His eyes didn't even move from the letter held before him. "Do you need something?"

"Um. No," she stumbled, completely unprepared for that reaction. "I just thought maybe you'd like to go for a drink. Or another walk?"

He didn't answer. Instead, he sighed and rested his head against his hands.

"But I, uh, I guess you're busy?"

He nodded.

"What are you up to?"

Every second that passed carved a tiny hole into her heart before he finally tore his concentration away from the letter and looked at her. His lips were pressed tightly together, his forehead was bunched up, and his eyes were brimming with utter dismay.

"What's wrong?" she asked. "Bad news?"

"You could say that." He stood up from his desk and tucked the letter into his pocket. "Listen, I have to go out for awhile."

"I'll come with you."

"No!"

The force of his reply surprised her. Jarro never raised his voice unless he was very upset.

"It's just a meeting with someone. Nothing important," he mumbled as he pushed past her.

"You sure you don't want me to come?"

"I'm sure. See you later."

She frowned, discouraged that he had left without her. So much for trying to recapture last night. So much for confessing her feelings. Sevy watched him longingly as he walked down the street, again craving the courage to run after him screaming, "Come back here, imbecile! I'm trying to tell you that I love you!"

Tonight then, she decided. She would tell him once he got back so long as her nerve didn't fail in the interim. After that, only the gods could predict what would happen, but at least she could say that she tried.

※

It was past sundown before he returned. She busied herself with a deck of cards, pretending that she had not been waiting by the window all day for him.

"Hello," she called as he came into the house. It appeared as though his mood had not improved. He was pale and held his head low. "What's wrong?"

"Nothing." He walked by without another word and went upstairs. Worried, she went after him.

"Jarro? How did the meeting go?"

"I don't feel like talking about it," he said, emphasizing his words by shutting her out of his room.

She shoved the door back open. "Too bad. What's wrong? What happened?"

"None of your business."

She folded her arms and gave him a look that made it clear she had no intention of leaving without an explanation.

He threw his jacket across the room, and then stared at the

crumpled clothing with a scowl. Sevy suddenly felt like crying. It was almost physically sickening to see him like this. Her beloved Jarro. Her sweet, sensitive farm boy. No one had the right to make him this upset, to make his beautiful face contort in this much anger and sadness and fear. She prayed for the power to make him smile again.

"Jarro, please."

"It was awful."

"How was it awful? Jarro? Talk to me!"

"It just was. I've never seen anything like that before. I didn't think it was possible. Gods, the smell! And those eyes! How does that even happen? And why now? Why me?" he asked, though it was plain he wasn't speaking to her anymore.

"But what—?"

"Sevy, enough! Gods, why can't everyone just leave me alone?"

His tone hurt her. Chastised, she turned to slink away like a whipped dog.

"Wait," he said, stopping her escape. "I'm sorry. I didn't mean to yell. It's just that I know you. I know what you'd want to do if you knew. So let me make this perfectly clear. You are not to get involved. Understand?"

She didn't answer. She was offended that he didn't trust her enough to confide in her. She glanced down at the floor and bit her lip.

"Hey, look at me." He lifted her face up gently. "I just don't want you to get hurt."

"It's that bad?"

"Yes. Not the kind of stuff I want us to get mixed up in. I turned them down. I told them to leave. Hopefully that's the last we'll hear from them. But listen, if you ever see anyone strange hanging around here, kill them. Got it? Don't hesitate. Not even for a second."

She nodded even though she really didn't understand what he meant or why he was so adamant about it. Killing random people was not something Jarro would normally condone, let alone advise.

Before she could make sense of his words, she was drawn forward into his arms. "This time next year none of this will matter. We'll be far away from here. We'll be free of all this. Just you and me, right, sweetheart?"

"Right."

"Sevy." His voice cracked with emotion. "I'm sorry I'm not a stronger man. I'm sorry that I didn't just...do what I should have done. Revik would have done it. He wouldn't have felt pity. Why do I always feel pity? Bolozi is right. They all are. I'm weak."

"Don't you dare think that. It's not even close to the truth."

He smiled. "Yeah, it is. That's just who I am. I was never meant for a life like this. I never wanted a life like this. But I'll do anything to keep you safe. You know that, right? I would give anything."

She was confused as to why he was so upset. Although she was dying to know exactly what had happened during that meeting, she decided it was best not to push him. Maybe when he was calmer, he would open up on his own. She bottled away her questions, and ran her finger down the thin white scar that lined the side of his face. "I know. You've always been my hero."

He kissed the palm of her hand before embracing her again. Her stomach danced when she felt his lips on her cheek and she almost moaned aloud as he wrapped his arms around her tighter than he ever had before. The yearning she felt for him was devastating, but she still could not get out the words she had been practicing all day. What good would tongue-tied, stilted mumblings of devotion do anyway? It wouldn't be right to force them on him when he was obviously so distraught. She had waited eight years to tell him. One more night wouldn't kill her.

He held her for a long time, almost as if he were afraid to let her go. When they finally parted, she was red with embarrassment and couldn't look him in the eyes. "I, um, you're probably tired, right? Get some rest. We can talk more tomorrow."

"All right. Goodnight, sweetheart."

Chapter 9

Later that night, her dreams were invaded with the smell of something burning. She rolled onto her back, trying to fight off the sensation that she was falling into a pit of flames. A noise from the outside world pierced her subconscious. She woke with a start, groggy and confused.

What was that?

Still bleary, Sevy looked around her room, thinking that she must have fallen back asleep because the fire scent remained. Then it came again. The sound that scored through her spine like a white-hot blade: a scream.

She leapt to her feet and burst out into the hallway. It was no dream. Another scream, louder and longer this time. Coming from Jarro's room. She raced down the hall and threw his door open, reeling back from the stench. She had found the source of the smell, but there were no flames or smoke to be seen.

"Jarro?"

No answer. She took a few steps in, letting her eyes adjust to the darkness. She made out the shape of something by his bed. It was him. He was lying half out of the bed with his face on the floor, almost as if he had been trying to get up.

"Oh gods! Jarro, are you all right?"

"What's going on?" Revik appeared in the doorway.

"Get a candle! Something's wrong with him. Jarro? Jarro! What's wrong? Wake up! Help me lift him."

Other voices. Other people coming in. The sound of candles being lit. Together, Sevy and Revik picked Jarro up and laid him on the bed. He was completely limp. They gasped at the sight of him in the candlelight—he was so pale, almost totally white. His face was shrunken in. His skin was pulled taut over his bones.

"Wake up!" She shook him. Nothing. She slapped him twice. He didn't react. She looked to Revik. "Do something! He's sick!"

Revik was gaping down at him with an expression of abject horror.

Sevy reached up and clawed at his arm. "Revik, do something! Get your herbs," she begged before turning to Jarro again. "Come on, wake up! Please. Oh gods, I don't think he's breathing. What do we do? What do we do?!"

Her scream seemed to stir Revik from his stupor. Hesitantly, he felt Jarro's throat. "No," he whispered.

"No?" Sevy demanded. "No what?"

"He...he's dead."

The word dropped onto her like a weight. "Dead?" She moved her head slowly from side to side in disbelief. "No."

"Oh my dear gods," Turlan mumbled as he came forward and put his hand on Sevy's shoulder.

"No. No, you're wrong. He's not dead. He's sick. Go boil some water. Get Revik's herbs. He's sick. He's just sick!"

No one moved. They had become as statues, staring forward with glassy eyes. Some of the women started crying. Some of the men shook their heads sadly. Sevy looked at each one of them, searching for someone who would help her.

"Why are you all just standing there? Help him! Please!" She grabbed Jarro's head with both of her hands and screamed into his face, "Wake up! Wake up!"

But she knew. She could tell by the coldness of his skin, by how limp he was in her arms. She backed away from him, putting her hand over her mouth to stop that dreaded word from springing out like a viper.

Dead.

The walls of the room were closing in on her. She couldn't get enough air. The voices around her became distorted, and she could no longer make out what anyone was saying. Someone caught her as she stumbled backwards.

"We've got to dress him. No. Wash him first. Right? That's what you do, right? And then dress him. And then, we need a...a coffin, and...and..."

She didn't know who she was telling this to. She just felt the need to do something and take control somehow. Why wasn't anyone doing anything? Why were they just looking at him, looking at her?

The sight of him made her feel faint. She had to get away. She ran out into the hall, pushing through the crowd of others who were lumped like mindless cattle around his doorway. She careened down the staircase and out into the courtyard where she promptly vomited.

When she opened her eyes she was in her own bed.

It seemed like a dream. It had to be a dream. Just a horrible, terrible nightmare. Then she remembered. In one excruciating spasm, she remembered everything. Revik had come outside. He had held her like a baby. They had cried together. He told her that it looked like the blood had been completely drained from Jarro's body, but he didn't know why. There were no marks, no evidence of a wound. Through her sobs, Sevy had told him that Jarro should be buried in Devenbourn, his home town. Ponarelle and two men had volunteered to take the body.

The body...

It was all too surreal. She couldn't believe that this was happening. This wasn't supposed to happen. But it was true. He was gone. She had seen them bring in the coffin. She had watched as they carried his body downstairs. The men toasted him and sang to him at the wake. She must have passed out. Someone must have brought her upstairs. She cursed herself. How could she have fallen asleep? How could she leave his side for an instant?

There was movement in the room and for the first time she noticed that Revik was there. He was watching her, wan face glistening with tears. They looked at each other for a long while before he spoke.

"It's time, Sevy."

She walked with him downstairs, leaning on him for support. The coffin was lying open on the table, a more grisly centerpiece than she could ever have imagined. She held her breath as she approached. Her entire body trembled. Her fingers curled around the edge of the casket, but it was awhile longer before she could force herself to look at him. When she finally did, she stared at the body before her, mystified. It was him and yet it was not. She knew every curve, every angle of his face. If she closed her eyes she could picture every detail in perfect clarity. This face was different. It was as though it wasn't Jarro lying there, just something that looked similar to him. It had the rough features, the basic likeness, but it lacked everything that made Jarro who he was.

For a second, she almost convinced herself that this wasn't him, that at any moment Jarro would come down those stairs with a big smile on his face. He'd call her sweetheart and they'd laugh about the strange thing lying there that resembled him. It was a nice little fantasy that she desperately wanted to hang onto, but knew she could not.

A droplet of water splashed against his cheek. She raised her hand to her face and was surprised to feel the tears driving down. She brushed them away and then carefully reached down to dry his cheek. The hardness that met her fingertips made her snatch her hand back in revulsion. She backed away and her breathing quickened, coming in short gasps.

"Sevy," Revik whispered, placing his hands on her shoulders.

Crossly, she shrugged him off and drew near Jarro again. She ran her fingers down his face, over his eyes, his nose, his mouth. She heard someone cry out, not realizing that the voice was her own.

"Oh no." Closing her eyes, she bent down and pressed her face against his, trying to ignore the chill. Her body wracked with sobs uncontrollably. "Please no! Please!" She kissed him over and over again, crying and calling out his name. Time slipped by. She forgot about the others in the room, blotting out everything except for him.

She felt warmth suddenly against her brow and her eyes shot open, thinking that by some miracle he was alive again. She frowned when the eyes that met hers were not deep blue, but fiery red. Revik was holding her, whispering something to her. She pushed away from him, stubbornly refusing to be comforted.

Revik tugged on her hand to guide her away from the coffin.

"Wait," she pleaded.

Sevy reached into her pocket and pulled out a worn old copper coin, smiling ruefully at the crude letter S carved onto one side. Very carefully, she placed the coin in Jarro's shirt pocket right over his heart.

One last kiss on his lips. One last look at his face. She had to rip her eyes away from him. She was vaguely aware of being ushered back upstairs. At her doorway, she resisted and continued down the hallway. In a daze, she entered his room. She crawled into his bed, whimpering when his scent drifted up off of the sheets, and clutched desperately at the pillow.

A bottle was put into her hand. She drank it down before burrowing herself deep into the bed. The pain took over then, and she cried herself to sleep.

⁂

Days passed. She didn't know how many. She stayed in his room, touching everything in it again and again.

He wore this, he used to read this book all the time, he touched this and held this and it was his and he was really here, but now he's gone.

People came and went, murmuring their sympathies, recounting stories about him, saying what a wonderful man he had been. Talk about the will of Annu-nial and how it had been his time. Sevy listened to them at first. Then she ignored them, but tolerated the visits. Finally, she threw everyone out and shrieked obscenities at anyone who dared enter.

She cried until there were no more tears, but the pain would not leave her so easily, nor did the recollection of his body lying there like a discarded husk. Every thought was consumed with that horrific sight. When she managed to sleep, she would wake up calling out his name, so she drank until she couldn't see, until she was so numb that she couldn't feel herself anymore.

A knock on the door elicited a growl from deep within her throat.

Turlan stuck his head in the room. "Sevy, honey, I brought some food."

"Go away."

She heard him shuffle towards her and place a tray of food on the bedside table. The smell of it made her stomach churn and acid came to her mouth.

"Take it away," she groaned.

"You've got to eat something," he said, sitting down next to her. He rubbed her back and pulled the pillow away from her head. "Come on, girl. Got to keep yer strength up."

"Why?"

He dipped a spoon into the bowl of soup and held it out to her. She knocked it out of his hand.

"I ain't going nowhere until you eat something."

Her shoulders shook with a sigh, and she reached down beside the bed, groping for another bottle of ale. Each one she came across was empty and she batted them aside angrily.

"You drank 'em all."

"Then go get me some more. And take that crap away, it's making me sick."

"Sevy, this ain't right. It's been two weeks. You can't keep going like this."

"Don't tell me what I can't do."

She found a bottle that still had a little liquid, and smirked in triumph. Turlan grabbed it as she raised it to her lips.

"Hey! Give that back!"

"No, it's for yer own good. You don't want to waste yer life on the bottle. It won't bring him back."

She laughed. "Oh, this is rich. A drunk trying to sober me up? That's just priceless!"

He looked slighted, but didn't back down. "You ain't getting another drop. Yer gonna eat this food, and then yer gonna get outta this bed. I know yer hurting—"

"You don't know anything."

"—but Jarro wouldn't want you to waste away like this."

"Don't you tell me what he would have wanted! Don't you even say his name!"

"Sevy—"

"Shut up! You know what he wanted? Huh? He wanted to leave! He wanted to take me and leave all of you useless bastards behind for good! And do you know why he didn't?" Turlan stared at her, speechless. Sevy felt like reaching over and shaking him, shaking that stupid expression off of his face. Instead she just laughed again. "Why, it's because of you, Turlan. That's why. He wanted to wait until you died. What do you think of that?"

Again, he just sat there like a mute and it absolutely infuriated her. "Who'd have thought that an old, drunken, washed up loser like you would live so damned long, huh? You tell me. Tell me why Jarro is gone, but you're still here. Can you tell me that? Can you explain to me why I shouldn't beat your sorry ass to a bloody pulp? Jarro is dead because of you!" she finished with a scream.

A single tear ran down his face and Sevy felt the slightest nagging of guilt, but she ignored it, preferring to focus on her anger instead.

"Funny world, isn't it? When filth like you get to bury a man like him."

Turlan opened his mouth—oh, how she wished he would protest—but then simply stood up and limped towards the door. She felt guilty again, which made her incredibly angry. Why should she feel any guilt? Every word she had spoken was the truth. Damn him for twisting everything around like that. She plucked a bottle from the floor and hurled it across the room so that it smashed onto the wall next to his head. It scared him. It made his old bones pop as he jumped, but he didn't look back. He left the room, quickly shutting the door behind him.

"Get back here and take this with you!" she yelled, flinging the tray of food onto the floor.

The door reopened. This time Revik came in. He looked at the broken glass and the spilt food, and then glared at Sevy.

"Unless you have more ale, get out."

His nostrils flared and his eyes burned. In three strides, he crossed the room and yanked her out of the bed.

"What the hell is your problem?" she cried.

"We've put up with you this long because we know you're in pain. But you've just crossed a line."

"Get off of me!"

"You had no right to talk to Turlan like that. He was only trying to help."

"Big help," she scoffed.

"You think Jarro would want you to treat Turlan like that?"

"You can leave now."

"Jarro loved that old man like a father. How dare you?"

"Go away and leave me alone."

"You selfish bitch! You aren't the only one who lost him. You aren't the only one who's hurting."

She stiffened, knowing that what he said was true. She was behaving shamefully and knew that Jarro would have been the first to call her on it, but that only served to spur her on.

"What do you know about loss?" she spat at Revik. "About pain? Stupid, self-righteous bastard! This must be quite amusing to you, huh? That someone would care so much about the life of a human."

"Are you even listening to yourself?"

"After all, what's a human life to you, hmm? We must be so insignificant to you and your kind."

"Sevy, stop."

"Hey, come to think of it. Dark elves. Tell me, what is it they like to do to humans?"

"Stop it."

"Oh yes, that's right. They like to suck out our blood. Well, isn't that interesting. And oh wait! What a coincidence. What is it you said about Jarro? That it looked like he didn't have any blood left in him?"

"That's a vicious lie and you know it. So just stop right there."

"All these years pretending to be our friend, just biding your time. So what happened, hmm? Jarro wasn't leaving fast enough so you thought you'd hurry things along? You and your kind. Vermin! Even the elves don't trust you. Guess now I know why!"

He slapped her, leaving her pride as well as her cheek stinging. His eyes were like flames and for a brief second Sevy was actually afraid. But not for long.

"You stupid bastard!" she shrieked before punching him in the chin. She swung again. This time he caught her fist and held it. She pulled free and screamed in rage, striking him over and over again. She wanted him to fight back, but he would not. He just stood there, taking each of her blows and looking down at her like he pitied her. She screamed as she hit him until she exhausted herself and fell sobbing against his chest. "You...stupid..."

He gathered her up in his arms. She tried to push away, but he refused to let go. He whispered something dark elvish into her ear and kissed her temple. Such gentle caresses even though she did not deserve them. It had always surprised her that someone so fierce could be so tender when he wanted to be. Leaning her head back to look at him, she saw her own grief mirrored in his eyes.

Revik, buy me a drink, take me dancing, sing me a song. Please. Anything to make me forget.

Before she knew what she was doing, she kissed him.

He jerked his head away. "No."

She frowned and kissed him again. Again, he pulled back.

"Please," she begged him.

This time he responded and tentatively returned her kiss. His lips were cool and soft, like a zephyr sleek with spring rain. She felt longing smolder deep within her and wanted more of it, wanted it to mask the pain. She draped her arms around his neck and pressed into him. Ah, but he was so tall and strong, and his hands were like anchors that could keep her secure against the storm of sadness that had caught her up. Revik, Revik, Revik. He was always there, wasn't he? He had always been there, waiting for her. Sevy walked backwards towards the bed, pulling him along.

He broke away. "No. This is wrong."

"I don't care."

She slid her mouth along his neck and tried to draw him onto the bed. He was still resisting, but she could feel him giving in, could feel the hardness growing against her hip. She snaked her hand down, grasping his length. He moaned and she knew she had him. They fell onto the bed together, and she cried out, thanking the gods for him, praising them for this moment where there were no memories, no regrets, no tears. Just his lips on her lips, his skin on her skin, his being siphoning into her, lending her his strength and his stability.

But when it was over, when the passion subsided and he lay panting on top of her, she was left lying in the wake of her own emptiness. Opening her eyes, she realized with dismay what she had done.

In his own bed. With his best friend.

Disgusted, she pushed Revik off and sat on the edge of the mattress, trying to stop the nausea that was coming on.

"I...Sevy, I..."

"Get out," she whispered, without turning to look at him. She couldn't. She was sickened with self-loathing. Revik didn't move. And now she cursed him and cursed herself, and for the first time, she thought she might even hate him. "Get out!" she repeated, this time yelling at the top of her lungs.

He dressed in haste and left. She couldn't fight the sickness anymore and threw up onto the floor.

Chapter 10

In her half sleep, Sevy heard sounds of shouting, of fighting. Was that someone screaming out her name? She didn't know if she was dreaming or not, but she couldn't force herself to get up. Eventually, the noise subsided and she fell back asleep.

It was hours later before she finally woke. Her head was pounding and her mouth tasted vile. The room stank of sweat, stale food, and vomit. Sevy stumbled over to the window and pulled the curtains back. The sunlight, though fading, nearly blinded her. She pushed the pane of glass open and stuck her face outside, breathing in the frosty air. It cleared her head enough so that she could function without passing out again.

She left Jarro's room and went to her own where she washed up and changed into clean clothes before heading downstairs. She wanted to apologize to Turlan. She wanted to make things right with him again. As for Revik, she didn't know what to say to him. She had used him horribly.

"Where's Turlan?" she asked one of the men, Graka, who passed her on the staircase. He didn't answer so she continued into the common room.

To her surprise, the room was in complete chaos. The furniture was overturned and broken. There were pools of clotted blood on the floor. She almost tripped on someone who was lying at the foot of the stairs. She didn't need to feel for a pulse to know what was wrong with him.

"What the hell is going on?" she cried.

"Sevy! You're back from the dead, eh?"

She scowled. "Bolozi. What happened? Were we raided?"

Bolozi sat by the fireplace with a gory sword resting on his lap. There was an ugly, purple welt sealing his eye shut and his right arm was wrapped with a blood-spotted bandage. Despite his injuries, he seemed content and relaxed. He even smiled at her. "So to speak. I heard what you said to Revik last night."

"You were listening?" she said, her anger springing to life.

"Well, yeah. It was wrong, I know. But it got me to thinking. Jarro's death was downright odd, don't you think? Not a drop of blood left and a dark elf in the house. Makes a soul wonder, don't it?"

"I didn't mean any of that! And you had no right to—"

He raised his hand to silence her. "You don't need to defend him. The boys and I had a chat about it, and well, we all agreed that it seemed fishy."

Panic flooded through Sevy as her eyes were drawn down to the bloodied floor again. "You didn't. Tell me you didn't!"

"Couldn't let ol' Jarro go unavenged, now could we?"

"You hated Jarro."

He laughed as he stood up. He swung his sword about casually before resting it on his shoulder. "Yeah. Yeah, I sure did. But now I got a lot to thank him for. And you too."

"What did you do with Revik, you bastard?"

"Not as much as I'd hoped. Ratty had a few more supporters than I thought, but I got him pretty good."

He gestured to the floor. Sevy gagged. The ragged remains of a blue-skinned arm still sleeved in blood drenched linen were draped across the doorway.

"Oh my gods!"

"Now you got a choice, Sevy," he said with such sadistic delight that it ripped her interest away from the arm. "You can stay on here so long as you can follow orders."

"I'd rather die."

"Like I said, your choice. I guess I can tell the boys that you were in on it with the rat. They'll buy it considering half the house heard you two go at it."

"You sick son of a bitch!"

She was unarmed and hung over. She could probably fight him and win, but then she'd still have to deal with his 'boys'. She could have laughed. Jarro had been right. Wasn't he always? Bolozi did have more friends than she would have guessed.

It would mean her death if she stayed here. The thought was appealing, but she couldn't give into it just yet. She darted outside. Bolozi's laughter chased her as she escaped down the street.

Where would Revik have gone? She had to find him. It was easy enough at first; there was quite a blood trail. She found a large splatter where he must have rested, but after that the droplets became less frequent. She had to backtrack often, hunting for the next bit of blood that would tell her she was headed in the right direction.

Where was he going? Where could he go? The guards wouldn't care about a dark elf, not many people would, but he must have had help to make it this far. The trail led her to the eastern gate. Tingarny. Of course. It made sense that Revik would come here. Lots of dark elves lived in Tingarny. Unable to find work within the city, the rickety, temporary hovels of the shanty town were all they could afford. Maybe Revik knew someone here, one of his own kind.

She lost the trail suddenly, and no matter how hard she searched she couldn't find it again. She kicked at the ground in frustration. She couldn't give up. She wouldn't. It was her fault. If only she hadn't said those terrible things to him.

She wandered around the dirt paths, peeking into doorways and windows as discreetly as she could. Revik wasn't stupid. He would be hiding. And in the meantime he could be bleeding to death, if he hadn't died already. She was running out of time and options.

It was not the occasion for prudence. She screamed out his name, was answered by angry yells in various languages, and had to duck the barrage of garbage that was thrown at her. In Eloria proper, Sevy had evolved into someone who inspired fear and deference from those she passed. But in Tingarny, she was nothing more than a weaponless human woman. Surrounded by the pariah race of Axlun, she was the perfect outlet for pent-up aggression. She wasn't dense enough to overlook this fact. She just didn't care.

"Revik! Where are you, Revik?"

"Girl, quit that," a familiar voice croaked.

"Turlan," she cried, spinning around to face him.

He was hunched in the entrance of a shed made of rusted iron sheets. "Get in here."

"Where's Revik? Is he all right?"

"He'll live."

Sevy followed Turlan inside. The shed was lit by a single lantern sitting atop an overturned crate; the metal walls seemed to absorb the light rather than reflect it. It was mostly empty aside from a few wooden boxes, but the shed also had a small cot set up in one corner. Revik was lying in it. What was left of his arm had been carefully wrapped. Sevy could smell burnt flesh and realized that the remains of his arm must have cauterized. She winced, suddenly reminded of the odd smell the night Jarro had died.

She knelt at his side. "I'm so sorry. I didn't want any of this to happen. Please believe me! I didn't mean what I said. I wasn't thinking. I didn't mean it, Revik!"

"I know." He sounded so small.

"What do you need? I'll get whatever you want."

"He'll be all right," Turlan said. "Thanks to his friends here."

"Friends?"

Turning, Sevy saw a line of dark elves, about ten of them, standing in the doorway. She bowed her head to them, but they didn't greet her in any way other than to sigh or roll their eyes. It was clear that they weren't happy about her presence here.

"They're gonna take him home soon as he's well enough to travel. I'm gonna go with him," Turlan said.

"But Eloria is his home."

She heard the dark elves behind her scoff. Turlan glanced at them before looking back at Sevy. "His real home. The mountains in the south where his family lives."

"They can heal him there?"

He shrugged. Sevy looked back down at Revik and a sob caught in her throat. She reached out to comfort him, but stopped herself, too ashamed to do anything other than stare at the bandaged stump.

"Come with us," Revik said, barely a whisper. His body trembled, threatening collapse, as he held out his remaining hand.

She took it and rubbed it tenderly as she considered the offer. Go with Revik and Turlan to the south. Finally escape Eloria like Jarro had always wanted. Run away with them the way she should have been able to run away with him. It wasn't right. None of this was right.

Everything she loved had been taken from her. Again. And the only people left who actually cared for her had almost been killed because of her stupidity. She felt anger replacing her sadness. That was preferable. It was easier to hate than it was to grieve.

She didn't know where she would go or what she would do, but she couldn't stay with them. She didn't deserve to. The darkness within her, the rage she had tried to keep suppressed would go unchecked now. She was tired of fighting it. And she was frightened to think of what more would happen to Revik and Turlan if she remained with them. They were safer without her. They were with people who would care for them. That would have to be enough.

She inhaled slowly, forcing back the tears so that her voice would remain clear and even when she said, "I can't. I'm sorry, but I just can't. Please understand."

"Idiot," Revik sighed, the only protest he could offer with what strength he had left. He let go of her hand after giving it a gentle squeeze.

"Goodbye."

"Goodbye? You're leaving us?" Turlan asked. "You won't even stay until he's better?"

"No. I'm sorry."

"Bloody bullshit."

"Turlan," Revik whispered, "don't."

"The hell I won't. Girl's being a soft-brained brat, and she ought to get put straight. So listen here, Sevy. I know what it's like to lose a love. How do you think I ended up being the 'old drunken washed up loser' that I am? But don't do this. This is just stupid."

Sevy grabbed Turlan's face between her hands. His eyes went wide; the milky one fluttered beyond his control. The fear poured out of him, and all she could do was laugh at it. She kissed him roughly, once on each of his cheeks, and then pushed him aside so she could stare at Revik. He tried to smile. She knew that he wouldn't hate her for her decision even if he didn't agree with it. Gods, why wouldn't he just hate her? She bent down and kissed him, pressing her mouth against his until they were breathing the same air, hoping to give back some of the strength her previous reckless kisses had stolen from him.

She did not stop for one final look at Eloria as she moved farther and farther away from the city walls, driven on by the bitter wind that lashed at her back. She wrapped her arms around herself, certain that no matter what happened, she would never be able to feel warmth again.

PART 3
SAVAGE

Chapter 1

The ground rose and fell in undulating waves of green that formed a convincing impression of a seascape. The clusters of white flowers that capped the crest of each hill and the rippling of the wind through dew glazed grass only heightened the effect. To the south, a forest of evergreens and birches stood proud, and to the north, Mount Lirra was painted against the sky, flanked by her sisters, Onsha and Dha Natsul. Far away, a storm waged a war of purple lightning with a rock face. For all its fury, the storm was impotent against the daughters of Ullydran who endured in might and majesty as they had for time immemorial.

Revik basked in the clover-scented air while the bleats of the flock bestowed the gentlest of lullabies upon him. It was a night for dreaming. Even those grounded in prose would find their thoughts borne away on wings of whimsy, and Revik, always the fanciful fellow, was lost amongst the clouds.

In all of five minutes, he had tamed the Beast of Kedinshir, vanquished the armies of not one but two evil empires, and rescued a beautiful maiden from certain death. She swore her undying love and whispered innuendo-sodden promises of his reward. Revik would be sure to claim that in due time, but right now the royals were going to honor him by naming him Hero of the Realm. Oh what the hell, by naming him King of the Realm.

He was just about to kneel to accept his crown when a small hand clasped his. Opening his eyes, he smiled at the child who stood gazing up at him.

"Hello, Yy'vran. Shouldn't you be in bed?"

"Mama wants you to come inside. She said it's too cold out for you."

"Tell your mother I'm fine. The flock needs tending."

"But Mama said you have to go in now."

"I don't care what she said!" Revik's rising irritation was immediately censured by the boy's trembling lower lip. He squeezed Yy'vran's hand and softened his tone. "Tell her not to worry. I'm fine."

"Come now," a husky voice boomed. Revik turned to face the source—a mustached, beefy man nearly four hundred years his senior. "You'd better go in before she gets upset. She sent me to take over your watch."

"Krelaan, I'm perfectly capable of—"

"I know, I know! You're a big boy. You can wipe your own arse and everything. But you know women and you know Yy'voury. I'd do what she says if I were you."

Revik felt his left hand constrict into a fist, felt his skin pulling tight over his knuckles. It was peculiar how the mind could fool itself so thoroughly. If he suddenly were to go blind, it would be an easy thing to believe that his arm was still there. He was almost more aware of it now than before its unexpected removal two years ago.

"Fine," he said, relenting, releasing the tension in both his real and imagined hands. "See you later. Come on, squirt. Let's go."

Revik bent down, allowing Yy'vran to scamper onto his back, and headed towards home. Though it was dark, he didn't need a torch to find his footing. There was no fear of falling off the bluffs to the west. He could find his way in his sleep. Leave the pasture, turn left at the crossroad, up the winding pebble-strewn laneway, and then directly up the hill. And just in case you were a complete oaf, there were signs posted every hundred paces. You couldn't get lost around here even if you tried.

And Revik had tried.

In the distance, a coyote called out and was answered by the yipping of its mate on the other side of the valley. "Did you hear that, Yy'vran? What was that?"

"Doggies."

"Are you sure?" Revik asked, making his voice high and squeaky. "I don't know. That sounded like a monster to me."

Yy'vran squealed and wrapped sticky little fingers around Revik's neck. "No. No monsters, Daddy."

"Oh no, it is a monster! Watch out, it's after us!"

He sprinted, bounced Yy'vran up and down, and then spun around in circles until the child exploded into giggles. Revik laughed with him and was able to prolong their return home by a good twenty minutes with his antics. But all too soon, the stone manor sprawled out before them, overwhelming the entire hillside with its sheer enormity. Revik was instantly subdued by the silhouette framed in the front door, that of a petite woman tapping her foot.

The scolding began before they were close enough to see the details of her face. "Yy'vran, get down this minute! You know better than that."

"Relax," Revik said. "Everything's fine."

Yy'voury scooped Yy'vran from Revik's back and nudged him into the house, stopping him long enough to place a peck atop his head. "Off to bed. Quickly now. It's long past your bedtime. And for the ancestors' sake, wash up! Don't think I didn't notice those jam hands, young man. And just where do you think you're going?" she said to Revik as he tried to sneak past her.

"To my room. Apparently I'm a child as well, seeing as I have a curfew."

She dismissed his sarcasm with a laugh and slung a handful of white braids and caramel-colored scarves over her shoulder. "Temper, temper. You know the night air is too cold for you at this time of year. You could catch a chill."

He didn't answer. If he could have rolled his eyes without her seeing, he would have.

"Besides, why spend the night outside when you can spend it with me?" she asked, standing on tiptoe to kiss him. She took his arm and turned to lead him up to her room.

Revik rooted himself to the spot. "I'm afraid I won't be much company tonight. You might as well go to one of the others."

"What's wrong? Don't you feel well? I knew you shouldn't have been out so late."

She put her hand against his forehead and searched his face for signs of illness. This time, he didn't care if she saw the whites of his eyes. "I'm fine." He pushed past her to move into the parlor. He wove round the furnishings and went directly to the hearth, distancing himself from her as much as the room would allow. "Go and get Trel. I'm sure you'll find him more accommodating."

He threw himself into a chair and stared at the flames, hoping that she would take the hint and leave him be. Instead, he heard her footsteps pad towards him. He groaned as she rubbed his neck, though not in pleasure.

"You're upset with me."

"No."

"Yes, you are," she said, chuckling.

He leaned his head back against an overstuffed cushion, scrunched up his shoulders, and kept his eyes focused on the fire. "No, I'm not."

"Don't you think I can tell? You read like a book, little husband. You're upset that I worry so much about you. Well, I'm sorry, but I can't help it. I love you. In spite of your obstinance."

"I am not obstinate and I am not a child. Stop treating me like one."

Go away, go away, just go away. The words became a mantra in his mind.

"Revik, how many times must we have this same argument?"

"Until you...never mind."

"I know you are proud, but sooner or later you must accept the fact that you are not as you once were. The loss of your arm weakened you consid—"

Enough was enough. "I am not weak!"

Since he had been compelled to return to his home in the Ullydran Mountains two years ago, forever disfigured by the blade of bigotry, Revik had been subjected to a harrowing brand of torture. The torture of being coddled and fussed over, unwittingly inflicted on him by the most insidious of adversaries—his loving family. Yy'voury, his wife of just shy of a century, was the worst offender.

Chief Mediator of the Ped-a-nor district, matriarch of the Sajene family, and the most affluent and prestigious dark elf this side of the Melacian Sea, Yy'voury was prized for her integrity and for her ability to remain impartial, no matter what the circumstances. Except, of course, when it came to the people she loved. In her presence, they dubbed her over-protective. Outside of earshot however, euphemisms were not employed. She was domineering, hypercritical, and neurotic. In short, she was a nag. And it was this type of behavior that had been a large part of the reason Revik escaped to Eloria in the first place. Well, that wasn't an entirely fair thing to say, but at the moment Revik couldn't care less about what was fair.

If there was one thing he could not endure, it was the feeling of entrapment. Revik moved through life taking his cues from the wind. At times calm, now and then tempestuous, perpetually in motion. He valued freedom beyond all else. And hysterical henpecking, as well intentioned as it may be, had proven more traumatic than the severing of his arm. The others were smart enough to sense this and didn't crowd him, but contrary to the notion that wisdom went hand in hand with age, Yy'voury could not, or would not, empathize with his suffering.

"Let me rephrase that, my darling," she cooed. "You cannot expect to do all the things that you did before. It's just not possible. You will only end up hurting yourself. Is that what you want? Do you really want to hurt yourself even more than you already are?"

He literally had to bite his tongue to keep from snapping back, "Of course I do! I enjoy that sort of thing. Pain is my favorite aphrodisiac." Luckily, before he could be nettled into saying something he'd regret, three of the children entered the room in a tizzy of youthful exuberance. Yy'voury gave Revik's shoulder a final squeeze before turning to them, apparently convinced that she had won that debate.

"Hello, my pets," she said happily.

Revik continued to stare at the fire, watching the curls of smoke that wafted up into the flue, but kept an ear open to the conversation. Yy'vinnen, a son not much younger than Revik, was protesting quietly as two of his sisters teased him about his latest girlfriend.

Yy'voury clucked her tongue. "And just who is this girl? What does her mother do?"

"It's Tehnishla, Mama. You know, her mother runs the trading post at the foot of the mountain," Yy'voura said.

"She's set to marry some boy from the lowlands," Yy'vry added.

"No son of mine will become the second husband of a trader! Yy'vinnen, what are you thinking?!"

Poor Yy'vinnen, Revik sighed to himself, although he was grateful that Yy'voury was picking on somebody else for the time being.

"Who says he's going to marry her? Maybe they just want some fun."

"Sylem," Yy'voury said, scolding the newest arrival to the parlor, "don't talk like that in front of the children. And Yy'vinnen, no decent family will ever consider you for their daughter if you start fraternizing with traders."

"Fraternizing. Is that what you call it?" The children's laughter drowned out Yy'voury's objections as well as her flustered shriek when Sylem goosed her before coming to sit in the chair next to Revik. "I thought you were out with the sheep tonight."

"I was," Revik said, cracking a smile for the first time since returning to the house. "Until..."

Sylem nodded knowingly. "Let me guess, it's too damp out?"

"Too cold. I could catch my death, don't you know."

"Oh, of course. I hear most deaths due to exposure happen in the summer."

"I can hear you, you know," Yy'voury said. "Imagine, being mocked in my own home. I've half a mind to send for Krelaan to come back in and beat some respect into the whole lot of you!"

"He might overexert himself doing that. Beating people is quite taxing to one's system," Sylem quipped, causing all to laugh once more. He didn't stop there. Once he had an audience, he would not let it go. "Ancestors above! I'm feeling the vapors just thinking about it. Yy'vry, be a dear and fetch Papa his smelling salts, won't you?"

Revik's foul mood dissipated like the musty air of an attic when opened up to a spring breeze. Good old Sylem. He was the only accomplice Revik had amongst the family of strait-laced co-husbands, submissive sons, and daughters who took too much after their mother. His teasing was always a welcomed respite.

Sylem continued his performance, which sent the two girls into a gale of giggles. For all her disapproving glares and head tosses, Yy'voury was powerless against Sylem's shield of wit. Yy'vinnen, now free of the maternal magnifying glass, took the opportunity to sneak out the front door, most likely on his way to visit the trader's daughter or some other equally scandalous tryst of which his mother would not approve.

Revik wanted to follow suit, but the mask of indignation on Yy'voury's face told him that he had a better chance escaping from a den of lions. The weight of that knowledge settled onto his heart. For no amount of fantasizing about heroic battles or daredevil exploits would be able to erase the awful truth that his wife, the woman he was supposed to love above all others, had become his jailor.

⁓⁓

Yy'voury sat at the head of the table with her head bowed as she listened to Yy'vry give the dinner blessing. The servants tiptoed around the room, looking terror stricken if they chanced to clink the cutlery, or bump against the door on their way back to the kitchen. It was no simple task to wait upon Yy'voury's table and Revik certainly didn't envy them. He sat beside Sylem, across from Yy'vran, and tried not to laugh as Yy'vran snuck a corner of bread into his mouth.

"And let us thank the ancestors for this bountiful meal. And let us thank Mama and our fathers for taking such good care of us," Yy'vry finished, after roughly ten minutes of 'and let us thank.'

"Nicely done, Yy'vry. And Yy'vran, if I ever see you eating during prayer again, you'll regret it," Yy'voury said with a pointed look.

Yy'vran shrank in his chair. Yy'voury had an uncanny ability of knowing when the children were up to something, even with her eyes closed. Five hundred years of motherhood and eleven children probably explained it. Revik chuckled and gave Yy'vran a kick under the table, both to tease and to bolster the boy. Then Yy'voury began to eat, a signal that the rest of the family could start as well.

"Looks delicious as usual," Krelaan said.

"Why, thank you, dear. The cooks really outdid themselves this time, don't you think? Although I will have to speak to them about these carrots! If I've told them once, I've told them a hundred times not to chop them so finely."

Revik ignored the family as they discussed the events of the day, or rather, while Yy'voury discussed the events of the day and everyone else ate in silence except for the occasional comment. He stared at his plate for a few seconds, then picked up his fork and stabbed at the food. As usual and despite his many objections, Yy'voury had insisted that the servants pre-cut every last piece of food into tiny bits. A suitable size for infants perhaps, but not for a grown man. He knew she was just trying to be helpful. It was difficult to cut food with one hand. But it was not impossible and this was just another irksome example of her babying.

"What's the matter? Need help with that?" Sylem asked, grinning from ear to ear.

Revik nudged the plate towards him. "Yes, please. I think I've forgotten how to chew."

The joke was cut short when it caught Yy'voury's attention. In their household, nothing drew suspicion like laughter. "What's that, dears?"

"I was just wondering how mediation went today," Sylem said innocently.

"Oh. Well, I had my hands full, let me tell you. Rikla and Odwimila were at each other's throats. It was a disaster. Rikla owns the flour mill, and apparently...Yy'vran, eat your vegetables...and apparently Odwimila is claiming ownership of poor dear Kirry's grain fields."

"Kirry was the one who died last autumn?" Trel, sitting between Krelaan and Sylem, asked.

"Yes, and with no daughters to leave the land to. Well, Odwimila feels she should have the land since her third husband is Kirry's first son. Yy'vran, don't slouch. This wouldn't be a much of a problem except that she wants to sell the grain for double what Kirry had been charging. Rikla decided to track down Kirry's sister, Kiranika. You know her, Sylem. She lives in the same village as your mother. So now this sister and Rikla have teamed up together against Odwimila, and it's causing quite a stir."

"What did you decide?" asked Trel.

"Considering that Kirry's land wasn't ancestral, Kiranika really has no claim to it. I decided in favor of Odwimila."

Krelaan raised his glass up. "A wise choice. Such a clever wife we have, eh boys?"

"Toady," Sylem whispered into his napkin, which made Revik choke on his wine.

"Oh dear, Revik! Are you all right?"

"I'm fine," he sputtered, wiping his mouth.

Yy'voury watched him for awhile longer before apparently deciding that he was telling the truth. Then she smiled and said, "Enough talk of business. We must be boring the young ones. Yy'voura, you mentioned that you had an announcement to make."

"Yes, Mama." Yy'voura, the only child that Revik could be sure came from his blood line, was his spitting image not only in looks, but in character as well. She was the rebel, the thrill seeker, the one who continuously ferreted out what little excitement the Ullydrans had to offer. Of course, being female she was granted more freedoms than he would ever be allowed to enjoy, so it was difficult to cheer her on without feeling a dash of resentment, as horrible as it was that he should begrudge his own daughter. She cleared her voice before continuing, "I've decided that I want to go on my first wander."

"That's great!" Revik exclaimed. "Good for you. Where were you thinking of going?"

"I'm not sure yet. Maybe east, to the coast. I'd like to see the ocean."

"That sounds wonderful! There is this amazing town by the Gulf of Hershal. They give tours of the harbor in these boats with glass bottoms. You really—"

"Revik!" Yy'voury said, interrupting. "Don't encourage her. Yy'voura, I don't think now is a good time for you to wander. Not at this stage of your life."

"Mama, Yy'vea was twenty years younger than I am now when she first left."

"Exactly. You should be thinking about marriage, not traipsing around like a vagabond."

"Your mother's right," Krelaan said. "You're nearly a century now. Don't want to wait too long to choose your first husband."

"But I want to see the world before I settle down."

"You should go, Yy'voura. You'll have a grand time," Revik insisted.

"They say the coast isn't safe. I've heard talk of pirate raids. The King has doubled his fleet to counter them," Trel said.

Revik laughed. "Pirates! The coast is as safe now as it's ever been. You can't live your life in fear. I knew a girl once who went up against pirates. She was only a child and she got away from them fine. I wouldn't worry about them. If you want to see the ocean, then you go and see it."

Yy'voura smiled gratefully at him before turning to gauge her mother's reaction.

Yy'voury did not look impressed, but Revik couldn't tell if it was from Yy'voura's request or from his insubordination. "Don't you listen to him. The way he talks, he'd have you become a pirate yourself! Oh, don't act so innocent," she said as Revik was about to object. "We've all heard more than enough about your dalliances with the criminal element. You fill the children's heads with dangerous ideas."

"I'm not recommending that she hop aboard the first three mast ship she comes across. I'm simply saying that she should be able to explore. There is more to the world than these mountains."

"And besides," Sylem added, coming to their defense, "Trel just got back from a wander and he didn't run into any trouble. Isn't that right, Trel?"

Trel looked petrified and promptly shoved a forkful of green beans into his mouth.

"Yes," Yy'voury answered for him, "but he was visiting family in the Northern Jungles, among our own kind. Not socializing with humans like Revik enjoys so much."

"There is nothing wrong with humans." Revik should have known the conversation would take this turn.

"Nothing? They are savages. Ignorant, violent, little savages. They'll run you out of their towns, Yy'voura. Is that what you want?"

"Not all of them are like that," Revik said.

"Oh really? Hacking off one's arm is a show of affection then?"

Everyone turned to Revik. He knew they were waiting for him to blow up, but instead, he calmly continued eating his dinner. He didn't look at any of them, not at the children, the other husbands, and especially not at Yy'voury.

After a few uncomfortable minutes, Trel began talking about the sheep and how he'd like the Barren Mage to come and bless them. Sylem and Krelaan started into an argument on the effectiveness of the Mage's protective spells. Sylem thought they were a waste as no less than three lambs and two ewes had been killed by predators in the last fortnight. Krelaan blamed the loss on Sylem, for not having enough faith in the ancestors. Trel tried to change the subject once again, but was shouted down. Finally, Yy'voury silenced them all by threatening to make them leave the table if their foolishness continued. This was a family dinner, not a free for all, and she would not tolerate her husbands setting such a poor example for the children present.

Revik ate his meal as a stoic, ignoring the lot of them. He was used to the squabbling. In a family of their size it was inevitable. But he was offended by Yy'voury's snide remarks. He knew she had never approved of his life in Eloria, a life which he hadn't bothered to keep secret from her. He wished more than ever that he was still there. It had been such an exciting time, full of fun and adventure. He loved Yy'voury and his family as it was his duty to love them, but he was forced to admit that he didn't really like any of them.

As the servants cleaned up after dinner, Revik didn't join the family by the fire. He had no interest in reading tales from the ancestors' chronicles, or gossiping about people from the village. He certainly had no desire to hear Yy'voury compare the humans he had come to think so highly of as little more than swine. Instead, he strolled around the veranda and listened to the wind coming up from the valley. How he envied the wind. It sang to him of far off places that he wished he could travel to; to be carried on its back to anywhere but here.

Yy'voury startled him by suddenly asking, "Did you come out here to sulk?"

"That depends. Did you come out here to pick another fight?"

"Why do you defend those humans? After everything they did to you."

"Only one did this to me. Why should I blame the rest?" He leaned against the railing and stared at the clouds of opal and amethyst that crowned the mountain range. "How many times do I have to explain this to you?"

"Well, I'm sorry! But how do you expect me to react to the monsters who tried to butcher my husband? A husband who would rather live amongst thieves and murderers than with his own family."

There was a quiver in her voice, one that he could tell she was trying to hide from him. He glanced at her in shock. Could it be that beneath her harsh exterior dwelt a spirit as broken as his? She moved to rush back inside the house. He caught hold of her arm.

"Yy'voury..."

"Don't try to deny it. I know you're not happy here. I know that you want to leave me again. I've known for months."

"No, that's not true." The words were unconvincing even to him.

"Yes, it is! As soon as you healed, I knew it was only a matter of time before you left again. The Barren Mage warned me about you. She said you had the wander lust in you, that you'd never be content to stay in one place, that you'd grow to resent me if I married you. And she was right. You hate it here. You hate me!"

"I...I..." he stuttered, not knowing how to respond to her sudden outpouring of emotion. She rarely let her true feelings be known. For a woman of her standing, it just wasn't done. "Please don't think that. It's just that I want things to be how they were before."

"You were never here before," she said, taking out a handkerchief to blow her nose. "And you only came back because you had to. I feel like I hardly know you. Am I so awful that you can't stand to be near me? Do you hate me that much?"

"I don't hate you. I get frustrated. I don't want to be treated like an invalid for the rest of my life. Can't you understand?" He brushed his hand against her cheek and wiped it dry.

"I know! And I'm sorry, honestly I am. I don't mean to annoy you so, but I worry. That I'll lose you. Now that you don't need me anymore."

"I'll always need you," he said, surprising himself that he actually meant it. He smiled and inclined his head to kiss her. "Just treat me like you treat the others, all right?"

"I'll try."

"And let Yy'voura go. Don't punish her because of me."

She frowned. "Well, I suppose. But honestly, I just do not understand the attraction of gallivanting all over the world like that."

"Maybe someday we'll go on a wander together. Who knows, you might learn to like it."

"Doubtful," she said, with a slight roll of her eyes.

He kissed her again, allowing the taste of her lips and the silk of her skin to distract him from the cyclone of bitterness that still twisted within his soul.

Chapter 2

The air misted against Revik's face as he strolled beside the flock. He lightly tapped wayward sheep with his staff, urging them along. Yy'voury had kept her promise and stopped objecting to his night watches. She hadn't been pestering him as much lately, although at times her body trembled as she battled against her nit-picking nature.

Across the meadow, Sylem's warbling voice could be heard. He was in the middle of a boisterous drinking song, one that Revik had taught him, and it made Revik smile. Yy'voury disapproved of such songs, but herding sheep was men's work. She was back at the house and would never know how all of the husbands, even the mousey Trel, reveled in the job away from her scolding.

Of course, Revik enjoyed it more than the others. He had more reason. He pictured Yy'voury as a clucking hen, forever pecking and scratching until there was nothing left of the man he had been. It wasn't a comparison he would likely reveal to anyone. Thoughts like that weren't productive or at all charitable, especially in light of her recent attempts to control herself. And besides that, she was a good wife. Revik had been lucky that his mother had consented to the match, considering that he had originally been intended for another woman. There had been a time, in the early years of their marriage, that Revik loved Yy'voury more than he ever thought possible. He loved her still, but he couldn't help wondering what life could have been like if they had never met.

His mind drifted to all the nights spent singing, laughing, and carrying on in taverns across the land. Yy'voury would have died of embarrassment if she knew some of the things he'd done. She would never understand the appeal of cheap ale or of sleeping under a blanket of stars, just like he would never understand her desire to remain shackled to one place. She had spent all of her long life on these mountains and seemed content to remain here until she died. Revik found that bewildering.

Wanders, as they were called by his people, were commonplace, especially among the younger generations. Most dark elves would go on a least a dozen or so during their lifetime. Yy'voury had never gone wandering. Not even once. That was unusual, just as the duration and frequency of Revik's wanders was unusual.

Revik had always been the adventurous one in his family and had left home shortly after his fortieth birthday, an age still considered part of childhood. For the next two centuries, Revik trekked the world over, returning only for the briefest of visits to rest and restock. At length, sick of the scandal his behavior caused, his mother insisted that he marry. She thought it would force him to mature and to gain some perspective, and for a time it had worked. Yy'voury was a beautiful woman after all, and with three other husbands, she certainly knew her way around a man. But less than a decade passed before the old longing returned and he struck out on his own once again. A reluctant Yy'voury let him go on the condition that for every year he spent away he must spend two at home. As far as he was concerned, it was an arrangement that had worked beautifully for most of their marriage.

Eloria changed everything. Originally, he had gone there to visit his cousin, who at the time was living in Tingarny. Revik hadn't meant to stay as long as he had, but the city was wild, just like him, and he found that intriguing. Because the population was predominantly human, he was liberated from the yoke of feminine authority. He didn't have to justify his presence, nor produce the letter that explained that he did in fact have his wife's permission to be there to any woman who assumed it was her business. When he introduced himself, it was as just plain Revik, not Sajene Yy'voury's forth husband, Revik, seventh son of Hamaris Revilawra. He was his own person.

Of course, he may no longer have been inferior in regards to women, but he was still considered far from equal. No one cared so much as to what was between his legs as they did the color of his skin. He was a dark elf and that was not something he could run from.

A month after arriving in Eloria, he was attacked at the Bloody Heart by a pack of humans who didn't appreciate his company. What hurt worse than the beating he received were the indifferent stares from the other people present. They continued to drink and to talk as though he didn't even exist. No one answered his pleas for help. Some even found it a source of hilarity. Except for one man.

It was a lucky thing Jarro had gone to the Heart that night or Revik may well have been killed. He broke up the fight and then nursed Revik back to health. To show such mercy and compassion to a stranger was unheard of, especially when that stranger was just a "rat." But that's just how Jarro was. When he looked at you, he didn't see your color. He didn't care what label society had pegged you with or what you were thought to be worth. He just wanted to help. That night, Revik made the best friend he had ever known.

And through Jarro, a new world of excitement opened up to Revik. Jarro had been making a living as a mercenary of sorts. He was an up and comer in the protection racket, and with Revik's help, managed to expand his business and increase profits. Revik hadn't meant to get involved, but it was just so much fun. The thrill of the fights, the adrenaline rush of sneaking past guards or breaking into a bank—he became intoxicated, not only from the ample supply of liquor, but from the whole lifestyle. He was ashamed to admit that if he hadn't lost his arm, he would have remained in Eloria for many years to come before even considering returning to his wife.

As it was, he stayed in the city for eleven years; time that had simply flown by when compared to the two years that he had been back home. If he stayed true to the bargain he made with Yy'voury, this meant twenty more years stuck on the mountains. Twenty years of mind numbing routine, smelly sheep, gossipy neighbors, and family fights. He could have cried. Would his memory and his imagination be enough to sustain him for so long?

Revik turned back to his flock with a sigh. There was no point dwelling on things that could not be changed. Just then, his attention was diverted. A cloud passed across the moon and veiled the meadow in darkness. Sylem stopped singing and Revik heard him talking to the sheep, reassuring them. He did likewise.

His eyes were accustomed to gloomy nights such as this, but for some reason, Revik felt uneasy. The air seemed to hang a bit thicker, and he fancied that he could smell burning meat although no fires could be seen. The flock felt this change too. They shifted, taking a few steps back and bleating before running forward then back again. Revik had difficulty keeping them together. They kept breaking off into smaller groups and heading in different directions.

It took all of his concentration to gather the sheep into a semblance of order. He lost track of Sylem and the next time Revik looked to where he had been, he saw nothing save for the fluffy white rumps of straying sheep. Sylem was not there to stop them. Revik peered through the inky blackness and called out. There was only the faintest muffled reply. He must have moved further away than first thought. Revik started towards the sound while Sylem continued to talk.

"Can't hear you," Revik shouted. "What did you say?"

His question was answered by another voice, low and feminine, but with an extra quality that made the hairs on Revik's arm stand on end. Suddenly, the flock went berserk. Their bleats turned into ungodly shrieks as they stampeded down into the valley below. Revik fought to keep his balance as the animals barreled past him in a chaotic mass of pounding hoofs.

The noise of the panicked animals moved into the distance, leaving behind a palpable hush.

"Sylem?"

A hiss. Like a giant snake from the jungles, a long drawn out hiss slithered through the air and bit into Revik's skin. He shuddered and grabbed a dagger from his belt. Then a piercing scream cut into the night.

Revik raced forward. The scream stopped, and so did he, spinning around the darkened meadow, trying to locate where it had come from. Another cry spurred him on again.

"Sylem!"

Then Revik saw him. Sylem stood rigid, arms out on either side, fingers twitching. He remained like that, a seizuring scarecrow, for another moment before slumping to the ground, hair spilling in a pool round his head. He was not alone. A figure cloaked in smoke was bent over Sylem, whispering to him.

Revik felt the hot breath of fear press against his chest. He couldn't bring himself to draw any closer. A glittering red mist rose from Sylem. It surrounded the shadowed figure. Revik heard a sigh, almost like a moan, and watched as the figure threw its head back in seeming pleasure while the mist coated its form, the red blending into black.

Revik stared, unable to move, unable to speak. The figure turned its head and looked straight at him. It smiled, fattened leeches of lips pulling back across its face. The pallid skin crackled and split with each facial movement, revealing streaks of pulpy musculature underneath. Hair draped the head in a great dried mass, forming a hood that seemed to merge with the ragged fabric that clothed the hunched form. It reached the shriveled bones that were its fingers towards Revik and took a step forward. The reek of burnt flesh oozed from it, smothering Revik in its repugnance.

"Demon!" he managed to whisper.

The thing laughed. "It's nice to see you too, Revik." The clarity of the voice surprised him, not matching the hag-like appearance. "What's wrong? Don't you recognize me?"

It laughed again then waved its hands in front of its face, murmuring in an unknown language. Instantly, the desiccated hair started to change. Vibrant red shot through it, coating the strands with rich color. It sprung to life, forming soft waves that fell smoothly down the creature's back. Ashen skin flaked off in large clumps like slag, revealing healthy pink flesh underneath. The blackened lips gave way to plump crimson that opened in a smile, revealing perfect white teeth. The crooked back straightened. The limbs lengthened. Only the eyes remained jet black and lifeless.

Revik blinked at the transformation. "Irea?"

"Yes, it's me." She giggled. "Granted, I've changed a bit since we last met. But then, so have you. What happened to your arm, dear Revik?"

Words were lost to him. All he could do was stare at Sylem lying prostrate at the creature's feet, unable to make the connection between the two. The thing that claimed to be Irea followed his gaze before turning its dead eyes back on him.

"Why, Revik, you look like you've seen a ghost. There's no cause to be alarmed. Your friend sated my hunger. For now anyway. I just want to talk to you. Let's reminisce, shall we? It's been such a long time. What's wrong? Nothing to say? No apologies?"

"What?"

"Have you forgotten what you did to me? I certainly haven't. Nor have I forgotten my promise to you. We've a debt to settle, you and I."

"What are you?"

"Much more than you could ever possibly understand."

"What did you do to Sylem?"

"What do you think?" she snickered. "I told you I'd get my revenge on all of you. I've taken my time, but the score will soon be settled."

Sylem...

Revik hurled the dagger at her. She melted, becoming black tendrils of fog that swirled around the knife as it moved through her. Once the dagger had passed, she reformed with a triumphant laugh.

"Can't get rid of me that easily, I'm afraid. Oh, this is so much fun, don't you think? Now let's see. Any more friends about the pasture that you'd like me to meet? Perhaps I should go up to the house and pay my respects to that lovely wife of yours."

Her words summoned his anger, replacing fear for the time being. "You stay the hell away from her!"

"Touching, truly touching. It's always nice to see men gallantly defending their weak womenfolk." She tapped a long, slender finger against her face in mock pensiveness. "Why, if I recall correctly, I do believe that Jarro said almost exactly the same thing."

The mention of his dead friend was unnerving. It was too much to take in at once. Revik struggled to make sense of it all.

Irea smiled coyly, looking as smug as a cat with a belly full of stolen cream. "Oh, didn't he tell you that I popped by for a visit back then? Well, I suppose he didn't want anyone to know. Especially not that dear little stray of his. He seemed most aggrieved by my presence actually.

It hurt my feelings."

"You saw Jarro," he said, mostly to himself as his mind reeled with this new information.

"Yes. And I'll tell you something else. I was so upset by his rudeness that I just had to pay him another visit later on that night. I'm sure you're clever enough to figure out what happened then."

The screams. Sevy's cries. The crumpled heap of the man Revik considered a great friend. It all rushed back to him in one horrible assault of memory. He shuddered, causing Irea to burst into more delighted laughter.

"Oh, you do remember, don't you? Isn't life just the funniest thing? How everything is interconnected? How each insignificant detail takes on new meaning as more and more of the design is revealed? I must say, I was worried that I wouldn't have the patience to carry this out. I've never been one for waiting. But seeing your face just now reassures me that I've made the right decision."

"What are you talking about?"

She said nothing, turning to look down at Sylem instead. "Is he one of your husbands? What's the name in your tongue? Quilorsha? Tell me, does it make you jealous to share your wife with other men? Or do you all just sleep together? Dark elves are such foul things. I wouldn't put it past you."

At the second mention of his wife, the urgency to protect her and the rest of his family suppressed Revik's own terror of the fiend before him. She seemed to notice this and cocked her head to the side, as if awaiting his next move. Would he challenge her? Could he? He was defenseless, his only weapon now lying yards away. He knew no magic to attack her with, and doubted that he could fight her off, handicapped as he was.

"Don't worry!" she said, apparently reading his thoughts. "If I wanted you and your precious slut dead, you would be. I'm here to talk. And unlike some people I could mention, I'm true to my word. You will die, my dearest Revik, though not today. I've got someone else in mind to feed my hunger and my vengeance. Now all I have to do is track the stray down."

His eyes widened in comprehension. "Sevy?"

"Mm-hmm. Any idea where I can find the bitch? No one in Eloria has seen her since your falling out with Bolozi. I do hope she hasn't thrown herself on her sword or some other melodramatic nonsense. That would be most disappointing."

"Don't you dare hurt Sevy!"

"Interesting. You still care about her after all this time, after all she did. If only you had been so loyal to me, you wouldn't be in this situation, now would you?" She grinned and, to Revik's surprise, dissolved. She blended into the cover of the night. Her voice came from all directions. "Farewell for now. Give my regards to your charming whore. I'll come visit you again once Sevy and I have a chat."

The shadow left the moon and the meadow was filled with light once more. The acrid smell dissipated. Revik was alone again, he was sure of it. Except, of course, for Sylem, lying lifeless on the gently waving grass.

Chapter 3

The wailing began at dawn and continued for the rest of the day, stopping only for designated breaks. Revik wondered how they were able to keep it up for that long. How could they still have tears left to shed? But they were professional mourners, the best the Ullydrans had to offer, so they must be used to it. Yy'voury had spared no expense. She was determined that Sylem would have the finest funeral the Ped-a-nor District had seen in centuries.

The Barren Mage and her apprentices had spent days preparing the body, rubbing it with oil from the Hulibra tree—a rare oil indeed as Hulibra only grew in salt water swamps—until Sylem's skin gleamed like polished sapphire. Painstakingly detailed lettering was drawn across his chest and back with iron powder, listing ancestors and tracing the lineages of both Sylem and Yy'voury. His long white hair was washed, combed through with oil, and arranged in plaits. This was an indisputable sign of power as typically men were not permitted to wear their hair in the style of women. No less than twelve porters were hired to carry his body up Mount Lirra to the cliff ledge belonging to Yy'voury's family. And there amongst the strewn remains of his wife's ancestors, Sylem was laid on a bed of opirss flowers, his final resting place until the beasts and the elements scattered him back into the Cauldron of Creation. He would not have to wait long. From countless crags and eyries, golden eyes and razor-like beaks keenly awaited the living's departure.

Revik stood back with Krelaan and Trel while the women and children gathered around the body and listened to the Barren Mage tell of Sylem's noble spirit. She spoke in the sacred language of women. Men were forbidden to learn it, although over the years Revik had picked up enough to understand the essence of what the Mage said.

Yy'voury knelt at Sylem's side and when the Mage finished the last blessing, she bent down and kissed his brow. A stranger would have thought that she wasn't grieving at all; she didn't weep or throw herself around like the mourners did. But Revik knew better. He could tell by the dullness of his wife's eyes just how much pain she was in. A woman of her rank was not permitted to show sorrow in public, and Yy'voury would never dishonor Sylem's memory by crying at his funeral.

Revik watched her, feeling more love for her at this instant than he had since the first passionate years of their marriage. For all her nagging, she was a wonderful woman, devoted to her family, always putting their needs above her own. To know that he was responsible for causing her so much grief tore at his heart. He cried freely, not only for the loss of a dear friend and fellow husband, but for the innocence that Irea had stolen from all of their lives.

Krelaan placed an arm around his shoulder and Revik smiled sadly at him before looking down at his feet. A sob caught in his throat as he thought of the loved ones he had lost in so few years. Sylem, Jarro, and Turlan.

The sweet old man had died shortly after they had made it to the mountains. Yy'voury, patient, gracious Yy'voury, had opened up her home to him. She herself had tended him in his final days. And though other women were outraged, she allowed him, a mere human, to rest on her ancestors' ledge. Family, she reminded them, was not defined solely by blood.

The funeral concluded. Led by the Barren Mage, the group began their descent as the mourners increased their wailing, performing one last show before the rites were considered final. One by one, the family moved away from Sylem until only Yy'voury remained, still kneeling. Revik wanted to take her away. Instead, he fell into line behind Trel, and left her to grieve in private.

It was hours later before she arrived home. She went into the kitchen as calm and composed as always and ordered the staff around. Revik, who was sitting by the fire with Yy'vran asleep on his lap, listened to her yell at one of the cooks for not having sliced the carrots to her liking. She was nothing if not consistent. Once satisfied with the dinner preparations, she left the kitchen and approached Revik.

"Walk with me."

He deposited Yy'vran onto the chair. The child mewed in sleepy protest, but did not stir. Then Revik followed Yy'voury outside. They walked in silence down the path, past the meadow and into the valley below. Finally, when they were almost to the woods that marked the border of Yy'voury's land, she spoke.

"Tell me again what happened."

"A shadow passed over the moon, we were separated and I—"

"No. Just...tell me he didn't suffer."

"He didn't suffer," Revik lied.

"Good."

She took his hand and they continued to stroll through the growing dusk. Their way was lit by tiny smudges of color as the evening pixies emerged from their nests amongst the trees. There were clouds gathering, but nothing ominous like the night of the attack. It was peaceful. Quiet, although not eerily so. Still, Irea's presence could be felt all over the Ullydrans.

Yy'voury had ordered double the usual amount of guards stationed around their house as well as the houses of all of her married children. No one was allowed to be alone, especially at night. She consulted with the Barren Mage at great length, and an exorbitant number of protective spells were purchased. Revik didn't have much faith in those. He couldn't see spells and guards doing much good against Irea, as no one seemed to know what she had become.

"Tell me more about her," Yy'voury said.

He had been expecting this line of questioning to come sooner or later. "She was an elf. From the north, I think. She was Jarro's woman all the time I knew her."

"Jarro was your human friend?" She knew this. Revik had spoken of him many times. She was just trying to sort things out, Revik supposed.

"Yes. They met in the city, but I don't know how. Probably just latched onto him because he had a bit of power."

"Typical elf."

He smiled and continued, "I never liked her. She was a sly one. She dabbled in magic. Read palms, made potions and the like for money. Nothing serious. But I never trusted her."

"She said she wants revenge." This was more of a question than a statement. She wanted Revik to skip to the end.

"She tried to have Jarro and Sevy killed. Sevy was another member of the gang. Irea was jealous of her."

Revik recounted the last time he had seen Irea, a story which he had never told to anyone. Not because of remorse or fear, but because it never had seemed important enough to mention. Irea had never seemed important enough. An error in judgment, he realized now. Irea was right: *Each insignificant detail takes on new meaning...*

He remembered her pleas. "Jarro, I...let me explain. It was Sevy! It was her and Duyan! Not me! I'd never betray you, Jarro! Never! I love you!"

"Get her out of my sight."

Revik wasn't sure what had happened, but he didn't need to know the details. He'd heard enough to know that Irea had turned on them just as he always expected. He grabbed her by the shoulders and hauled her outside.

"Let go of me!" He held tight, forcing her forward. She strained to look around him and screamed back towards the open door, "Jarro! Jarro, please! Listen to me, it was all Sevy!"

"Keep walking!" Revik commanded.

She stumbled ahead a few steps and then dug her feet into the ground, refusing to move. She clawed at his tunic. Tears drenched her face. "Revik, you don't understand! Please, let's just talk about this! Be reasonable!"

He couldn't help but smirk. She was pathetic, groveling at his feet as though he could be so easily fooled. He had always known that she was treacherous, using whoever she could to get what she wanted. Jarro had been tricked by her beauty, but not Revik. And now the truth had come out, and his mistrust of her proved justified after all.

"I am being reasonable, so keep walking. I'll drag you if I have to."

She narrowed her eyes and hissed through her teeth. "You," she said, her voice low and full of hatred. "It was you and that girl! You poisoned his mind against me!"

"You did that yourself. Be grateful he is who he is. Any other man would have your head."

She scratched him across the face, drawing thin lines of blood. He grabbed her wrists as she tried to strike again. Twisting her arms behind her back, he forced her forward, applying pressure if she resisted. In this way he led her through the streets, ignoring her protests and the stares of those they passed. Fortunately, not many seemed eager to intervene, and a sharp look was enough to dissuade any would-be heroes. The city guards ignored them. Quarrels between nonhumans were none of their concern.

"What are you going to do with me?"

"I should kill you. I'd certainly like to. For Jarro's peace of mind, I'll let you live. I'm taking you to the Northern gate and you're going to leave the city. Permanently. If I ever see you here again, you'll regret it."

"You can't do this to me, you arrogant bastard!"

"Careful now or you'll hurt my feelings."

The gate came into view and he loosened his hold on her arms. She jerked free, spinning round to face him. "You can't make me leave!"

"Fine. Have it your way." Revik loved the faint zinging noise his sword made as he pulled it from its sheath. He twirled it in his hand. The light danced upon its length while Revik waited for Irea to fully appreciate her predicament.

"Everything all right there?" A blacksmith had come out of his shop and watched Irea and Revik with worry.

"Help me! He's mad!"

"Everything's fine. This is none of your business."

"Wait! Wait," she pleaded. "Please! Can't we talk about this? I was only trying to save our lives. Jarro and that bitch were going to get us all killed. Duyan was out for blood."

Revik laughed. "How stupid do you think I am?"

"Fine! I wanted Jarro gone. Why do you care? He's just a human. After everything humans have done to your people, you'd still side with them over one of your kindred?"

"Kindred? Shut it, elf. We're nothing alike."

"Aren't we? Our skin may be different colors, but we're the same inside. Our races are forever linked. And we share a common enemy. Humans have taken over. They treat us like animals! We should band together against them!"

"You'll say anything, try any angle. You're pathetic. Get going." He pointed his sword towards the gate.

"But this is my home! Where will I go? What will I do?"

"I really couldn't care less."

"It's not fair! I had everything and that little bitch took it all away!"

"You're blaming everyone but yourself. As usual."

"You don't know anything about me!"

"I'm losing patience. Leave now, or regardless of Jarro, I'll kill you."

She sputtered with rage, but they both knew that she was no match for him. Dejected, she turned and walked forward a few paces. He sheathed his sword and watched, waiting for her to exit the city. Just then, she paused. He thought she was going to continue to whine, but instead she darted over to the blacksmith and grabbed a pair of glowing red tongs from the forge.

Screaming, she flew at him. He readied his sword and blocked her wilds swings. She didn't know how to fight; fending off her blows was effortless. In one simple thrust, he knocked the tongs from her hands.

He waited for her next move. Now that Irea was disarmed, Revik assumed she would turn and run. Not so. She came at him again, screeching, her face contorted with fury. She tried to wrench the sword from his hands, and he laughed at her feeble attempt before pushing her off.

"Last warning, Irea."

He sheathed his sword again and stood with arms crossed. He found all of this to be quite amusing; the once proud elf reduced to shrieking and flailing around like a drunken harpy.

"I swear by the gods, one day I'll have my revenge on you. On all of you!" She spat at him.

He backhanded her across the face, a little harder than he intended.

It was enough to incapacitate her. She landed face down on the ground, and to his surprise, began to scream. She rolled onto her back, clutching her face. Revik could smell burning flesh. The tongs! They were still scorching and she had fallen on top of them.

He yanked her shaking hands from her face, recoiling at the sight. The skin along her right cheek was charred. It bubbled and peeled, exposing muscle.

"Here, quickly," he said as he tried to drag her to the smithy's bucket of cool water. Instead, she pulled away and ran.

He didn't follow. What good would it have done? She wouldn't have trusted him to help, and quite frankly he didn't really care. To his mind, she had still received less than she deserved.

Returning to the house, he didn't tell Jarro or anyone else what had happened. Knowing Jarro, he would have felt so much pity that he would have gone looking for her. It was best that he didn't know. He and Sevy had left Eloria soon after on the first of their travels, and Revik had put the matter out of his mind. He had never expected to see or hear of Irea again.

A light drizzle started and the cool droplets splashed against his face, waking him from his memories. Yy'voury pulled the hood of her cloak over her head, but remained at his side. He couldn't look at her. The pain she felt, the pain they all felt—it was his fault. If he had only killed Irea when he had the chance, none of this would have happened. How many lives had been destroyed because he had failed to act?

"Yy'voury, forgive me."

"There is nothing to apologize for. This man, your friend Jarro, he was right to show mercy to his enemies. You did well to follow his example. Blood begets blood, nothing more."

"No, I should have killed her. Jarro showed mercy and look where it got him."

"Don't dwell on the past. You had no way of knowing what would happen." She reached up and gently wiped his dampened hair from his face. "Do not bear the guilt of this evil, little husband. It is hers alone. Now come, the meal will be ready soon."

She tugged on his hand, but he stood in place. "Yy'voury..."

"Don't say it," she whispered. "Please."

"I'm sorry, but I have to go and warn Sevy. You know that I have to."

"Why?" she demanded, her voice rising in pitch and her eyes blazing. "Is she so important that you would risk your life? I've not even begun to mourn one husband and now I am to lose another?"

"I have to go. I owe it to her, and to the memory of Jarro."

"You care more for those humans than your own family! Who's

to say that Irea won't come back and slaughter us all? Who's to say that Sevy is even still alive? Nothing that monster elf said can be trusted."

"I know that, but we won't be safe until she's dead. I'm a liability as long as I stay here. She said she'd be back for me eventually. If nothing else I'll draw her away from you and the children. You'll be fine, you have protection. You have the guards, the spells. Sevy is all alone."

"You don't know that."

"I'll find Sevy and then I'll find Irea and kill her. She won't be allowed to hurt anyone else. I swear it."

But was that the real reason he wanted to leave? He concealed the unseemly hint of exhilaration he felt at the prospect of another wander, another adventure. It was wrong to take pleasure in this time of pain. What sort of man was he?

A good man wouldn't feel his heart race with excitement like this. A good man would comfort his wife. Revik embraced Yy'voury and kissed her. Her chest heaved. Neither spoke for a long while.

Finally, she glanced up at him. "At the very least, don't stay away for so long this time."

"I won't."

"We'll go to the Barren Mage in the morning. She can help you find your friend. But for tonight, I get to fuss over you all I want. Understood?"

"Understood. I love you, Yy'voury."

She smiled wistfully. "And I love you, little husband."

Chapter 4

They sat side by side on an uncomfortable bench in the anteroom of the Barren Mage's house. Her apprentices bustled about, some cleaning or carrying various supplies and mystical ingredients, others doing nothing more than trying to appear busy, but the Mage had yet to make her appearance. Revik tapped his foot and Yy'voury gave his knee a gentle slap.

"Patience. She's a busy woman."

"We've been waiting all morning. What could she possibly be doing?" he grumbled.

He tried to peek into the next room as an apprentice went through the door, and he saw glimpses of colored glass jars neatly arranged on shelves. He was always impressed with how organized and clean the Mage's house was. It was quite unlike the dark, cluttered apothecaries and magic shops of Eloria. Here, the walls were freshly white-washed and the floors were covered with luxurious wool rugs.

The apprentices were likewise spotless in appearance. They wore crisp linen dyed the same hue as their skin; their heads were freshly shaved and waxed, the mark of the Barren; and they smelled like sweet grass. The Mage demanded that all her apprentices be meticulous in every detail of their lives.

Revik caught site of Yy'veera, one of Yy'voury's oldest children. The girl was clearly fathered by Trel. She had his slight frame and docile nature, behaving more like a son than a daughter. She didn't notice her mother or Revik as she had her nose stuck in a rather large tome, mumbling under her breath.

"Hello, Yy'veera," Revik called.

She glanced up and smiled before turning back to her book. Revik admired her devotion to her studies. She had been quite young when she first entered the order. Her first marriage only lasted a decade, during which time she suffered multiple miscarriages. A divination by the Barren Mage revealed that Yy'veera was unfruitful, so her husband was given back to his family, and Yy'veera became an apprentice. Yy'voury was beside herself with pride that the ancestors had bestowed this honor on their family, and swore that Yy'veera was so talented that she surely would become the next Mage.

Unfortunately for Yy'voury's bragging rights, the Barren Mage was just as tardy crossing over into the Cauldron of Creation as she was for their appointment today. She had surpassed her predecessor's reign by over two hundred years and showed no signs of slowing down.

Finally, the door opened and the Barren Mage stood, beaming down at them. She was a willow of a woman, graceful and poised. She reached out her delicate hands to welcome them.

Yy'voury bowed before her. "Lonely One, thank you for seeing us."

"Hello, my sweet child. How are you feeling today?"

"Fine, thank you."

She patted Yy'voury's hand then turned to Revik with a disapproving toss of her head. "Well, come in."

They entered the Room of Nascence. The walls were lined with the glass bottles Revik had seen earlier, and sunlight from the many windows caught in them and reflected their colors around the room, which gave it a cheery, nursery-like feel. The Mage motioned for Yy'voury to take a seat while she ushered Revik towards a rectangular piece of onyx that was standing in the corner. It was nearly as tall as he was and was buffed so that he could see himself and the Mage in it.

"Your wife tells me that you are planning a suicide wander," she said, forcing him to kneel before the onyx by pulling on his hair.

"It's not suicide," he protested. "I will find Irea and kill her."

He watched the Mage's reflection as she swept away. She stood next to a low wooden table and began grinding something in a mortar.

"If you were my husband, I'd whip you for even thinking of attempting this. It's pure foolishness. This thing, this perversion of nature, it is unknown even to me. I have tried to find her, but she is beyond the sight of the ancestors."

"So you have no idea what she is?" He turned to look at her.

"I didn't say you could move! Don't look at me!" she screeched, throwing a spoon at him. Once he resumed his position facing the onyx, she regained her composure. "I have an idea of what she is, but I know nothing in certainty. I have my girls consulting our people's oldest records, but I doubt they'll find much. I believe this witch of an elf has delved into ancient magiks. Older even than the Grave Chasm which split the Alfar people, our oldest ancestors, into the two races known today as light and dark elves."

She selected a bottle of violet liquid from the shelves, poured it into the mortar, and swirled the mixture together with her finger as she came towards Revik again. "Here, drink one mouthful."

He did as he was told, grimacing at the sour taste. She took the bowl from him and splashed the rest of the mixture onto the onyx slab. Then she turned back towards the table and continued to speak.

"There are legends of demons that roamed the earth in the time of the Alfar, but these tales are few and incomplete. I wonder where this Irea would have found such a spell so as to transform herself."

Instead of dripping down, the concoction she had poured onto the onyx congealed on the smooth surface, and Revik was unable to see the Mage in the reflection anymore. He listened as she moved about the room behind him, and although he was curious about what she was doing, he didn't dare turn again to watch her.

"As a man, you have little knowledge of our history, but legend states that the gods were to blame for the Grave Chasm. The five true gods, having grown bored with their eternities, began to spend more and more time in the mortal realm. They lost sight of their responsibilities and as time passed these gods became as mortals. Petty, jealous, indulgent, and cruel. They developed a fixation with worldly pleasure and the Alfar, being the most beautiful of mortals, caught the gods' eyes. One group of Alfar reveled in this new attention. They cast spells to gain favor, bargained with their flesh and their souls. They became as whores to the gods in their desperation for prosperity and the ability to change one's fortune. As time went on they became elves.

"Another group of Alfar despised the gods for losing their sanctity. They would not barter for their destinies. This group stopped all worship and began to rely only on themselves and, in time, on their ancestors for guidance. This is the group that we are descended from. The gods showed their displeasure by branding us 'dark' and perpetuated lies about our kind. Lies which persist to this day.

"They say that we feast on blood and that we live in shadow. Interesting how your demon, Irea, does both these things. It is my belief that the myths concerning dark elves actually come from a beast, one that was known to the Alfar before the Chasm. Likening dark elves to these demons must have been a great insult at the time."

She appeared at his side with a tray that was filled with clay pots of colored powder. "Pick the one that most reminds you of the friend you seek."

His fingers moved over the rows of color, finally settling on one. "Green. For her eyes."

The Mage returned to the table. "Of course, this is all speculation and does nothing to explain what the demon is, or how you can stop it. Perhaps there are libraries that you can consult, other Mages across the land who could give you more help. If you can stomach it, you could even confer with a wizened old elf," she said with a scoff. "Maybe their kind has more detailed records on the subject. They glory in harping on and on about the Chasm. They call it their Time of Sagacity."

Revik heard an indignant huff from the corner. He had forgotten that Yy'voury was there. The Mage approached once more and handed him a long, thin pipe made of bleached bone. She sprinkled the green powder into the chamber and held a flame in the bowl until the powder smoldered.

"Smoke it. Blow the smoke onto the onyx," she commanded, and Revik did so. "Now I want you to stare at the stone and think of your friend. Think of her face. Think of her voice. Think of the first time you met her and the last time you saw her."

He thought of Sevy as a young girl. She had been so lanky and awkward, but full of nerve. He remembered her bursting into the Bloody Heart and bossing around Vipin, the surly barkeeper. Then he thought of her as a woman, tall and tough and full of strength despite her sorrow. She was still as bold and cocky as she had been as a child, but had become tempered with time and experience.

As he thought about her, an image formed in his mind—Sevy, sitting at a table, a glass of ale raised to her lips. She was looking around, seemingly disinterested but alert at the same time. Her hair was shorter, the lines around her mouth and eyes were deeper, but there was no mistaking that familiar scowl.

"I see her!" he cried. "I think she's in a tavern."

"All right, now see what she sees. Try to make out the details of the room, the people."

He was able to see three dwarves sitting at the table next to her. Then he saw a barmaid walk by, fair and blonde, carrying a tray of mugs. He could smell the barley. He saw the bar, and a number of men sitting at it. He heard strains of several conversations that blended into indecipherable racket.

"I see the room. I see lots of different people."

"Good. Now see past the room. Move outside. Can you read a sign perhaps? Or make out a landmark?"

Revik squinted as though that would make a difference. He moved away from the people to a door just ahead of him. In his mind, the door opened and bright light streamed in. He blinked as though the light was actually hitting his eyes. Outside, there was a beaten-down dirt path lined with small wooden buildings. Up the road was a green blur. He concentrated harder. The blur was actually trees and bushes. A forest.

He frowned. "All I see are trees. She could be anywhere."

"Focus!" the Mage said, as if he hadn't been doing that all along.

He sighed and tried again. He turned from the trees and looked back at the buildings. There was a butcher shop; he saw the carcasses hanging in the window. A barber shop. Someone inside was getting their tooth pulled. He looked back towards the tavern door. There was a mark on it. He stared at it until it formed a discernable shape.

"I see a drawing of a pig lying on its back with crosses on its eyes." The image of it jogged a memory. "I've seen that before. I've been there before."

"A pig?" Yy'voury asked.

"Wait. No, not a pig. A hog," he said slowly. "A dead hog? No, it's not dead. It's passed out. That's it! She's in Allerough! She's in The Drunken Hog in Allerough!"

"Well done." The Mage slapped Revik across the face.

"Hey! What was that for?"

"Quickest way to bring you back out. Now you know where she is. Bully for you."

"Now show me Irea!"

She rolled her eyes. "Yes, because I hadn't thought to try that. I've already told you that she is beyond my sight."

"Oh." He sat back on his heels and sighed.

"'Oh' he says," the Mage muttered, pulling him to his feet by his hair again. "Like I didn't just grant him a vision. 'Oh' he says like a spoiled child."

"Forgive him, Lonely One, he is merely a man, and a rather impertinent one at that," Yy'voury said. "We are most appreciative of your help."

Revik seethed, but kept his mouth shut. Considering he was leaving her the next day, he decided not to say or do anything that would embarrass his wife.

Yy'voury kissed the Barren Mage's hand and then they both turned expectantly to Revik.

"Oh, right." He bent to kiss her hand as well. "Thank you."

The Mage tossed her head again before shooing them both out of the Room of Nascence.

"How far is Allerough from here?" Yy'voury asked as they walked through the village to the path that led home.

"Three weeks, maybe two if I hurry."

"You may take a horse. I'll find a good, strong one for you. But what will you do if she's gone by the time you get there?"

"I'll pick up her trail."

"And once you find her, how will you find Irea? If not even the Mage can?"

"She'll find us, most likely. But don't worry," he added quickly, seeing the fright on Yy'voury's face. "We'll be ready for her. Sevy is a strong fighter, I trained her myself. Irea won't stand a chance."

This, of course, was far from certain. Revik didn't know what would happen once they faced Irea again, but there had to be a way to stop her. If what the Mage said was true then this kind of demon had existed for eons, and if there was no way to kill them, wouldn't the world be overrun? It didn't matter either way. He would kill her or die trying.

He took Yy'voury's hand in his. He would leave in the morning, maybe for the last time, but for today he was still Yy'voury's little husband.

Chapter 5

Sevy dipped her hands into the basin and watched the water turn red. She felt as she always did afterward—disconnected and numb. It had been too easy. There was no struggle. He hadn't even turned around. Just the flash of her blade, a gurgling sound, and the warm wetness of his blood spilling over her fingers. Nothing to it.

There was a mirror hanging on the wall, but she avoided her reflection as she finished washing her hands. Without a final glance at what she had done, Sevy climbed back out of the window and scaled down the side of the house. It was the middle of the afternoon, but it didn't matter if anyone saw her. None of these pathetic townspeople were a match for her.

She held her head high as she stomped along the dusty street. She glared at anyone who stopped to look at her, presenting them with an unvoiced challenge that no one seemed eager to take. A cry sounded. No doubt the body had been found. She jeered at the wailing. Just another drop in a sea of death, what did it matter? Nothing mattered really. Not when you stopped to think about it. She pushed a troublesome pang of guilt deep down inside of her and continued her dissertation on mortality. Everyone dies. Everyone deserves to die. So she had given Annu-nial a helping hand, so what? And besides that, the pay was good.

Following the village's only road, she reached the outskirts of the Gouldrion Forest and started down a deer trail, preferring it to the cleared and marked path that was sure to be populated with a variety of nuisances. A breeze sailed through the trees. Sunlight caught in the fluttering leaves. Her route was dotted with shifting patterns of green that provided an atmosphere of calm and tranquility. Not that she needed calming. The events of this day were no different than any other.

Sevy hiked for hours, lost in thought, surrounded on all sides by massive oaks, adrift in the forest's depths. The great leafy arms of the trees reached out and tangled together, blocking the sun, casting the trail in shadow. The forest was huge. It could be days before she emerged from it depending on which direction she headed. And at present, she couldn't care less where she was going. It felt good to be in the solitude of the trees.

Cocky birds chattered insults to her as they hopped on the forest floor. Every now and again she heard some small animal rustling around, camouflaged within the undergrowth. Or perhaps it was a fairy. She couldn't tell. Part of her hoped that it was a fairy, or maybe a troll. She could have a fight then. Might help make things more exciting. The thought made her smile.

The trees thinned and she found herself looking upon a small lake. Wind skated along the water and she watched tiny waves ripple across the surface. A chorus of frogs and insects hidden within the bulrushes provided an uncanny serenade. The germinating smells of life and growth were all around her, and coincidently enough smelled a lot like death.

A familiar notion, one as worn and comfortable as an old pair of boots, filled her head. It soon blocked out all other thoughts. Wouldn't it be nice not to remember anymore, not to feel anymore? She was so tired. Before she realized it, she was at the lake's edge, allowing the water to lick at her feet. It was better than she deserved, but at least it would be an end. Delivered from the haunting curse of memory, she would finally be able to sleep. She walked forward into the murky brown water until it covered her thighs.

She paused, staring down at the water as it swirled soothingly around her, reassuring her of the liberation it could provide. She took another step then paused again. Her hands balled into fists, nails digging into her palms. She scowled. Another tentative step forward. Her boot sank in the mud and she yanked her foot up against the suction.

"Coward," she whispered. With a sunken heart, she waded to the shore. She walked away from the lake and back into the womb of trees. Her hands were warm and sticky. Looking down, she saw small half-moon imprints of her fingernails cut into her skin. Droplets of blood seeped out and pooled together in the center of her palms. She shook her hands and the blood sprayed the foliage, a shocking splash of red against the world of green. "Fucking coward."

※

The ale slipped down her throat. She had a nice little buzz going and wanted it to last, so she rapped on the bar with two knuckles until the bartender handed her another glass.

The tavern was too noisy and too dark, but it would do for now. She surveyed the room, observing the men lurch about and the whores work their charms. A drunken musician, egged on by the clink of coins in his tip jar, squeaked out a shrill tune on his flute. Too many people in such a small place. It made her nervous.

She waved a barmaid over. "How much for a room?"

"We're full up, honey, unless you wanna share with someone," the girl drawled. Sevy made a face and the barmaid laughed. "Suit yourself."

So it was the woods again tonight. Her shoulders drooped. She downed the rest of her drink then pushed her way outside. Smoke from the tavern's several chimneys created a haze that hurt her lungs. She coughed, hiked up the pack on her back, and started down the road.

The tavern was nestled on the side of a busy crossroads. She had come up from the south, from the Gouldrion Forest and Allerough. She didn't have any particular place to go. She'd simply walk until she found more work. West led to the borders of Axlun and Belakarta, north led to the jungles, and east...

East led to the farmlands and beyond that to Eloria. She stared at the signpost and felt something inside pull her in that direction. She ignored it. She'd go north. She had heard there was trouble in the jungles. The gold miners were clashing with some dark elf villages and there was talk of a revolt. Changes in land ownership always resulted in plenty of business opportunities for Sevy. It made sense to go north. It did not make sense to go to Eloria. All that was left there was a pain best kept at arm's length. Still, the city called to her. Maybe it would be good to walk down those streets again, see some familiar faces.

She punched her leg. Who was she expecting to see? Bolozi? Although, she had to admit that driving a piece of metal through his heart might cheer her up considerably. The thought had crossed her mind more than a few times over the years, but she just couldn't bring herself to confront the city, confront the past. But maybe she didn't need to. Maybe the only closure she needed was to see that useless slug eat the end of her sword. East it was then.

The sun began to set, throwing a coral brume over the tops of the trees and bringing a hint of a chill to the air. Once she moved far enough away from the crossroads, the sounds of other travelers subsided. Soon she heard nothing but the chirping of crickets, the hum of pixie wings, and the crunch of her boots on the gravel. As she walked, she tried to whistle before realizing that the only melody she could think of was the irritating one the tavern musician had been playing.

She made camp a few hours later and resumed her journey at dawn. She passed a few people throughout the morning. Merchants mostly, carrying large bundles on their backs. She ignored their greetings, and her dirty looks were enough to deter them from bothering her further. A lucky thing for them. Had the right mood struck her, she would have robbed them and left them for dead.

Slowly, the landscape changed. The impressive oaks and maples were replaced by their scrub cousins and twiggy, bristly shrubs. The ground dipped then flattened, and Sevy could see far off into the horizon. As the day wore on, tiny farmhouses began to pop up, circled by well tended fields of swaying grains.

As the sunlight waned, dull rhythmic thudding woke her from her walking doze. A growing dust cloud appeared in the distance and she heard the whinny of a horse. A rider was rapidly approaching. She moved to the side of the road to let them by.

Sevy kept her hand on the hilt of her sword just in case. One could never predict when bandits would make an appearance. The king's army did precious little to protect the roads this far south of Wilrendel and many a traveler had vanished along the way.

The rider quickly overtook and passed her. Just as she relaxed her grip on her sword, the rider yanked on the reins and forced his horse to turn around. *Interesting*, she thought. Maybe she could gain a horse out of this. She squared her shoulders and waited.

The rider threw off the hood of his cloak, yelling, "Sevy!"

She blinked. "Revik?"

He leapt from the horse, ran to her, and embraced her before she had a chance to react. "I'm so glad I found you! I've been searching for weeks!"

"Revik?" she repeated. "What are you doing here?"

"Looking for you. Thank the gods you're safe."

"Looking for me? Why?"

His happy smile turned grave. "We need to talk. Let's get off the road."

She followed him into the fields, watching with curiosity as his gaze darted about. It was almost as though he expected someone to be hidden within the long grass. And even more peculiar, he sniffed the air.

"What are you doing?"

"Just checking."

He let the horse roam and straight away it began grazing, quite content now that it had a chance to rest and eat. Revik flopped onto the ground and pulled out a pouch of water. Sevy cringed as he fiddled with the cap; he couldn't get it opened with just his one hand.

"Let me," she said, reaching forward.

"I can do it!" he snapped. After a minute, he managed to pop the cap off, and took a long drink. He held the pouch out to her, but she shook her head. She sat down next to him even though she longed to run away from him as fast as she could.

"How have you been?" he asked, smiling again at her. It made her uncomfortable. Two years without any contact, and now here he was acting like nothing had happened. She realized that she was staring at his stump and hurriedly averted her gaze.

"Fine. What's going on? What are you doing here?"

He exhaled and looked up at the sky as if gathering his thoughts. "I don't really know how to tell you this. I've been thinking about it since I left home, and I still don't know how."

"Then just say it."

"I know what happened to Jarro. I know who murdered him."

Her breath hissed between her teeth. She had not heard anyone say that name since she left Eloria. She hadn't even allowed herself to say it. It was too sacred to just blurt out. And to hear that hallowed name paired with such an ugly word as 'murdered' made her want to vomit. She felt as though the air had been kicked out of her. A fine sweat broke out across her brow and her mouth went dry.

Revik was suddenly very close to her, peering into her face. "Are you all right?"

"Who?"

"You've gone pale."

"Who?!"

"Irea."

Irea, she puzzled, staring at the ground. That bitch elf? With the ease of a wobbly-legged fawn, Sevy rose to her feet.

"Where are you going?" Revik asked.

"To kill her."

"Wait. Just wait!" He grabbed her belt and pulled her back down. "There's more."

Sevy sat in deadened disbelief as Revik recounted what had happened. It sounded so preposterous. Irea, a woman who Sevy had only known for a matter of months years ago, had secretly come back as a demon and murdered Jarro out of spite? And now, after even more time had passed, Irea was out for Sevy's blood as well? Good. Perfect. Sevy prayed Irea would show herself, the sooner the better, so that Sevy could make her beg for mercy and scream in agony before cutting her heart out.

"I'm surprised she hasn't found you yet. I thought I'd be too late," Revik finished.

Sevy stood, dusted off her trousers, and walked back towards the road.

"Hold on!" Revik ran to fetch the horse who had wandered off in search of sweeter grass. Once it was trailing behind him, Revik raced to catch up to her. "You've got a plan, I take it?"

She kept her focus on the road. "Yeah. The plan is for you to go back home. I'll take care of this."

"Not bloody likely. I'm coming with you."

"No, you're not. Go home."

"Make me."

Sevy stopped and crossed her arms, glowering at him. "Don't try to cross me, Revik."

"Oh, get over yourself. If you think that I'm just going to twiddle my thumbs...err, my thumb...while you go and get yourself killed, you've got another think coming."

"This isn't your fight."

"The hell it isn't! Irea came after my family! And in case you're too blinded by self-pity to remember, Jarro was my friend too. This is my responsibility. I should have killed Irea when I had the chance."

"Damn straight you should have."

He sighed. "I'm sorry. I'm sorry that all of this happened. If I could go back and change things, believe me, I would. The only thing I can do now is to stop her from hurting anyone else. I owe it to Jarro."

Despite her better judgment, she agreed. There wasn't really any way she could stop him short of tying him up and sticking him on a caravan back to the mountains. They walked in silence and she tried not to take notice of the glances he snuck at her face. He obviously had more that he wanted to say. She wondered if he was thinking about the way she treated him, about the last inappropriate hours they spent together. Did he hate her for it as much as she did?

Revik broke the quiet by raising his voice, "So where are we heading?"

She was relieved by the question. She had been expecting something more personal. "You said she mentioned Bolozi. I find that odd considering they never met so far as we know. She must have gone looking for us in Eloria at first. She must have met him there. Maybe he'll know something."

He nodded. "Good idea. You were headed there already, weren't you?"

"Mm-hmm."

"You go back there often?"

"No."

"Oh."

There was another extended, uncomfortable pause. The horse snorted suddenly, afraid of a branch that was lying across the middle of the road. Sevy and Revik both jumped at the chance to comfort the horse and ease it around the branch. Even something that mundane was a welcome distraction from having to, heavens forbid, talk to one another. Sevy sighed. This was going to be a long journey.

Revik laughed and made a comment about how timid horses can be. Sevy smiled half-heartedly, but didn't reply. It had been quite some time since she had made small talk with anyone. And given their past, what could she say to him that wouldn't sound spurious and contrived? It pained her that there was such awkwardness dividing them. They had been good friends before she wrecked everything with her selfishness and stupidity. She peeked again at his arm. What was left of it was tucked away within the fabric of his tunic. The sleeve had been shortened and stitched closed. She wondered who had done that for him.

"I'm sorry about your friend," she ventured. "Or was he your brother?"

"He was my wife's husband."

"Come again?"

"It's customary for our women to have multiple husbands. Sylem was Yy'voury's third husband. I'm her fourth and last."

"Oh. That's...interesting," she said lamely, causing him to chuckle. "I, um, how long you have you been married?"

"Ninety four years."

She choked. "Ninety four years? But you never told me you were married before!"

"It never came up."

"Never came up?" she cried, completely flustered.

"Relax. We view marriage differently than humans do."

"Apparently! Got any kids?"

"Yeah, eleven of them. Although," he added when she gasped, "probably only two of them are actually mine. In fact, most of them are the same age as I am, if not older."

"That's bizarre."

"I suppose. Anyway, what about you? What have you been up to? You were pretty hard to track down. I lost your trail in the Gouldrion Forest. Thought I'd never find you."

"Nothing. Traveling. That's all."

"For two years? What have you been doing for money?"

She frowned. This was definitely not a subject open to discussion. Although she had convinced herself that becoming an assassin didn't bother her, and she doubted it was possible for Revik to think any less of her than he must already, she still didn't want him to know about it. "Odd jobs," she replied finally.

"Like what?"

"Like none of your goddamned business, that's what!"

She stomped ahead. Revik sped up to match her pace.

"Sevy—"

"What?!"

"It's good to see you again." He smiled. "I missed you."

Her shoulders sagged and she smiled meekly back at him. "You too, Revik."

"Even if you are still a pain in the ass."

Chapter 6

"Are you all right?"

"Sure, why wouldn't I be?"

They stood in front of the Bloody Heart for the first time since their less than glamorous departure. She felt nauseated, but refused to let it show. At least she could take comfort in the fact that Revik seemed to be feeling the same uneasiness. He had grown quiet. The hold that this neighborhood had on them was still strong, even after all this time.

They went to the house first, and Sevy nearly cried out when she saw it in ruins. Only one wall remained upright and it was thoroughly scorched, evidence that a large fire had swept through. Judging by the amount of garbage on top of the rubble, the house had been destroyed months ago. Even the courtyard tree that shaded her room was gone, chopped down. Revik sifted through the debris, but found nothing of significance. Nothing to suggest what started the fire or what happened to those inside.

In a way, it was a relief. It probably would have hurt more to see the house as she remembered. At least now she couldn't imagine that Jarro was still somewhere inside. There was no opportunity for flights of fancy, for thinking that they could simply pick up where they left off and step back into their old lives. Like a gravestone, the ruins of the house marked the death of the past that Sevy had cherished so dearly.

The Bloody Heart looked the same as it had before, although maybe there were a few more scuffs and scratches on the door. Revik walked in first, and after a beat Sevy followed.

It reeked of sweat and blood, but she breathed it all in, comforted by the familiarity. The smells and sounds drew out memories long forgotten. Happy memories that made her eyes mist.

She studied the faces around her. Some she recognized, but most were unknown to her. She didn't see anyone from the old gang. The only one she could place for certain was Vipin, still as fat and as surly as the day she met him. As Sevy and Revik approached, his eyebrow rose.

She could tell he recognized them too, although he tried to conceal it.

"What'll you have?" he asked carefully.

"Information." Revik flicked a gold coin onto the counter. "What happened to the house down the street?"

"Burnt."

"Well, obviously. When? How?"

Vipin crossed his arms and smacked his lips, considering his reply. "About a year ago."

Sevy sighed. This was getting them nowhere. She leaned across the bar and grabbed the front of his apron, jerking him towards her. Face to face, she stared him down until he looked away.

"Where's Bolozi?"

"I, uh, can't say as I know that name."

"Bullshit! You know Bolozi, just like you know who we are. Tell me what I want to know, or I'm going to take you for a walk outside."

"Sevy." Revik touched her arm.

"I'm warning you, old man. I don't like having my time wasted," she continued, ignoring Revik.

"Sevy!"

"What?" She turned her head to yell at him and saw that they were now surrounded by ten men. A couple of them cracked their knuckles. One ran his finger down the blade of a knife. Despite their glares, Sevy was unimpressed by their little displays of dominance. She let go of Vipin and stood tall, her hand sliding to the hilt of her sword. "Got something to say, or are you just going to stand there gawking like half-wits?"

A heavily muscled man stepped forward. He smelt like the oil rich women used to style their hair, and either he had the thickest eyelashes she had ever seen, or he was wearing kohl. She found it humorous that this pretty boy appeared to be the leader of this group.

"Take your business elsewhere. We don't deal with his kind," he said, looking Revik up and down in disgust.

Revik laughed. "And just who might you be?"

"Name's Orius and this is my neighborhood."

"Really?" Sevy asked, her interest sparked. "Well then, maybe you can be more helpful than this old idiot. We're looking for Bolozi."

He moved closer, towering over her, an obvious intimidation tactic. "I guess you didn't hear me so good the first time. I said get out."

Sevy pouted playfully before kicking him in the groin. When he folded over, she grabbed his head and cracked it against her knee. He fell face first onto the floor, blood gushing from his nose.

Two of his men leapt at her. Revik pulled out his sword and cut them down before they reached her. He beheaded another who came at them from the side, and then in one light jump, he crossed the room and impaled two more men before they had a chance to draw their weapons. He looked down at his blade with a smile, obviously impressed with himself. The remaining thugs, not so brave now that their numbers had been reduced, took off running.

Sevy turned back to Vipin with a sweet smile as she dug the heel of her boot into Orius' hand. The barkeeper watched, terrified, as Orius writhed.

"Where's Bolozi?" she repeated.

"I dunno," Vipin gasped. "He left after the fire!"

"Tell me exactly what happened." She pressed her foot down harder, and Vipin flinched as the bones snapped.

"The redhead came looking for you. You know who I mean? Bolozi and her had words, I don't know what about. Then the men started dying."

"How?"

"Just like Jarro. Bolozi said it was you," Vipin said, with a nod towards Revik. "He put a price out on both your heads, said someone would pay for your whereabouts. But then the house burnt down. Weren't many that got out alive. Bolozi did though. I seen him running fast as he could, even while his men screamed and burned."

"Where is he now?"

"I hear he's holed up in Lornian. Lives above a dancing parlor or something. And that's all I know, I swear."

Sevy turned on her heel, eliciting one final whimper from Orius before she stepped off his hand. She heard Revik throw another coin at Vipin before following her outside.

They didn't speak until they reached Lornian. The change there was dramatic. Without Jarro to look out for them, the madams hadn't the strength to maintain their sanctuary. It was now a slum, like any other. The girls standing on the corners were black-and-blue and toothless, eyes glazed over with shame and fear. Sevy wondered what had become of Ponarelle. Imagining that nice old lady subjected to living like this was terribly saddening. It was too much to hope that she had escaped the city, so Sevy prayed that she was dead.

They spent more time in Lornian than Sevy cared for, scouring through brothels and dance halls, coming up empty handed each time. Her mood grew fouler by the minute, though Revik seemed to be enjoying himself. He ordered a drink at each place they visited and paid more attention to the working girls than he did to the men hanging around.

Sevy finished searching the upper level of a particularly ratty building that had once been a stately home and, coming back downstairs, was infuriated to see Revik chatting up one of the whores. She grabbed his cloak and yanked him outside.

"Hey, watch it!" He pulled free.

"Bolozi's not here. Let's go."

"I wasn't done talking to her."

"Oh yes, you were. Honestly, you're as bad as Jarro," she muttered, before realizing what she had said.

Revik chuckled. "I'll take that as a compliment. But listen, I was asking her about Bolozi. She knows him. He lives in the apartments above the hall."

"I just went through those rooms. He wasn't there."

"You wanna bet? Don't you remember how fast word travels around here?"

She followed him back inside and up the stairs. Revik put his finger to his lips and she rolled her eyes. Obviously she wasn't going to start talking. Did he think she was new at this? He motioned her towards a doorway while he took the one opposite.

He began counting to three, mouthing the words silently, but she didn't feel like playing this stupid cloak and dagger game. If Bolozi was there, she'd find him. She kicked the door in.

From the hallway, she heard Revik curse her. She scanned the room. It was empty like she knew it would be. She clomped back out into the hall.

"He's not there."

"Would you just shut it for one minute?"

He pressed his ear against the remaining door and closed his eyes, listening. She tapped her foot. Without looking at her, he lifted his hand and flicked her forehead. She had to laugh, even though it smarted. Suddenly, he pulled away from the door and banged it open.

The room was just as empty as the other. She was about to mock him, but then Revik darted across the room, unsheathed his sword, and poked it into the back of a fireplace.

"Ah! Watch it!" a familiar voice cried.

"Come out of there, you stupid ass."

Bricks scraped together as they were pushed aside, and soot rose in a thick cloud. Bolozi crawled out, filthy and fat. The years had not been kind to his waistline. Sevy was surprised that he had been able to squeeze his girth into such a small space.

He scrambled to his feet and eyed them nervously. "Uh, hello."

Sevy burst out laughing. "Hello? Is that all you've got to say?" She retrieved her dagger from her boot, nice and slow, so that Bolozi had time to appreciate his situation. "How about 'I'm sorry'? Or even better…'No,

Sevy, please don't kill me!'"

He gulped. "I...I'm sorry?"

She grinned and pressed her blade into the folds of skin on his throat, drawing a thin line of blood. Revik put his hand on her shoulder. Although she wanted to gut the pig right then and there she knew that they needed him. For now anyway.

She stepped back and watched as Revik paced in front of their captive. "We need to know a few things," he said. "And you're going to cooperate with us, aren't you?"

Bolozi gave a frantic nod.

"Tell us what happened back at the house. And you'd better tell us everything."

"What do you wanna know?"

Sevy stepped forward again. "Irea. We know she showed up. What did she say to you?"

"Irea? You mean the elf? She showed up about a year after...after you left. She said she'd pay for information about you two. I told her not to get her hopes up because I didn't think the ra...Revik was still alive."

"Go on," Sevy growled.

"She didn't believe it. Said she knew you better. And she said that we'd better start looking, or else."

"Or else what?"

He gulped again. "She said she'd do like she'd done before. And then she turned into a monster. All roasted and dead looking. Killed one of my men, just like she did Jarro." He shifted his eyes towards Sevy. "Then she says she's staying in the city and wants us to report to her. But she didn't wanna wait. She got angry when we couldn't find you. Killed a bunch more men. Burned the place down. I barely got out. She's mad, that one."

"Where was she staying?" Revik asked.

"I dunno. And I ain't seen her since. Not that I went looking."

Revik and Sevy looked at one another. Bolozi began to inch himself towards the door. "She's probably still around. I can try to find out for you. I've still got some contacts. You wanna get her, right? For Jarro? I can help you."

"No, I think that's all the use we have for you. Revik?"

Bolozi's jaw dropped, which pushed all of his chins together so that he looked rather like a bullfrog. "Now, Revik, I know I did you wrong, but I've paid for my mistakes. I mean, look at me! Look at this place. I've got nothing left!"

"That's not entirely true," Revik said as he twirled his sword around. "You do have one thing left that I don't."

Sevy barely saw the blade as it struck out and cut Bolozi's arm off. She grimaced at the spray of blood that hit her face. It was slimy, just like him. Bolozi shrieked. He fell to his knees and clutched at the gory stump with his remaining arm.

Revik watched the spectacle with cold, unblinking eyes for a long moment before turning and leaving the room. "Coming?"

"I'll be right there."

Sevy bent down and grabbed Bolozi's chin, forcing it up so she could look him in the eyes.

"Please," he sobbed, "help me!"

She blew him a kiss and rammed her dagger deep into his throat. Blood flooded into his mouth, choking him. She yanked the dagger back out and stepped to the side so that she wouldn't cushion his fall. Then she wiped her blade off on the back of his shirt, and spat on the body before joining Revik outside.

※

Sevy tried to hide her pity when Revik announced that he was going to write a letter to his wife. Little actions, as simple as untying his pack to retrieve a sheet of parchment, a quill, and a bottle of black ink were drawn out ordeals for him, but he didn't utter one word of complaint. Sevy absorbed herself in what was left of her dinner to keep from yanking the quill from his hand. She knew he was too proud to accept her help, and he did seem to have everything under control. He placed a wine bottle on the top corner of the page to hold it steady, and began writing furiously.

She wondered what he was telling his wife. Since learning that he was married and had children, she had been trying to picture Revik as a family man, but it was impossible to reconcile that notion with the man she knew. The same person who taught her how to fight and kill, changing diapers and reading bedtime stories? It just seemed wrong. Fathers were supposed to be, well, fatherly. Revik was too wild for that sort of thing.

And then she began wondering what type of woman Yy'voury was. Did it bother her that Revik had lived in Eloria for over a decade by himself? Did it bother her that Revik was here now? Though with so many husbands to manage, maybe she was happy for a break. Curiosity nibbled at Sevy, and she tried to sneak a peek at what Revik was writing. She leaned forward, pretending to yawn and stretch so she could get a better look.

"Can I help you?" he asked.

She sat back, embarrassed. "No. Sorry. I just, um..."

"I didn't know you could read Femoanese."

"What? Uh, no. I can't."

"I'm telling her about our progress," Revik offered, as he continued to write. "But I'm leaving out the part about Bolozi. Even though she doesn't like humans, she's not one for revenge or violence. It upsets her."

"She doesn't like humans?"

Revik looked up at her with a strange smile. "Not many of us do."

"Really?"

"That surprises you?"

"Huh? Well, no. Just never thought about it, I guess."

"But of course, you should know by now that I don't share the same prejudices that most of my people do."

"Right. Of course. Yeah, I know that."

He bent his head back down, dipped his quill in fresh ink, and resumed his letter. Sevy fiddled with her cutlery and plate until a barmaid came and took them away. Bereft of that distraction, she leaned her chin against her hand and watched Revik again. "What's your wife like?"

Another odd smile. "She's a good woman, a good mother. She's strong. Stubborn. Kind of like you."

Sevy pouted. "I am not stubborn."

"No, of course you're not."

"Does she know that I'm here with you? Does she know about...?" Sevy realized that she was skirting around an uncomfortable subject, and began stammering. "What I mean is, does she have a problem with me? I mean, because I'm human? You know, since she doesn't like humans."

"She knew I was looking for you. She knows all about you. I've told her everything. In fact, I'm not allowed to tell any more stories about the gang. She got sick of hearing them. Thinks that they'll be a bad influence on the children."

"Oh, so she knows about that. I was wondering. About that. So she knows...everything?"

He held her eyes for a moment. "Everything."

Sevy didn't quite know how to respond.

Revik finished the letter. It took some time for him to maneuver it into the envelope and then seal it with wax. Once he was done he called the barmaid over. She promised to post it for him, but only after he placed a few coins into her waiting hand. That task done, he poured himself another glass of wine and relaxed into his chair.

"I was thinking about something the Barren Mage told me."

"The who?"

"The Barren Mage. She's like a priestess. She said we should consult with an elf scholar to learn more about the demon Irea's become."

"Why? I know enough."

He rolled his eyes. "So we can find out how to kill her. She was able to mist through my dagger. I don't know if weapons can hurt her."

"Maybe you just weren't fast enough."

"What's that supposed to mean?"

"Nothing! Fine, we'll go interrogate an elf."

"Not interrogate. Just ask a few questions. There used to be an old one at the Royal Library. I forget his name, but Jarro used to mention him, remember? We should talk to him."

"All right." She rose from her seat.

"Not right now! I want to finish my drink first."

She sighed. She had forgotten how bossy Revik could be. Sevy had never been very good about taking orders from anyone. Anyone except Jarro that was.

Jarro...

She tried to force him from her thoughts. She didn't want to think about him. It was too distracting. She should think about Irea, about how great it would feel to butcher her. She needed to focus on her anger, to call forth the incredible fury that had been repressed for two long years.

But it was too late. She was already summoning his face to her mind. That big smile that always came so easily and so often to his lips. The sound of his laugh. She missed that laugh. The world was meaningless without it.

Her chest hitched and Revik turned to look at her. "Something wrong?"

She tried to fake a smile. "Don't mind me. Just a little drunk is all."

Revik regarded her in sympathy before reaching over and squeezing her hand. "I'm sorry. This must be hard on you."

She shrugged and looked away, hoping that he wouldn't see the tears forming.

"You don't have to hide it, Sevy. I know how much you loved him."

"What? Love? I didn't. I mean, I..."

"Don't be embarrassed. He loved you too. Everyone could see it."

"What? No." She jumped to her feet, but tripped over her chair. She didn't let Revik help her up. "No. He was my friend and—"

"Where are you going?"

"I need some air."

Sevy rushed out of the tavern, knocking people out of her way. Just as she had done as a child, she ran from what she feared, ran from what she didn't want to accept. Street after street, alley after alley, stopping only when her legs insisted upon it. Then she slumped against a wall, breathless and shaken. Bunching her hands into fists, Sevy pressed them to her eyes to stop the flood that spilled down her face.

Stupid! You're so stupid!

What was wrong with her? It had been two years. Why did she still feel like this? Why couldn't she let go? And why did Revik say those things? Was he trying to drive her mad? She tried to calm down and suppress her cries, but they escaped her throat in strangled sobs.

"Sevy?"

She hurriedly wiped her face with her sleeves before glancing up. Revik was beside her. He pulled her into a hug and forced her head against his shoulder.

"It's all right," he murmured. "It's all right."

Sevy couldn't control the emotions that came pouring out. Gripping Revik's tunic, she wept longer and harder than she had since Jarro's funeral. She could picture Revik as a father now. It made perfect sense. He was so gentle, so devoted. Even after all the pain she had caused him. Gradually, her cries lessened and she sniffled softly.

"It's all right," Revik said again. "You aren't alone anymore."

He always knew just what to say. Gods, she had been such a fool to abandon him. As he held her, she felt warm and protected, something she had not felt in a long time. Not since that night.

She stiffened. This was dangerous. And wrong. So very wrong.

Revik kissed the side of her head. She jerked free.

"Sevy? What is it?"

"What the hell was that? Just what are you trying to do?"

"What do you mean?"

"Don't play dumb!" she yelled, pushing him away. "You know what I mean. You kissed me. Why did you do that?"

"I was just trying—"

"I know what you were trying! And here I thought you were my friend. I thought you actually cared."

"I do care!" he protested. He raised his hand to stroke her cheek. She slapped it away.

"Don't touch me! I know what you were trying to do!" She stormed down the alley, muttering over her shoulder. "Well, you're out of luck. It's not going to happen. Not this time!"

"Excuse me?" he said, raising his voice. He took hold of her with that damned iron grip he was so good at, and made her face him. "If you're talking about what happened that night, as I recall, you're the one who started it."

"I was grieving. You took advantage of that."

"Oh please! Like anyone could ever take advantage of you. What is wrong with you?"

"You're what's wrong with me!"

"Oh, go fuck yourself! You're even more deluded than I thought if you mistake me trying to comfort you for coming on to you!"

"I am not deluded!"

"Right. Whatever you say." He pushed her aside and marched up the street.

"Where are you going?"

"Anywhere to get away from you."

"Wait!"

"Why?"

"Because...because..." She just couldn't force the words out. She frowned at her feet. Revik started laughing and she glared back up at him. "What's so funny?"

"You are, you lunatic."

"Jackass."

"Bitch."

Her mouth twitched into a grin. "One-armed freak!"

"Finished? Then let's go."

"Where?"

"To the library, stupid."

They walked half a block before she built up enough nerve to stop him. "Revik?"

"Yeah?"

"Thank you."

Chapter 7

The Royal Library towered above the crumbling mansions of the western quarters. It was a massive structure, dwarfed only by Eagleborn Castle itself. In its day, it had been the pinnacle of extravagance, a symbol of the prosperity and influence of the royal family. The king used to spend hours there, though not actually reading, just being out among his public. To see and be seen. It had been more of a social setting for the well-to-do than an actual place of learning.

Since leaving Eloria for the northern city of Wilrendel, King Grewid had allotted fewer and fewer grants for the upkeep of the library, and over time it had become a mere shadow of its former glory. The once imposing columns were deteriorating at their bases. It wouldn't be long until they collapsed and brought down the entire entablature. The gargoyles and statues nestled in amongst the massive walls were pock marked by the weather, their features more unrecognizable each year.

The soggy smell of mildew overpowered Sevy and Revik as they ventured inside. They walked through the aisles, gazing up at row upon row of rotting books that probably had not been opened since they were bound. It was depressing and claustrophobic, but Jarro had loved it. He had spent many afternoons here, rummaging around. Sevy smiled, remembering how excited he'd be when he found a long sought after book hidden amongst the stacks. Knowledge was better than any treasure, he would tell her. She never fully understood what he meant by that. You couldn't buy food with knowledge.

Today, the library was deserted save for a few beggars and the occasional world-weary student. Sevy exchanged a look of surprise with Revik when they turned a corner and saw two miniscule gnomes sitting on the floor, leafing through a tome almost as large as they were.

"Hello," Revik said. "Maybe you can help us."

The gnomes hopped up and dusted each other off. "Who are they, do you think?" the bigger one said.

"Couldn't tell you," the other replied.

"And I couldn't tell you."

"Better just ignore them then." They nodded, sat back down, and returned to their book.

"Hey!" Sevy said. "Maybe you didn't hear him. He said we need your help."

The gnomes jumped again as though they had completely forgotten that Sevy and Revik were there. They stared up at them with wide eyes. Sevy sighed. *Gnomes!*

"We're looking for the elf that used to work here a few years back. Is he still around?" Revik said, trying to keep a straight face.

The gnomes bent their heads close to each other and conferred quietly before one of them answered, "Yes."

"Well then, can you take us to him?"

They whispered together once more. Sevy growled with impatience. Finally, they looked back up. "Yes. Follow us."

The gnomes continued to whisper to one another, and shot nervous glances over their shoulders as Sevy and Revik followed them through the maze of books. After minutes of twists and turns, the gnomes suddenly stopped. They scratched their heads and looked confused.

"Is there a problem?" Revik asked.

"That's a loaded question if ever I've heard one."

"Yes, loaded indeed."

The bigger gnome looked at Revik. "Which problem did you have in mind?"

"Sorry?"

The gnomes clucked their tongues and stroked their beards. "How can we say if a problem is there or not if you don't even know which one you're asking about?"

Revik looked at Sevy in bewilderment, and then laughed. However, she was not so easily amused. She bent down and grabbed the taller gnome by the beard. "Listen, you little twit, enough with the double talk. Bring us to the elf!"

The gnome squeaked and pulled away. He embraced his friend as he glared at her. "No double talk! Why would we double talk when you don't look smart enough to single talk?"

"Yes, not smart enough at all!"

"Oh, for..." She put her hand to the hilt of her sword.

They squealed at the top of their lungs, clutching each other in fear. Revik put his hand on her shoulder. "Leave them alone."

"They're fucking with us!"

"No, no, Miss! We would not do that!"

"No, Miss, most assuredly not! You are far too unattractive for that!"

Sevy's mouth dropped open and Revik fell against the shelves from the force of his laughter. "They're just gnomes, Sevy."

"They'll be dead gnomes if they don't start cooperating."

Revik crouched down and whispered something, after which he and the two gnomes all turned to look up at Sevy. The gnomes sniggered behind their hands, and then started walking again. Revik followed and Sevy trailed behind, grumbling to herself.

After another five minutes, they arrived at a doorway. "See?" Revik said. "You just have to use a little common courtesy."

The gnomes scurried off while Revik knocked. Sevy muscled him out of the way and banged on the door.

"Come in."

Sitting behind a massive desk, piled with parchments and books, was an elf. His skin was pasty. Obviously, he spent more time with his books than he did outside. Dust speckled the top of his corkscrew of blond hair.

He looked up from the stack of papers and adjusted his spectacles. "Yes? What can I do for you?"

"I take it you're the resident librarian?" Revik asked.

"Who else would I be?"

"We need some information and thought you might be able to help us out."

"I am very busy, as you can plainly see."

Revik raised his hand up to stop Sevy before she could yell. He pulled a bag of coins out of his pack and plunked it on top of one of the books on the desk.

"We'd like to know about the Grave Chasm. My village's Barren Mage thought that an elf scholar would be able to tell us about it."

He snorted. "A barren mage? I daresay I can tell you more than those old biddies ever could. What exactly did you need to know?"

"She spoke of an ancient demon. One that lives in shadow and drinks blood. She believes that it existed prior to the Great Chasm, and that the Alfar people knew of it. Can you tell us anything more?"

"As per usual, the ignorance of dark elves comes shining through. Your mage would do better selling love charms and hexes than teaching history she clearly knows nothing of."

"Then please enlighten us if you're so damned smart," Sevy said.

"I know the demon of which you speak. It is too foul to merit a name. They did not exist prior to the Time of Sagacity...or the Grave Chasm, if you prefer," he said with a smirk. "Rather, they are a product of that era."

He sat back and smiled smugly, basking in the knowledge he held over them. Clearly it wasn't every day he received an audience to his brilliance—he was as much a relic as the entire library was—and so he was greatly enjoying himself. Sevy tapped her thumb on the sheath of her sword, waiting for him to continue.

"They are creatures of Chaos, born from the Dark God to upset the balance of nature. Their souls exist in a state between this realm and the next."

"So your gods created these monsters?" Sevy asked.

The elf sighed and shook his head. "You would not know this, human, but there are five gods. Five true gods. Not the multitude of spirits and specters that your kind reveres. Humans. You'd worship a rock if the mood struck you."

"Get on with it!"

"There are four gods of balance, each controlling an aspect of the universe. Nature, knowledge, fortune, and justice respectively. They keep the world constant. The fifth god, Chencholor, is the God of Chaos. He revels in disrupting the work of the other gods in any way that he can. This is why he is known as the Dark God.

"At the Time of Sagacity, the gods of balance took pity on mortals. They descended from their divine sphere so that they could better hear the prayers of their followers. They taught us ways to bend the universe to our favor. My people remained devout while yours," he looked down his nose at Revik, "chose the way of the heathen. We embraced the wisdom granted us, but the dark elves began to think of themselves as equals to the gods. Worshipping their ancestors...it's appalling."

Sevy bristled. "Mind the insults or you'll regret it."

"Just let him talk."

Exasperated, she paced back and forth, kicking at random piles of clutter.

"Please, continue," Revik said.

"While the attentions of the other four gods were distracted, Chencholor was able to seize a handful of strength from Reyla, the goddess of nature. He then forged an alliance with the dark elves. In exchange for promises of immortality, he was given living sacrifices. With Reyla's stolen strength, he poisoned these lives, twisting them into demons that are neither living nor dead. By doing so, not only was the balance of nature disrupted, but the balances of justice, fortune, and knowledge as well.

"Reyla was alerted to the presence of these demonic forms. She and Chencholor waged a great battle and she emerged victorious, regaining her full power. While she could not undo the damage he had done, she was able to reinstate some degree of control by placing the final fate of all mortal beings upon the demons. While they may exist outside the laws of nature for a time, their bodies inexorably rot. They soon wither and die. Balance is then restored. And so Chencholor's scheme was undone.

"The demons appealed to Chencholor, and he did manage to find a way to extend their unholy lives. By devouring blood, they are able to retain their bodies for a longer period of time. But this only prolongs the inevitable. They will eventually return to Reyla's embrace."

Sevy pursed her lips. "That's a nice little bedtime story, but it doesn't tell us anything useful. How do we kill these things? How do we track them?"

"That I do not know."

"What? Why not?"

"These demons died out millennia upon millennia ago. They are merely a footnote in history. Some claim they never actually existed. There is no need to know how to fight them."

Sevy grabbed his robes. "I have a need, so you'd better crack open your books and get me an answer!"

"Sevy, let him go."

"No! I'm sick of these stupid games. First those damned gnomes, now this asshole elf. I don't have time for this! You hear me?" She shook the librarian, and then slammed him into the back of his chair.

"That's enough!" Revik said.

She spun round, eyes narrowed into slits. "Whose side are you on?"

"Just calm down."

"I am calm!"

The elf rose from his desk and tiptoed towards the door. Sevy leapt after him. "Where do you think you're going?"

"I...I was going, I mean, I have to consult the...consult the books..."

"Sevy—"

"Shut up, Revik! Listen, elf, I'm warning you, you better tell me what I want to hear!"

"Sevy!"

"What now?"

"Do you smell that?"

What a ridiculous thing to say at that moment. But then she began to smell it too. A kind of burning, very potent and harsh.

"So?"

"That smell. It's the same as the night Sylem was killed."

She released the librarian, pushing both him and Revik to the ground, and raced out of the room.

"Goddammit, Sevy! Wait for me!"

"No!" She paused to slam the door shut, and used her dagger to jam the handle. "You stay there!"

There was something ahead of her, a wispy shadow that danced along the book shelves. She chased after it. She could hear Revik calling for her, pounding against the door, and she cursed him. Why didn't he just do what she said for once? This was her fight. He'd only get in her way.

She was now lost within the stacks of books. The shadow disappeared, but she could tell from the smell that it was still near. She slowed to a walk. Someone giggled, and then a handful of books fell down on Sevy's head. Wet wind raked across her side. Touching her face, she felt four cuts burnt into her cheek. Scratch marks.

The aisle ahead of her darkened by several shades and a squeal rang out. Moving forward cautiously, Sevy turned the corner and almost tripped over one of the gnomes.

"Get out of my way!"

The little thing stood stock still, transfixed. She followed his gaze to the next aisle where the other gnome was lying face down on the ground, twitching and shuddering. A shimmering red shadow hovered over top of him.

As she watched, the shadow solidified. The trunk of a body formed first. Next came an arm, and then another. A head appeared out of the swelling blackness. It laughed before suddenly speeding towards her. There was no time to react. Sevy was knocked off her feet.

The shadow shrouded her, and she gasped for air as it filled her mouth and nose with its foul stench. Her vision blurred. All she could see were bright red beads rising up into the air. Before she could guess what they were, excruciating pain devoured her mind. It felt as though she were being ripped apart, one piece at a time. The last thing Sevy was aware of before losing consciousness was black eyes staring at her, watching her with glee as the thing consumed her blood.

Chapter 8

She awoke with a groan. She tried to put her hands to her head, but found that she couldn't move. The best she could do was wiggle her hands, which made needles of pain shoot from her fingertips all the way to her shoulders.

"Wake-y, wake-y!" someone called to her in a singsong voice.

Sevy opened her eyes. It took some time before things shivered into focus. She was in a darkened room with roughly cut stone walls. A fire in a pit across from her gave just enough light to see a shadowed figure sitting on a bed in the corner.

"Who are you?" Sevy asked.

The figure rose from the bed and stepped into the firelight. It was a wrinkled, withered hag covered in rags and reeking of scorched flesh. "Three guesses."

"Irea!"

"Clever girl. Welcome to my home. It's so nice to see you again after all this time."

The rage surged swiftly, violently, instinctively. It compelled her to attack, but when she attempted to rush forward, she was jerked back. With a glance to her side, she realized she was chained to the wall.

Irea giggled and crossed the room to stand just inches from Sevy's face. The stink of sulfur overwhelmed Sevy, bringing tears to her eyes as she glared at Irea. Revik had been right. There was little left of the elf they once knew. The lovely amber eyes that Sevy remembered were replaced by dead pits, and the perfectly shaped rose of a mouth was now gnarled and wasted and twisted into a mad grin.

"Simmer down. I just want to talk to you, not fight."

"I'll tear you apart, bitch!" Sevy screamed and pulled against the chains, testing them, seeing if she could wrench free so that she could make good on her threat. "You killed Jarro!"

"Quit your squawking! It's unbecoming. Listen, I've had a long time to think things through, and I've come to a conclusion." She paused, obviously awaiting Sevy's reply.

Sevy refused to give Irea the satisfaction of talking with her and playing along with whatever sick game she had concocted. Instead, she twisted her hands again, trying to slip them from the shackles.

"My conclusion is that the two of us are not as unlike as I once thought."

Sevy snorted.

"No, it's true. We're just two women trying to get by in a man's world. Aren't we, Sevy darling? And we've both been terribly misused."

"My heart is bleeding for you, bitch."

"Oh, you! You're just being stubborn. Think about it, won't you? We both have done things we're not proud of. We've both made mistakes, but that's only because we know what we want and we'll do anything to get it."

Irea hobbled across the room and sat back down on the edge of the bed. She rummaged around in the covers until she pulled out something small, circular, and metal. Sevy saw the firelight shine off of it as Irea twirled it around her fingers.

"Poor, poor Sevy. You've had such a hard life. All you ever wanted was to be safe and loved. I realize that now. I forgive you for the way you treated me."

Sevy laughed. "Listen, if you're going to kill me, just go ahead. Otherwise shut your fucking mouth!"

"And really, when you think about it, I did you a favor by killing Jarro."

"Come closer and say that again," Sevy whispered, convulsing with hatred.

"What do you honestly think would have happened? Don't you know that history is doomed to repeat itself? He loved me once, you know. And look how easily he threw me aside. He would have done the same to you."

"Shut up! Just shut up!" Blood dripped from Sevy's wrists and dashed onto the stone floor from her struggles against the chains.

"All I ever wanted," Irea said quietly, ignoring her captive's frenzied attempts at freedom, "was to be in control of my own life. To not be at the mercy of a man's whims. This world is cruel, isn't it? You can't count on anyone but yourself."

"Am I supposed to feel sorry for you? Murderer! Demon!"

"Let me finish! I wanted power. I wanted strength. And now look at me. I have become much more than I ever dreamed possible."

"I still see the same whore you've always been."

Irea slid her tongue over her lips, wetting them enough to be able to grin as she weaved the metal object through her fingers again. "I've become strong. I've become the hunter. I've seized the power I used to beg for. There's just one problem. This body, this abomination that I've been transformed into...it's weakening. It decays with each passing hour. That's why I need you."

"Hah! You expect me to help you? You can rot in hell!"

"You'll help me. Because I have something you want."

"There's nothing I want except to see you die."

"Oh really?" Irea held up the metal object. It was an old copper coin, green with rust and mold. "Here. I believe this is yours."

She placed the coin in Sevy's hand, quickly pulling away before Sevy could sink her nails into Irea's rotten flesh. Disappointed that she had missed such an opportunity, Sevy frowned at the coin. Then she flipped it over.

Carved onto the opposite face of the coin was a large letter S. Sevy was struck with the sudden memory of that morning in the kitchen, of his smile, of his arms around her. It was followed by the memory of his cold skin, of kissing him one final time. Bile rushed into her mouth and she stared wide-eyed at Irea. "You monster! What have you done?"

Irea cackled, doubling over and clutching at her stomach as she caroused around the room in hysterics.

"What have you done?!"

"See for yourself!" Irea ripped the covers from the bed.

Sevy's squeezed her eyes shut, hoping that what she had seen wasn't really there. She couldn't resist looking again. A skeleton lay on the bed. The skull rested on the pillow and the boney arms were folded across the rib cage as if it were awaiting burial. Some scraps of skin were still clinging in spots, seemingly grafted over the withered tendons and ligaments that remained. Two rows of gleaming teeth gave the appearance of a macabre smile. The nose and eyes had long since sunken in, and all that remained of the hair was a matted mass plastered against the top of the skull. But it was him.

"Oh my gods," Sevy moaned. "Jarro! Oh my gods!"

"Behold your love in all his glory!" Irea shouted before collapsing with laughter against the wall.

"You sick fuck! You sick fuck!" Sevy teetered on the edge of madness. She banged her head back against the stone wall to break herself out of this sickening nightmare. Tears streamed down her face and she felt like she was suffocating.

Above it all was a blinding fury, more intense than anything she had ever experienced before. She gnashed her teeth together and strained against the chains, praying with all her might to hear the metal creak, to hear it break, so that she could pounce on Irea and choke out what little life remained in her.

Irea's laughter stopped. She grabbed Sevy's face in her claws. "Do you understand yet? Do you understand?"

"Get your hands off of me!" She was so angry that she couldn't speak further. Her words garbled together, forming an incoherent protest that she shrieked at the top of her lungs.

Irea punched her across the face to quiet her. It didn't work. She struck again and again, and tried to yell over Sevy's cries, "I'll give you him! I'll give you everything you've ever wanted! I'll give you him!"

Sevy stopped screaming. Her throat burned as she panted for breath.

"I have the power to bring him back to you," Irea purred. "All you have to do is help me."

Sevy darted her eyes to Jarro's body. Was it possible? "What...what do you want?"

"You and Jarro, you betrayed me. You cast me out. But I don't care about that now. I could have gotten by just fine if not for Revik."

"Revik?"

Irea put her hand to her cheek and looked at the fire. "You call me a monster. It was Revik that made me one. He mutilated me. He took away my beauty, my livelihood. No man wanted me. I was a disfigured freak. What else could I do except go back home and convince my family to help me? Even they refused me. So I prayed. I prayed and I prayed. And I suppose I went a little mad." She giggled. "After four hundred years, you'd think I'd have known that the gods don't listen to prayers. That is, all the gods save one. Chencholor took pity on me. He came to me in the night and whispered secrets to me. Magiks that could restore my beauty. That could make me powerful and could help me get revenge on my enemies." Irea looked down at her hands, so wasted that the firelight shone through them. "Revik made me a demon. And you are going to help me change that."

"How?"

"Chencholor still whispers to me. He told me of a spell that will let me keep the strength this form allows me, and have none of the weaknesses. I just require two final ingredients. The Eye of Annu-nial. Have you heard of it?"

"Yes." She paused and looked warily at Irea. "Why can't you get it yourself if you're so powerful?"

"I can't enter the temple. It is protected against me. Only a human can retrieve it for me."

"Why me?"

"You never take anything on faith, do you? Very wise. It's quite simple, really. Because Revik trusts you."

Sevy frowned and Irea sighed in disdain. "Come on, Sevy, keep up! Revik is the final ingredient. Chencholor doesn't help mortals for free. He requires a sacrifice."

"You want me to betray Revik? Never!"

Irea shook her head in exaggerated slowness, and walked over to the bed. She looked down at Jarro's body and placed her hands on his. Closing her eyes, she spoke in an odd tongue. The steady rhythm of the words suggested that it was some sort of chant or incantation. Sevy watched in disgusted fascination as Irea used one of Jarro's skeletal fingers to slit her wrists open. Dark clots oozed out of her, and she continued to mumble as his chest cavity filled with her blood. She glanced over her shoulder at Sevy. "You will bring me the Eye and you will bring me Revik. In exchange..."

The blood twinkled in the firelight and suddenly took on a life of its own. It spread across the body, coating each bone and every bit of remaining flesh. The body quivered, just slightly at first then increasing in vigor until it shook so much that it moved about the bed. Irea held her hands above it and raised her voice, continuing the spell. The louder she spoke, the more the body thrashed.

The blood grew thicker. It solidified and gave Jarro's body proper form. The concave chest rose, the hollowed nose took shape, the bones were no longer visible. They receded, giving way to muscle and sinew. Amongst the glittering wetness of jellied blood, tiny shoots of flesh snaked out, forming a mesh that resembled skin. Within a matter of minutes, in place of the desiccated skeleton lay Jarro, just as Sevy remembered him.

Irea grinned. "Impressive, no?"

Sevy could do nothing, say nothing. Her mouth was open though no sound would come out.

"Now watch this!" Irea bent down and appeared to kiss him. Instantly, his chest heaved. He was breathing!

"What do you say? Do we have a deal?" Irea was at Sevy's side, holding up a key. She began unlocking the chains, but stopped to give Sevy a stern look. "A word of caution. Don't try anything foolish. You have a choice. Help me and Jarro is yours forever. This means, of course, that Revik will die. You can't have them both. I gave Jarro new life and I can take it away any time I want. His life is bound to mine. If I die, he dies. Understand?"

Sevy was mesmerized by each breath he took, each movement he made. She was vaguely aware that Irea had undone the locks. Now free, Sevy staggered towards the bed. "Jarro?"

"Do we have a deal?"

Gods forgive me...
"Yes."

Chapter 9

For two years, night after lonely night, Sevy had dreamed of this moment. She played it out in her head, fantasizing about every last detail. She knew exactly what she would say, and exactly how he would respond. It would be beautiful. A magical storybook ending to share with their children and grandchildren.

Yet now that it was happening, all of her carefully rehearsed words were lost. She remained motionless on a chair next to the bed. How long she had been sitting there, staring at him, she couldn't say.

Jarro slept uneasily, trembling and sweating, crying out every now and again. She wanted to comfort him somehow, to reach out and touch him. She longed to hold him and feel warm, living flesh instead of the cold hardness she all too vividly remembered. But she was terrified that if she did touch him, the spell would be broken and he would fade into nothingness again.

The fire crackled and popped, casting shadows around the room, but lighting him up perfectly. She studied his face, searching for some sign that this was Jarro and not some cruel deception Irea devised to torture her with. He was exactly as Sevy remembered. His face, his hair, the scar on his cheek. He even smelled the same.

She couldn't sit here like this forever. She had to know the truth. Timidly, she reached out to touch his hand.

Before she could, his eyes fluttered open and fixed onto the stalactites on the ceiling. She froze, fingers just inches away from his. He didn't show any sign of knowing she was there next to him, and Sevy wasn't sure if he was truly awake or not. But then his chest moved up and down in violent gasps—he was panicking.

Sevy touched his hand and moaned at the warmth. He didn't react. "Jarro?"

He blinked twice, but she couldn't tell if he had heard her.

"Jarro?" she repeated, pressing down on his hand.

His breathing slowed, and without turning his head, he looked at her. Oh, but those eyes! The exact shade of blue she remembered. A tear rolled down her cheek as she leaned forward. "Can you hear me?"

His lips parted, trying to form a word. Nothing came out except for a small puff of air. He frowned and tried again. "Sevy."

It was too much to bear. She hid her face against his arm. Suddenly, she felt something touch her head. It was Jarro, caressing her hair with his free hand. How had it come to pass that a dead man was trying to comfort her? And how like Jarro it was. It gave her hope that this wasn't just a trick.

"Is it really you?" she asked.

His chin trembled as he gaped at her in confusion. Was it that he didn't understand the question or that he didn't know the answer? "I think so."

"How can I be sure?"

"I...where am I?"

"Tell me your name," she said, forcing him to focus on her instead of his surroundings.

"Jarro."

"Where are you from?"

"Devenbourn. How did I get here?"

"Where am I from?"

"What? Sevy, I..."

"Answer me!"

"W-Willing's Cove."

"Tell me something that only you and I would know."

"I..."

"Please," she whispered.

Silence. Jarro stared at his hands then touched his face, his throat, his chest. He grimaced, shutting his eyes and opening them again as if he expected the room to have changed in the interim.

Sevy was about to repeat her question when he looked back at her and said, "I wanted to kiss you."

"What?"

"By the fountain. I wanted to kiss you."

"Oh gods." Sevy buried her head against him again. She held him tightly, almost cruelly, afraid to let go, afraid he would slip away again.

"I don't understand. Where am I? What happened?"

Her eyes widened. What was he asking? How much did he remember? She didn't want to upset him. He seemed so frail.

"You're with me now. Rest."

"I remember eyes," he whimpered. "Her eyes in the dark. And, and pain."

"Ssh." Sevy stroked his cheek to soothe him as best she could.

"Was I...? I was...dead. Wasn't I?"

After a moment, she nodded. He swallowed and turned to stare back up at the ceiling.

"Jarro? Are you all right?"

"How long?"

"Two years."

He closed his eyes. "Is there any whiskey?" he asked finally.

She laughed, crying at the same time. "It is you! I thought I'd...oh gods, Jarro! You don't know how much I've missed you."

He squeezed her hand, but said nothing.

"Without you, I did terrible things. I wanted to die with you. I couldn't...without you, I..." She dissolved into tears.

He tugged on her hand. That was all the prompting she needed. She joined him on the bed and wrapped her arms around him. Breathing in deeply, Sevy held onto Jarro as to a lifeline in a squall. The smell of the grave still clung to him, but she pushed it aside.

"Irea," he said. "She did this. I feel her. Inside of me. Where is she?"

She was frightened by the implications of his words, but did not let him see this. "I don't know. She left awhile ago. She said she'd be back in the morning."

"I don't understand. How? What happened?"

"She has some sort of power now. Don't ask me to explain. I don't really understand it myself. She used her magic to bring you back to life."

"Why?"

Sevy leaned up on her elbow and looked away while she conjured an answer. She didn't want to lie to him, but she couldn't tell him the truth. The basic facts were enough, she decided.

"She's sick and wants me to help heal her. She needs me to get her the Eye of Annu."

"And that's all?"

He couldn't know about Revik. He wouldn't allow it. He wouldn't be able to live with himself if he knew.

"Yes," she said, swallowing the sear of the lie. "That's all. And then she'll let us go. We can be together again, like before."

He shook his head. "We can't believe a thing she says. You can't help her."

"But—"

"No!"

Why was he arguing? Why was he making this harder than it had to be? "What choice do I have? I won't lose you again, Jarro! Never again! I can't!"

"Do you honestly think she'll let us live in peace?"

"We'll run away. She won't be able to find us," Sevy said, clutching him desperately.

"She'll find us. I feel different. It's like she's a part of me. Inside my head. In my blood. Sevy, this feels wrong."

"I don't care! I won't lose you again! I won't! You don't know what it was like! Oh gods, Jarro, please! Please don't leave me again! Please!"

"Ssh, sweetheart, don't cry."

He kissed her. His lips were warm and soft against her own. Breaking away for an instant, she looked into his eyes, reassuring herself that this was actually happening before kissing him again.

She ran her fingers through his hair before trailing one hand down, brushing the side of his face and coming to a rest on his chest. With her help, Jarro rolled over onto his side and embraced her again. A shiver swept through her body and the blush rose to her cheeks, but this time it wasn't from schoolgirl embarrassment. She pressed against him, relishing the feel of him.

"I love you."

The words fell from her mouth so effortlessly. Why had she never managed to say them before?

"I love you too."

She could taste the saltiness of her tears on his lips. He traced the curve of her collarbone before running his hand down the length of her side, gently, carefully, as though she were a porcelain doll. Yet his touch still managed to shatter something within her. Any doubts she had were broken, the remnants borne away on a wave of bliss.

Sevy pulled back once more. "Tell me this is really happening."

"It's really happening."

He smiled at her, though it was not the smile she had dreamed of for so many nights. It was subdued and weary, shaded with sorrow. That was all right. That was nothing to worry about. Sevy would get him to smile again. Things would return to normal and everything would be fine. Everything would be wonderful.

She kissed him again. And again. She looked deep into his eyes and begged him to call her sweetheart, begged him to tell her again that he loved her.

"I love you, sweetheart," he willingly whispered after each of her requests.

Sevy laughed and wept and called his name until he silenced her with another kiss. This was better than anything she had ever imagined. This was real. He was real. He was alive. And he loved her.

Nothing else mattered. No one else mattered. And no one was ever going to take him from her again.

Chapter 10

With a disgusted snort, Irea closed the door and locked it behind her. They were too consumed with one another to notice that she was watching their nauseating reunion. Listening to them whisper their clichéd declarations of love really was enough to make one sick. That tawdry stray hadn't wasted any time, had she? Slut. The temptation to rush back in and bleed her dry was so very enticing. But she resisted. After all, she'd waited a decade to get her revenge on those two. She could wait a little longer.

For tonight, Irea would let them linger in one another's embrace. It would make it that much sweeter when she ripped them apart again. Besides, she was too exhausted to fully enjoy herself right now. Reviving Jarro had taken too much out of her. She was sluggish. Her feet felt as if they were weighted in lead. Becoming mist and shadow was impossible, which she found disconcerting. It left her far too vulnerable. Worst of all, each movement she made drove searing bursts of pain through every inch of her body.

She cringed as she plodded down the sepulchral-like corridor. Her footsteps were much too loud for her comfort and made her ears ring. Her senses had been heightened the night of her rebirth, but at times like this, they were excruciatingly acute. Even the lone torch that lit her way hurt her eyes so she threw it in a puddle on the ground where it sputtered into soothing darkness. Better, but not by much. Irea needed something to stave off the pain before it grew completely out of hand.

She lingered in front of one of the doorways and rested her head against it, shuddering. A rich, heady aroma filled her nostrils, more toothsome than any confectioned goody. This one was perfect. She'd saved the best of the bunch just for such an occasion as this. How delicious it was that he was still alive. She really couldn't remember the last time she fed him. Trivial details like that were hard to keep track of.

His scent was so distracting that she fumbled trying to find the right key. Anticipation made her giggle as she pushed the door open.

"Hello, my darling."

He cowered in the corner and scarcely looked up at her when she entered the cell. He began to weep, sounding like a wee fledging, still pink and sightless in its nest.

"There now, don't cry. Why don't you come lay your head on my shoulder and tell me what's bothering you?"

His cries grew louder and he rocked back and forth, which put a damper on her good cheer. It wasn't as much fun when they didn't fight back. He could have at least put up a semblance of effort. She observed his feeble throes, the knuckles smacking against his forehead, the meaty vestiges of his nails clawing at the wall, and was filled with loathing. Humans. Such brainless, pathetic, polluted creatures. An example of the gods' warped senses of humor. Only their numbers kept them in power and that would change if Irea had anything to say about it.

"Come now. What was your name again? I forget. Oh well, it doesn't matter. You're behaving atrociously! I'd expect more resilience from the Captain of the Guard. The rest of your men had so much more backbone. What would they think of their captain now, hmm?"

His response was to cover his head with his arms and groan.

"Very well then. Have it your way."

Irea stood over him and spread out her arms. Drool escaped from the corner of her mouth, and her tongue whisked out to lick it up before it ran down her chin. She could not wait a second longer. The hunger was too fierce.

Her fingers splayed and immediately she felt that luscious pull. She called to the blood, urging it, beckoning it to meld with her, to coat her parched cells with its warmth and vitality.

It seemed to take forever. Her energy was so depleted that her lure took longer than normal to seize hold of him and the delay was maddening. Finally, crimson speckles emerged on the surface of his skin, like the heads of worms peeking out of the earth after a rainfall. He screamed. It was glorious. To her ears, it was a song, an ethereal aria composed and performed for her alone.

The droplets rose and suspended themselves in the air teasingly before ascending into her. Pleasure crested as the blood saturated her, filling each pore, coursing through each membrane. She laughed and her head lolled back in rapture.

Then all too soon the song ended. He was dead. Drained without another ounce left in him to give. Her chest throbbed with disappointment. While it had done wonders for her strength, it had not satisfied her hunger.

She left his body where it had fallen and moved back out into the corridor. Smell of rot, smell of death, but unfortunately the only smell of blood persisting in the dungeons belonged to Sevy and Jarro. Hot and fresh. Salted with sex. It smelled so good. No. She could not give in. She had plans for those two. She rushed up the stairs to distance herself from their intoxicating perfume.

She climbed a spiral of stairs until she was atop the castle wall, looking out over the parapet. Eloria lay twinkling beneath her, a cornucopia of plethoric delights. The slums were the easiest targets, but did not appeal to her palate. The people there always tasted so, well, so poor. Why settle for tripe when one can sup on tenderloin? She turned her ravenous scrutiny to the mansions that surrounded Eagleborn.

"While I'm at it, I can pick up some pretty baubles for myself," Irea said with a puckish grin.

After all, the fruits of her arduous labors were coming into sight at last. She deserved a little celebration.

Chapter 11

In the morning, Irea freed the gag-inducing duo and beckoned them to follow her by the crooking of a cadaverous finger. She had gorged on blood all night, which allowed her to maintain a look of morose disinterest even though their beating hearts sang to her like sirens. Sevy's especially. She was strong and young. Irea definitely wouldn't mind another sample of that hothead's blood. It had been most pleasing. Jarro's blood, mixed as it was with Irea's own, was less tantalizing, but still distracting nonetheless.

It wouldn't do to loiter in their company for too long, but they seemed unaware of their predicament. Sevy was so focused on Jarro that she let down her guard completely, and Jarro was too weak to worry about anything other than standing upright. He shook terribly and had to rest every few steps. Sevy fussed and fretted so much that Irea finally pushed both of them up the remaining stairs.

"Easy!" Sevy yelled. "Leave him be!"

"Relax. I'm only trying to be helpful."

"It's all right, Sevy," Jarro said. "I'm fine."

Irea frowned. He was avoiding her. When she had first entered their cell, he averted his eyes and hadn't said anything to her at all. That irritated her more than she cared to admit. She had been hoping for something more. A frantic apology, maybe a pledge of atonement. Falling at her feet and begging for his life would have been nice, but any sort of acknowledgment would do compared to this obvious snubbing.

She tried to conceal her disappointment as she guided them through the snaking passageways and cobwebbed chambers that led to the throne room. The men that had been left to mind the castle when King Grewid departed had been shoddy housekeepers. The marble floor was swathed in dense layers of dirt. The velvet banners were faded and torn, and the throne was in need of a vigorous polishing. Not entirely the look of majesty Irea hoped to convey, but it seemed only right to address her guests here. She was the queen of this castle now, even if the spiders and mice were her only subjects.

She perched herself on the arm of the throne and watched them huddle before her. Jarro looked like he would collapse at any minute. Sevy held him and whispered something trite into his ear. What a wretched little pair.

"Now then, Sevy," Irea said. "You'd best be on your way. If you aren't back in ten days I will consider our deal null and void. Understand?"

"I think Jarro should come with me. He needs someone to take care of him."

Irea's head flopped to the side with her riotous laughter. "How stupid do you think I am? He stays, you go. I promise that I'll be a good hostess and watch over him while you're gone."

"If you hurt him in any way—"

"Yes, yes. You'll kill me, you'll make me writhe in agony, and so on and so forth. Honestly! Considering that I'm the one who came up with this little bargain, I do understand how it will work. Do as I've asked, and you and Jarro will be free to go."

"Don't listen to it, Sevy! Kill it!"

"It? Well, that's just uncalled for!" Irea sprang to her feet. She took a moment to collect herself before continuing. "I'm losing my patience. Either you go now or..."

"I'm going!" Sevy said, and then offered a weak smile to Jarro. "It'll be all right. You'll see. I'll be back as soon as I can."

"No, please listen to me. Don't do this! Promise me you'll run away. Promise me you won't do what it wants."

"I have to. It's the only way."

"I don't belong here. You know this isn't right," Jarro protested as Sevy led him across the room and sat him on a bench against the wall. Irea stuck a finger into her mouth when Sevy bent down to kiss him.

"I love you," she whispered before walking away.

"Sevy! Sevy, please, don't do this!"

"Oh, will you just be quiet?" Irea said, frowning. "You're giving me a headache."

She sank down into the throne, coughing as dust billowed up off the cushion. Then she made her hands into a temple in front of her face, and watched Jarro as he stared despondently at the door Sevy had exited through.

"Well, my darling, looks like we're alone at last."

He ignored her.

"I said it looks like we're alone at last!" she repeated, letting her voice ricochet off of the high walls.

Very slowly, he turned his head and regarded her in silence. She couldn't tell what he was thinking. Was it fear or anger she saw in his eyes? Whatever it was, it incensed her.

It was the same look he had given her when she met with him two years earlier.

Why she had wanted to talk to him instead of just slipping back into that house and slaughtering the lot of them, she couldn't say. At the time she had convinced herself that it was a good idea. She needed help, and who would be more understanding than Jarro? Sweet, predictable Jarro, always looking out for those less fortunate. Surely after all the time that had passed he would have softened a bit. Besides, he had never been able to say no to her before.

She knew full well that Sevy and Revik would have chomped at the bit to finish her off if they had known she was there—those two pompous imbeciles, she couldn't wait to see them squirm, but first things first—so she had sent Jarro a letter. In it, she asked him to meet with her, alone, at a bakery across town, alluding to her desperation and to a danger that concerned them all.

As was expected, he arrived precisely on time. She had picked the bakery to cover up her smell, which would have clued him in to the change in her as soon as he caught wind of it. It was just carelessness, she would explain if he asked. A batch of meat pies had been forgotten in the oven. It was not wholly a lie. Pies had been left to burn, but not due to neglect on the baker's part. He and his pretty wife lay dead in the pantry after providing Irea with enough power to try out her latest trick. She mouthed the words of the incantation Chencholor had taught her, "As was, now will be. As was, the fool shall see," and once finished, stepped out into a beam of flour laden sunshine. She would know soon enough if it worked.

"Hello, Jarro."

"Irea."

She could barely contain her excitement. The glamour had worked. He saw her as he had known her, before the ruin and decay, even before the disfiguring burn Revik had given her, from a time when she was flawlessly beautiful, the desire of every man who set eyes upon her. She wished that, even if only for an instant, she could see what he saw.

"Thank you for coming," she purred as she sashayed up to him. "I wasn't sure if you would."

"What do you want? I thought Revik made it clear you aren't welcome here anymore."

"I've missed you. It's been so long."

She placed her hand on his chest and was surprised when he

snatched it off and took a step away from her.

"Jarro! There's no need to be short with me. I'm not here to cause trouble. Isn't it time we let bygones be bygones?"

"You tried to have me killed. I'm just supposed to forget about that?"

"It's so easy to play the victim, isn't it? I admit that I made a mistake. A terrible one. But I'm not the only one at fault and I thought that you would have the decency to own up to your culpability in the matter."

"Hah! I don't even know why I came here. Goodbye, Irea."

"Wait! Please don't go. I need you, Jarro, I need your help."

Now that caught his attention, just like she knew it would. He crossed his arms and glared at her, clearly suspicious, but at least he wasn't leaving. For good measure, she quivered her lips and sniffed.

"These years have been so hard. I've been so alone and I've missed you so much. Please say you've missed me, even just a little? We were so good together, weren't we?"

"Get to the point."

"Oh, Jarro!" she cried, throwing her arms around his neck. "Can't we start over? Can't you find it in your heart to forgive me? We loved each other once. Let's find that love again!"

The bastard pushed her aside. "You never loved me. You used me."

"How can you say that? How can you stand there and say that to me?"

"You used me, and then when you thought you could do better you tried to get rid of me."

"But only because of Sevy! I saw the way she looked at you. And you liked it too, didn't you? Having her fawn all over you. That bitch."

"Don't try to twist things around. It shouldn't have mattered what Sevy or anyone else did or didn't do. You should have trusted me. You should have known that I would never have hurt you. I loved you. I really did. Gods, I can't believe how stupid I was."

She stamped her foot and yelled in frustration. This wasn't going the way she had planned. And then, unexpectedly, she felt woozy. She reached out to grab at the counter to steady herself. The room became hazy and she couldn't stand upright anymore. Resting her head in her hands, Irea tried to regain focus.

"My gods!"

She glanced up and saw that Jarro was staring at her in shock. His hand covered his mouth, and his eyes were wide with fright. The glamour must have worn off when her thoughts became unfocused. He was seeing her in her true form.

"Jarro, I—"

"What...what are you?!"

"You don't understand! You weren't supposed to see me like this. Not yet. Please don't go! You have to help me! You have to!"

But he wasn't listening. He was too terrified, too disgusted. It was the same with everyone who saw her, and the saddest part was that she couldn't really blame them. She looked down at her wasted breasts, her skeletal arms, and she could have cried.

"You see what you've done to me?" she groaned. "This is all your fault! You and that bitch and Revik! You see how you've destroyed me."

"What's wrong with you? Why are you...? What happened? What did you do?"

"I had no choice! What else was I supposed to do? You left me with nothing! I had no choice!" She couldn't stop the shrillness in her voice. She couldn't stop the trembling in her hands. Her anger demanded that he realize the magnitude of his sins. She clawed at him, desperate to make him understand. "Now you have to make things right. You have to help me find a way!"

"Find a way to what?"

"You have to help me. I can't do it by myself. He needs a sacrifice and he needs some kind of relic and then...and then—"

"Sacrifice? What are you talking about?"

"Chencholor! He needs it. He needs the blood to break Reyla's Curse, and then I'll be myself again. Only better."

"No!" Jarro cried, shoving her away. She was so weak that she lost her balance. The skin on her knees burst open when she hit the floor. She curled into a fetal position as though that would somehow make the pain go away.

"But you have to!"

"No. I don't know what you've gotten yourself into, but I don't want any part of it."

"You'd do it for her though, wouldn't you? Wouldn't you! You'd do anything for that stupid, simpering stray! Maybe I'll go pay her a visit and then we'll see if you're ready to cooperate!"

His eyes darkened. He grabbed her shoulders and hauled her up. "You stay the hell away from Sevy, do you hear me? If you so much as look at her..." He threw her back down and stalked away. "Get out of Eloria, Irea. If I see you again, I will kill you."

He left her there, crying in defeat. He had just walked away. How dare he refuse her? Who did he think he was? She screamed and beat her fists on the ground until she passed out.

When she awoke, her body was smoldering with pain and hunger. She roamed the streets, taking life after life, but they did not quell the inferno inside. Her pride demanded vengeance as much as her body demanded blood.

She slithered back to the old house. She drifted through his open window as a shade, unseen by the others. He was asleep in his bed. She sat down next to him and waited.

After a few minutes, he stirred, sensing someone was there. "Sevy?" he murmured.

She laughed. "Not quite!"

The second he realized it was her, the instant that his eyes enlarged and he inhaled a quick, sharp breath, she took him. It had been absolutely delectable. His screams had filled her soul with bliss.

One would think that he would have learned from his mistake. One would think that he would treat her with more respect now that he knew what she was capable of. She had taken his life and given it back, yet here he was, staring at her like she was some sort of vile insect. She dug her nails into the arms of the throne, cracking the aged veneer.

Maybe she'd just kill him now. Maybe she'd string up his body so that he could greet Sevy on her return, a gruesome welcome back gift guaranteed to drive Sevy into madness. But no, she must be patient. The rewards would be so much greater if she could only hold out just a little while longer.

Then without warning, Jarro lurched to his feet. He slowly crossed the room, coming towards her.

"And just what might you be up to?"

"If she won't kill you, I will."

"Oh please! You can barely walk. Maybe if you hadn't spent all night fucking that bitch you'd have more energy today."

"Then I'll kill myself."

She paused. Now that was something she hadn't considered. She got up from her throne and sidled over to him. "Do that and I will keep her alive for months, years even, before I finally take her life. By the end, she won't even be able to scream. I'll break her again and again until there is nothing left of her. Is that clear?"

"Monster!" he hissed between clenched teeth.

"You know, I'm getting tired of hearing that word. Oh, for the days when people had more imagination. But you are only human after all, I suppose. Your narrow little mind can't even begin to comprehend what I've become."

"And what's that?"

"A goddess!"

He laughed and she struck him in reply. The force of it sent him reeling and he landed in a heap. He didn't move again for a very long time.

"My, how the tables have turned, hmm? Now it's your turn to beg at my feet just like I begged at yours."

"I'd rather die."

"You know, Jarro," she kneeled down beside him, "you don't have to be my enemy. I don't blame you for what Sevy and Revik did. I forgive you. I know this isn't really you talking. You're hurting. I wasn't strong enough to bring you back without any pain, and for that I'm sorry. But once my destiny is fulfilled, we can be together. Like we were before that miserable stray came into our lives."

He laughed yet again, quieter this time, though just as caustic. "I don't want you, hag."

She knew better than to be provoked by his insults, but she couldn't resist. Summoning her strength, she began a soft chant and although she couldn't see or feel any physical change, the expression on his face told her that her glamour was taking hold.

"Don't be so fooled by appearances, lover. It's true that I am weak now, but once Sevy brings me the Eye of Annu I will become as a god. I will be strong and vibrant, with all of the wondrous powers Chencholor has granted me. Reyla will be denied. I will live forever and I will be magnificent.

"You're insane," he said, crawling backwards. "Get away from me!"

She lunged at him with a snarl. His head cracked against the marble. He struggled against her, but was too feeble to push her off as she lay down on top of him.

"Tell me something. All these years, all that build-up, you finally had her last night. So tell me, and be honest now, was she worth it? I bet she doesn't know half of the tricks I do. I bet she didn't get you to scream the way I used to."

She covered his mouth with hers, and when he tried to turn his head, Irea grabbed his face with both hands to hold him steady. She ground her hips against his and shivered.

"Ah, you feel so good. So strong. So handsome," she said, licking him.

"Stop it!"

"What's wrong, darling?" She giggled. "Aren't you enjoying yourself?"

"Get off of me!"

"Don't fight. Didn't you used to love it when I was on top?"

He pulled hard on her hair, yanking her head back. "I said get off of me, you disgusting piece of shit!"

With a deafening shriek, Irea allowed herself to disintegrate into shadow form. As a black cloud, she raged about, knocking over the throne and ripping down the tattered banners. She slammed into the walls, smashing off chunks of granite. The grime and grit from years of neglect lifted and spun around the room, caught in her wake.

"How dare you?" she screeched. "You could have had everything! Now you can rot with that precious bitch of yours!"

She encircled him and lifted him off of his feet. Ignoring his cries, she carried him back down to the dungeons and threw him into his cell.

"Enjoy what time you have left, bastard. When Sevy returns I'll show you what real pain is!"

She slammed the door shut and locked it behind her, convulsing with anger and exhaustion. Moaning, she sunk to the floor. She had over-exerted herself again. So much so that she didn't know how she would be able to make it up the stairs, let alone go out and hunt. She needed blood. And Jarro was close, so very close.

A dull hum throbbed in her ears. She smiled.

"I hear you, Lord," she whispered. "You've come to help me once more?"

And suddenly Irea felt herself rising to her feet and climbing the stairs. She shuffled out into the courtyard of unkempt topiaries, and devoured the air. Blood. It was there somewhere, hidden amongst the wind-rustled hedges. She could feel it.

A human child, no more than six or seven years old, appeared from behind what used to be a sculpted swan. He examined her with eyes that seemed impossibly large for his tiny face, but he did not try to run.

"Thank you, Chencholor. He's beautiful," she murmured as she opened her arms to receive the exquisitely ruddy gift of her god's love.

※

The keep would do nicely. The room at the top of it was the highest in the castle and it had a panoramic view of the entire city, a proper backdrop for her numinous ascension. Let Eloria serve as witness to the coming of a new era. The city that broke her would be broken in return, crushed under her heel like an overfed maggot.

She dragged a table out from the wall. Though the wood was splintered and pitted, it would function as a suitable altar. Rummaging through a canvas sack, she found the four candles of the Gods of Order that she had stolen from an elvish cathedral.

She inspected each one. They were simple, plain columns of beeswax standing about a foot in height. The only difference between them was the insignias carved into their bases—a tree surrounded by flames for Reyla, goddess of nature; an open eye with two pupils for Harsidia, goddess of wisdom; an overlapping sun and moon for Korinium, god of fortune; and a hand holding a small round mirror for Bedethal, god of justice.

Irea lined the candles side by side on the edge of the table. She stared at each in turn as her ire seethed then knocked the lot of them over. They clattered to the floor.

"That's what you get, pigs. I will beat all of you down for betraying me. How many nights did I waste crying to you? How much did I endure while I pleaded for your grace?"

Memories glimmered—the days spent in writhing as Revik's burn became septic, the biting flies attracted to the globs of pus that seeped from the eschar. Too nauseated to eat, too frail not to. She had no money, no friends. Revik, Sevy, and Jarro had seen to that, hadn't they? Luckily, she knew enough herb lore to brew a draught that would slow the infection, and in time cure it, but she did not know enough to be able to heal her disfigured skin.

She hid her face behind a veil as she journeyed by caravan, paying her way by bedding fellow travelers. At least with her face as it was they did not try to kiss her, but small mercies being what they are, that fact really did not make it any easier. She made no pretence to act as if she was enjoying herself, not that any of them cared. If only she knew who they were. She could track each one down and have her way with them, see how they liked it, but they were just nameless memories, too numerous to count.

It was weeks before she reached the northern borders of Axlun, and weeks more as she journeyed deep into the Kingdom of Vasurach to the home of her birth. By then, her face had scabbed over and revealed the form that it would remain in for the rest of her life. She could not bear to look at herself in the reflection of her parents' front door.

"And you told them not to help me, didn't you?" she ranted to the prostrate candles. "You wouldn't speak to me, but you spoke to my father. After all, why show pity to a diseased whore when you can conspire with an Elder Mystic? Isn't that right? How benevolent of you!"

Irea remembered groveling before her father, a tiny man compared to most elves, who only had a few strands of red hair remaining on his spotted head.

"Please, Father. I've learned my lesson. I have been humbled. Won't you please accept me back?"

She was garroted by the lies and the humiliation. And how her father had smiled. So smug and self-righteous. Her mother stood behind him, wringing her hands, as pathetic and spineless as ever.

After what had seemed like ages, her father spoke. "I knew it was only a matter of time before you came crawling back. What's wrong, slut? Are the men not as pliable as they once were?" He rose up from his chair and sauntered over to her, lifting the veil from her face. "Ah, now it becomes clear. I suppose it doesn't matter how wide you can spread your legs when you have a face like that."

Her mother gasped and clutched at her breast, feigning swoon. Irea simply bowed her head even lower while her father laughed in contempt.

"Very well. You may stay here. But there are a few stipulations. First, you mustn't tell anyone that you are my daughter. My parishioners must never know that a man of my standing begot a godless harlot. And second, you must earn your keep. We could use another charwoman, I suppose. Couldn't we, dear?"

And so it came to be that Irea worked as a maid in her own home. She lived amongst the other servants, humans mostly, but a few dwarves for the heavy labor. She rarely saw either of her parents, which suited her fine. When she did happen to pass them in the halls, their reaction was always the same. They would look at one another and then her father would laugh and her mother would sigh.

"And you, did you laugh at me? Did you laugh? Did you even notice me at all?" Irea whispered sadly, swatting at the candle of justice.

Months stretched into years. Over time she grew mute, often going days without uttering a single word. Her life became an endless cycle of droning drudgery by day and fervent prayer by night.

She did not miss any of her father's liturgies, not even one, and she prayed until the words lost their meaning. On days of penance, she would bathe in ashes and whip her ankles with rushes. She read fortunes to earn enough money to buy talismans of luck which she kept on her person at all times. In spite of her efforts, she saw and heard nothing from the gods, not even the slightest inkling of their presence.

Not until one night when a low hum caught in her ears. It persisted for days, irritatingly constant, following her into her dreams with its whine. As no one else seemed to hear it, Irea assumed she was going mad.

Then miraculously, while cleaning her father's study, the hum began to make sense. Words emerged from the incessant drone. Phrases took form. It was then that she realized her prayers had been heard after all.

She fell on her knees and wept. Chencholor comforted her and kissed her mind. Life would be different now, he promised. Her faith made all things possible. With his guidance, she was drawn to one of the leather-bound books on her father's shelf. The cover was emblazoned with the mark of Chencholor, a knot of serpents within a broken circle. Its clasp worked itself free. The book fanned open to expose blanched vellum and red ink, which at first was illegible until Chencholor explained how to decipher the swirls of script.

Irea pulled the very same book out of her canvas bag now and set it upon the altar. She flipped through it until she came to the spell that had transformed her into a demon. The Transmogrification of the Profane. The magic behind it was fairly simple, though certainly not for those with weak stomachs.

She hadn't needed much persuasion to convince her of what needed to be done. Betrayal, Chencholor explained, was the sweetest elixir. It was a decisive expression of chaos and proved how far one was willing to go to subvert harmony.

Irea had remained in the study, awaiting her father's return from evening supplication. He looked startled when he saw her standing by the fire.

"Good evening, Father."

"I told you to never address me like that," he said gruffly as he took off his ceremonial headdress. "What are you doing in here?"

"Cleaning. That's what you pay me for, right? Oh. Wait. You don't pay me at all."

"Hurry up and get out."

"I'm all done, Father, except for one tiny little thing. I have a question for you."

"I don't care to answer it."

"Really? Not even...not even in exchange for something?"

His eyes lit up as a greedy child's. "What kind of exchange?"

The veil concealed her grin. She moved to the door and closed it, clicking the lock into place before turning back to him. "Just like old times, Father."

Smirking, he approached her. The revulsion was difficult to hide as she allowed him run his hands over her chest. He leered at her. "Pity about your face."

"Isn't it though? Now then, what is Reyla's Curse?"

"Hmm?" he mumbled, distracted.

"Reyla's Curse."

"Oh. Yes. Well, it's a relic from ancient days." He circled behind her, lifted her hair from her neck and kissed her. Her stomach churned.

"What does it do?"

"Something to do with immortality. Reyla trapped the key to immortality within it so the cycle of life and death would go on uninterrupted."

"I see," she said as he began to untie her dress. "Where is it now?"

"Don't know. It was lost to the humans some centuries ago. They don't know what it is, stupid things. They just know it has power. It gets passed around between their gods, and they use it for their fruitless rituals."

The heat from the fire nipped at her as her dress slid into a puddle at her feet. He sighed in satisfaction and pressed against her, his enjoyment all too obvious despite its laughable size.

"Which gods, Father?" She jerked away. "Which gods?"

He frowned at the loss of contact. "Eewerel, their god of birth. Yemet, I think he's the god of harvest. They have so many. Annu-nial, goddess of death..."

He kissed her roughly. She pulled back again. "One moment, Father. I think I need a drink first."

"Don't pretend to be such a prude. I know you better than that."

She removed her veil and smiled before plucking a large, jewel-encrusted goblet off one of the shelves.

"You can't use that," he protested. "That's for the purification rites!"

He grabbed at it, but she held it out of his reach. She made her other hand into a fist which she placed before his face. "Let the ruination commence. I offer up this sacrifice to you, Chencholor—"

"What are you doing?"

She opened her hand, revealing a pointed shard of glass. "—in the hopes you will judge me worthy."

"You stupid girl! Stop this immediately!"

Again he tried to grab the goblet so she used it to bash him across the head. He fell dazed against the bookshelf. While he was stunned, she sliced the shard across his neck. Blood bubbled out as he grasped at the gaping wound, but his fingers could not stop the flow. Irea filled the goblet to the brim.

"Consecrate me in the fires of chaos," she continued, staring into the foaming fluid. Her father fell. She turned away from him, and kicked him when he blindly clawed at her leg. "With this unholy libation grant me the power of anarchy, the power of those divided from the will of the gods!"

She raised the cup to her lips and drank the blood down. Immediately, she felt a strange dizziness. The scar on her face throbbed and she clasped a hand against it. Heat spread from her wound, coiling round her head, her neck, down her body. The pain ripped through her so greatly it sent her into seizures.

Then gradually the burning lessened. She was able to stand again and felt strangely invigorated. She stared down at herself in awe. Her skin had become pale and felt gritty, as though she were covered in ashes. She was thinner too; the bones of her cheeks jutted out so that she could see them if she looked down. Chencholor sang her praises. She had done it, but just what she had done was still uncertain.

There was a knock at the door. "Dear? Are you all right? I heard screaming."

Irea cocked her head, confused by the luscious smell that wafted in. What was it? She had never smelled anything so succulent. Her mouth salivated as she undid the lock.

"Hello, Mother."

Irea sighed and closed the spell book, waking herself from her reminiscences. She stood to survey Eloria. She could smell them all down there. Humans, elves light and dark, trolls, dwarves—they each had their own unique flavor, some more satisfying than others. But the blood never tasted as sweet as it had that night.

As time passed it became harder to quench her thirst, harder to maintain the vitality that she felt in the beginning. Chencholor told her that was to be expected. Until she found and broke Reyla's Curse she would continue to deteriorate. Odd that he had failed to mention that piece of information before her transformation.

That's why she had returned to Eloria, and why she had pleaded for Jarro's help. She didn't feel strong enough to do it on her own. And when that idiot rejected her, it was Chencholor who stayed her from draining Sevy and Revik the very night she killed Jarro. They could prove useful, he said. He was right.

She had left that night in search of Reyla's Curse with the sound of Sevy's screams still ringing in her ears. The trail was convoluted, leading her from one city to another, from one god to another. It was months before she located it, secreted away in a woodland temple dedicated to Annu-nial.

Unfortunately, the humans there were not as dimwitted as her father had believed. The priestesses seemed to know of its history, and refused her entry. Not to worry, Chencholor assured her. It was only a temporary setback.

As was tracking down Revik once she returned to Eloria to find both him and Sevy missing. Her panic had risen as the weeks plodded on and she grew feebler, but through it all Chencholor remained confident. He said that he had visions of her greatness, and that she should believe him when he said that he would never let anything happen to her. He had been true to his word.

Irea looked to the northwest, to where the temple lay in the midst of the Mindervale woods. Sevy would retrieve the Eye of Annu. She would bring Revik. She would do the dirty work that Irea was not capable of doing. There was no question of that.

A great grin spread across her face. It was all coming together now. All of her suffering and sacrifice would be rewarded and her enemies would at long last be held accountable for their trespasses. She would join Chencholor in the heavens and together they would bring the world

to its knees. Never again would she be a slave to men.
   It was all too delicious.

Chapter 12

"Sevy! You're alive! I...I..."

Words failed Revik. He was left stammering, dumbfounded, completely amazed to see Sevy walking up the steps to the library. He had spent the night presuming her dead, devoured by Irea while he toiled to break down the door he had been locked behind. It was a miracle. He ran to her and threw his arm around her. Sevy did not return his embrace. Her body was tense, muscles taut like a cat on the prowl.

"What happened? Are you all right?"

"Yeah," she said, blinking her eyes away from his.

"I heard you screaming, but by the time I got out you were gone."

"Irea took me. I managed to escape."

"How? Tell me everything. Did you kill her?"

"No. When she left the room, I, ah, picked the locks."

"Where is she? I'll finish her off."

"No! I mean, you can't. She's too strong."

"Are you sure you're all right? What did she do to you?"

He scanned her for signs of injury. She appeared unscathed aside from bruising on her sallow face and bandaging spotted with dried blood on both her wrists. Revik would tend to her wounds later, but right now what was most startling was the exhaustion he saw in her.

It didn't make sense. Why hadn't Irea killed Sevy, or at least kept her in a more secure location? He was also incredulous that Sevy hadn't died fighting rather than let Irea get away. Something was not quite right here, and even though he was overjoyed that she was safe, it gave him pause. It wasn't every day that someone returned from the dead.

Sevy fidgeted under his inspection. "Come on. Let's go."

"Just a second." He leaned into her and sniffed.

"Stop that," she said, slapping him. "What the hell are you doing?"

"Just making sure you're you. You could use a bath, but you don't smell like her."

"Um, thanks?"

He hugged her once more. "I was scared you were dead. Don't ever do that to me again!"

He expected her to shy away. She could be so strange about physical affection. But she didn't object. Instead, she slipped her arms around his neck. Her shoulders shook, and he heard her sigh.

"Are you crying?"

"I'm sorry," she mumbled into his chest.

"For what?"

She didn't answer so he just held onto her, willing to be her anchor if that was what she needed from him. He had been her friend for years, but could honestly say that he had never truly known her until the night of Jarro's death. Before that, she had seemed a caricature, switching from gaiety to anger and back again at manic speeds, keeping the world at bay with her capriciousness. But he knew that those who display the greatest strength usually bear the deepest heartache.

Seeing Sevy cry called to mind the image of a hawk, born to soar over open waters, abased to a pitiable flopping travesty by a broken wing. He wished he could find a way to heal her, to take away her sadness, but knew that the only person who ever had that ability was now just a memory.

Her cries lessened and she turned away, bashfully wiping her face dry. "I'm sorry for, um, scaring you like that."

"You don't have to apologize. It wasn't your fault. Although, if you hadn't been so pigheaded and waited like I told you to, this wouldn't have happened."

He hadn't meant that to sound harsh. He didn't want to add to her grief, but now that she was safe, he could not keep his own hurt camouflaged. She never would have locked him away like that before he lost his arm. She saw him like Yy'voury did, like they all did. And for some inexplicable reason, Sevy's patronization was more upsetting than everyone else's.

He waited for her to protest, call him a few names, and be her regular aloof self. It was troubling when she only gave him a faded smile.

"Lots of things happen that shouldn't," she said, cradling her head in her hands.

"What?"

"Nothing. Forget it." She breathed in and out so forcefully that her whole body quaked. "Come on, Revik."

"Where? To Irea?"

"No. Not yet. We need something first."

"All right, but listen. The librarian looked up more information. He said that Irea can be killed. We just need to weaken her, get her to use her powers. Between the two of us we shouldn't have much trouble wearing her down."

"The two of us," she said, trailing off into a train of thought she would not share.

He saw motion out of the corner of his eye. The surviving gnome peeped at them from behind a column. Another life marred by the misery that Irea wrought. Revik raised his hand to wave goodbye, an apology perhaps, for bringing evil to the little creatures that had been secure within the bosom of their books. He wondered what the poor thing would do now without its friend to chatter with. The gnome gave an alarmed squeak when it realized that it could be seen, and scurried back into the library.

"Damn that Irea," Revik said under his breath.

There was another horse, pawing and jumpy, tied next to his in the stables he had rented. Sevy didn't offer an explanation for its procurement and he didn't ask. He knew it couldn't have been lawful. She didn't have the funds for that. As Sevy climbed onto its back without wasting words to reassure it, she seemed to be on the verge of crying again.

Had she been anyone else, Revik would have demanded to know what was wrong. But this was Sevy. Though her emotions sometimes slipped through the chinks in her armor, nothing could compel her to speak about them. Whether that was from pride or from fear was anyone's guess.

"Where are we going?" he asked, trying to distract her from whatever unhappiness she was dwelling on.

"Irea told me some things. Wanted to brag, I think. She needs a relic to stay alive. I know where it is. I'm going to get it first and…"

The tears built again. She sucked them back down and transformed her face into a sheet of ice, her signature stare that must have been perfected in the days of her stolen childhood.

"And then I'll do what needs to be done."

The trees and the birds held more frequent and lively conversations than Sevy and Revik did as they traveled to Mindervale. Two days after leaving the city, anxiety took hold of him. Sevy was acting strange. Even for her.

He questioned her more, but she kept her answers glaringly succinct. Not only did she not want to discuss her time with Irea, she did not want to talk at all. When she did speak, she went out of her way to be polite. She ignored blatant opportunities to insult him. She agreed with every suggestion he made—which route they should travel by, where to stop at night—instead of arguing with him simply for the sake of arguing. It was abnormal to receive such compliance from Sevy.

Oft times he would catch her watching him, looking so miserable and hopeless that it tore at his heart. Now and then, she would confound him with the smiles she gave to herself, her cheeks in full blush, oblivious to everything except for her apparently pleasing thoughts. Although she had been a moody girl for as long as he had known her, her current behavior was perplexing and Revik found himself worrying about her more and more. Maybe Irea had done something to her after all.

One night, after they made camp, he studied her through the licks of fire as she sat drawing pictures on the ground with her finger. She hummed to herself and had a faraway look in her eyes.

"Sevy?"

As though she were waking from a dream, she turned to him. He could read nothing in her expression.

"I was just thinking. When this is all over maybe you'd like to come back to the Ullydrans with me? You could stay for as long as you'd like. I think it would be good for you. You know, to just rest awhile."

She chewed on her lower lip. "No."

"Why not? If you're worried about Yy'voury, don't be. She doesn't care about that night. That sort of thing doesn't mean much to my people. And you'd be doing me a favor too. She'd have someone else to pester."

"Pester?"

"She's, how should I put this? A little overbearing. She's been a mother for so long I don't think she knows how to stop. But it makes her happy. She likes to feel needed."

"Does she love you?"

"Yes."

"Do you love her?"

His answer was a smile. He really did love her, in spite of it all. Looking on the positive side, he'd say that recent sorrows had taught him to appreciate Yy'voury in ways he never had before. Her desire to shelter and protect those she cared for, to make choices for them that they wouldn't make for themselves, was understandable to Revik now that he felt himself wanting to do the same for Sevy.

"Come home with me," he said. "It'll be fun to have you in the family."

Sevy sent a spray of sparks into the air as she kicked at the campfire. She stomped off into the forest, deaf to his concern. Revik could hear her breaking branches, tossing them about, lashing out at whatever stood in her way. Her fit disturbed a nest of pixies, and they swarmed into the clearing, shaking their tiny fists at her.

"What's wrong? Come back here, Sevy!"

"It's just not fair," she yelled as she emerged from the trees, ripping twigs and leaves from her hair and flinging them into the fire.

"What's not?"

"No matter how hard I try, no matter what I do, it doesn't make any difference at all, does it?"

"What doesn't?"

She screamed at the sky. "A single scrap of happiness! That's all I ever wanted! Is that too much to ask for? Is it? I mean, what is this? What the hell is this? It's a fucking joke, that's what it is!"

"Calm down."

"No! This time, I'm going to get what I want. I deserve it! And no one is going to take it away from me. Not you," she pointed accusingly at him, "not anyone!"

"Sevy, please, try to relax. Here, sit down. I'll make you something to drink."

"Don't! Just stop it. Leave me alone!"

"Sevy—"

"Hit me!"

"What? No."

"You know you want to. I'm the reason you lost your arm. Don't you hate me? Don't you want revenge?"

"You little fool."

"Don't you dare walk away from me. Hit me! Right here. Go on. Do it!"

Revik sighed. She was such a simpleton. She closed her eyes and stuck out her chin. It was tempting. Maybe he could knock some sense back into her. But in the end, he simply leaned over and kissed her.

"That wasn't a pass," he said when her eyes shot open. "Now sit down, shut up, and let me make you something to drink."

"Please," she whispered. "Please stop being so nice to me."

"Don't tell me what to do. If I want to be nice to a violent, melodramatic idiot, then that's what I'm gonna do." He laughed before growing serious again. "I know how much you're hurting. So if you need to cry then cry. And if you need to yell then go right ahead. But stop trying to push me away. I'm not going to let you go through this alone. I will always be here for you. I promise."

She trembled, and for an instant Revik thought she was either going to faint or vomit or both. He helped her down onto her bedroll, crouched beside her, and cupped her chin in his hand.

"Here's another promise. Irea will pay for what she did to Jarro. And maybe it will take awhile, but someday you'll meet someone else and you'll be happy. Just trust me on this one, all right? You will be happy again."

He didn't expect his words to instantly reassure her, she was far too stubborn for that, but he did not anticipate the reaction he received. Just when it looked as though she would surrender to grief, the thoughts and feelings swimming in her eyes sunk deep down within her. When she spoke, it was in a dull, flat, lifeless tone. "Yes. I will."

Had he said something wrong? Had he done something to hurt her even more than she already was?

"You should get some sleep. I'll take first watch," he mumbled, not knowing what else to say.

"No, I'll do it. I'm not tired. Goodnight."

She sat with her legs crossed and her spine rigid, and settled into inertia. Her torpid demeanor made Revik uncomfortable. It was almost vicious in its vacantness.

Lying down, he tried to reason with himself to control the dread intensifying inside. She was just upset and frustrated. Obviously, she had never recovered from Jarro's death and facing Irea must have affected her more than first thought.

He turned his head to look at her again. She sat as a statue, staring into the fire. He preferred her rage or the heartbreak of her tears to this. This was unnatural. It was unhealthy.

She'll be all right. Once this is all over, she'll be fine.

He could only pray that was true.

They reached the Temple of Annu-nial at dusk the following night. The horses whinnied their disapproval as Revik and Sevy dismounted and tied them to a tree. The woods were alive with eerie eyes, white-gold or green, reflecting the night back at him. They were unsettling, though it was probably the trepidation Revik already felt that granted them their sinister quality.

A goddess of death. Why would anyone want to worship that? Humans were so morbid.

As he didn't care to know much about this particular religion and wasn't sure what to expect from these priestesses, he waited for Sevy to give the signal to approach. Instead, she brushed him aside and threw the door open.

He frowned. She really did need to learn some patience. There was a proper panache to this type of thing, but Sevy had never really understood that. She was too brash for her own good. With a sigh, he followed her, stooping to get through the low doorway, when suddenly a huge pressure seized his chest, like a vice cinching his heart and lungs. The force drew him slightly forward then threw him back more than a foot.

"What the...?" he groaned as he picked himself up.

"What's wrong?" Sevy asked.

He approached the door cautiously and reached out his hand. Blue streaks of lightening trailed from his fingertips as he moved them about the space and he heard a low crackle of power. Some kind of energy was erected here, blocking his entrance. No matter how he tried he could not penetrate the opening.

"Magic," he said. "A spell."

"Ah, so that's how they did it," Sevy said cryptically.

"How who did what?"

"Nothing." She shrugged, apparently unaffected by the energy.

Revik peered in after her, careful not to get too close lest the enchantment worked into his eyes. Sevy circled a fountain of water in the center of the room and kicked over the candles that were lying about. He couldn't see beyond that; it was too dark.

"Can I help you?" a timid voice asked.

A blonde human had appeared. There must have been a door somewhere back there in the gloom that she had come through. She smiled at Sevy and looked baffled when her greeting was not returned.

Sevy got straight to the point. "I'm here for the Eye of Annu. Give it to me."

Obviously that was not a request the blonde expected to hear. She twisted her hair around her fingers. "Oh, I can't do that. The goddess would be so upset with me."

"Tell her to let me in," Revik called.

The blonde gave him an uneasy smile. She was a half-wit. That was evident. And Sevy's unwavering stare was agitating her. She shuffled from foot to foot, and her words became almost incoherent. "The...the goddess..."

"You should be worried about upsetting me, not your stupid goddess. Hand it over. Now!"

"But...but..." the woman stuttered as Sevy backed her against the wall.

Revik didn't like this. There was no need to be so rough with the poor thing. Her soft spoken objections did not warrant it.

"Leave her be."

"Shut up, Revik. I remember you. Your name is Leonetta, right? I'll say this nice and slow so you can understand. Give me the Eye or I'll cut your throat out."

The woman gasped and covered her neck with handfuls of hair.

Revik's heart drummed. Surely Sevy was just bluffing, but there was something in her tone that was completely alien, a deadness that made him shudder.

"What's going on here?"

His eyes were drawn to another woman, again materializing from the shadowed inner doorway.

"Hello, Aliss," Sevy said.

"Do I know you?" the woman asked.

"Not really. I brought you a crystal a few years ago. I'd like it back."

This one was no simpleton. Her eyes glistened, showing an internal strength akin to that of the Barren Mage's. She had power, this woman, and Sevy better take heed of it, especially since Revik was impotent to help her if things got out of hand.

She gathered herself up in defiance. "Go ahead and take it. It's there in the fountain."

"Nice try," Sevy chuckled. "I'm not touching that damned thing. I remember what happened the last time, and I'll bet you've got just as annoying a hex here too. Take it out and give it to me, and we'll be on our way."

"We? Ah, an elf," Aliss said, noticing Revik. "Enjoying my spell? Did you think you'd be immune because of your skin? How stupid do you think I am? Light or dark, it makes no difference."

"That's fascinating, really it is," Sevy said. "Now hand it over."

"Is your blood cursed, elf? I should have known when that demon first appeared that more would follow."

"Do you mean Irea?" Revik asked. "She was here?"

"Annu-nial will have you one way or another. The Eye will not save you."

"Save me?"

"He's not one of them," Sevy said, interrupting. "Quit stalling and give it to me."

"Never. I am sworn to protect it and I'd rather die than help you. Let the elvish ghouls rot!"

"So be it."

There was a history here that Revik didn't know about. Sevy had been keeping more secrets than expected. Before he could ask what the two of them were talking about, Sevy pounced on Aliss, clamped her hands around the priestess' neck, and squeezed. The blonde screamed, but was so frozen with fright that she could not move to help her friend. Underneath the shrill din, Revik could hear Aliss' stifled attempts to breathe.

"Sevy, let her go!" He pushed against the invisible barrier, but was thrown down once again. He shook his head clear and ran back.

Sevy's knuckles were white from the effort of strangling the priestess, who was now on her knees, clawing at Sevy's wrists. Then Sevy dropped the woman onto the ground. Aliss coughed and hacked. It sounded so raw that he winced in sympathy.

Sevy looked at Leonetta, who was still cowering, and smiled sweetly at her. Revik's stomach heaved at the suddenness of a wet thud. Sevy had kicked Aliss in the forehead. Blood erupted from the split skin as Aliss groped at the floor and tried to pull herself away. This was escalating into something horrifying.

"Enough!" Revik shouted. "Stop it!"

She ignored him. "Last chance. Give me the Eye."

Aliss tried to speak, but was unable to do anything but croak and spit out the blood that trailed into her mouth as it poured down from her forehead. Her face was awash with it, like a macabre second skin.

"Leonetta," Revik called, "let me in!"

But Leonetta had lost all reason. She rocked back and forth in a frenzy, chanting some kind of protection prayer. Sevy paid her no mind. She grabbed Aliss by the hair and dragged her to the fountain.

She dunked Aliss' head under the water. The priestess thrashed her arms and legs about, but to no avail. Sevy's grip was too tight. After a minute, Sevy lifted her sputtering back into the air, but did not release her hold.

"Leonetta, you can end this now if you want to. Just give me the Eye and I'll leave Aliss alone."

The blonde said something, a squeak of acquiescence perhaps, and started towards the fountain. She plunged her arms in and splashed about, searching the bottom.

"D...don't," Aliss managed to rasp.

Leonetta stopped and with terrified eyes stared at Aliss then at Sevy. Revik shared her fear. Sevy's face was so blank. He couldn't tell if she was actually serious. He pounded against the bewitched door. "Don't do this!"

"Will you shut up?" She forced Aliss' head under again and looked to Leonetta. "Well?"

Leonetta had been taught her lessons of obedience too well. When it was clear that no response was forthcoming, Sevy pushed Aliss deeper.

"Time's up."

Revik and Leonetta's screams blended together as Sevy continued to hold the woman down. Aliss ceased her struggles. Her body went slack. And then the only sound left in the room was the echoing drip of water.

"What have you done?" Revik whispered.

Leonetta lay face down on the ground, blubbering and pummeling her head with open palms. Sevy pushed herself up by pressing one last time on Aliss' back. The dead woman's head sank then bobbed to the surface again. Her dark tresses floated around her, wrapping through her outstretched hands as though she had been drowned in the tangle of her hair.

"Get me the Eye."

"Sevy," Revik cried. "Why are you doing this?"

Leonetta continued her wordless wail, so Sevy hoisted her up. She screamed even louder until Sevy belted her across the face.

"You wanna end up like her? Get me the fucking Eye!"

She threw Leonetta into the fountain. Foundering, Leonetta was unable to get her footing and accidentally bumped into Aliss. This elicited another scream. Sevy growled impatiently and booted Leonetta in the chin. She fell backwards, stunned. Blood dribbled out of her nose and swirled into the water.

"Stop it! Stop!"

Revik beat his hand against the door. This couldn't be happening. The woman standing there, so poised and unemotional, torturing that pitiful girl, could not be his friend. She had not just murdered in cold blood. He shook his head, praying that it was all a horrible mistake, never feeling so helpless in his life.

Leonetta, fearing the wrath of Sevy more than that of her goddess, resigned herself to surrender. Trembling, she reached down and lifted out a crystal about the size of her fist.

Sevy snatched it out of her hands and sneered. "Pleasure doing business with you. So sorry about the mess."

Leonetta collapsed into hysterics as she clung to the edge of the fountain. Sevy made no move to help her. She wiped her hands dry on her trousers and rammed past Revik as she exited the temple.

"We're leaving."

"You bitch!"

"I really hate that word, you know," she muttered as she mounted her horse.

He planted himself in her path. "How could you do that? You murdered that woman! Gods, Sevy, what are you thinking?"

"Are you going to fight me?" she asked with a smile.

"Why? Why did you do that? I don't understand."

"You don't have to. Let's go."

"No! Sevy, I—"

"Why all this fuss? It's not as though you've never killed anyone before."

"Not like that. That was..."

"That was what? Dead is dead."

"You're mad!"

It was obvious. Clearly, she had lost her mind. Revik formulated a plan. He'd bring her to a healer. She'd rest for awhile. She'd recover. Yy'voury would help. She could buy the right spells, the right potions. They could purge the dark waters from Sevy's mind. And when she was well again, Revik would help her make amends to the poor half-wit priestess.

"I'm going to help you. Don't worry. Everything's going to be all right."

Sevy clucked her tongue and trotted her horse forward a few steps. Although she was still smiling, a fat tear fell down her cheek.

"No, Revik. Everything won't be all right. I'm sorry."

He didn't see her boot fly towards his face. The next thing he knew he was on his back, gagging at the taste of copper that suddenly filled his mouth. Through sparks of light and swirls of darkness, he saw her bending over him. There was a blur of motion as she struck again, and then blackness swallowed him.

Chapter 13

As Jarro stretched out onto the ground, the grass brushed against his back, providing a verdant, aromatic blanket that tickled as much as it cushioned. The breeze that skipped round the meadow was crisp. It cooled and caressed the bare skin toasted by the heat of the afternoon. He closed his eyes and relished the incense of earth and wildflowers, the smell of comfort, of home.

Her warmth came down upon him, bringing a smile to his face. "Sevy."

"Ssh," she murmured as she ducked her head to kiss him, amazing him with the sweetness of her lips. He sighed as she leaned back again. Her hair was loose, bobbing beguilingly on her shoulders, and the sun was a halo behind her. If he had been an artist, he would have painted her just like this, to capture this moment of perfection for the ages. Had he been a poet, he would have woven her beauty into words. But Jarro was neither of these things, so he simply gazed at her, enchanted that at long last she was his.

"I love you," she whispered, tracing feathery patterns on his chest with her index finger.

"I love you too, sweetheart."

He touched the hollow of her neck before trailing downward, skimming the sensitive skin between her modest but charming breasts, and settling on the flat of her stomach. Her muscles shivered.

"That tickles!"

He grinned and wrapped his hands around her waist, pressing her down against him. Her lips hovered above his. He lifted up his head to kiss her again, but she teasingly pulled away at the last instant.

With a low growl, he flipped her over and rolled on top of her. He crushed his mouth against hers. Her back arched. She moaned when he massaged his thumb over her breast, plumping the roseate nipple to a delectable point. It was all he could do not to take her right then, but he wanted this to last. After everything they had been through they deserved this time together, savoring one another the way they had wanted to for so long.

"Oh gods, I love you, Sevy." He sighed, burrowing into her neck. He nibbled her earlobe as she ran her hands through his hair, each stroke multiplying the shock wave of desire that coursed through him.

Suddenly, she drew away from him. "Your face is bleeding."

As if to illustrate her point, a scarlet bead splashed onto her, startling them both. He sat up and put a hand to his cheek. It was true. Somehow, his old scar had reopened and it was just as fresh as the day it was made. The blood oozed at first, then trickled. Soon the flow increased. It gushed out, covering his body and soaking the ground.

"Sevy," he cried, looking to her for help. She was nowhere to be seen. The wind picked up, blasting him in the face, netting drops of blood and then spraying them about. "Sevy! Where are you?"

He tried to stand, but slipped. Where was the grass, the sun? They had been replaced by soggy red earth that squelched under his feet and a black sky stippled with his own blood. The merciless wind flung him around, forcing its way into his mouth and nose so that he couldn't breathe. It deafened him as it roared into his ears. He squinted, but could only see the blood as it pelted his eyes. He was helpless in a tempest of wind and gore.

And then, from deep within him, came scorching agony. He was being burnt alive from the inside out, his organs reduced to char and his skin bursting into flames. He gagged on the metallic smell of cooked blood and the choking reek of ash.

His eyes shot open and he gasped for air. When he jerked his hand to his face, he found it intact. It took time for the fog of confusion to clear. He was lying on a bed, not the ground. There was no field of grass and wildflowers. He was in the damp dungeon cell, where he had been all along. Someone was in the room with him. He turned to them, desperate to see Sevy, but instead his eyes were locked to those of a shrunken, perverse horror.

"Irea," he said, sickened by the sight of her.

"I brought food. Eat it."

She gestured to a bowl on the floor and nudged it towards him with her foot. Her idea of encouragement, he supposed, as if he was merely a dog. But he was hungry. His stomach twisted expectantly at the sight and smell, but he wasn't willing to go near her to pick the food up. He lay back down on the bed and turned away from her.

"Listen, you can starve for all I care, but I doubt your stupid sweetheart would appreciate that. Eat it."

Jarro stared at the coarse stone bricks in front of him and tensed his body, awaiting her approach. He had to fight back a shudder when he thought about that monster touching him, kissing him again. Her taste of charcoal and mold had remained with him for hours. But she made no move to come to him. Finally, he heard her leave the room and lock the door behind her. He relaxed and flopped onto his back.

It took a moment to gather enough energy to sit up then he swung his shaking legs to the floor and tested them against his weight. He could tell by their quavering that he wouldn't be able to walk. He would have to crawl.

Since Sevy left, he had grown so very weak. The fire had long since burnt out, and the cell quickly turned frigid. A single lantern provided the only light and warmth, and even that meager source was beginning to die as the flame lapped up the oil gluttonously. Irea rarely brought him food, sometimes disappearing for what felt like days before she'd show up again. He didn't know how long it had been since her last visit. He couldn't even tell if it was day or night. There was only dark and darker, cold and colder. The passage of time had lost all meaning down here in the bowels of Eagleborn.

A wet rattle had settled in his chest, and he hacked up sticky, thick fluid as he dragged himself towards the food. Every movement was painful. Every breath burned. He didn't know how much longer he could last.

He prayed to Annu-nial that he would just die. That would be the best thing. Without him as a bargaining chip, Sevy would fight Irea, and he knew that she was strong enough to win because the witch was deteriorating just as much as he was. With each visit, Irea's shoulders became more slumped, her frame more withered, her voice more muffled. He could feel her blood dying inside of him where at first it had blazed through his veins, fortifying him even as he suffocated in its poison.

If only Sevy would heed his warnings and stay away. Let the two contaminated corpses waste away in this castle together, forgotten by the realm of the living. It would be a fitting end for Irea, and Jarro was never meant to be here anyway. As strange a thought as it was, he was meant to be in his grave. Just a memory that his loved ones could look back on with a bittersweet smile. It wasn't fair and it wasn't right, but that's the way it was.

Finally making it to the bowl, he devoured what he presumed was some type of stew. It tasted off. It probably had been sitting out for a week or more, but that was the least of his worries. He licked up every last bit of it, probing the cracks in the wooden dish with his tongue for any trace of food remaining, and then rolled on his back, far from satiated.

His stomach lurched. He had eaten too much too quickly. He fought to keep the food down, breathing slowly and deliberately, waiting for the queasiness to pass. It was then that a rich, meaty aroma wafted into his nostrils. His mouth salivated until he detected the rot underneath.

It was the smell of the fetid flesh of other prisoners that Irea had kept down here. The distinct odor had been recognized days earlier when he still had enough strength to try to pick the lock. The stench had drifted in and given him flashes of battlefields years past. The blood, the pulp, the flies buzzing about joyously. It had sickened him at the time, but now he was even more appalled to discover that he was so hungry it was starting to smell good.

With that revelation, the nausea could not be staved off any longer. He heaved onto the ground, shoulders wracking violently, emptying what little he had in him until only yellow acid was brought up. He sobbed. There was nothing but pain and sickness, and he couldn't take it any longer.

To calm himself, he imagined Sevy. Sevy coming back and saving him. Sevy holding him and soothing him, lying next to him, telling him that she loved him. This was just make believe and "Ssh, love, everything is all right now."

But that was selfish. He was already dead. His suffering did not matter. Only Sevy mattered now and he had to make sure that she would be safe. Jarro knew she'd return for him, even though he had pleaded with her not to, and once she did Irea would kill her. He was convinced of that. Desperation may have duped Sevy into believing Irea's promises, but he knew better.

Jarro crawled to the door and used the handle to help himself upright. After a few deep breaths he called out, "Irea? Irea!"

She was still nearby. She had to be. Please, gods, let her be nearby.

"Irea!"

He screamed her name until he was hoarse. After a few agonizing minutes, he heard her footsteps in the corridor. The door banged open and her lifeless eyes bored into him.

"What?"

"Come and talk to me. Please."

Leaning against the wall for support, he hauled himself back to the bed. He slumped down, exhausted, before turning to smile at her.

She raised an eyebrow at the gesture. "Why?"

"I'm lonely. Won't you sit with me for awhile?"

He patted the bed. He could see her agitation as she debated, searching out the deceit in his request. Finally, she sat next to him.

"I've been doing a lot of thinking. Not much else to do down here." He gave her the most charming smile he could. "Thinking about my life, the things I've done. Things I should have done differently."

He caressed her face. She baulked, but then relaxed and allowed the touch.

"I should have treated you better. I'm sorry."

"You're many things, but you're not a very good liar."

He laughed and waved away her scorn. "Oh, I'm not lying. I mean it. A woman like you has certain needs. I should have taken you from Eloria. Maybe gone to Wilrendel and given you the kind of life you wanted. You weren't happy living like a thief. I tried to make you something you weren't. You deserved better. If I hadn't been so selfish I would have recognized that, and maybe none of this would have happened."

"And what about your stray? Hmm? You don't fool me."

"Sevy? Well, what can I say? I'm a man. I'm weak. It was nice on the ego to have a girl throw herself at me all the time."

"It was appalling how she wormed her way into our home. And you bought right into that little innocent act of hers."

"I know. I know. That must have hurt you a lot. I don't know what I can say. I have no excuse. But you know," he inclined towards her, "you were right on all counts. Maybe it's just because I'm so sick right now, maybe that's why I couldn't really get into it, but being with her was nothing compared to being with you. She's a cold fish, that one. But you, you're like fire. We sure had some wild times together, didn't we?"

She grinned, revealing the scummy raisins that were her teeth. He brushed the straw-like hair back off of her shoulders and she sighed.

"Do you remember that night when we first met? The tavern? They kicked us out for making too much noise."

"Oh, I had forgotten that," she said with a girlish giggle.

"You forgot? How could you forget that? I was sore for days afterwards!"

She threw her head back with delighted laughter. He laughed with her until he began to cough uncontrollably, choking on the phlegm he brought up. He collapsed onto the mattress. His muscles ached as he fought to regain some degree of composure. Irea leaned over him. He was surprised to see the concern in her face.

"It hurts so bad," he whimpered.

She nodded her head in sympathy. "I know."

"Before I die, I want you to know how sorry I am. For everything. If only I'd never met Sevy. Things would be so much better if only I'd never met her."

"There's still time to make things right." The black pits of her eyes twinkled.

"What do you mean?"

"When Sevy returns I'll regain everything I lost. And you can too.

My offer still stands."

He struggled to sit up. "You mean after everything I did to you, you'd forgive me? You would take me back?"

"Provided, of course, that you do me a small favor first."

"Anything."

"I want her to pay. I want her to suffer. When she gets back, I want you to break her heart before you kill her. Can you do that for me?"

"Yes."

He hoped that she didn't hear the vitriol in his voice. She smiled and kissed him. Revulsion consumed him, but he kissed her back. Her tongue was a slimy mass, sloppily slapping the sides and roof of his mouth, lathering him with feculence. His eyes rolled back into his head as he suppressed the urge to vomit. Her hands groped at him, trying to coax his desire. He groaned in disgust, masking it as passion, as he laid her down.

"Wait, not like this," she whispered. She recited strange words and her form changed so that she was radiant and young. This was exactly what he was hoping she'd do.

"You're so beautiful," he said as he kissed her again.

She sought to undress him, but he kept her at bay, stalling and teasing her with light touches and kisses. She shifted in pleasure beneath him, oblivious to his loathing. Finally, just when he thought he couldn't take another second of it, he felt Irea's magic waver like the hot breath of a flame burning itself out.

When next he opened his eyes, he was greeted by raw, roasted flesh. He pretended not to notice and she was too distracted to care. He ran his hands up her arms, cringing when a chunk of her skin sloughed off at his touch.

Jarro seized her neck. He pressed down as hard as he could, driving her into the mattress. Creamy black liquid squirted as his fingers sank into her. He couldn't tell whether he was choking her or ripping out her throat, but either way she'd be dead.

But then his throat felt like it was closing in on him. He couldn't breathe. The room spun. As his grip slackened, she threw him off. He flew back across the room and was knocked out cold.

When he came to, Irea was standing above him, tenderly rubbing her neck.

"Tricky boy. You think you're oh so clever, but you forgot one thing. I made you!" she screeched as she lifted him into the air by the front of his shirt. "I own you! Without me, you are nothing! You can't kill me, you stupid bastard!" She threw him down again and stepped over him. "Poor Jarro, in so much pain. Don't worry, lover. It will all be over soon enough."

She paused for a short time, resting against the door before slamming it shut behind her.

"Dammit," Jarro screamed once he could speak again. He balled his hands into fists and pressed them against his eyes. Despite his best efforts to maintain control, he broke down into tears. His one chance wasted by weakness. There was nothing he could do to save Sevy. He had failed her, the way he always failed those he loved.

"I'm sorry, I'm so sorry," he moaned.

His only hope now was that she wouldn't return, but there was little chance of that. Sevy would never dream of abandoning him, and because of that devotion, she was condemned to death. Irea's revenge would be complete. There was nothing he could do to prevent it. The only question that remained was which one of them Irea would kill first.

Chapter 14

It took every last shred of willpower she had to not kill him right then. How dare he? Who did he think he was that he could treat her like that? And how dare he choose that obnoxious stray over her? Again. It was preposterous.

Chencholor hummed in her ears. She squirmed as he pulsated through her temples, increasing his heated pitch to a sharp whine.

"I know, Lord. I'm sorry. That was silly of me. It won't happen again." Her voice was a mumble as she pulled herself up the dungeon steps. "I just was thinking about the delicious look on Sevy's face if she had seen Jarro at my side. It would have destroyed her. But you're right. It was pure vanity. It won't happen again."

Chencholor continued to lecture as she crawled into the throne room and robed herself in one of the fallen banners. She murmured her agreement though her thoughts were less than godly. They wandered back to the man dying in the room below. Why had she been so blind? She hadn't counted on Jarro resorting to deception. That just wasn't like him at all.

And it wasn't like her to be so easily fooled. Perhaps she had simply enjoyed the attention. It had been too long since a man looked at her or touched her without recoiling. She missed the sense of power she used to get directing them around by their sordid, lustful instincts. She consoled herself with the fact that things would not be like this for much longer. She'd have the world in her thrall once the spell was complete.

Then Jarro would lament his choice. Just wait until he saw Sevy return with Revik. What would he think of his sweet stray then? Let him die knowing that the woman he had thrown Irea aside for was a vicious, cold-blooded bitch. Let him die knowing that he had refused the most exceptional gift he'd ever been offered.

If Irea was to blame for anything, it was for being too generous. To think that she even considered forgiving him after what he had done to her. He wasn't worthy of her. No one was. The gods had played a cruel trick allowing Irea to be born into this life of servitude when she knew that she was meant to be a queen, but not to worry. Chencholor would make sure that no one ever took her for granted again. Her name would become synonymous with sovereignty.

She felt so weary. It was best to sleep for now, and collect her energy for Sevy's return. And then what fun she'd have. First Revik then Sevy. She'd save Jarro for last, ending his life only after she had taken away everything that had ever meant anything to him, just like he had done to her.

"Ah, my Lord," she whispered. "How wise you are. You knew all along what had to be done. I'm sorry I ever doubted you. I will be reborn in their blood. I will be the instrument of your chaos, and you will reign supreme."

Her words seemed to appease him. The shrill hum abated and was replaced by a purr of tranquility, promising vengeance and conquest. She drifted into sleep, soothed by the soft strains of Chencholor's lullaby.

Dawn broke in glorious splendor. The sun, peeking up over the horizon, kissed the tops of the buildings that bordered the castle grounds with violet-pink lips. In this light, Eloria almost seemed picturesque rather than dilapidated. A balmy wind blew in from the west, pushing away the stink of the Elor River. It was perfect. The ideal day to herald a new goddess.

Before the sun had fully risen, Irea scampered into the suites of the late ladies of court. She scoured their wardrobes, picking through forgotten dresses for one that suited her. She fingered the delicate silks, rubbed her cheeks against the fur stoles, all the while consciously overlooking the blackened smudges her skin left behind. Finally, she chose a fetching number in purple satin with a sweeping hem and outrageously low neckline.

Irea ripped off her rags and stifled a sob when she beheld her naked form for the first time in recent memory. Her feet were mere fans of bones. Her knees appeared bulbous and swollen next to the gaunt of her legs. And her waist...she had to look away. She hadn't realized she had decayed to that degree. Her spine was visible through the front of her abdomen, flanked by the jutting wings of her hip bones. She was as skeletal as Jarro had been the night she dug him up from his grave.

She could have been lost to hysteria at that moment, but she persevered. The purple gown was thrown over the atrocity of her body. It sagged fretfully, but once the ritual was complete, she would be able to fill it as it should be. She toyed with the idea of experimenting with the ladies' pots of rouge, but decided that should probably wait until her skin had returned to its natural hue. As a finishing touch, she donned a ruby necklace that she acquired from her last victim. It would complement her hair quite nicely as soon as it was restored to its previous glory.

Once her toiletries had been completed, she fetched Jarro from his cell. Though he could barely breathe, he still tried to fight her as she carried him upstairs. It was amusing and infuriating at the same time.

His labored breathing filled her ears, grating on her every last one of her nerves as even the smallest sounds were magnified and threatened to overpower her if she let them. Beneath the rasping, she could hear the feeble beating of his heart and the flow of blood through his veins. It was hypnotizing, promising a reprieve to her anguish.

With unsteady hands, she held off her hunger and forced Jarro to sit, lashing his wrists to the arms of a chair. Lugging him up to the room at the top of the keep had depleted the last reserves of her strength; she solidified, having lost the ability to transform into shadows again, perhaps for good. Her limbs felt encased in stone. Each movement made was elephantine and clumsy. Should Jarro strive for one last display of heroics, Irea was in no position to defend herself. It was of paramount importance to be cautious even if he did look like he was about to die.

He shivered and sweated with fever. His eyes and nostrils were crusted over with dried mucous. It was almost painful to see him like this, her dashing young lover of yore. Irea's recollections of him were not entirely disagreeable. There had been a time when she had felt a degree of fondness towards him, something just shy of love. But then she ran her fingers over the wounds he inflicted the day before, a malicious reminder that he did not deserve her trust or her sympathy.

"I guess I should have taken better care of you. Do you think Sevy will be upset with me?"

He glared at her from under heavily lidded eyes and she saw the hatred that burned within them. That was encouraging. Where there was hate, there was life. The fool better have enough decency to survive until Sevy returned.

Sevy would be here soon. She would not risk breaking her deadline. Irea was positive of that.

She paced back and forth, glancing out the window at every transient hoof beat that sounded in the streets below. Doubt gnawed at her as the day waned. Maybe Sevy had decided not to help her. She could be scheming with Revik right now. That would be disastrous. Irea shot a glance to Jarro, who had either fallen asleep or fainted.

No, she'll be here.

After all, how could she resist when Irea offered such enticing bait? She knew Sevy. As much as it irked her, she conceded that the two of them were cut from the same cloth. They were survivors, fighters, and they were both willing to go to extremes to get what they wanted. And what Sevy wanted, had always wanted, was Jarro. When Sevy first arrived on their doorstep in the dead of night so many years ago, Irea understood exactly what made that stupid stray's heart beat.

Irea herself had been like that once, believing that salvation could be found within a man. Until the score of heroes that paraded themselves through her life had each proven false.

But that did not matter now.

To distract herself from these melancholy musings, Irea fingered through the spell book. She knew the words by heart, having read them so often. It was surreal that soon she would be speaking them aloud, that she'd be transformed by these outwardly innocent passages. Wouldn't her father be proud of her now? She would invoke magiks the likes of which he had never dreamed possible. Her mystical prowess would go beyond anything that perverted old man ever attempted.

Movement in the room—Jarro had awoken and was trying to slip his hands free.

"Stop that. You'll hurt yourself." She laughed at the dirty look he gave her. "You've grown so hostile. You used to be more pleasant. Been hanging around that stray for too long. She's been a bad influence on you. What a shame."

He tried to say something, a pedestrian slur no doubt, but his mouth was too dry.

"What's that?" she sneered. "Cat got your tongue? Speak up, darling. It doesn't do to whisper in the presence of a deity."

More hoof beats from outside. Irea ran to the window and delight blistered the putrefied remains of her heart.

"She's back!"

Jarro perked up at that. He raised his head from his chest and looked towards the window. Though she knew she could not afford the exertion, she danced around him in glee.

"And you'll never guess who she's brought with her."

Chapter 15

"Well now, isn't this marvelous? The four of us reunited again after all this time. It brings a tear to my eye. Oh no, no, no! You leave him right where he is," she scolded as Sevy began to untie Jarro. "He's been a naughty boy."

"He's sick! I told you I should have taken him with me."

"Leave him there. He'll be fine. Now then...Revik! Dearest! You're so quiet. Are you seeing ghosts again?"

Revik, as he had since coming into the room, stared at Jarro in awe. One of his eyes was swollen shut and nicely bruised. He was bound and gagged, quite ingeniously Irea thought, considering he only had one arm to bind. Sevy had dragged him from his horse and up to the keep, applying force as necessary. Irea had to hand it to her. She was efficient. If only all lackeys could be so methodical.

"Why is Revik here?" Jarro asked while Sevy wiped his face with a damp cloth. "What happened to his arm?"

Irea smirked as Sevy avoided the question and continued to dote upon him. "Didn't she tell you? My, my, she certainly is a secretive little thing, isn't she? Well, I'm not entirely clear on all the details, but Bolozi did fill me in a little."

"Irea," Sevy warned.

"Shortly after your unfortunate and untimely demise, Sevy and Revik had a fling. Quite the scandal really. They didn't even have the decency to wait until you were properly mourned. I've always said that dark elves are vulgar. Pair them with a human and that's the kind of depravity you wind up with. Anyway, I suppose Revik didn't make much of an impression on her because she turned the gang against him."

"Irea, shut your mouth!"

"And to answer your first question," Irea continued. "Isn't it obvious? Sevy's been kind enough to bring me a present. Isn't she thoughtful?"

"Sevy?"

She blushed and bit her lip. "It didn't happen like that."

"Listen to me," Jarro said, rousing some fortitude from whatever stores he had left. "I don't care what happened. You cannot help Irea. Kill her!"

"No. I have to do this. I have to. I can't lose you again. I love you, I need you!"

"No. This isn't right. I won't let you."

Irea laughed. "You don't have much of a choice. This is between Sevy and I. Isn't that right, sweetheart?"

Sevy stood up and though her face was leaden with shame, she looked into Irea's eyes evenly. "Jarro and I are leaving now."

"You can't. Not yet."

"Why not?"

"Because you haven't fulfilled your end of the bargain, you goose."

"But I did what you asked. I brought you the Eye and...and Revik."

"There's one more teeny tiny little thing. Don't fret, it won't take long." Irea paused for dramatic effect, consummately enjoying how the three of them were riveted by her words. "Just this one last thing, and then the two of you can run away together with my blessings."

"What do you want?"

"I want you to kill Revik."

Silence. Sevy gawked at her. "Wh...what?"

"You heard me."

"No," Jarro yelled. "No!"

"That wasn't part of the deal."

"Oh, did I forget to mention that? Oops, how silly of me. Let me make this perfectly clear. If there is any chance of this working I'm going to have to have complete focus on the rites. I need you to assist me."

"But I can't! No. I won't."

"I'm surprised at you. Don't you want to save Jarro? Look at him. He's dying just like I am. Reyla's Curse is eating both of us alive. I'll be dead within the month, if that. And Jarro, well, we're lucky he's lasted this long. The ritual must be performed to save both our lives."

"But...but..."

Irea threw her arms up. "I don't see what the problem is. You knew that Revik was going to die when you accepted my offer. You brought him here knowing full well what I intended to do with him."

"But I didn't think that—"

"Oh, I see. You don't want to get your hands dirty? I've got news for you, darling. You reek of death. I can smell it all over you. And you choose now to get squeamish? I thought you loved Jarro. I thought you'd do anything for him. What's Revik to you anyway? How can his life possibly mean more to you than Jarro's?"

"No, Sevy, don't do it!" Jarro pleaded. "Kill her!"

Sevy trembled. Irea folded her arms and leaned back against the wall, content to wait. She knew Sevy could not refuse and watching this tragedy unfold was almost orgasmic.

Revik would not look Sevy in the eyes. He bowed his head, resigned to his doom. He knew just as much as Irea did that he didn't stand a chance. He had always been the sidekick, the second thought, purely a passive spectator in the drama that was Sevy and Jarro. Irea had hoped that he would struggle more, perhaps make an impassioned plea for his life, but he didn't. Damn the pride of dark elves. It spoiled the fun.

"All right," Sevy said finally. "I'll do it."

She sunk to the ground and laid her head in Jarro's lap as they both wept. With his fate sealed, Revik straightened his shoulders and held his head high, apparently hoping to go out with an iota of dignity. Commendable, Irea thought, but fruitless. By the end, he would be howling for mercy.

"Excellent! Then let's begin, shall we? On your feet, dear."

"Sevy, if you love me you won't do this," Jarro said.

"Be quiet or I'll muzzle you too. Now come on." Irea yanked Sevy up. "Tie him to the table."

Sevy hesitantly took hold of Revik's arm. "I'm sorry."

He snorted into his gag. Sevy tugged him, but he refused to budge so she pushed him from behind. He stumbled forward a few steps then held his ground again, resisting as Sevy tried to compel him to lie down onto the table. She steeled herself and punched him, once across the face and once in the stomach, wincing not because of her actions, but because they made Jarro gasp and sob.

As Sevy fought with Revik, Irea rested her head atop of Jarro's. She whispered into his ear, "What do you think of your sweetheart now, hmm? Do you finally see her for the bitch she is?"

"How can you do this? Please, just let them go."

"Ha! What do you take me for?"

"It's me you want. I'm the one who hurt you. Let them go."

"Enough with the martyr act, Jarro. It's long out of fashion. I'm going to make Revik squeak like the rat he is. And this is only the beginning. Just wait until you see what I've got in store for Sevy."

"No, you can't! Leave her alone. I'm begging you. I'll do anything!"

"Too little, too late. Take a good long look at them. Their deaths are on your head. I want you to remember that as I feast on your soul."

"Sevy, stop! She's going to kill us all! Please stop this!"

"Don't listen to him," Irea said, raising her voice and her head.

"He's only trying to be noble. A bargain is a bargain. Once this unpleasantness is finished, you are both free to go."

She winked at Jarro and he thrashed in his chair. Concerned, Sevy started towards him.

"Don't pay any attention to him. He's just having a temper tantrum." She handed Sevy a dagger. "Cut Revik's clothes off."

Sevy ripped through the linen of Revik's tunic as Irea arranged the four candles of the gods around his head. She was so excited, she fumbled and dropped one of them onto his face.

"Sorry about that, dear. Light the candles, would you please, Sevy? I don't trust my fingers."

Irea held up the Eye of Annu-nial, Reyla's Curse, and kissed it lovingly. It was even more beautiful than she imagined. Pity that the spell would dissolve it. It would look sensational set into her crown. Her crown. Yes, she would have to have one commissioned immediately. Second hand would just not do. She could scarcely believe it. It was really happening. All these long years of torment were coming to a close.

Her head buzzed. Chencholor was near and he was just as excited as she was. He was not alone. There were new voices humming in her ears, just as animated, but for a different reason. The voices belonged to the four gods of balance. They were singing to her, commanding her to stop.

"Oh, I see. Now you'll come to me. Now you'll make yourself known. But when I was pleading with you, when I was begging for your help, where were you? Where were you then?"

"Who are you talking to?" Sevy asked.

Irea hadn't realized she was speaking aloud. She flipped her hair back, a bit embarrassed. "Never mind. Just do everything I tell you to."

She took the dagger from Sevy and, laughing, sliced her own palm open and coated the Eye with her blood. At once it sizzled, and she balanced it on the dip of Revik's abdomen.

She raised her arms over him. "Hear me, oh gods in the heavens! Your time has passed. With this sacrifice of betrayal and blood, let the seal between life and death be broken. With the birth of His most unholy child, let Chencholor rule above all others. Bow down before the terrible throne of chaos!"

Irea spoke first in the ancient language of the Alfar, then again in the tongue of the King for the benefit of her guests. After all, they deserved to know what they were dying for, did they not?

"Cut his chest. Not too deep. Just enough to draw blood."

Sevy touched the tip of the dagger to Revik's skin and looked at Jarro. She squeezed her eyes shut as she sunk the blade in. Despite his best attempts at detachment, Revik let out a muffled cry.

"Hear his cries, my lord. They echo the cries of Harsidia, weeping for the lifetime of wisdom that dies with this dark elf. Weeping for the knowledge I've stolen from Her holiest of scriptures. Words written for blessed eyes alone will be defiled and contorted to your will, Chencholor."

Irea clenched her hand into a fist and held it over the candle of Harsidia until a dollop of blood leeched out, extinguishing the flame. There was a harsh noise, like the shriek of a blizzard, and then one of the voices became so faint it was barely perceptible. The other gods murmured in anger, and Chencholor spurred her on.

"Cut him again."

"Stop! Stop it!" Jarro exclaimed.

Quickly, Sevy pierced Revik once more.

"Hear his cries, my lord. They echo the cries of Korinium, mourning for the destiny that dies with this dark elf. Mourning for the fortune I've stolen to raise myself beyond that which He ordained. The workings of fate will be defiled and contorted to your will, Chencholor."

Irea spattered out the flame of Korinium's candle. Again she heard wailing and Chencholor's voice grew stronger yet. The room darkened. The air felt more compressed. It was working!

"Again!"

"Sevy, please don't hurt him!"

Sevy whimpered as she cut into Revik a third time. Blood collected in a sticky puddle on the curve of his naval, bathing the crystal. It bubbled and hissed in the rich red liquid. The smell of it made Irea light headed, but she would not be distracted, not now.

"Hear his cries, my lord. They echo the cries of Bedethal, lamenting for the equity that dies with this dark elf. Lamenting for the justice I've stolen so that those He would deem praiseworthy are laid to waste before the feet of the corrupt. Righteousness will be defiled and contorted to your will, Chencholor."

As Bedethal's candle was doused, Irea was nearly knocked over by the screeching within her head. Now only Reyla and Chencholor were left. She could feel them battling within her, phantom blows glanced off the inside of her skull. Without the strength of the other three, Reyla was weakening.

Irea felt the oddest tingle shimmy through her, beginning at her head. She looked down at her hands and out of curiosity she rubbed them together. The blackened hide flaked off and healthy fresh skin emerged.

What was this feeling? This lightness? She blinked in disbelief. She remembered this. This was what it was like to be free of pain. This weightlessness, this vigor—she had forgotten what it was like.

She jiggled Sevy's elbow zealously. "Again!"

Tears flowed from Revik's eyes as he bore the pain, not only from the four gashes, but from the propagation of Irea's burden within him. The Eye of Annu seared into his skin. She could smell the flesh frying. She could see the blisters forming beneath the blood.

"Hear his cries, my lord. They echo the cries of Reyla, grieving for the essence that dies within this dark elf. Grieving for the lives I've stolen to elude the mortality She imposed upon me. Natural order will be defiled and contorted to your will, Chencholor."

Reyla bellowed as her flame was drowned in Irea's clarifying blood. Chencholor threw Reyla down and trod upon all four of the bested gods, grinding invisible heels into nonexistent heads. He laughed and this time the sound of it wasn't restricted to Irea's mind. Sevy jumped as his voice reverberated about the tower.

"Let my curse become his," Irea yelled. "Let my blood be cleansed with his. With his death I am reborn. Come now, Chencholor, and with this offering supplant the gods of order. Break them in the fires of chaos! Now, Sevy! Strike him down!"

Sevy put a hand to her mouth, her resolve faltering now that it came down to it.

"Now!"

"I...I..."

"Do it! Or I'll kill Jarro!" Irea yanked his hair and slammed his head against the back of the chair.

Sevy's body rocked with the might of her panicked breaths. "Don't hurt him! I'll do it."

"You can't," Jarro groaned piteously.

"I have to!"

Irea cheered as Sevy turned back to Revik. She cut the gag from his mouth. Revik swallowed as she brushed the hair from his face.

"I'm so sorry."

Revik didn't speak. He simply gazed up at her, then over to Jarro. A faint smile came to his lips as the two men beheld one another. The look that passed between them spoke volumes, even to Irea, telling of affection and loyalty, a statement of love that wordlessly said, "I would gladly die for you, my friend."

"Sevy, no!"

Irea backhanded Jarro across the face to quiet him. "You have no choice, bitch! Do it now!"

Weeping and shaking, Sevy gripped the dagger with both hands. She placed it against Revik's chest, above his heart.

"Forgive me," Sevy whispered. She lifted the blade.

Revik closed his eyes. Jarro screamed. Irea flung her arms up and her head back, awaiting the miracle.

There was motion. There was a cry. Irea felt very cold suddenly. She hadn't expected to feel cold. The room resonated in silence as Chencholor ceased his laughter.

Confused, she looked at Sevy. The miserable expression she wore meant the deed was done. Didn't it? Then what was this awful sensation? Like the gelid burn of ice. Irea bent her head down, each vertebra in her neck taking its time responding to her command. The hilt of the dagger stuck out from her chest. Her hands fell to her sides.

She plucked the dagger out, mystified. And then the ground rushed up to meet her. She couldn't feel anything anymore, not the floor beneath her, nor the warmth of her own blood which blanketed her.

"Chencholor," she whimpered. "Help me."

He was gone. She was alone again, feeling the world speed past her, up into the sky. An immense light, greater than any known to the earth pierced her eyes. She wanted to raise her hands to shield herself, but could not. They lay beside her, purposeless now.

In awesome brilliance, arrayed in the mantle of the sun, Reyla appeared before her, descending from a stairway of ether. The goddess seemed to be laughing though Irea could hear no sound save for her own failing heartbeat. She writhed in terror. Lost now in the desolation of her own soul, Irea could not even scream as she was engulfed within Reyla's fervent embrace.

Chapter 16

Sevy swept Jarro up in her arms, using the discarded dagger to free him of his binds. Carefully, she eased him to the floor and cradled him as an infant. His head slumped back. She couldn't tell if he was breathing.

"Jarro? Oh no. No! Jarro!"

She pressed her lips against his clammy skin and nearly fell over in relief when she felt his eyelashes flutter against her chin. She kissed him again.

He smiled. "Thank…"

"Ssh, save your strength. It's all right. Everything's going to be just fine." Then why were the tears falling?

"Sleepy."

"No! No, you stay with me, Jarro. Stay with me. Fight it, Jarro, I know you can."

His eyelids drooped. "Love you…swee…"

"I love you too. I love you!"

He tried to lift his hand. She scooped it up in hers and held it against her face.

"Please," she begged in a hoarse whisper. "Don't go."

"Sevy…love…"

Beside her, Irea gasped one final time. Jarro exhaled, draining his lungs of air, of life. His body turned limp. Those beautiful blues closed forever. Sevy crushed him against her chest, and rocked him back and forth.

For the briefest, most shining moment, he had been hers. That he had seen beyond her shell of hostility and believed that the woman stowed away inside was beautiful had made her feel that anything was possible. She was irascible. She was cruel. She was a bitch. And still he had loved her. He was the finest thing that ever graced her life, the only thing that made living worthwhile.

And now he was gone. Again.

Words were pointless. Time was meaningless. She held him and wept into the waves of his raven hair. When she spent all the waters of sorrow that were to come, Sevy looked lovingly down upon his sweet face, tracing the gentle curve of his last smile.

"Jarro..."

                                  ~

"Our hearts overflow with thankful praise as the remains of Jarro Destan, dearly departed son of Baywyn and Didrianna, brother of Lon, can now be laid to rest once more. Let him be granted the peace of Annunial. May she bear him on swift wings back to the land of Promyraan. May he be remembered for his kind deeds and gentle manner, and through his memory may those who loved him find solace."

Sevy barely heard the words of the priest. She stood with clasped hands and bowed head, sightlessly staring at the mound of freshly turned earth. She was distracted by the townspeople shuffling behind her. All of Devenbourn was in attendance, though not all to honor him.

It had been quite the scandal when his grave was found emptied. Great discussions were held as to who the likely culprit could be. There were those who said Jarro's old army general dug up the body to put on display as a deterrent to other would-be deserters. Some said that it was an enemy from Eloria, a rival gang with a grudge that extended beyond death. Still others whispered of demonic forces, monsters that prowled the night and ate human flesh.

Certainly, having a dark elf show up in town did not help to quell the rumors. Children ran screaming from Revik and hid behind their mother's aprons. The men held meetings. The local clergymen offered prayer services to help in this fearful time. It was ridiculous. Sevy expected them to form a mob at any moment.

It must have been a terrible burden for Jarro's parents to bear, seeing their son defiled like that, and then have their friends and neighbors use it as a source of morbid entertainment. The Destans' gratitude and grief were evident the morning the wagon carrying Jarro's second coffin arrived on their doorstep, and it was then that Sevy learned the origins of his compassionate heart. Despite public warnings, his parents had extended an invitation to both Sevy and Revik to stay with them until the body could be interred again. Sevy had refused.

Jarro's mother, Didrianna, was a small woman, soft-spoken and mild. She must have been a great beauty in her day, though her face now had more than its fair share of wrinkles. From age, from woe, who could say? But her eyes—they were so much like Jarro's that they wounded Sevy.

Baywyn, an imposing man, was what Sevy considered to be the archetype of a father: firm but fair, reserved yet receptive. Though his black hair was mottled with grey, he was still hale and sound. He looked how Sevy pictured Jarro would have had he lived into autumn years.

They were both exactly as Jarro had always described them to be. Sevy was drawn to them and yet she also felt great resentment. If they had not insisted that he join the army, if they hadn't made him feel like he couldn't return home, perhaps he would still be alive. He would have had the life he always wanted. He never would have had to become a criminal. He never would have met Irea. And he never would have met Sevy.

And if she had somehow managed to survive those first years in Eloria, Sevy wouldn't be feeling the pain she felt now. She would have lived and died never knowing what it was to love him, what it was to lose him. But no, she wouldn't have wanted that. The pain was worth the store of memories she had of a love that comes only once in a lifetime.

Everything was worth it because of you.

The crowd thinned as the priest concluded the funeral. Soon only Jarro's parents, Revik, and Sevy were left in the sleepy graveyard, listening to the lonesome cry of a hawk gliding overhead.

Sevy stiffened when Didrianna approached her. "Thank you for bringing him home," she managed to whisper through a throat thick with tears.

Sevy smiled and looked towards the sky. Baywyn gave Revik a clasp on the shoulder and nodded to Sevy before leading his wife away, past a pair of wilting lilac trees that guarded the gates and down a path that cut through an endless sea of rippling grain.

Sevy waited until they were gone before kneeling. She rested her head against the stone and idly moved her fingers over the engraving that humbly read 'Jarro Destan.' She could still feel his presence, though not from the grave beneath her feet. He was everywhere. He was the earth and the flowers, the trees that sighed in the wind. The sky held the shade of his eyes and the sun gave the warmth of his smile. He was at peace now, she knew.

Revik startled her by dropping a bundle of yellow daisies onto the loose soil. She had forgotten he was there.

"Sevy, I..." he began before trailing off into uncertainty.

"Your wife must be missing you. You should go home to her. Please ask her to forgive me for keeping her husband away for so long."

"I'm so sorry."

"Do not apologize to me. I'm the one who's sorry. For what I did to you. For what I almost did."

"I don't blame you. At least, not entirely. I can't imagine how hard that was for you. If it had been me, if I had to choose between you and

Yy'voury, I probably would have—"

"No. You wouldn't have."

If he only knew the lengths she had been willing to go. If he only knew how close she had come to murdering him.

"I know what you're thinking," Revik said. "And the answer is no. I don't hate you. I promised you, didn't I? You'll always be my friend. No matter how many times you almost get me killed."

"You're too forgiving."

"Maybe. I guess I learned from the best." He gazed down at Jarro's grave.

"I don't deserve your friendship."

"That's not true. You're a good person, despite what you might believe. I know it, Jarro knew it. He loved you very much."

"I know," she said, wiping her eyes with the back of her hand. "I hope someday I'll be worthy of his love. And yours. Goodbye, Revik."

They embraced each other. They kissed once then again, and Sevy finally understood what Revik's kisses had been trying to tell her for years.

"Won't you come with me?" he asked. "Even for just a little while?"

"Thank you, but no."

She could see the worry creased into his brow. "You're not going to do something foolish, are you? Promise me you won't."

"I promise."

He didn't look like he fully believed her. "I just hate to think of you all alone."

Sevy hugged him again. To think that this was the same man she once feared. She remembered the night they met. "She's got quite a pair," he had laughed. She was glad to have made such a friend. She was happy that despite her selfishness and stupidity, there would always be someone willing to laugh with her and cry with her and set her straight whenever she acted like an idiot.

She reached into her pocket and pulled out an old, worn coin marked with a letter S. Clutching it against her heart, she closed her eyes and felt the sun place a gentle kiss on her forehead.

He was right; Sevy did have quite a pair. She looked up at Revik and then smiled into the sun.

"I'm not alone."

The End

About the Author

Sarah-Jane Lehoux has always had a passion for storytelling. From grade school tales of cannibalistic ghosts, to teenaged conversations with God, to her latest fantasy adventures, she's attempted to share her love of the quirky and unconventional with her readers.

Sarah-Jane currently resides in Ontario with her husband and horde of cats. With a degree in anthropology and a diploma in animal care, she is employed as a veterinary technician. In between wrestling with rottweilers and fending off fractious cats, she has continued to craft stories that will entertain and provoke. For more information, please visit wwww.sarah-janelehoux.com

LaVergne, TN USA
28 March 2011

221799LV00001B/1/P